'Your fees do not present a problem.' Matsuo Noda continued, 'This afternoon a retainer of one hundred thousand dollars was deposited in your personal account at Chase.'

'*What in hell . . .*'

'Money is of no consequence in this matter, Mr Walton. Time is.'

'You seem awfully sure I'll agree.'

'We expect your involvement to begin immediately. I cannot stress too strongly the urgency of what you will undertake.' He smiled thinly. 'I also feel confident a man who enjoys a challenge as much as you do will find our undertaking . . . intellectually rewarding.'

Seems I was hired and I hadn't even said yes.

Thomas Hoover

The Samurai Strategy

SPHERE BOOKS LIMITED

SPHERE BOOKS LTD

Published by the Penguin Group
27 Wrights Lane, London W8 5TZ, England
Viking Penguin Inc., 40 West 23rd Street, New York, New York 10010, USA
Penguin Books Australia Ltd, Ringwood, Victoria, Australia
Penguin Books Canada Ltd, 2801 John Street, Markham, Ontario, Canada L3R 1B4
Penguin Books (NZ) Ltd, 182–190 Wairau Road, Auckland 10, New Zealand

Penguin Books Ltd, Registered Offices: Harmondsworth, Middlesex, England

First published in Great Britain by Michael Joseph Ltd 1988
Published by Sphere Books Ltd 1989
3 5 7 9 10 8 6 4 2

Made and printed in Great Britain by
Richard Clay Ltd, Bungay, Suffolk

*Most events in the following story are entirely imaginary . . .
so far.*

ONE

New York, New York. Friday, early September, dusk. Heading uptown on Madison. Sheets of icy rain washed the pavement, heralding the onslaught of autumn and the freezing winter to come. The city was poised for its cruellest months, that twilight of the spirit when strangers arm-wrestle for taxis, nobody has time to hold a door and you cherish every fleeting human kindness.

Bring on the blizzards, the holiday madness. This winter I was planning something long overdue. To treat my daughter Amy, the Madame Curie of her ninth grade, to a real vacation. Just us. We'd leave at Thanksgiving and stay gone through the Christmas break. She got to live with me three months a year, and December was by God going to be one of the months. School? She'd already skipped a year; maybe she was a little too fast-track for thirteen.

Since Joanna, my ex, had already lined up her own holiday excursion (Amy the spy claimed it was with some divorced Tishman VP), she hadn't bothered inventing the usual roadblocks. Clear sailing. We'd open the house down in St Croix and spend a month getting reacquainted. Work on the tan and some post-graduate snorkelling, a strategic move while I still enjoyed a small sliver of her attention, before a certain 'totally terrific' skateboard virtuoso finally got around to noticing *her*. Only a couple of jobs needed finishing, but they'd be wrapped up with weeks to spare.

That night, in truth, had its moments of nostalgia. The destination was Sotheby's auction house, a place where Matthew Walton was greeted by name at the cashier's window. Home away from home for obsessive collectors. I leaned back against the vinyl seat of the Checker, letting the rhythm of the streetlight halos glimmer past, and reflected on all those happy nights I'd made the trek with Joanna. She'd had no real interest in my collecting hobby, Japanese *samurai* swords and armour, but she was always a decent sport about it. Besides, she had her own passions. While I was agonising over long blades and short blades, she'd sneak off and browse for something French and nineteenth-century and expensive. Fact is, I'd usually plan ahead and have something of my own on the block just to pay for that little sketch, or print, she suddenly had to have. Out of habit I'd even shipped up a couple of mistakes for the auction this evening (a hand axe and a lacquered-metal face guard).

Though tonight's sale had only a few odd items in my speciality, the slim offerings actually suited the occasion. It left the evening open, time for the real agenda — getting things rolling with a new client who'd inexplicably handed me a job as simple as it was strange.

The man, name of Matsuo Noda, had rung all the way from Japan the Friday before last, introduced himself in generalities, then declared he had a pressing legal matter requiring both speed and confidentiality. Inquiries had led him to me. Would I have time to help him locate an office building to buy? He claimed he was head of a Kyoto consulting outfit that called itself Nippon, Inc. and he was looking for something in midtown, seventy-million range.

Honestly I couldn't quite believe he was serious at first. Why this job (just a little legwork, really) for somebody he'd never even met? I could swing it, sure, but now that Japanese investors were snapping up US property right and left, who needed some ex-Texan turned New York lawyer knocking around? There was no rational reason to engage a corporate attorney.

'Out of curiosity, why aren't you working through one of the Tokyo firms here in New York, say Hiro Real Estate or KG Land? Surely they could . . .'

'Mr Walton,' he interrupted smoothly but firmly, 'allow me to say I have my reasons. May I remind you I stressed confidentiality.'

'Merely asking.' I took a deep breath. The connection was

distorted, a high-pitched hum in the background, as though he wasn't using commercial phone lines. 'If you want, I can look around and see what's on the market ... and in the meantime how about sending along a prospectus, just for the file?'

'Assuredly,' he said, 'and I do look forward to working with you.' After a few more polite nothings, he abruptly closed out the call.

Peculiar. That wasn't how the Japanese road show usually did business. From what I'd seen, Tokyo invests very cautiously and deliberately, sometimes 'researching' a deal half to death. I momentarily wondered if it wasn't just one of the jokers from my old partnership pulling my leg.

He was real enough. A brochure arrived by overnight air, bound in leather, with a flowery covering letter. Two problems: most of the thing was in his native tongue and what I *could* read didn't tip his hand. From the looks of its public disclosures, Nippon, Inc. was merely some kind of money manager for Japanese investment banks; it had almost no assets of its own. All I could find listed were a few million dollars, lunch money for a Japanese outfit, mostly cash parked in some short-term Euroyen paper. That, and a head office in Kyoto, was the sum of it. What's more, Noda only worked with Japanese banks and firms. No foreign clients.

So why did this man suddenly require space in New York? An entire building. I honestly couldn't figure it. On the other hand, with any luck the whole deal probably could be put together with a few phone calls.

By way of introduction, let me say that I worked, technically, as a straightforward attorney-at-law. I say 'technically' because I was, in fact, a freelance defensive back in the corporate takeover game, which these days is anything but straight. You'd have to go back to the roaring twenties to find so many creative screw-jobs.

Some people are drawn to power; guess I'm more attracted to the idea of occasionally whittling it down to size. So when some hotshot raider found a happy little company whose break-up value was worth more than the current stock price, then decided to move in and grab it, loot the assets, and sell off the pieces — one of the players apt to end up downfield was Matt Walton. For reasons that go a long way back, I liked to break up the running patterns of the fast-buck artists. It's a game where you win some and lose some. The trick is to try and beat the odds and I suppose I'd had my share of luck.

Give you a quick example. Back in the spring, a midsize cosmetics outfit called me in as part of their reinforcements to fight an avaricious rape, better known as a hostile takeover, by one of their biggest competitors. After looking over the balance sheet and shares outstanding, I suggested they divest a couple of unpromising consumer divisions — namely a 'male fragrance' line that made you smell like a kid leaving the barbershop, and a 'feminine hygiene' product that could have been a patent infringement on Lysol — and use the proceeds to buy back their own common shares. We also threw together a 'poison pill' that would have practically had *them* owning anybody who acquired more than twenty per cent of their stock. Our move scared hell out of the circling vultures and reinforced my reputation on the Street (unduly harsh, I thought) as a give-no-quarter son of a bitch.

Another fact worth mentioning is that I worked without the benefit of a real office; after selling off my piece of the law partnership, I operated out of my place downtown, with a telephone and a couple of computers. A kindly grey-haired dynamo by the name of Emma Epstein, who had a rent-controlled apartment down the block, dropped by afternoons and handled correspondence, filing, matrimonial advice, and the occasional pot of medicinal chicken soup. The only other member of my staff was a shaggy sheepdog named Benjamin, who served as security chief, periodically sweeping the back garden for the neighbour's cat. That was it.

Oh yes, one other item. Crucial, as it turned out. I'd always been a collector of something — once it was antique spurs, for chrissake — but about ten years earlier I'd started to get interested in things Japanese, and ended up going a little overboard about old swords and such. Joanna's unscheduled departure managed

4

to burn out a lot of my circuits, and what had been merely an obsession grew into something a little crazy. For a year or so I became, in my own mind at least, a sort of American *rōnin*, a wandering *samurai*.

You see, the Japanese warriors had a code that said you ought to live every moment in full awareness of your own mortality. When you adopt this existential outlook, so they claimed, all regrets, emotions, complaints can be seen as an indulgence. You're ready to meet life head on, to risk everything at a moment's notice. That's the only way you ever discover who you really are and it's supposed to make you marvellously detached.

Almost enough to make you forget how your raven-haired, brilliant, sexy mate packed it in one New Year's Eve twenty months past ... when you called late from the office, again ... after declaring that was the goddamn last straw and apparently the only thing you could find worthy of undivided attention came printed on goddamn computer paper and she was goddamn sick of it — which she demonstrated the next day by slamming the door on her way out.

Add to which, she used my momentary disorientation to get custody of Amy. So while I was battling corporate Goliaths, I let her walk off with the only thing I would have given my life for. The more time went by, the more I wanted to kick myself. Alex Katz (of Walton, Halliday and Katz — now minus the Walton) read the custody agreement the day after I signed it, sighed, glared over his smudgy half-lenses, and announced that this kind of unconditional surrender should only be signed on the decks of battleships. What did he have, a law partner or a fucking *schlemiel*?

He was right, for all the wrong reasons. Not long after, I cashed in my piece of the firm and went independent. Win or lose, it's best to sort things out on your own. I was then forty-three, six-one, and weighed in at an even one eighty. There were a few lines on the face and several more on the psyche, but the sandy hair was mostly intact, and I could still swim a couple of miles if absolutely essential. Maybe there was still time for a new start. Part of that therapy was going to be our trip.

Perhaps I should also add that I'd had a brief 'rebound' fling, for what it was worth. The lady was Donna Austen, a name you'll recognise as belonging to that irrepressibly cheerful 'Personalities!' host on what Channel Eight likes to term its *Evening News*. She'd called about a segment on the subject of the cosmetics company takeover, then very much in the local press, and I'd said fine. She ended up downtown, and soon thereafter we became an item. She was the closest I'd had to a girlfriend, and at that it was mostly an on-again off-again thing – which terminated in an event reminiscent of the Hindenburg's last flight. In the aftermath I went back to chatting with Amy every day on the phone, putting together stock buyback packages and collecting Japanese swords.

Anyway, while the cab waited for a light, worn-out wipers squeaking, I fumbled around in my coat pocket and extracted the *meishi*, the business card, one side in English, the other Japanese, that had been included with Noda's letter. He'd personalised it with a handwritten note on the side with English print. Now, I'd kept track of the new Japanese investment heavies in town – Nomura, Daiwa, Nikko, Sumitomo – since you never know when a corporation might need some fast liquidity. They were starting to play hardball and these days (with all that cheap money back home) they would underbid a nine-figure financing deal before Drexel Burnham could spell 'junk bond'. But Nippon, Inc.? Never heard of the outfit.

Well, I thought, you'll know the story soon enough. The driver had just hung a right on Fifty-seventh and was headed east towards York Avenue. I'd called that afternoon to lower the reserve on one of my lots and had been told that because of some union squabble the preview would continue till just before the sale, now scheduled to kick off at eight-thirty. It wasn't quite seven yet, so we would have at least an hour to run through my list of prospective buildings.

As the cab pulled up next to the chaste glass awning, I took a deep breath, shoved a ten through the Plexiglas panel between the seats and stepped out. While the battered Checker (lamented remnant of a vanishing species) squealed into the dark, I unbuttoned my overcoat and headed up the steps. A few grim-faced patrons milled here and there in the lobby, but nobody looked familiar. There was even a new girl at the desk by the stairs, ash blonde with tasteful smoked pearls, pure Bryn Mawr art history. A class act, Sotheby's.

It appeared that most of the Japanese crowd was already upstairs, undoubtedly meditating on their bids with the meticulous precision of the Orient. I was headed up the wide, granite steps myself when I decided to check out the downstairs one last time.

Hold on, could be there's a possibility. Waiting over by the coat check, thumbing the catalogue, was a distinguished-looking guy, retirement age, wearing a light charcoal suit. Italian. Unlike the usual Japanese businessmen, he clearly didn't assume he had to dress like an undertaker and keep a low profile. No, probably just some Mitsubishi board member thinking to diversify his portfolio with a few *objets d'art*.

Abruptly he glanced up, smiled and headed my way. I realised I'd been recognised.

'Mr Walton, how good of you to come.' After a quick bow he produced his card, a formality that totally ignored the fact he'd already sent me one. As convention required, I held it in my left hand and studied it anew while I accepted his hearty American handshake. 'It's a pleasure to meet you. At last.'

At last?

I let that puzzler pass and handed over a card of my own, which he held politely throughout our opening ritual, then pocketed.

Noda had a mane of silver hair sculptured around a lean tan face and he looked to be somewhere between sixty and seventy. Though his dark eyes were caught in a web of wrinkles that bespoke his years, they had a sparkle of raw energy. He moved with an easy poise and the initial impression was that of a man eminently self-possessed. He had that sturdy, no-nonsense assurance usually reserved for airline pilots. If you had to entrust somebody with your wife, or your life savings, this man would be your pick.

Well, my new client's a mover, I told myself. All the same, I accepted his hand with a vague twinge of misgiving. What was it? Maybe something about him was a little too precise, too calculated.

'Mr Walton, permit me to introduce my personal consultant.' He laughed, a slight edge beneath the charm, and more wrinkles shot outward from the corners of his eyes. 'I always seek her approval of major acquisitions, particularly those of the Heian period, her speciality.' He turned with what seemed obvious pride and gestured towards the tall Japanese woman standing behind him. I'd been so busy sizing him up I'd completely failed to notice her. 'I must confess she is, in fact, my ... niece. I suppose that ages me.' Another smile. 'You may possibly be familiar with her professional name, so perhaps I should use that. May I introduce Akira Mori.'

Who? I stared a second before the face clicked into place. And the name. They both belonged to a well-known commentator on Tokyo television. Only one slight problem: her 'speciality' had nothing to do with art.

'*Hajimemashite*. How do you do, Mr Walton.' She bowed formally and, I noticed, with all the warmth of an iceberg. No surprise – I knew her opinion of Americans. She did not bother meeting my eye.

She looked just as I remembered her from the tube. A knockout. Her hair was pulled back into a chignon, framing that classic oval face, and her age was anybody's guess, given the ivory skin and granite chin. She was wearing a bulky something in black and deep ochre by one of the new Tokyo designers. For some reason I was drawn to her fingernails, long and bronze. The parts, a mixture of classic and avant-garde, did not seem of a piece, the kind of detail you didn't notice on the TV. But there was something more important than her looks.

I'd been to Tokyo from time to time for various reasons and I'd heard a lot of stories about this lady. Fact is, you didn't have to be Japanese to know that Akira Mori was easily Japan's most listened-to money analyst. You've probably seen her yourself in snippets of that weekly chat show she had on NHK, which used to get picked up by the networks here when they needed a quick thirty seconds on *Japan This Week* or such. Her ratings had little to do with the fact she's a looker. She was, talk had it, an unofficial source for official government monetary policy. Akira Mori always had a lead on exactly what was afoot, from the Bank of Japan to the Ministry of Finance, even before the Prime Minister broke the news.

Miss 'Mori', whoever the hell she was, had some very well-placed friends. Tell you something else, she didn't go out of her way to find flattering things to say about how Uncle Sam handled his bankbook these days. Her appearance made Noda's un-orthodox office plans even more perplexing.

'We both appreciate your taking time from your schedule to meet with us.' He bowed again. 'We've been looking forward to having you join us at the sale.'

While Akira Mori appeared to busy herself with a catalogue, Noda and I got things going with that standard formality pre-ceding any serious Japanese professional contact: meaningless chat. It's how they set up their *ningen kankei*, their relationship with the other guy, and it's also the way they fine-tune their *honne*, their gut feeling about a situation. Any greenhorn foreigner who skimps on these vital niceties runs the risk of torpedoing his whole deal.

In response to my pro forma inquiries, Matsuo Noda declared he liked New York, had even lived here for a while once, honestly found it less hectic than Tokyo, usually stayed these days at the Japanese hotel down on Park but sometimes picked the Plaza when he needed to be closer to midtown. He adored La Grenouille and thought La Tulipe overpraised. When I pressed him, he declared his favourite Japanese place to dine was Nippon, over in the East Fifties (maybe he merely liked the name, but it was my pick as well).

After he had in turn solicited my own views on Sotheby's, a couple of the galleries down Madison, and various North Italian eateries, he suggested we go on upstairs and preview the lots.

All the while Miss Mori appeared to ignore us, standing there like a statue of some Shinto goddess, except for the occasional tug at her dark hair. Maybe she didn't give a damn about this obligatory small talk, thought it was old-fashioned. Or possibly she liked the idea of being the only one not to show a hand. And as Noda led the way up towards the exhibition rooms, she trailed behind like a dutiful Japanese woman – while we, naturally, continued to talk of everything except, God forbid, why we were there.

In the first room we were suddenly in my arena – *samurai* swords and battle gear.

'This is your special interest, is it not, Mr Walton?' Noda smiled, then turned to admire the row of shining steel *tachi*, three-foot-long razors, now being watched over by a trio of nervous guards. Sotheby's didn't need some amateur Toshiro Mifune accidentally carving up the clientele. 'I understand you have a notable collection yourself.'

What? What else did he know about me?

Easy, Walton. Play the game. I knew what a Japanese would expect in reply.

'Matter of fact, I've lucked onto a couple of items over the years.' Then the standard disclaimers. My own painstaking collection was merely a grab bag of knick-knacks, the fumbling mistakes of a dabbler, etc., etc.

Noda monitored this culturally correct blarney with satisfaction. 'As it happens, Mr Walton, I was in Nagoya last year when several of your pieces were on loan for the show at the Tokugawa Museum. I still recall certain ones, particularly that fine fifteenth-century *katana*, attributed to the Mizuno clan. Unusual steel. No date or mark of the swordsmith, but a remarkable piece all the same.' A split-second pause. 'Your reluctance to part with it was most understandable.'

This man had done his homework! Or maybe *he'd* been the one who had tried to buy it. The steel was unusual, too heavy on copper. I'd even had a little metallurgical testing done on it down at Princeton, just to prove that hunch. But it was no big deal, merely an oddity that had fallen my way via an estate sale. There was an anonymous inquiry shortly after the exhibition opened, with an insistent offer, but I'd turned it down.

Poker time. 'I was honoured. Your figure was more than generous.'

He laughed – bull's-eye. I watched as he glanced back at Miss Mori, maybe a bit nervously. Then he returned his attention. 'Merely a small gesture for the museum. I felt it should be back in Japanese hands.' He continued, his voice now sober. 'You do understand?'

'Certainly.' I just stared.

'Good. I see I was right.' He had paused to examine a large monochrome screen. It was eighteenth-century and he inspected it with only mild interest, then moved on.

I was still knocked over. Could *that* be why he'd retained me as his US legal counsel? Because of some damned antique sword? OK, I was already getting the idea Matsuo Noda might be a trifle eccentric, but all the same . . .

'Interesting.' He was pointing at a long picture, part of a series locked in a wide glass case. 'Hontō ni omoshiroi, desu ne?'

Miss Mori was already there. In a voice scarcely above a whisper she proceeded to give him a rundown of pros and cons. It was the first time I'd noticed any enthusiasm out of the woman all night.

I checked my catalogue. The piece was a Heian hand scroll, said to be 'exceedingly rare'. After a few moments Noda motioned me over. 'Perhaps you could give us your opinion. What do you think?' He pointed down. 'The subject is intriguing. These are ladies-in-waiting for the Emperor. Fujiwara. Notice the delicate refinement of the colouring, the matched fabrics, each enhancing the other like flowers in a bouquet. That was eight centuries ago, just before the rise of the first Shogun, the first "Generalissimo" who would rule in the Emperor's name.'

When he said 'Shogun', niece Mori shot him a quick admonitory glance. There was some kind of unmistakable electricity passing. Something left unspoken.

'The Heian era ended with the great conflict between the Heike and Genji clans that led to the death of the ruling Emperor in 1185 and the loss of the Imperial Sword at sea.' Next he said something in guttural Japanese to Mori, obviously very intent, and indicated one corner of the painting, where the Emperor sat. Her reply was quick and curt. Now, I only know a little of the language, maybe a couple of cuts above Berlitz level, but I did manage to pick up she wasn't talking about the painting. Something to do with the Emperor himself, though I missed the rapid-fire delivery.

In response to Noda's question I tried to sound intelligent, saying the ink colouring looked well preserved, or some such auction house mumbo jumbo. It wasn't my thing really, which the man surely knew. He seemed to know everything else about me. After he listened politely, they switched back to Japanese and finally settled on a bid. I watched as she marked it in the catalogue – low six figures.

Walton, I thought, you're dealing with a pair of heavy-weights.

By then I'd decided not to bother bidding on anything. There were too many curious twists, not to mention the building deal. Surely the ritual had gone far enough, the *samurai* negotiating ploy of making your adversary be first to reveal his game plan.

Why not bring up why we were there, just for the hell of it?

When I did, Noda betrayed a fleeting smile. 'But of course, the building.' He made it sound like some kind of trivial annoyance, a nuisance to get out of the way so we could all get back to the serious work of admiring the pretty pictures.

Touché, I thought. Round one to Noda, on points. 'I assume you've had a look at the package of materials I messengered up to your hotel yesterday?'

A broker friend had put together some listings for office buildings around midtown – it turned out the market was softening a touch due to the latest construction binge – and I'd hoped that maybe something would catch Noda's eye. Matter of fact, there were a couple of real bargains over near Sixth.

'My people have examined it in detail. We would like to move forward on the twenty-storey building on Third Avenue.'

For a second I thought he was joking. Sure we'd tossed in the

12

write-up, because it fitted his profile, but it was a crazy all-cash deal, and they wanted ninety million, firm.

'Did you read the terms on that one? It's all . . .'

'There *is* a vacant floor, is there not? Available immediately?'

'Well, yes, but . . .'

'There may be a few items to clarify — we would like your legal opinion concerning the leases of the existing tenants — but nothing major. If the seller is prepared, I think we could even go to contract early next week, while I'm here. I would like very much to close as soon as possible. If some of my staff can meet with the seller's attorneys over the weekend, perhaps we can start work.'

Over the weekend? No counter bid, no haggling? Now, you didn't have to be a brain surgeon to realise this was a fast-track deal; Matsuo Noda was a man in a hurry. 'Looks like you just may have yourself a piece of property. I'll try and get hold of them in the morning, if I can, and start the ball rolling.'

'Excellent.' He hesitated a moment, as though framing his words, then continued, 'But in fact, Mr Walton, we'd actually wanted to meet you tonight for an entirely different purpose. I'd hoped we might be working together on, well, some additional matters.'

'Something else?'

'As you might surmise, we are not enlarging our presence here to no purpose. Tonight I wanted to tell you something about the objectives of Nippon, Inc. And then let you decide if what we propose merits your participation. Your financial expertise could make you a great asset to us.'

Hang on, I thought. This thing is starting to go a little fast.

'What do you have in mind?'

'First let me say you are a man I have long admired. Your style is not unlike my own. We both understand the importance of moving cautiously, of keeping our adversaries off guard. Most of all, there is a rigorous discipline about your work. That is the style of *bushidō*, the way of the warrior.' He smiled, and his tone lightened. 'I think we could cooperate very effectively.'

Already I was wondering whether I really wanted to

'cooperate' any further with Matsuo Noda. Something about the man, and Miss Mori, made me very nervous. Besides, I was trying to finish off work now, not begin more. But he'd found out the one line that would keep me listening. He'd somehow discovered I was a deep admirer of the old-time military strategists of the East — such as Sun Tzu and Miyamoto Musashi.

Like a hostile takeover bid, the ancient Japanese way of combat was ritualised, as mounted warriors rode out, announced their lineage (to the SEC?), then matched up with men of equal renown. The *samurai* prized flexibility over brute strength; they had steel swords that handled like scalpels and body armour that was a woven mesh of lacquered-iron scales laced together in rows to create a 'fabric' of metal. Those weapons and armour made for agile movement, easy feints, fast changes in strategy — all trademarks of mine on the corporate takeover battlefield.

As a result, I fancied myself some kind of *samurai* too . . .

The question was, how did Noda know this?

For some reason just then I glanced over towards Akira Mori. She appeared to be studying a scroll with the detachment of a Zen monk in *zazen* meditation, but she wasn't missing a syllable.

'Care to run through whatever it is you have in mind?' I indicated one of the ottomans along the side of the room, now clearing as bidders rose to go inside. I watched as the dark-suited Japanese businessmen filed past, none with Noda's sense of style, and noticed that several seemed acquainted with him, pausing to offer obsequious bows.

'With pleasure.' He settled himself. Mori, now looking over some screens, still didn't elect to join us. 'First, may I presume you already know something of Nippon, Inc.?'

'No more than what I gleaned from that package you forwarded. Almost nothing, really.'

He laughed, a flash of even teeth. 'Perhaps I should be pleased. These days too much visibility in the US can sometimes stir up "friction".'

'Your prospectus indicated you help banks manage capital, so I assume you're looking to enter the financial picture here.'

That was the funny part, recall. There was no indication of *any*

US action in his prospectus. Yet I knew that, overall, Japan's US investment, private and public, was in the tens and hundreds of billions. Pension funds and industries were building factories, financing corporations, snapping up Treasury paper. Japan had become a major source of fresh money for the US and for the world. But Nippon, Inc. wasn't one of the players.

'Yes, we intend to be concerned, initially, with the position of Japanese capital in the US. We are particularly interested in the matter of Treasury debentures.'

That was what anybody would have figured. Just that week the *Journal* had noted that Japanese investors were expected to cover almost half of our Treasury overdrafts for the year. They were advancing us the bucks to keep up that spending spree known as the national deficit. They sold us Toyotas; we sold them federal IOUs, using the proceeds to buy more Toyotas. In effect they were financing the good life, supplying us the 're-volving credit' to buy their cars and VCRs and semiconductors.

'Treasuries always make a lot of sense.' I picked up the thread. 'Full faith and credit of the US government, all the rest.'

'Quite so, Mr Walton, but since all things are theoretically possible, over the past few months I've undertaken a small programme through subsidiaries of Nippon, Inc. to begin cushioning Japan's exposure in your Treasury market somewhat.' He paused. 'Now that my effort may be expanding significantly, I was wondering if perhaps you might consent to serve as our American agent in that endeavour.'

For a second I didn't grasp what he was driving at, probably because my involvement seemed totally unnecessary. Surely he realised Treasuries were bought and sold here every day on the open market through dealer banks? No big deal. Why bother hiring a middleman?

'I can make this quick. Why don't you just contact some of the authorised Japanese brokers here in New York? You must have used them before. Nomura Securities is well respected. There's also Nikko Securities. And Daiwa Securities America. They're all primary dealers in Treasury paper now. Buy or sell whatever you like.'

Noda nodded. 'Of course. But we both know the financial markets can be very delicate. Impressions count for much, which is why I have chosen to keep a low profile. Consequently, I would prefer to continue to operate for a time outside normal channels. And in that regard, I now believe it would be desirable to have an experienced American financial specialist assist us. You, in particular, would be ideal.'

I studied him. 'Let me make sure I understand this. You're asking me to step in and begin fronting for you here in the Treasury market?'

'That is correct, Mr Walton.' He rose and strolled over to the row of *tachi* swords, where Miss Mori was still standing. They were lying on a spread of dark velvet and she was scrutinising them with a connoisseur's eye.

Now, I'd like to think I was a quick study of a situation, but this one was definitely out of whack somehow. If all Noda wanted was to roll over a little government paper, why the hush-hush? More to the point, why a whole building in midtown? He could easily do it from Tokyo. The scenario didn't compute.

'Before this conversation goes any further, I'd like a better idea of the kind of activity you're talking about. Selling Treasuries? Moving the funds into corporate bonds or munis? Commercial paper, equities?'

'Sell?' He abruptly paused to watch as the staff began carefully assembling the weapons to take inside for the sale, and his mind seemed to wander. 'You know, Mr Walton, the sword always has held the greatest fascination for me. To make one of these, layers of steel of different hardnesses were hammered together like a sandwich, then reheated, hammered out, folded, again and again, until there were perhaps a million paper-thin layers.' He pointed to one of the long blades now glistening in the light. 'You cannot see it, of course, but they used a laminate of soft steel for the core, harder grades for the cutting edge. And whereas the edge was tempered quickly to preserve its sharpness, the core was made to cool very slowly, leaving it pliant.' He suddenly smiled with what seemed embarrassment and turned back. 'I take great inspiration from the sword, Mr Walton. The man holding one must learn to meld with the spirit in the steel. He must become like it. What better than to meet the world with your hardest surface, yet maintain an inner flexibility, able to bend to circumstance as the need may arise?'

He stood a moment as though lost in some reverie then chuckled. 'Sometimes I do tend to go on and on. I believe it was selling you asked about. The fact is you would not be actually selling Treasury obligations.'

'Then what . . .?'

'Are you familiar with interest-rate futures?'

'Of course.' The question was so unexpected I answered almost before I thought. Futures contracts were part of the big new game on Wall Street, although most of the action was still out in Chicago, places like the Merc and the Board of Trade, left over from the old days when farmers sold their crops in advance at an agreed-upon price. The farmer 'sold' his grain harvest to a speculator while it was still nothing but green sprouts. He was worried the price might drop before he got it to market; the speculator was praying it would head up. The farmer, interestingly, was selling something he didn't yet have. But even if the price of wheat suddenly tanked, he was covered.

These days futures contracts were traded for all kinds of things whose value might change with time. High on that list were financial instruments such as Treasury notes and bonds, whose resale worth could drop if interest rates unexpectedly rose. If you owned a bond and were worried it might go down in value, you could hedge your exposure with a futures contract, in effect 'selling' it in advance at the current price and letting somebody else assume the risk of future market uncertainty.

Modern finance being the marvel it is, you could even sell bonds you didn't own, just like the farmer's non-existent grain. The Wall Street crowd called this a 'naked' contract, since you were obligated to go out and acquire that bond in the open market on the day you'd agreed to deliver it, even if the price had skyrocketed in the meantime. Or you had to try and buy back the contract. Of course, you were betting that price would go down, letting you pocket the difference.

Pious spirits on the futures exchanges called these deals high finance and risk hedging. They operated, however, remarkably like legalised gambling. Dabbling in interest-rate futures was not for those with a dicey heart.

'Our objective,' Noda went on, 'is to cushion Japan's exposure somewhat.'

'With futures contracts?'

'Precisely. US Treasury obligations are held by a variety of investors in Japan, but up until now we have made very little use of the protection possible in your futures markets. Nippon, Inc. will concern itself with that.'

I listened thoughtfully. 'So you're saying you want to create an insurance programme for Japanese investors in case the price of Treasuries weakens?'

It made sense. If interest rates went up, reducing the worth of their government paper, then the value of his futures contracts would rise to offset the loss.

I glanced over at Japan's monetary guru, Akira Mori, who was carefully examining her bronze fingernails. Was *she* the one behind all this sudden nervousness about America's financial health? What could these two know that we didn't? I wondered. It was all a bit mysterious.

One thing was no mystery, though. Whatever was going on with Matsuo Noda and Akira Mori gave me a very unsettled feeling.

'I'm flattered.' I looked him over. 'But afraid I'll have to pass. This fall I plan to take off for a while and . . . catch up on some personal matters that . . .'

'Mr Walton,' he cut in, 'I would urge you not to lightly dismiss my proposal.' He was staring back at me intensely. 'I can only say for now that issues are involved . . . well, they encompass matters of grave international consequence.' Another pause, followed by a noticeable hardening of tone.

'Your other obligations cannot possibly be as important. It would be in your best interest to hear me out.'

Want the truth? At that moment all my negative vibes about Matsuo Noda crystallised. He wasn't threatening me exactly. Or maybe he was. The large viewing room was all but empty now. Maybe he'd deliberately waited before getting down to his real agenda.

'My other "obligations" happen to be very important to me just now.'

'Then please consider rearranging them.'

'Besides, my fees can be substantial.' They weren't all *that* substantial, but I was looking to slow him down.

'Your fees do not present a problem.' He continued, 'This afternoon a retainer of one hundred thousand dollars was deposited in your personal account at Chase.'

'What in hell . . .'

'Money is of no consequence in this matter, Mr Walton. Time is.'

'You seem awfully sure I'll agree.'

'We expect your involvement to begin immediately. I cannot stress too strongly the urgency of what you will undertake.' He smiled thinly. 'I also feel confident a man who enjoys a challenge as much as you do will find our undertaking . . . intellectually rewarding.'

Seems I was hired and I hadn't even said yes.

This guy had another think coming. Besides, he could get anybody to do what he wanted. He didn't need me. As I stood there, I started trying to guess the dimensions of Matsuo Noda's financial hedge. Taken all together, Japan probably had roughly a hundred billion and change tied up in US government paper. No way could he be thinking of covering more than a fraction of that. I knew plenty of law clerks who could do it, for God's sake. A few phone calls to a couple of floor traders in Chicago . . .

'Look, the most I can do for you is recommend some very competent brokers I know to help you out. There shouldn't be too much to it. You'll just have to go easy. You can't hit the market makers in Chicago with too much action all at once. Prices get out of kilter. Then, too, there are exchange limits . . .'

'That is why we will be trading worldwide.' Noda withdrew a folded sheet of paper from his breast pocket. 'Perhaps you'd like to glance over our programme. These are cumulative totals, which include our activity to date, but we will begin moving much more rapidly as soon as I've completed all the financial arrangements with our institutional managers at home. Perhaps you will see why we need a monetary professional.'

I was still chewing on the 'financial arrangements' part as I took the paper, opened it, and scanned the schedule of contracts. While I stood there, the room around us sort of blurred out. I had to sit down again. All his talk about *samurai* and nerves of steel was for real.

Matsuo Noda had a programme underway to sell a pile of futures on US Treasury bills, notes and bonds he didn't own, 'naked', in an amount I had trouble grasping. I knew one thing, though: if interest rates headed down, raising the value of those presold obligations, he'd be forced to cover awesome losses. He'd be in a financial pickle that would make Brazil look flush. On the other hand, if some disaster occurred and US interest rates suddenly shot sky-high . . .

Numbers? The CBOT's long-interest contracts, notes and bonds, are in denominations of a hundred thousand each; the Merc's short paper, bills and CDs, are in units of a million per. Finally I did some quick arithmetic and totted up the zeros. Something had to be wrong here. Nobody had balls *that* big. I decided to run through the figures again, just to be sure.

It was along about then that I realised all Noda's pious talk about sheltering Japanese widows and orphans had been purest bullshit. Resting there in my hand was the biggest wager slip in world history. Assuming enough players could be found worldwide to take his action, he was planning to advance-sell US Treasury IOUs in the amount of five hundred *billion* dollars. A full quarter of our national debt.

His bet: something or somebody was about to push America over the brink.

TWO

'Yo, counsellor. Get thy butt over here and buy me a drink.'

I was standing in the smoky entry of Martell's, on the way back downtown from Sotheby's, when I heard the voice, a Georgia drawl known from Wall Street to Washington. And sure enough, leaning against the long mahogany bar, the usual Glenfiddich on the rocks in hand, was none other than Bill Henderson.

Long time, no see. I'd actually stopped by for a little 90-proof nerve medicine myself, not to pass the time with America's foremost cowboy market-player. But the idea of bringing in a Wall Street pro was most welcome. If anybody could dissect Noda's game, Bill was the man.

What was I going to do? I'd stalled on giving Matsuo Noda a final answer, telling him I needed time to think. Then just to make sure the whole thing hadn't been some sort of macabre hoax, I'd checked at a Chase bank machine on Lex. He hadn't been kidding. A retainer had been deposited all right, presumably by certified cheque since it had already cleared. I was on the payroll, ready or not.

Noda was right about one thing. What he planned to do had grave international consequences. The problem was, his game had just one payoff. The way I figured it, he won if, and *only* if, the US suddenly went broke. As international consequences go, that seemed reasonably grave.

Henderson was the perfect guru to take apart the scenario. Assuming he was sober. Tell the truth, at first glance I wasn't entirely sure. The guy looked a mess. I assumed he was holding some sort of private celebration, or maybe it was a wake. What was the occasion?

'William H., welcome back to town. Thought you'd decamped permanently down to DC.'

'Packed it in. Back to start making a living again. Could be I've just set some kind of new world record for the briefest tenure ever seen on the Council.' He eased over to make room, while the jukebox began some Bobby Short standard about incomparable NY. 'So where's your TV star tonight? Sure love that gal.' He toasted Donna's memory. 'If tits were brains, she'd be a genius.'

Sexist? Tasteless? That was merely Henderson warming up.

I hadn't actually set eyes on Bill since an ill-fated birthday dinner Donna had thrown for him in midsummer, a favour to a producer friend of hers at the station who'd wanted to try vamping a real live millionaire. That evening he'd arrived with a serious head start on the whisky, his meditation on the concept of birthdays, and then proceeded to regale those assembled with his encyclopaedic repertoire of farmer's-daughter and travelling-salesman vignettes. In the aftermath, Donna swore she'd kill him if he ever set foot in her place again. When I made the mistake of speaking in his defence, she critiqued a few of *my* character defects as well, then added me to the list.

'Friend, no small thanks to you and that sordid evening, I haven't seen Donna since.'

'That was a dark moment in my history. After listening half the night to that air-head producer she put next to me, I was in mourning for the hearts and minds of America.' He revolved back to the bar. 'What're you drinking?'

'Something serious.' I pointed towards the single malt. 'Laphroaig neat.'

Just then Bill paused to watch as two women in bulky raincoats brushed past. They receded towards the other end of the bar, settled their coats across an empty stool and ordered drinks. One was a youngish blonde, a bit nervous, having some tall coloured potion that looked as if it could use a cut of pineapple and a plastic monkey on the glass. But the other one, brunette, was a different story. Pained eyes, with a psychic armour that could only be called battle-weary New York. Joanna, all over again. Tanqueray martini. Straight up.

'Hot damn, sure is good to be back in this town.' He was trying, without conspicuous success, to catch the younger woman's eye.

'Henderson, you're standing next to a man with some news that could well alarm you considerably.'

'Like maybe this dump might run low on booze?'

'Not likely.' I reached for my new drink. 'I've got to make a decision, fast. So try to keep a clear head and see if you can help me out.'

In my estimation Henderson was a phenomenon — sober or loaded. He'd emerged from the red clay hills somewhere in north Georgia, former football All-State ('I only did it for the pussy'), and ended up at Yale Law — where we shared an apartment for three whole years. By the time we'd finished our degrees, I figured I was ready to tackle real life, but Bill had hung in and gone for a PhD in economics. Although his athlete's physique hadn't survived Yale — an early casualty of the single malt and the Dunhills — Henderson still had the delusion he was twenty-five. Easter before last he'd arrived at my place down in the islands with some leggy print model half his age and a case of Jack Daniel's Black. Did the redneck routine bamboozle the cautious hearts of his admiring ladies? Probably. Right under the radar.

All that notwithstanding, it was a commonly accepted fact that Bill was the sharpest private currency-trader on the East Coast. If tomorrow the dollar was about to dive, the guy who'd already sold it short tonight from Hong Kong to Zurich was invariably Henderson. That part of his life had been all over the papers the previous spring, after he got tapped for the President's Council of Economic Advisers. I guess some genius on the White House staff — urged on by that wily Senator from New York, our mutual friend Jack O'Donnell — concluded the Council needed a pet 'contrarian' on board for appearances and Henderson looked to be a sufficiently probusiness prospect. Wrong. After a couple of interviews he was forbidden to make any more public statements. He'd failed to grasp that the national interest required fantasy forecasts just before elections. Bill may have been a master of subtlety when he was trading, but otherwise he tended to call a spade a spade, or worse.

'What's up?' He was about to punt with the blonde after one last try.

'Maybe you'd better go first.' I took a sip, savouring the peaty aroma. Let Henderson decompress in his own good time, then sound him out on Noda's chilling proposition. 'What *are* you doing here?'

'Call it modesty and discretion.' He turned back.

These were not, as you might infer, the first descriptors that leapt to mind whenever I thought of Bill.

'Care to expand?'

He slid his hand across the bar, extracted another Dunhill from its red pack, and launched a disjointed monologue starting with the goddamn traffic in DC, then proceeding to ditto coming in from La Guardia.

All this time his cigarette had been poised in readiness. Finally he flicked a sterling silver lighter, the old-fashioned kind, and watched the orange flame glisten off the mirror at our right. 'So, old buddy, that's it. All the news that's fit to print. History will record this as the moment yours truly bailed out. I figure it like this. If I can't read the signals myself these days, what in hell am I doing giving advice? Time to hit the silk. Get back to making a living. Don't know how long this party's going to last, but I figure we'd all better be saddled up and ready to ride, just in case.'

As it happens, self-proclaimed ignorance was a crucial ingredient in Henderson's deliberate 'country-boy' camouflage, designed to disarm the city slickers. I estimated the professional dirt farmer next to me, Armani double-breasted and gold Piaget timepiece, was now worth about forty million, including a chunk of an offshore bank. Yet for it all, he still liked to come across as though he'd just moseyed in and wished somebody would help him through all this fine print.

'Don't bullshit me, Bill.' I toyed with my drink. 'What you're really saying is you couldn't get anybody else to agree with you.'

24

'Have to admit there were a few trifling differences of opinion about the shape we're in.' He positioned his Dunhill in the ashtray and washed his throat with more Scotch. 'You can't cover up fundamentals with cosmetics. Things like a megabillion trade shortfall, a debt nobody can even count, and a dollar that don't know whether to fish or cut bait. We're still selling the suckers of the world more funny-coloured paper than Czarist Russia did. There ain't no quick fix for this one.' He took another sip, then turned back. 'But fuck it. Remember that old saying I used to have about being a lover, not a fighter. I always know when it's time to call in the huntin' dogs and piss on the fire. I'm back in town to stay. I got hold of my boys and they're coming in tomorrow to start getting everything out of mothballs. We're going back on-line.'

As anybody who knew Bill was aware, he'd installed a massive computer bank in the converted 'maid's quarters' of his Fifth Avenue apartment, hooked to the major futures exchanges and financial markets around the world. Running his operation on a moment-to-moment basis were a couple of young fireballs, his 'Georgia Mafia', who did nothing but watch green numbers blink on a CRT screen and buy and sell all day. He and his boys talked a language that had very little to do with English — jargon about comparing the 'implied volatility' of options on this currency against the 'theoretical volatility' for that one, etc. On any given day, they were placing 'straddles' on yen options, 'butterfly spreads' on pound sterling futures, 'reverse option hedges' on Deutsche marks, and on and on. Half the time, Einstein couldn't have tracked what they were doing. Add to that, they leveraged the whole thing with breathtaking margins. To stay alive in Henderson's game, you had to be part oracle, part Jimmy the Greek. You also had to have ice water in your veins. It wasn't money to him, it was a video game where the points just happened to have dollar signs in front. The day I dropped in to watch, he was down two million by lunch, after which we casually strolled over to some shit-kicker place on Third Avenue for barbecued ribs and a beer, came back at three, and by happy-hour time he was ahead half a million. In the trade Henderson was part of the breed known as a shooter. Up a million here, down a million there — just your typical day in the salt mines. A week of that and I'd have had an ulcer the size of the San Andreas fault.

He liked to characterise his little trading operation as 'a sideline to cover the rent'. I happened to know what it really paid was the incidental costs of a lot of expensive ladies. Could be Bill's entertainment fund was in need of a transfusion.

'Back to business?' I asked. 'Like the good old days?'

'Bright and early Monday morning. Got a strong hunch the Ruskies'll be in the market buying dollars to cover their September shorts on Australian wheat futures. Might as well bid up the greenback and make the comrades work for their daily bread. Then round about eleven, I figure to unwind that and go long sterling, just before London central figures out what's happening, shits a brick, and has to hit the market for a few hundred million pounds to steady the boat.'

Well, I thought, Henderson the Fearless hasn't lost his touch.

'Bill, I want to run a small scenario by you.' I sipped at my drink. 'Say somebody'd just told you he was taking a massive position in interest-rate futures? What would that suggest?'

'Tells me the man's getting nervous. If he was holding a lot of Treasury paper, for instance, he'd probably figured rates were about to head up and he didn't want to get creamed. See, if you're holding a bond that pays, say, eight per cent, and all of a sudden interest rates scoot up to ten, the resale value of that instrument is gonna go down the sewer. But if you've already "sold" it using a futures contract, whoever bought that contract is the one who's got to eat the loss. You're covered.'

'I'm not talking about standard hedging.' I was wondering how to approach the specifics. 'Say somebody started selling a load of bond futures naked. Nothing underlying.'

'Well, thing about that is, the man'd be taking one hell of a risk.' He swirled the cubes in his glass. 'Anybody does that's bettin' big on something we don't even want to think about. Some kind of panic that'd cause folks to start dumping American debt paper.'

26

I just stood there in silence, examining my glass. That was precisely my reading of Matsuo Noda's move. 'But I can't think of any reason why anything like that's in the cards, can you?'

'You tell me. It's hard to imagine. The economy's like a supertanker. Takes it a long time to turn around. But if you want a special Henderson shit-hits-the-fan scenario, then I can give it a shot. Say, for instance, some Monday morning a bunch of those hardworking folks around the world who've been emptying their piggy banks to finance our deficit suddenly up and decide they'd like their money shipped back home. That'd create what's known as a liquidity crisis, which is a fancy way of saying you don't have enough loose quarters in the cookie jar that morning to pay the milkman and the paperboy both. The Federal Reserve would have to jack up interest rates fast to attract some cash. Else roll the printing presses. Or of course' – he grinned – 'we *could* just default, declare bankruptcy and tell the world to go fuck itself.'

'Nobody would possibly let it go that far, right?' I toyed with my Scotch. 'Particularly Japan. We owe them more money than anybody.'

'Wouldn't look for it to happen. Remember though, right now the US Treasury's out there with a tin cup begging the money to cover its interest payments. If the national debt was on MasterCharge, they'd take back our card. So let some of those Japanese pension funds who're shovelling in money start getting edgy, or the dollar all of a sudden look weak, and you could have a run on the greenback that'd make the bank lines in '29 look like Christmas Club week.'

'That's thinking the unthinkable.'

'Damned well better be. But don't ever forget, paper money is an act of faith, and we're in uncharted territory here. Never before has the world's reserve currency, the one everybody uses to buy oil and grain and what have you, belonged to its biggest debtor nation. We're bankers for the world and we're ass over elbow in hock. Everybody starts gettin' nervous the same day, and the bankers on this planet could be back to swapping shells and coloured beads.'

'Offhand I'd say that's pretty implausible.'

'And I agree. The system got a pretty good shakeout in the October Massacre of '87 and things held together, if just barely. Stocks crashed but the dollar and the debt markets weathered the storms. Nobody dumped. Japan doesn't want its prime customer to go belly up. Who else is gonna buy all that shiny crap?'

I studied my glass again. If Henderson, who had pulse-feelers around the globe, wasn't worried, then maybe Matsuo Noda *was* just a nervous, spaced-out old guy. A loony-tune with an itch to gamble. Funny, though, he appeared the very essence of a cool-headed banker.

About then, the two women across the bar waved for their bill and began rummaging their purses. Sadly enough, the brunette had done everything but send over an engraved invitation for us to join them. She and I had looked each other over and we both knew what we saw. The walking wounded.

It made me pensive. More and more lately I'd begun to wonder about the roads not taken, the options that never were. What if all our lives had started out differently? Where would you be? Where would I be — playing lawyer now, or maybe driving cab? It was the kind of woolgathering that drove Donna Austen insane.

It was on my mind that first afternoon I met her, when she brought her sound guy down to record some 'voice-overs' to use with shots of the house. She made the mistake of asking for a little background, so I decided to go way back and give her the big picture. It turned out to be a little kinky for the six o'clock news.

I started the tale by telling her about my father, once a rig foreman in the oil patch out around Midland, Texas. I was still a kid when he started tinkering around weekends with drill bits out in his shop, and I was no more than about ten when he came up with a new kind of tip. Turned out it could double the life expectancy of a bit, not to mention the life expectancy of a lot of roughnecks who had to change them every few hours. He patented the thing, and next thing you knew, he was 'President' of Permian Basin Petroleum.

'Your father was a successful inventor?' She'd set her Tab down on the living-room table and perked up. Here was some 'colour' for her profile.

'More than that. The man was a believing capitalist.' Was she really going to understand the significance of what happened? 'You see, since no banker would risk loaning out venture capital back in those days, he had to take PBP public. He needed money so badly he sold off 60 per cent of the company.'

'Like those entrepreneurs who created home computers in their garage?' She brushed at her carefully groomed auburn hair. Maybe here was her hook, the grabber.

'Close. He took the money, several million, and started production. And guess what? The bit he'd invented was *too* good. Next thing you know, another outfit that will remain nameless here came along and infringed on the patent, saying "sue us" — which he began trying to do. But since they were already tooled up to manufacture, they undercut his prices and drove PBP's stock down to zip. Then came the kill. They staged a hostile takeover and — since PBP now owned the patents, not him — axed the lawsuit. Bye, bye, company.'

'How does this story relate to what you do today?' She was checking her watch, no longer overly engaged.

'Well, by the time all this happened, I was off studying engineering at the University of Texas. But when I graduated, I decided to do something else. I headed for Yale Law.'

'If you can't lick 'em, join 'em? Something like that, Mr Walton?'

'Not exactly, Ms Austen. I wanted to find out if the Bible's right: that guys who live by the sword had better be ready to die by the sword. After the sheepskin, I shopped around and found the Manhattan law firm that handled the biggest oil-field service outfit in the country, then applied to that firm's corporate department. A couple of years and a lot of memos later, our oil-field client somehow got the idea they ought to go vertical, acquire their own source of equipment. Next I ran some numbers and showed them how profitable it would be to acquire a certain tool company that now owned the patent on a terrific drill bit.

29

Of course, it would require a hostile buyout, but with a little restructuring they could swing it financially.'

'And?'

'I worked nights and weekends for six months and personally devised the takeover. By oddest coincidence, when we were through we decided to strip all that company's overpaid executives of their "golden parachutes" and dump them on the street. My graduation present to the old man.'

She rolled her eyes and waved at her sound man to shut off the mike. 'Mr Walton, I think our viewers would be more interested in personal stories.'

What did she want? I wondered. This was the most 'personal' story I had.

'What do you mean? What I eat for breakfast?'

'I do personalities.' She looked around the living room. 'Are you married?'

'I was.'

On came the tape. But she didn't get what she wanted. Joanna wouldn't appreciate being critiqued on Channel Eight's evening news. And Amy would have killed me. So I just plunged ahead and finished off the other saga.

'There's a bit more to this intimate bio. Guess I'd seen enough quick money in the oil business that I'd forgotten you were supposed to be impressed by it. Or maybe I'd just never mastered the art of kissing my elders' asses convincingly. You'll find, Ms Austen, that those are two attitudes whose rewards are largely intangible; Wall Street compatibility definitely not being on the list. After five years the Management Committee offered a partnership, but by then I'd decided to go out and try making it on my own. Be my own man.'

She waved the sound man off again. 'You mean you quit?'

'Couldn't have said it better. I hung up a shingle ... and started playing the other side of the scrimmage line.'

'I understand you've been in quite a few takeover fights.'

'Let's say I've fought a lot of takeovers, Ms Austen. There's a subtle but important distinction.'

Donna Austen turned out to be more interested in my marital

status than in anecdotes about corporate mayhem. Thing was, beneath all that glitz I found her a challenging woman. Amy, on the other hand, despised her. But then she never likes anybody I bring home. The real problem, however, was that I kept thinking more about Joanna than I did about Donna. As witness this evening, when that sadder-but-wiser brunette headed out the door reminded me of her more than a little . . .

'Hate to see that young specimen depart without a good-faith offer of condolence.' Henderson was wistfully eyeing the young blonde. Definitely his type. 'Trouble is, I couldn't locate the equipment tonight with a compass and a search warrant.' He hoisted his glass, then turned back and reached for another Dunhill. 'So tell me what brings you uptown. Never knew you to venture this far into civilisation just to stand a drink for your oldest and wisest confidant.'

Back to reality. 'William H., you will undoubtedly find this difficult to accept, but I just got asked to front some Treasury action for a new client. Selling futures.'

'Where do you find your suckers?' He grinned. 'That's never been your game.'

'Hey, at least I know the rules. Corporations have been known to hedge their debt offerings, my friend. But what I've done up to now's been strictly bush league compared to this.'

'So what's the play?'

'A foreign outfit that wants low profile. And PS, they're talking substantial numbers.'

'What do you mean, "substantial"?' Suddenly Henderson's input file was on red alert.

'Probably wouldn't impress a high roller like you, Bill.' I paused. 'Half a trillion dollars.'

'Jeezus.' He went pale. 'Who's putting up the earnest money for this shot? Let interest rates head the wrong way, you couldn't cover the margin calls on a position that size with the GNP of South America.'

'What if it happened to be some of our friends from across the Pacific? An outfit that calls itself Nippon, Inc.' I looked at him. 'Ever hear of it?'

'Nope.' He just stood there, examining his drink as though it suddenly had acquired an enormous insect. 'But you've got a surefire knack for really messin' up an evening.'

'I guess this is what's meant when people talk about the big time.'

'Christ Almighty. Tell you one thing, that's a hell of a number to put on the table. I'd sure like to see those boys' hand.'

'Maybe somebody's paying to see ours.' I finished off my drink and signalled for another. The more I thought about Matsuo Noda, the more I realised I needed it. 'You know, this half scares the crap out of me.'

'Matt, old buddy, do yourself a favour. Stand clear. Just back away.' He was getting more sober by the second. 'You'd be lifting up some kind of big rock when you don't know what's under it. I never do that. Ironclad rule. Same as I always cut losses at ten per cent and never let a long position ride over a weekend. And I'll tell you something else. Nobody lays down a bet like that unless he knows the casino's fixed.' He paused. 'I wonder if maybe we oughtn't to give Jack a call?'

'O'Donnell?'

'Low key. Just touch base. Inside word is his Finance Committee's going to be holding hearings on foreign investment, maybe in a couple of months. Besides, I know for a fact he owes you a few.'

That was true. Senator Jack O'Donnell was headed for re-election headaches. He was America's corporate nightmare – a former professor of labour law at Columbia who'd gone out and bought some tailored suits, shed thirty pounds, dyed his hair, and actually gotten elected to the US Senate. He was despised on Wall Street for good reason. O'Donnell was the Grand Inquisitor of the corporate scene, hauling CEOs in front of his committee every time he sniffed some new scam to shortchange stockholders. Since we saw eye to eye a lot, I'd made it a point to lean on a few of my clients and come up with some campaign bucks for him, telling them it was good 'insurance money'. Still, if I leaked this to Jack, I'd probably be reading it tomorrow in the *Washington Post*.

'Henderson, I can't bring him in. Nobody's talking anything illegal. Still, I'm beginning to think I ought to keep an eye on this from the inside.'

'Matt, you haven't been listening. Let me pass along a major working principle on how to keep your ass intact in this world. Write it down and tape it to your phone: staying on the sidelines is a position too. That applies to Wall Street, and it damned sure applies to life.' He stretched for a Dunhill, then leaned back. 'Ever tell you about that feisty 'coon hound I used to have, Redtick I called by the name of Red?'

'Only about a hundred times.' Red was his favourite sermon text.

'Well, ol' Red somehow conceived the idea he was just about the meanest fucker in the county and he was always out to prove it. Then one night he made the mistake of treeing a big old mama 'coon, up in this little sycamore we had down by the creek. I heard him barking and raising hell and I knew I wouldn't get a wink if I didn't go down and see about it.'

'Henderson, *Christ*, I've already heard this.'

'Well, I'm gonna finish it anyhow, by God. Sounds like you could use a refresher course.' He took a drink. 'Now then, after I made it through the copperheads and briars and got down there, naturally the first thing I did was shine that tree with my light and count the eyes. Turns out that mama raccoon had a bunch of her little ones up there too. So she was in a real disagreeable frame of mind. Her eyes were bright red and I could tell she was thinking she just might eat herself a smartass hound for supper. I tried to explain this to Red, call him off, and get him to come on back up the house, but no sirree, nothing would do but he had to take her on. So I figured it was time he had a little reality contact. I chunked a couple of rocks, got lucky, and down she tumbled. Next thing ol' Red knew, he thought he had his ass caught in a brand-new John Deere hay baler. I finally had to kick her off him and get her back up the tree before she really got mad.'

'Henderson, I hear you.'

'Listen up, friend. There's a moral. You see, ol' Red didn't have enough expertise that night to know when to stand off. But I'll tell you one thing: he learned real fast. Next time he chased that particular mama up that sycamore, he took one sniff and just trotted right on back to the house.' He sipped again. 'Every time I come across a tree full of something I don't know about, I remember old Red and just turn around and walk away.'

'I'm taking your warning under advisement.' I threw down a fifty, glanced at the soundless Mets game on the TV over the bar, and reached for my coat.

'You'd damned well better.'

'Henderson, get some sleep. As a friend and colleague I must in all honesty advise you you look like absolute hell.'

'I've always valued your candour.' He waved for another drink. 'But I've got some heavy thinking to do.'

'OK, get home safe. Let's keep in touch.'

He saluted with his glass. 'Tell you what, Matt, maybe I'll just do a little sniffing around myself, see if I can't get a fix on what's up the tree.'

'OK.' I was putting on my coat, checking through the window to see if the rain had stopped. Looked like it had. 'Let's both sleep on it.'

'You do that.' He wasn't smiling as I headed out the door.

Henderson, who could slumber like a baby when he was down a million for the day, didn't look like he had much rest ahead that night. For all my brave talk, I didn't either. Now that the rain was over, I wandered over to Fifth to look at the trees sparkling in the streetlights. And to think. If you're from West Texas, you love to see green things wet.

Then I hailed a cab downtown, still with lots of unanswered questions on the subject of Matsuo Noda. What had happened to my country that could make it so vulnerable to the financial shenanigans of a single white-haired foreign banker? Was this what people meant when they talked about the tides of history? Was the free ride over?

Back when I was a kid, I'd accepted as an article of faith that America was the greatest, that we were destined to lead the world forever. Was that hubris? Now I had this sinking feeling we were about to begin learning a little modesty. Maybe Amy didn't know it yet, but her America was going to end up being a lot different from mine. All of a sudden folks all over the world were about to be richer than we were. It was going to take some painful adjustment.

That's when I finally decided. Yes, by God, I would track this one. And when I figured out what Noda had up his sleeve, I'd blow the whistle. Somebody needed to stand guard over this country, and if not me, who?

Matt Walton *vs* Matsuo Noda.

As it turned out, the evening still wasn't over. Things continued to go off track, beginning with when I walked in my front door. I guess by now everybody's pretty blasé about urban crime, but it's still always a shock when it happens to you. I also think it's getting worse. I can remember five years ago when Joanna and I never bothered even to latch the street windows. These days they have bars – a small precaution following an evening on the town during which everything we owned with an electric cord attached walked out into the bracing Manhattan night. That was my first experience with the hollow feeling in your gut when you realise your sanctum has been plundered. It's not the lost toys, it's the violation that gnaws at your karma.

This time, though, it appeared to be minor. No forcible entry. Somebody had actually picked the front-door lock, a fact I only established to my satisfaction after every other possibility had been considered and dismissed. Truthfully, I probably wouldn't have noticed anything at all that night if not for a wayward train of thought on the way home.

I'd been meditating on a particular sword in my collection, a *katana*, which was totally without distinction except for a little oral history. Reportedly the blade once tasted blood in a rather arcane episode. Noda probably would have approved. The story was, the *samurai* who'd commissioned it decided he liked it so much he didn't want the swordsmith telling anybody how he'd forged it. So after he'd thanked the guy graciously, deep bows and all the rest, he picked up the sword, bowed one more time, and then hauled back and sliced him in half, clean as a whistle.

The *kesa* stroke, left collarbone straight through the right hip. It's said a *samurai* could do things such as that in the old days.

My meeting with Noda had made me want to look it over, to refresh my memory concerning that Japanese capacity for the unexpected. So after I let myself in through the front foyer, I tossed my raincoat over a banister, headed down to the kitchen to pour myself a nightcap and proceeded upstairs to the 'office'.

I clicked on the light and then . . .

Jesus! The place had been trashed. Drawers open, files tipped over, piles of paper askew. After the first numbing shock, that perception-delay your senses impose before you can actually accept what you're seeing, I quickly started taking an inventory. OK, what did they get this time?

Well, the computer and printer were both intact, cordless phone was there still, the little nine-inch Sony in the corner was untouched . . . Hey, could it be they hadn't actually lifted anything?

Then I remembered why I'd come upstairs. Off to the side, under the back stair, was a big walk-in closet I called my 'sword room', always kept under lock and key. I glanced over at the door.

Hold on. It was hanging open slightly. I strolled over and checked it more closely. The mechanism had been jimmied, professionally but with enough force that the metal frame around the door was askew. Not a blatant entry, but a determined one.

My heart skipped a beat. That's why they didn't bother with TVs. These guys knew where the real action was, the lightweight, very expensive loot. I opened the door, took a deep breath and felt for the light.

You could have heard my sigh of relief all the way out in the street. From the looks of it, nothing was missing here either.

Be sure now. I quickly glanced down the racks, mentally cataloguing the pieces. Everything had a place, and all the places were still full. Strange. This stuff was worth thousands. Burglars break in to steal. So what happened? Maybe something scared them off. My sheepdog Benjamin, the fearless terror of the streets? He was now snoring at the foot of the stairs, but who knows . . .

Walton, you lucky stiff, this could have been a major hit. I cursed at the thought of having to have the door and lock repaired, made a mental note to remember to call the locksmith over by Sheridan Square in the morning, and pushed the damaged door closed.

What a hell of a night. I pulled the Sotheby's catalogue out of my pocket, recalling the auction that had inaugurated this fateful evening, and turned to chuck it in the file cabinet where I kept all the records for my hobby: prices, news clippings, correspondence, the rest.

The cabinet, one of those cheap tin jobs you buy at discount office supply places, was slightly askew. What's this? I yanked open the top drawer and saw chaos.

Uh, oh. I went down the row, checking. Tell you one thing, my intruders had been thorough. Every drawer was a mess, just like the office. Then I got to the bottom, the one with backup data on the collection. Appraisals, provenance of the pieces, that kind of thing.

It was empty.

But of course! Any pro would know that half the value of a collection such as this would be in all the documentation. Which meant my methodical thieves were no dummies; they'd started with the paperwork, the valuations and authenticity info . . . which meant they weren't through. I must have somehow interrupted their . . .

My God! They could still be here.

I edged for the phone and punched 911, the police emergency number. Next I went back and pulled down a sword, just for protection, and swept the empty house. It was all nice and tidy.

Finally New York's men in blue showed, an overweight Irishman and his Puerto Rican partner, both with moustaches. I actually knew them, having once received a ticket for walking Ben off the leash. We went through the formalities, lots of questions with no answers worth writing down, and then they offered to send around a fingerprint squad in the morning. Sure, why not. And you'd better get new locks for this place, Mr . . . Walton. Right. We all thanked each other and I saw them out.

Then I headed back down to the kitchen. What was this all about? Stealing files? Paper? Those documents, lovingly and painstakingly assembled, were what made the swords somehow uniquely a part of my life. Something that actually wasn't going to decide to take a hike the next week. The stuff had no value to anybody except Matt Walton.

Or so I thought.

THREE

Some people will swear life runs on coincidence. Is it true? If so, here's one for the history books. It's the tale of an old flame. Before my ex-wife Joanna, before my later ill-starred adventure with Donna Austen. The lady's name was Tamara Richardson, and she was a professor at New York University. When I knew her, though, she was merely an assistant prof with a shiny new PhD, fresh out of Columbia's graduate school and very much starting out. I was too. Best I can remember, we met shopping for green groceries at Balducci's, just up Sixth Avenue from my place, and we saw each other a few times. It had to be at least fifteen years (how time flies) since our brief episode.

Tam Richardson, however, was not easy to forget. There was a kind of under-the-surface intensity about the woman that seemed always close to the ignition point. When you were around her, you were always worried somebody might accidentally light a match. However, she had no shortage of men in her life and eventually we each went our own way. Ships that passed in the night. I never expected to hear of her again.

Things didn't quite work out that way, however. She started getting famous, as a thorn in the side of America's lackadaisical corporate management. Somewhere along the line, Tam Richardson had taken it upon herself to single-handedly kick some overpaid ass in America's plush boardrooms, and she wasn't trying to win any popularity contests doing it. She was the kid in the story who pointed out the Emperor had on no clothes, while everybody else was claiming his tux was a great fit. Guess you can't fire somebody in academia merely for saying what everybody knows to be true but doesn't have the guts to verbalise.

Then about a year ago, I noticed a full-length profile of her in an airline magazine spread about 'America's New Achievers'. No escaping her. Between the lines, I got the definite impression she hadn't really changed all that much over the years. She was around five seven, high cheekbones, dark hair that looked like it could use a brush, and eyes that made you think twice about giving her a lot of bullshit. Reminded me of, say, the young Glenda Jackson with a heavy spike of Debra Winger. For my money, though, she was just about ideal in the female department. Trim bottom, nice little twist in her stride, just enough cleavage to make you wonder. She didn't go out of her way to advertise, but you figured the goods were on board. My recollection in a nutshell? Tam Richardson was a better than average looker, damned smart, and she knew no fear. None.

There was something about her, though, that always left people puzzling. Where'd she come from? American, sure, but no way could she have been corn-fed Midwest like her surname. The answer was, she had a slightly more exotic, and probably painful, history than most of us. Maybe that was part of the reason she always seemed to be a loner, never went along with the crowd. The one time she'd tried that, it hadn't worked. I got to know her well enough to hear a bit of the story, but I'd sort of repressed the details.

Maybe I'd do well to come clean and admit I still thought about Tam from time to time. What's more, I gleaned from the magazine piece that she still lived right around the corner. Made me think briefly about giving her a call, get together for a drink, the old days, etc. But I finally decided I'd had enough high-spirited women for a while. Time to mellow down. Why go looking for lightning in a bottle?

She'd always liked three things: good-looking men, telling the high and mighty unpleasant truths, and interior design. Consequently it was no great surprise that the magazine devoted a photo spread to her rambling six-room apartment. The place was in one of those NYU-owned buildings on the west side of Washington Square Park, and it was definitely a knockout. She'd played off the old classic interior, a generously proportioned thirties layout, turning it into an environment that blended technology and design. Not for Tam, though, the utilitarian 'high-tech' look so trendy a few years back; no ugly 'state-of-the-art' machines. It was eclectic — modernism here, deco there.

Take her library-office. I smiled when I noticed that next to the latest IBM PS/2 was a 'streamlined' Raymond Loewy-designed calculator, pure thirties. Same old Tam. On the other hand, just to keep it all from getting too serious, she also had a collection of kitschy salt and pepper shakers scattered among the books — a dog peeing against a hydrant, a naked babe with spicy boobs . . . she told the writer it was her 'tribute to America'.

The place was everything she was, a pot-pourri of the world, a mishmash of styles, and she clearly loved it. I probably missed a good half of the insider gags, this outrage up against that one, but I must say she brought it off with appreciable élan. Truthfully the place was a perfect reflection of the Tam I remembered — a woman who did her own thing.

She was now, so it said, a full professor at the university. Undoubtedly she deserved it. She was also director of their new Center for Applied Technology, which she'd founded. When the interviewer asked her which department the Center was under, she'd apparently shrugged and said 'certain people' at the university wanted to bring it in under the School of Business. But the Center had outside funding, was doing vital work, and she was darn well going to stay independent.

Whoops. That ballsy crack, although perfectly in character, meant she was now giving the back of her hand to university politics. Mouthing off in a national publication about some departmental power play is no way to endear yourself to college deans. It lays bare all their petty empire-building. Didn't seem to worry her, though; just like in the old days, she said exactly what she was thinking and let the chips tumble.

Her major occupation in recent years, as anybody who reads the op-ed pages around the country knows, was to shame American executives into getting off their duffs, to make them start diverting some of their executive perks into the serious problem of getting this country competitive again. She had plenty of ideas where the corporate-jet money could be better invested.

Over the years she'd knocked out half a dozen books on technology and the American workplace – office automation, computer-aided design in engineering, robots and computer-integrated manufacturing, that kind of thing. Tam Richardson still believed America would whip the world, but it would take more than speeches and flag-waving. Her latest exposé of America's corporate fat cats, which actually got a sidebar in the story, claimed they'd better start cutting their million-dollar salaries and putting the money into creating American jobs, or we'd all soon end up fetching coffee for the new Pacific Rim dynamos and buying our goodies at East Asia's company store.

Only she didn't bother to say it that nicely. Worse than that, the book actually supplied a long list of America's more notoriously overpaid CEOs. I suspect there were a lot of corporate contributors to the university who'd just as soon have seen her muzzled. Good luck, Tam.

Now the coincidence. The Saturday following my Friday night episode with the inscrutable president of Nippon, Inc., an event occurred that would soon bring Tam Richardson back into my life. Random luck? Fate? Anybody's guess. As it turned out, however, while I was on the phone leaving messages at country clubs for the building's attorneys, a mere five blocks away from my place Dr Tamara Richardson was putting the final touches on preparations for an evening dinner party – destined to throw us together again only weeks later.

The dinner was supposed to be strictly social, to celebrate the beginning of her sabbatical – academic talk for a year off with three-quarters pay. There were a few dinner debts to square away, so the timing was perfect. She had several articles lined up; she'd finally axed a stormy year-long affair with a colleague in Economics named David Mason; and she was scheduled to begin a book on intelligent robots. She was trying not to think too much about academic politics and the real possibility her department chairman might consign her to some kind of academic hyperspace, there to teach freshmen for the rest of her tenured days.

By mid-afternoon she was down to the last-minute refinements on the evening's plans. Since the overnight rain had purged the soot from the air, she was feeling great. She put on a new Vangelis CD, worked a few modern-dance moves into her routine as she cleared the loose books out of the living room, and continued trying to convince herself that breaking off with Dave Mason had been a smart move. After a while, though, she wasn't humming any more, just thinking. OK, it had only been a week, but why had she invited him to come to the dinner? Just to be a good sport?

The thing about it was, they'd actually had a more or less unspoken understanding not to inquire too closely into each other's occasional little diversions. They were both adults, right? This time, though, Dave had pushed it too far. He'd finally broken the rules, bringing one of his admiring grad students up to the apartment – *her* apartment. She bumped into them coming down in the elevator, and this one was a prize – stage make-up, bleached hair, the works.

Out of bounds. She'd nailed him right there in her marble lobby: you want to bang some Queens debutante, you'd better not be doing it here. This place is my home. She then told him to pack. The apartment was hers and she wanted all signs of him out by Monday.

Then she'd invited him back for the dinner. Why? Could Humpty-Dumpty be put back together again? Crack eggs, make an omelette . . . she half smiled at the odd way your mind connects absurdities when you're a little overworked . . .

That was when the phone rang.

Was it Dave, dropping out at the last minute to prove he could still piss her off, one more time? She headed for the kitchen, so she could at least chop some veggies while they argued for half an hour on the phone.

It wasn't Dave. Instead it was a scratchy old voice, one she loved. Shouting into a pay phone at Kennedy was Allan Stern, who announced in his staccato tones that he'd just stepped off a JAL flight fresh from some conference in Tokyo. He *had* to see her tonight.

'Tonight?' When it rains, it pours, she thought. 'Allan, I'd love to, but I'm having some people in from school ... What? ... Well, sure, nothing that special ... *Allan*, I adore you dearly, but you wouldn't know any of the ... OK, OK ... Can you get down by eight?'

'See you then, Tamara. You're a dear.'

Stern was an old, old friend, and a guy everybody in the country had probably heard of vaguely. Any freshman in computer science could tell you he was one of the unofficial founders of the field known as artificial intelligence, now usually shortened to 'AI'. As it happened, she had convinced him the previous spring that they ought to collaborate on a book about the growing use of smart robots in the workplace but for some reason his input had never made it past the talking stage. She'd decided just to go ahead on her own with the writing.

Well, she thought, maybe he's decided to pitch in after all. Great. That would mean it might be adopted for a lot of college courses. Allan had plenty of respectability with the establishment.

He was probably the closest friend she had, her mentor alnost. They went back to a Denver conference fifteen years ago, when he'd stood up in a session and challenged the conclusion of the very first paper she ever gave, though he'd come in midway through. Even then he had been a powerhouse in Washington, chairing one of the technical committees that reviewed federal grant applications submitted by university researchers. The inside talk on campuses was: love him or hate him, but think twice before you cross the opinionated bastard.

She was so mad she didn't care. She had sidled up to him at the coffee break and introduced herself, saying what an honour it was to meet a scholar so highly regarded, a man whose reputation was so well established. He nodded in absent acknowledgment, sipped at his styrofoam cup, and stared over her shoulder. She then proceeded to advise the celebrated Allan Stern that he'd missed the whole thrust of her talk, which she'd explained in the introduction, and furthermore – judging from the data at hand – he struck her as a pompous asshole.

Such forthrightness, which was entirely new to Dr Allan Stern's

44

sheltered existence, so astonished him he apologised on the spot. By week's end he was trying to recruit her out to Stanford. He still was.

Allan was always punctual, to the minute, and that Saturday night was no exception. The doorman downstairs announced him at eight sharp. When she met him at the elevator, her first impression was he looked a trifle worn down. America's foremost futurist was gaunt, as always, but his trademark shock of white hair streamed over a lined face that was more than usually haggard. His hard eyes, which could bore through screw-off Congressional staffers like a pair of Black & Decker drills, were actually bloodshot. In sort, the man looked awful. Then she remembered he'd just come in on the 747 directly from Narita. Into the teeth of the latest baggage-handlers' slowdown at Kennedy. Give the poor old guy a break.

She made him a drink and then asked, 'OK, Allan, what's up?'

'Later, Tamara. It's a long story.' With which he lapsed silent. Very out of character.

About then everybody else started coming up, reasonably on time since Tam was known far and wide to hate the concept of 'fashionably late'. Also, she was a great cook. Bottles of bargain wine with the prices scraped off collected on the table in the foyer and coats amassed in the second bedroom. Given that everybody knew everybody, it was mostly elbow patches and open collars. Only the women had bothered to dress. Simpson from Computer Science, whose wife worked in Admissions; Gail Wallace from Business, whose pudgy, skirt-chasing husband had guided two companies into bankruptcy; Alice and Herman Knight, who both taught in Economics (she was dean of the undergraduate college) and published as a team; Kabir Ali from Mathematics and his browbeaten little Iranian wife Shirin who seemed frightened of the world – and her husband. Only Dave had the nerve to be late and hold things up.

While they waited, they knocked off a little Scotch and white wine, trashed the administration and complained about all the committees on which they were being pressured to serve. Then around a quarter to nine Dave finally appeared, sandy curls askew to let her know where he'd been. She didn't even bother offering him a drink, just announced that everything was ready so let's adjourn to the dining room.

There're two kinds of dinners: ones that follow the rules and ones that break them all. Tam's were the latter. This time it would be real tallow candles and everybody's wine, including her own. Somehow her craziness always seemed to click; they inevitably came back for more. Tonight she'd decided to pay an offhand tribute to autumn and American cuisine. Cheddar cheese soup, marinated Ottomanelli's quail broiled with fresh sage, sweet potato scallops and baby peas, homemade corn bread and then, as a change of pace (keep 'em off balance), an endive salad spiked with coriander. Dessert was an apple-walnut casserole, washed down with pots of McNulty's dark Haitian coffee. At the end she produced an ancient cognac you could inhale forever. By eleven-thirty everybody thought they'd just ascended to paradise.

She ordered Dave to take care of the dishes (since he'd been acting as if he owned the place, let him help), then led everybody back into the living room. In the park below the weather was perfect, and marijuana sales were in overdrive. A couple of joints also appeared around the room, accompanied by withering glares from Allan. Then, while Ed Wallace was chatting up Shirin and everybody else was drinking and smoking, Allan picked up his cognac and motioned her in the direction of the study.

Finally, she thought. This must be some story.

She was right.

It wasn't her book he wanted to discuss. Instead, he wanted to tell her about what he'd just seen, and not seen, in Tokyo.

'Loved dinner.' He settled into a leather chair, the one next to her long bookcase, and drained his snifter. 'I was afraid I was turning into a fish over there.' He laughed, but only briefly. Social hour was over. 'Tam, I wanted to ask you if you could maybe help me out with something.'

'What do you have in mind?'

'Well, you know I've always thought I was on top of what Tokyo is doing, but now I'm not so sure any more. I'm afraid things are starting to get away from me.'

'Such as?'

'OK. It's no secret I've been to Japan a lot. I've got my share of friends over there, people I respect and admire very much. But this trip started to get very strange. It's as though I'm suddenly an outsider. Just another *gaijin*. I'm puzzled, and I wonder if maybe I ought to be worried.'

Gaijin. That sounds familiar, she thought. But it wasn't something that usually bothered Allan. She brushed her dark hair back out of her eyes and studied him. He'd never been more serious.

'What happened?'

He paused. 'You know about their big artificial-intelligence effort, called the Fifth Generation Project? If it goes the way they're saying, before too much longer they'll have programs, software, to *design* the next generation of computer technology.'

This was supposed to be news? Come on, Allan. Everybody knew. It was the talk of the industry. Japan's goal was computer logic capable of replicating human thought processes, a monumental, maybe impossible, undertaking.

'Allan, don't you remember we discussed doing a chapter on it in the robotics book? And if you . . .'

'Tamara, bear with me. You also know very well that project is Japan's attempt to leapfrog American technology. Added together with all their R & D on chip technology. In my opinion, by the way, our response is definitely too little, too late. More and more we're having to buy essential components for missile guidance systems from Japan. The Department of Defense is already nervous, but not nervous enough. We may have dug our own grave. And now I think our worst fears may be about to come true. Something funny seems to be happening, only I'm not sure what.'

'What do you mean?'

'Let me close that door.' He got up and did so, then turned back. 'Maybe first I ought to tell you about the odd experience I had last week.'

'Go on.' She heard somebody in the living room put on one of her old Beatles albums – still the middle-ager's idea of hip.

'Well, as always, I scheduled a stop at the Fifth Generation lab

47

to get up to speed on how their effort's doing. But all of a sudden it seems I'm too darned famous to be bothered with the shirtsleeve stuff. I tried to get in there for three days running. It was always the honourable Stern-san this and the celebrated Stern-san that and you must meet the head of every damned ministry and we have to set up this formal dinner and blah, blah, blah.'

'Allan, you're the Grand Old Man these days.' She laughed. 'Get used to it.'

'Wash out your mouth, Tamara Richardson. I'm not grand and I'm most decidedly not old.' He sniffed. 'No, it's as if they were very politely cutting me out. OK, they didn't exactly say the project was off-limits now or anything, but there never seemed to be a convenient time to drop by the lab.'

'Who knows? Maybe they just didn't want some American partisan poking about the place any more.'

'Could be. But why? I'm scarcely a spy for DOD, or the CIA. They know I only do pure science. OK, maybe I'm old-fashioned, but Dr Yoshida at least has always claimed to respect me for that. I used to spend hours with him going over his work there and vice versa. We swapped ideas all the time. Now all of a sudden there's this smokescreen.' He paused, sipped at his brandy, and then leaned back. 'Which brings me to that favour I need.'

'What?'

'Well, I was wondering if maybe you could try and get into the Fifth Generation lab yourself, check around a bit. See if you can find out what's cooking.'

'Go to Tokyo?'

'I realise it's a lot to ask, but who else can I turn to? Tam, you're the only person I know who could pull this off. You know the technology, and they respect you. Also, you understand the language. Maybe you can cut through all the politeness and the translated PR. If you'd like a little *per diem*, I'll see if I can't shake loose the money from somewhere.'

'Allan, really, don't you think you're maybe going overboard just a little? What if Dr Yoshida was just tied up? The last time I visited the lab, he showed me everything, completely open.'

'Ho, ho.' He set down his brandy, and his eyes hardened. 'I still haven't told you the clincher. There's some new guy in charge now.'

'That's hard to believe. Yoshida practically invented the Fifth Generation Project. He's the director . . .'

'That's just it. Kaput. All of a sudden he's not around any more. They said he's now "technical adviser". But you know what that really means. Removed. *Sayonara*. Promoted upstairs or downstairs or some damn thing. That in itself is mystifying. He's one of the most competent . . . oh, hell, the man is a genius. Why would they do that?'

'Very strange.'

'Exactly. But now he's out. Couldn't even see me. "On vacation." The new director is some bureaucrat by the name of Asano. I spent a little time with the man, and I can testify he's a smoothie. Lots of pious generalities about "technical cooperation". But I got the distinct feeling he didn't want to talk details with me. Actually, I wondered if maybe he wasn't even a bit afraid to say anything.'

Asano? Oh, shit. She took a deep breath. 'Was his name Kenji Asano?'

'Ken. Right, that's his first name. Maybe you know him. I think he used to be a flunky with some government bureau over there. But now he's just been put in charge of the Fifth Generation work. It's more than a little curious.'

She puzzled a minute. From what she knew about the Fifth Generation, and about Kenji Asano, he had a lot more important things to do than run that lab. The 'government bureau' he worked for was none other than MITI, the Ministry of International Trade and Industry. In fact, at last count he was Deputy Minister for Research and Planning, a top-ranked executive slot. Could this mean that Japan's ambitious artificial-intelligence effort was being moved in on by MITI, their industrial war room?

'Allan, I'll tell you the truth. You may not have heard, but I'm in a fight now at the university. I expect to win, but I've got a lot on my mind. Notes for the book. I can't just suddenly . . .'

'Tam, I need your help. Look, maybe they've had some new

breakthrough that none of us ever imagined.' He paused. 'Just between us, I lifted a strange MITI memo I found lying around an office when Asano took me on an escorted tour up to the labs at Tsukuba Science City.'

She looked at him. 'Was it classified?'

'How would I know? There was something about it. My sixth sense told me it was a document nobody was supposed to see. When I get back to Stanford, I plan to have a postdoc over in Physics make me a quick translation.'

It was very unlike Allan to walk off with confidential memos uninvited. Which could only mean he must suspect something he wasn't telling.

'You'd better give me the whole story.'

'Not now. Not yet. It's only guesswork, Tam.' He glanced away. 'Nothing to bore you with at the moment. But if you can find out anything, we'll write it up as a report I can circulate around the Hill. This could be important, believe me. Already Cray has started having to buy critical chips for its supercomputers from Japan. And while the Department of Defense is pouring billions into research on semiconductors that will withstand nuclear radiation, Japan is forging ahead on speed and miniaturisation – what really counts. I think they could be about to have us by the balls, pardon my French. If they've now somehow incorporated AI . . .'

'Allan, it doesn't add up. I once met Asano. In fact it was a couple of years ago at that Kyoto University symposium on Third World industrialisation. He spent a lot of time trying to pick my brain about our specialised silicon-chip manufacturing here. But he wasn't the slightest bit interested in artificial intelligence.'

'Well, prepare yourself for a surprise. He's plenty interested now. And knowledgeable. But still, it's not like the Japanese to do something like this, install some government guy to run an R & D programme.'

'That's certainly true.' She strolled over, looked down upon the park and began to want a brandy of her own as she chewed over the implications. Was MITI setting up some new high-tech industrial assault? If the Fifth Generation had been taken over by Kenji and his planners . . . 'Allan, let me think about this for a couple of days.'

'Don't think too long. I'm convinced somebody over there is suddenly in a very big hurry. I need to find out the real story. Am I just starting to go nuts in my old age? . . . well, make that my prime.' He grasped her hand for emphasis. 'And you really should make it a point to see this Asano fellow. If you already know him from somewhere, I'd say that's even better.'

She started to respond, then stopped. She knew Kenji Asano all right. From a little episode at that conference, when he had invited the panel members of a session he chaired to a late-night tour of the endless tiny bars in Kyoto's Gion district. She remembered all the steaming sake and being ignored by flustered bar girls who were pretending that another woman wasn't around. They had no idea what to do about a member of their own sex there in their sanctuary of male flattery. Ken apparently had staged it mainly to watch their reaction and hers.

Part of the scene was that Ken Asano was actually something of a hunk, as Westernised as they come and attractive in that way seemingly reserved for men of great wealth or great power. He may have had both, but she was sure only about the second. Whenever he handed out that *meishi* with the MITI logo, even millionaire industrialists and bankers automatically bowed to the floor.

A lot of sake later, after the other panel members had piled into a cab for their hotel, she decided to show Kenji Asano a few things about women he wouldn't learn from giggling bar girls. She'd always heard that Japanese men were pretty humdrum in bed, quick and self-centred, at least in the opinion of a woman she knew who'd done exhaustive field research on the topic. After her own experience with Ken, though, she wasn't so sure. Still, it had been a passing thing. The next morning she awoke in her own room in the Kyoto International and half tried to tell herself it hadn't really happened — just a dream, a chimera of the sultry Kyoto night, brought on by all those quaint little side streets and red paper lanterns.

The truth was she still thought about him from time to time. He was a talented lover – she certainly recalled that part well enough – and he was a charmer. In fact, she could use a little of that charm right this minute.

What she didn't admire was the organisation he worked for: the infamous MITI. Behind a smokescreen of 'fair trade' rhetoric, MITI's intentions clearly were to extinguish systematically Japan's world competition, industry by industry. And so far they were batting a thousand. They'd never once failed to knock off a designated 'target'. What was next? Had MITI finally concluded that, down the road, intelligent computers could be the drive behind some massive shift in world power?

Maybe she should go.

She poured another dash of cognac for Allan and they wandered back into the living room, just in time to see the Simpsons out. Everybody else followed except for Dave, now perched by the windows and glaring out into the dark. She decided to ignore him as she walked over, opened one a crack and looked down. In the park below, commerce was tapering off and the Jamaican Rastas had begun toting up receipts for the night. No sounds, except the faint strains of reggae from a boom box.

Funny, but every once in a while she'd stop everything and watch the kids in the playground down there. What to do? The damned shadows were growing longer by the minute. Maybe Dave wasn't so bad. Trouble was, he needed mothering too.

Think about it tomorrow, Scarlett. She sighed, poured herself a cognac and headed for the bedroom to get Allan's coat.

After she'd put him on the elevator, she came back and checked out Dave, now slouched in the big chair by the lamp, his eyes closed. He looked positively enticing, and she sounded his name quietly. Nothing. Then she realised he was sound asleep. Snoring.

The bastard. This was it. She grabbed his coat, pushed him out the door, poured herself another stiff cognac and plopped down in the living room to think.

All right, Allan. You've got a deal. Could be you're on to

something. I seem to remember there's a conference in Kyoto starting week after next on supercomputers. Kenji Asano will probably show. Good time to catch him off guard and try to find out what's suddenly so hush-hush.

Yes, by God, I'll do it.

She didn't bother with any of Allan Stern's funding. This trip would be strictly off-the-record. She wrapped up some loose ends, called a few people she knew in Tokyo, lined up half a dozen interviews that might be helpful on the new book, packed her toothbrush and tape recorder, and boarded a Northwest flight for Narita.

She had no idea then, of course, but she was Alice, dropping down the rabbit hole. A fortnight later she was dining with the Emperor of Japan.

FOUR

Allan Stern's alarm about Japan's semiconductor challenge reflected only part of the picture. There was also plenty going on with Japanese research in addition to information processing. Superconductivity was getting a big push, as was biotechnology, optoelectronics, advanced materials. Although we in the West think of Japan as a newcomer in the high-tech sweepstakes, it actually has a long tradition of innovation. A typical for-instance: in the area of advanced materials those of us hooked on swords know the Japanese were already creating 'new materials' hundreds of years ago that still haven't been bettered. Back then it was flawless steel for *katana* blades; today it's, say, gallium arsenide crystals for laser-driven semiconductors. How, one might inquire, did all this expertise come about?

To stick to materials research, if you think a moment you realise it's a discipline that actually must have begun in the latter days of the Stone Age. 'High technology' in those times meant figuring new ways to use fire and clay to create something nature had neglected to provide. Not integrated circuits, but a decent water pot.

And the Japanese have been making terrific pots for a thousand years. As it happens, some historians claim the very first Japanese pottery was made in the province of Tamba, near Kyoto. Why mention this? Because, then as now, technology and politics had a way of getting mixed together in Japan, and Tamba was a perfect example. Tamba's artisans made great use of a special oven known as a climbing chambered kiln. Whereas ceramics kilns elsewhere in the country were narrow and high, Tamba's climbing-hill chambers were wide and low, thereby allowing the fire to touch the clay directly. The result was a rugged, flame-seared stoneware that pleased the manly eye — powerful earthy greys, burnt reds, greenish-browns, all with a hard metallic lustre. Thus Tamba was a locale much frequented by the warrior Shoguns.

Which may be why Tamba province has another claim to history as well. It is the location of the one-time warrior castle-fortress of Sasayama, once a regional command post of the Tokugawa strongmen in Tokyo. You won't find overly much about Sasayama in the usual guidebooks since it has the kind of history that's more interesting to Japanese than to tourists. The place has no gaudy vermilion temples, no bronze Buddhas ten storeys high. Fact is, very little remains of the fortress itself these days except for a wide moat, green with lotuses, and a few stone walls lined with cherry trees that blossom an exquisite white for a few breathtaking moments each spring.

Although the castle is now burned down, a few homes of the *samurai* retainers of its various warlords remain. If you stand on the rocky edge of the moat at its south-west corner and look down through the cherry trees you'll see an old-style house built some two hundred years ago by the twelfth *daimyō* of Sasayama for his most loyal retainer. Its walls of white plaster are inter-spersed with beams of dark wood, its thatch roof supported by the traditional ridgepole. Think of it as the home of the *samurai* most trusted, the guardian of the gates, the warrior nearest the fount of power.

Perhaps it should not be surprising, therefore, that this ancient *samurai* residence, in the Shogun stronghold closest to ancient Kyoto, was now home base for a powerful warrior of modern Japan. Matsuo Noda.

Samurai had once battled in Sasayama's streets; many's the time its castle had been stormed by raging armies; much blood had been shed and much honour lost. But the event that occurred in Sasayama precisely two weeks after Tamara Richardson's dinner in New York was a historical moment more important than any in its thousand years prior.

It began shortly after dawn, a cool September grey just ripening to pink over the mountains. The early sounds of morning — birdsong, the faint bell of the tofu seller, the steam whistle of the autumn sweet-potato vendor — were only beginning to intrude on the quiet. Noda was where he always was at this moment: on the veranda overlooking his personal garden, a classic Zen-style landscape whose central pond was circled by natural-appearing rocks, trees, bushes, paths. It was, of course, about as 'natural' as those sculptured hedges at Versailles. In order to create the illusion of perspective and depth, the stones along the foreshore of the pond were bold, rugged, massively detailed, while those on the opposite side were dark, small, smooth — a little trick to make them seem farther away than they were.

It's a game heavy with nuance. For example, the stone footpath on the left side of the pond may look as if it goes on forever, but that's just part of the art: the stones get smaller towards the back, curving in and out among the azalea bushes till they make one last twist and disappear among the red pines and maples at the rear. Which trees, incidentally, have themselves been slightly dwarfed, again enhancing the illusion of distance, just as the back is deliberately shaggy and dark, like the beginnings of a forest that goes on for miles.

Noda's Zen garden, which deludes rational judgment by manipulating all the signposts we use to gauge distance and space, appeared to be limitless. The secret was that nothing actually ends: everything simply fades out and gets lost. It was a closed space that seemed for all the world as if it went on and on if you could only somehow see the rest of it. Yet peek only a few yards away and you've got the mundane streets of sleepy Sasayama.

This special dawn, as a few frogs along the edge of the pond croaked into the brisk air, he knelt on the viewing veranda in a fine cotton morning robe, a *yukata* emblazoned with his family crest (an archaic Chinese ideogram meaning 'courage') and began to centre his mind. He'd left his Kyoto headquarters early Friday evening, skipping the usual after-hours-drinking obligation of Japanese executives and grabbing the eight-thirty San-in Express to Sonobe, where his limo waited to bring him the rest of the way home. Now he was up before daybreak and readying his usual morning ritual. As he sat there, gazing across the placid water dotted with lotuses at the foreshore and framed with willows at the far horizon, his silver hair contrasted with the marine blue of the robe to create a presence easily as striking as the garden itself.

For a time he merely knelt, silently contemplating the view and listening to the metrical drip of water from a bamboo spout situated just at the edge of the steps. Finally he turned and picked up his *sumi* stick, a block of dried ink made from soot, and carefully began to rub it against the concave face of an ancient inkstone, till its cupped water darkened to just the proper shade. When the fresh ink was ready, he wet a brush in a separate water vessel, dried it by stroking it against a scrap of old paper, dipped it into the dark liquid and looked down.

This was the moment that demanded perfect composure, absolute control. Before him was a single sheet of rice paper, purest white, and now his hand held the brush poised. He was waiting for that instant when his senses clicked into alignment, when the feel of the brush merged with his mind, much the way a *samurai's katana* blade must become an extension of his own reflexes.

Although he would stroke only a few *kanji* characters, scarcely enough for a telex or a memo, the moment required discipline acquired through decades of practice. His Zen-style calligraphy allowed for no hesitation, no retouching. It must be dashed off with a spontaneity that was, in itself, part of the art. As with the swordsman, there could be no time for conscious thought, merely the powerful stroke guided by intuition. No decision that confronted him throughout a business day would demand half so much mental control, inner resolve.

Just then, at the far end of the pond, the first sun flickered through the wisteria. Suddenly, without his consciously knowing the exact moment had arrived, as a Zen archer's arrow must release itself of its own will, his hand struck. The dark tip of the brush pirouetted down the paper, starting at the left and laying down a mere five lines, twenty-two syllables.

57

Inishie ni   Once held,
ari kemu hito no   it's said, by
moteri cho   men of long ago,
omitsuwa wo   my ancient prize —
ware wa mochitari   at last is near!

It was done.

He sighed, leaned back, and reached for the cup of green tea that rested beside him on the polished boards. The verse was in an archaic style, a few syllables longer than a haiku, modelled on an eight-hundred-year-old work by a court poet of the Heian era. The strokes were perfectly nuanced, the flow of the brush precise, the intuitive strength as natural as a waterfall.

Noda drained his tea, then rose to go back inside. His antique house was tastefully 'empty': its *tatami*-floored rooms, measured in multiples of those standard three-by-six reed mats, were barren, a museum to times past. They also were open to each other, their sliding doors, *fusuma*, being pushed wide. The walls, too, were vacant expanses of white plaster with only an occasional mounted six-fold screen depicting poetry parties of the Heian era, that courtly civilisation portrayed in *The Tale of Genji*. And there were no overhead lights, merely an occasional cypress *andon* floor lamp to augment the pastel glow of the rice-paper *shōji* windows.

'*Asa-han.*' He curtly ordered his grey-haired cook to bring breakfast, then turned to mount the ancient stairs.

'*Hai.*' She nodded and was gone.

Although he kept the lower floor exactly as it had been two centuries past, the upstairs was a different matter entirely. It had been converted into a high-tech office, hooked through a maximum security TeleSystems TCS-9000 direct uplink (via the mid-Pacific Mareks-B satellite) to the mainframe of his new NEC information management system in the Kyoto headquarters, an augmented NEAX 2400 IMS, which handled voice, data, text, image. He had scarcely flipped on the system when the woman who managed his kitchen appeared, bowing, and deposited a tray bearing *miso* broth, rice, an uncooked egg and more tea.

He grunted thanks as he was checking a CRT screen for the current rate on Fed funds, the cost of the money American banks lend each other overnight to meet reserve requirements. No surprises. Then he turned and cracked the egg over his rice, adding a leaf of dried *nori* seaweed. As he leaned back, chopsticks in hand, he quickly glanced through the Tokyo papers, followed by *The Asian Wall Street Journal* and the satellite edition of London's *Financial Times*. Finally he tossed them aside.

This was always the moment when he liked to take measure of the three photos standing in a row across the back of his teak desk. The first was his deceased wife Mariko — long-suffering, deferential, resignedly selfless. A model Japanese woman. He still thought of her with fondness, but as was expected of a Japanese helpmate, she always ran a distant second in his affections. His work came first.

The next picture was very different. This woman's face was white, her hair a lacquered wig, her lips a tiny red pout. Her name, Koriko, had been assigned years ago in the Gion district of Kyoto and she was holding a three-stringed lute, a *samisen*, and intoning some classical melody from centuries past. These days she purchased thousand-dollar kimonos the way most office girls bought jeans, but she worked for the money. She was a *geisha*, a real one, an artist whose calling required years of training and commanded the awe of even the most modern Japanese. Like a prizefighter or a matador, she'd spent long painful hours perfecting style, technique, art. She had been Noda's one-time protégée, beneficiary of his patronage. Now, though, she had other 'patrons'. He still missed her, but the memory was fading.

The third photo was a face familiar to all of Japan's avid TV viewers — Akira Mori. She was wearing a dark blue Western suit, her hair a glossy pageboy cut, the conservative look of times past. It was the occasion of her graduation from the School of Law, Tokyo University (Tokyo Daigaku, or Todai as it's known), an important moment. Todai's alumni represent a network, a *batsu*, of the country's ruling élite, who compete with each other for the choicest, most prestigious government ministries. Although she had chosen a more visible career, she still relied heavily on her contacts in this governing clique, heads of the leading ministries, including Finance, Foreign Affairs, and of course the Ministry of International Trade and Industry, MITI.

Matsuo Noda himself had, in fact, once headed MITI, probably Japan's most powerful ministry. He came from ancient *samurai* stock – fittingly perhaps, since the bureaucrats of modern Japan are mostly of that class. The *samurai* caste, men who served a liege lord and were forbidden to engage in trade, were actually Japan's first public servants. In between civil wars they became sword-carrying bureaucrats. Many a modern bureau chief has ancestors who wore two swords and sliced up a peasant or a merchant now and then with impunity, which may help explain why the average citizen still views government officials with such nervous awe.

A Todai honours man himself, Noda was a natural for MITI, which runs what is in many ways a covert operation. The head offices are in a nondescript, soot-covered building of tinted glass and limestone near Tokyo's Hibaya Park, guarded by armed, helmeted members of Japan's National Police. Inside it's mostly open floors and lines of grey steel desks; no plush carpets and mahogany suites. MITI has twelve bureaus, each devoted to a major industrial sector. If its officials decide Japan's strategic interests would be served by a certain manufacturing group's cutting production, lowering prices, altering product lines, these 'recommendations' are passed along. And it happens.

Noda began his career there by circulating through the different sections, 'going around the track' as it's called, after which he proceeded to run the General Affairs office of various bureaus, by which time everybody had him picked for a mover, on the 'élite course'. Eventually he was promoted to section chief in the International Trade Bureau, next on to bureau chief, and finally at age forty-seven he made the top. Vice-minister.

After he reached the pinnacle, he held the job for a mere five years, then routinely left. He had to go: early fifties and you're out. MITI is no country for old men. He moved on to head the Japan Development Bank, JDB, where he financed various high-tech start-up industries. Finally he retired and went out on his own.

Unlike most other retired government officials, however, he didn't accept any of the lucrative private offers he received, the suddenly 'vacant' spot on a conglomerate's board of directors. No, he had his own smouldering vision. In a dazzling and successful departure from usual Japanese convention, he founded Nippon, Inc., an adjunct to Japan's major financial players, with headquarters in the commercial centre of Kyoto. His new organisation immediately became a financial fixture in the new post-industrial, high-tech Japan and now, five years later, Nippon, Inc. was a thriving force in the management of capital. These days even the new generation at MITI routinely called him up for 'consensus'.

For Matsuo Noda now, everything was in place; he was at last ready to pursue a lifelong dream. He'd never forgotten the end of the war, that last day on Okinawa when Ushijima's 32nd Army was a dazed remnant. He'd been in the cave above Mabuni when the general radioed his farewell to Imperial Headquarters, then severed his own spinal cord. Matsuo Noda, with anguish he could still remember, had burned the regimental flag and told those remaining to scatter, to become guerrillas — repeating Ushijima's last command to 'fight to the last for the eternal cause of loyalty to the Emperor'. Noda had declared that their struggle would continue on for a hundred years if need be.

He had overestimated the difficulty. The plan now poised had required less than fifty.

As usual for a work-at-home Saturday (just another business day in Japan), he was wrapping up loose ends from the week, finishing reports, signing off on audits. Two printers were running, since he preferred to work with hard copy, and he was reviewing the list of outstanding loans NI was in charge of monitoring, checking for any early signs of trouble. Had any credit ratings slipped? If a receiving corporation was publicly traded, had its stock faltered? What was the overview: securities, unamortised discounts on bonds, cash on hand? Next he paged through the weekly updates from the Small Business Finance Corp, the National Finance Corp, the Shoko Chukin Bank, various credit associations and savings banks. It was all on his Kyoto information base, pulled off the new fibre-optic network that linked Japan's financial centres.

He was about to ring down for fresh tea when a priority override flashed on the screen for his eyes only. This meant a coded message that could only be unscrambled using a special module in the computer. The Kyoto office knew he was on line, but they hadn't wanted to route the information directly.

Highly irregular.

He punched in the code, called up the receiving routine and waited for the message.

There had been a call from ship-to-shore phone, the communications line linking him directly with Dr Shozo Takahashi, director-in-charge of his top secret 'project' in the Inland Sea. The director was requesting that Noda-sama contact him immediately via scrambler. Top security. He felt his pulse begin to race as he digested the news.

It had been so *easy*. Almost too easy.

He sat perfectly still for that timeless, historic moment, gazing at the photograph of Akira Mori. A promise kept, from long, long ago. Four decades now, and he had never forgotten what he had said he would do for her.

He called down for tea, waited till it had been delivered, then punched on the phone and switched it to the security mode.

But even on the scrambler, Takahashi began circumspectly. As the esteemed Noda-sama was aware, their 'project' had, over its three years, contended with great difficulties and many disappointments. They were working at the very limits of undersea technology. As Noda-sama also knew, he went on, their early attempts at seismic vertical profiling had been a complete failure. Takahashi took personal responsibility for that. Next they had changed strategy and utilised state-of-the-art microwave radar, hoping that minuscule changes in density along the bottom might indicate what they sought. That too, Takahashi apologised, had been unproductive from the start as Noda-sama had been informed, and he, Takahashi, took full blame for the failure.

Noda cut in at that point, impatient and wanting to circumvent the litany of apologies. Why was Takahashi calling?

The director paused dramatically, then declared he wished to inform the august Noda-sama that their latest approach, the use of a new digital magnetometer, had at last borne fruit. Only this morning they had detected and brought up an 'item'. In the treacherous straits east-north-east of Shikoku. It was a watertight gold case embossed with what appeared to be a sixteen-leaf chrysanthemum or *kiku*. The Imperial insignia.

Other confirming inscriptions? Noda nervously reached out and clicked off the humming computer.

Yes, the formal script across one end appeared to be no later than tenth century. Although they dared not open the gold case for fear of damaging its contents, at this moment preliminary analytical procedures were underway and the early results, including a makeshift attempt at shipboard X-ray crystallography, suggested that the steel inside, which clearly showed traces of copper alloy, contained less than a hundredth of one per cent of iron oxide. In short, it was possible the 'item' might be perfectly preserved.

It was theirs, Takahashi said, in that breathy, clipped language inferiors use to signify great importance and great deference. It was his extreme honour to announce to the esteemed Noda-sama that the most important archaeological find in the history of Japan now belonged to Nippon, Inc., and they—

'*Chigau,*' Noda cut him off, in the curt tone expected of superiors. Incorrect: it belonged to its rightful owner and would now be returned.

And furthermore, he added, Nippon, Inc. had just ceased to exist. Since the name for ancient Japan was Dai Nippon, 'Great Japan', as of this moment Nippon, Inc. had just become Dai Nippon, International. A complete reorganisation would begin immediately.

Finally he ordered a total blackout. Radios silenced. No shore leave for crew or scientists.

He clicked off the phone and, repressing a tremble, descended the stairs.

And there on the garden veranda, using a new brush and perfumed *sumi* ink from his rare collection, Matsuo Noda composed a very elaborate letter, long swirls of black down a perfect sheet of thick, flowered paper hundreds of years old. It was then sealed in a silver case and hand-delivered by special messenger to a fortress in the centre of Tokyo.

Five days later its recipient read it before a nationally televised press conference, and Japan exploded.

FIVE

'Kami wo araitai no desu ga. Ii desu ka?' Tam peered through the doorway and nodded hello to the girl in the blue Imperial Hotel uniform. The hair salon was almost empty. Perfect.

'Hai, sō.' The girl, startled at the *gaijin*'s accentless Japanese, bowed to the waist. *'Dōzo.'*

'Manikyua mo onegai shimasu.' What the heck, Tam thought, why not go all the way, get a manicure too.

'Hai. Dōzo.' Another bob as the girl ushered her forward.

There was the plush, padded chair. Big, grey, and voluptuous. She sighed and settled back. Heaven. Perfect peace in the middle of hectic Tokyo. She knew that here for an hour or so she would be an honoured guest, smothered with attention. One of the most incredible experiences in Japan.

While three of the girls began shampooing her hair, they went back to chattering about the new husband a matchmaker had just arranged for the petite assistant in the back. The bride-to-be was blushing and there were plenty of giggles all around, hands over mouths. Tam realised, though, that the girls were being a little circumspect. Who was this strange brunette *gaijin*, speaking Japanese with no accent? Maybe she understood what they were saying.

She did.

The woman who would become Tam Richardson was born Tamara no-name in Kobe, Japan, the somewhat embarrassing result of an evening's diversion for an anonymous GI. Her mother, equally anonymous, had prudently given her over for adoption rather than face the social awkwardness of raising a fatherless, half *gaijin* child.

She was eventually adopted by Lt Col Avery Richardson, US Air Force, and his wife Mary, proud Iowa stock, six years after she'd been stuck in the orphanage. That was during the latter days of the Occupation, but they'd stayed on in Japan through '54 while Lt Col Richardson served as adviser for the rearming of what would be the Japanese Self Defence Forces. He'd also become a Japanophile by then, so he left her in a Japanese school rather than subjecting her to the 'army brats' on the base. Finally they returned to the States, with a dark-eyed little daughter who'd spoken Japanese for almost a decade and, being the achiever she was, read it virtually as well as a high-school graduate.

The thing she remembered best from all those years, though, was one word. *Gaijin*. It wasn't exactly that the modern Japanese consider *gaijin* inferior. They no longer dismiss Westerners as 'red-bearded Barbarians'. No, *gaijin* were merely unfortunate, luckless folk not part of the earth's elect tribe. You were either born a part of Japan, a full *nihon-jin*, or you were forever outside it, *gaijin*.

But knowing it was one thing, and living it as a kid was something else. She wasn't one of *them*, and they made sure she got the message. Finally, though, she discovered the hidden secret of Japan — most Japanese get very uncomfortable around a *gaijin* too fluent in their language or customs, since that outsider has penetrated their life without the constraint of relationships and obligations. No *gaijin* can ever entirely belong to their seamless culture for one simple reason: no outsider could ever be held accountable to the powerful social and family interdependencies that allow a population half that of the US to get along in a place functionally smaller than California. So to survive there if you're not *nihon-jin*, you just play that fact for all it's worth. Then, like everybody else, you've got a niche; yours merely happens to be outside the system. As an almost-*nihon-jin* you're threatening; as a *gaijin*, you're safe. She'd finally learned this the hard way, from all those unsmiling little girls in blue school uniforms who used to hiss '*gaijin*'. But thanks to them, Tam Richardson learned to be a permanent outsider. And a survivor.

Well, here she was again, ready for another bout. Round-eyed 'Tama-chan' all grown up and still on the outside.

Though she knew Tokyo well from times past, she was still trying to readjust. After checking into the Imperial Hotel in Tokyo's Hibiya section, she'd showered, changed and headed out for some jogging – the best way she knew to see a lot of the city quick. Her major puzzle: where to look for the new impulse behind Japan's big drive, their meteoric move towards the target of *dai ichi*, 'Number One' in the world. Try to feel the vibes, she told herself, be a tourist and see the 'New Japan' through fresh eyes. If it had been winter, she'd have gone straight over to Shinobazu Pond in Ueno Park to watch the migratory Siberian waterfowl diving for fish amongst the clumps of floating ice. In spring she would have first monitored the radio to find out which park had the finest cherry blossoms, then gone somewhere else to avoid the sake-swilling crowds. And if it had been summer, she probably would have headed for the cool of the Imperial Palace East Gardens to catch the pink and red azaleas.

Autumn, though, was a time for swallowing the city whole. She started with the Meiji Shrine, that garish tribute to Japan's Westernisation, then moved on to the Imperial Palace, itself a place that, like Tokyo itself, had something for all seasons. She passed through the East Gardens watching provincial honey-mooners snapping pictures for the parents back home, then worked her way across toward the Sakuradamon Gate so she could follow the Palace moat as she made her circuit back to the hotel. Along the way she passed the Diet Building and the Supreme Court, then decided to look in on the Yasukuni Shrine, buried in its own exquisite grove of cherry trees and mixed foliage. The massive bronze *torii* arch leading into the shrine was always surrounded by stalls selling those marvellous little rice cakes, sweet and leaden, she remembered as a kid. She stopped and bought two.

By then she was experiencing advanced jet lag, so she decided to head on back to her crisp-sheeted bed at the Imperial. Tokyo this time around was as impossible as always, maybe more so. Where do you start? The garish Ginza, the self-conscious trendi-ness of Roppongi, the skyscrapers of Shinjuku, solemn Mar-unouchi – all of it engulfing, awesomely materialistic. Each trip the city seemed to get bigger, louder, more everything. More cars, more neon, more . . . yes, more money. She could remember, almost, a time when this town was a burned-out ruin. Now . . .

She needed some time to think, to work out a game plan. Sure, clues to the phenomenon of modern Japan were everywhere – drive, self-confidence, competence – but how did they fit together? Change was coming like an avalanche. Who could keep track?

The best thing, she'd told herself, was to start with a clear head. Back off for a while. After all, the last year had been much toil and little play, with the latest book coming out, hassles at the university. She needed some unwinding. Maybe a little time spent thinking about nothing would be best of all.

So for a day she lived off room service, immersed herself in the local papers, magazines, TV and just relaxed. She let Allan's hints about some ominous new development slip way down the scale.

One of the things she couldn't help noticing, though, was an odd stirring in the newspapers, something very much between the lines but all the more real for that very reason. In typical fashion, signals were going out that a major event was in store. The government, she knew, always used a kind of early-warning system for important shifts. Very Japanese. If the Bank of Japan was about to raise or lower interest rates, a move that would impact thousands of businesses and banks, for days in advance various unidentified 'officials' would be quoted as speculating that maybe a change in rates might be possible. Of course they didn't actually say it was going to happen; they merely hinted it could be an idea to consider, it was plausible, conditions might well warrant . . . Anybody with any sense knew immediately this meant the decision was already made and citizens were being alerted to cover themselves posthaste.

Consequently, if 'government sources' start hinting an event is conceivably possible, you can usually assume it's as good as fact.

But what was this about, she wondered, all these allusions to a new 'interest' of the Emperor's? The standard elements were all there: leaks, guesswork, columns, unnamed 'high sources'. No doubt, something major was pending. And just to make sure nobody missed the importance of whatever it was, there was even speculation His Majesty might actually hold a press briefing.

That last possibility, she decided, was clearly farfetched. Just not done. A picture session, maybe, but that was it.

After a day of unwinding, she was ready to get out and start gathering some information. This time around, however, she wanted a different image. A shift from the staid-professor look to high-tech Japan. Start with a few clothes, something smashing/expensive/ designer Japanese. And the hair. Right. A cut, a different style, a *something*.

Thus around noon the third day she finally got into street clothes and headed down to the lobby, then teeming with lagged-out Aussies in funny tour hats. She took one look, ducked around them, then made for the lower arcade and the shops.

And here she was. Already feeling recharged. Relaxed and . . .

Just then a short, excited hotel porter ducked his head in, bowed and announced he'd just heard that the Emperor was about to be on TV.

His Majesty? The salon froze.

At first Tam thought the porter must just be playing some kind of local prank. Arcade high jinks.

Then she remembered the speculation in the papers. Could it be true? She glanced at her watch; it was a couple of minutes before twelve.

The girls immediately dropped everything and clicked on the big Toshiba digital set suspended over the mirror. Service halted in midstream, just as in a *soba* noodle shop when the sumo wrestlers on the corner tube had finished glaring, thrown salt three times and were ready to lunge. Then one of the hairdressers remembered Tam and − maybe still believing no *gaijin* could understand her language − reached down to snap on the small black-and-white Sony attached to the chair arm, tuned to CNN's Tokyo service. It was currently scrolling temperatures in the US.

Now on the big Toshiba overhead, NHK (the government channel) was announcing they were about to switch to a remote broadcast, live, from the sacred Yasukuni Shrine.

Uh, oh, she thought. Yasukuni! Has everybody here gone crazy?

Back before 1945 Yasukuni had been a memorial to the 'master race', official home of the new 'State Shinto'. Japan's militarists had revised traditional Shinto, a simple nature-reverence, to include violent nationalism, Emperor worship, 'the Yamato spirit', the 'way of the *samurai*': every warlike aspect of national character. These days Yasukuni enshrined the names of Japan's two million heroic war dead, a roll call recently enlarged to include Tojo and others the US later executed as criminals – which had turned the place into a political hot potato, resulting in an enormous flap when the Prime Minister tried to appear there in his official capacity. So, for the Emperor to show up suddenly, with heavy press coverage, was almost unthinkable. Besides, she'd just been by the place and hadn't noticed anything. This was very sudden.

Then the remote came on. The front of the shrine was roped off, right across the bronze *torii* gate, with only cameras and press allowed inside. On screen was a shot of an elaborate new dais where an official from the Imperial Household Agency, the government bureau that kept His Majesty under its care and scheduled his appearances, was just finishing up a long-winded introduction. Then it was the Prime Minister's turn. After what seemed half an hour of absolutely contentless oratory (a Japanese politician's most respected skill) on the subject of the country's majestic Imperial past, the PM finally stepped aside to allow a tall, strikingly handsome Japanese man to approach the speaker's podium. Since the occasion had official significance, his walk was ceremonial, with his feet wide apart in the jerky *samurai* swagger necessitated in days of old by the two swords at the waist. Meanwhile, everybody around him was bowing low.

His Imperial Majesty, wearing a formal male kimono equivalent to morning dress at Ascot, looked truly august. He was also carrying a long silver box, filigreed.

When he finally started to speak, the girls around Tam gasped in astonishment. She noticed immediately that he wasn't using modern Japanese. Instead, his language was an archaic, highly ornate dialect: the court speech of long ago.

After his brief, almost unintelligible prologue, one of the Household officials opened the box for him and took out a long, scrolled document. The cameras did a quick close-up, showing a page of antique, flowered paper inscribed with brush and *sumi* ink.

It turned out to be a letter in modern Japanese from the president of a financial organisation called Dai Nippon, International. As the Emperor read it to the cameras, it began with a recounting of the loss of the Imperial Sword in the Inland Sea during the 1185 battle of Dan-no-ura. That sword, it declared, signified Japan's physical link to a divine past . . .

What? History 101 on TV?

Then came the bomb.

Abruptly CNN cut into their normal late-night programming for a live satellite report. Their reporter, grasping a mike and standing in front of the milling mob around the podium, was reading from a press handout that provided an English summary of the letter. Since the CNN signal was being flashed to the US and then back to Japan on the 'bird', effectively circling the globe, it was a few milliseconds behind the NHK broadcast. She turned up the sound.

. . . noon here in Tokyo, and at this shrine sacred to all Japanese, His Majesty, the Emperor of Japan (*Cut to shot of the Emperor speaking. Reporter voice-over*), has startled the nation by announcing that marine archaeologists working for an investment organisation called Dai Nippon, International have just succeeded in recovering a famous symbol of early Imperial rule. A three-year secret project in the Inland Sea, funded by DNI, culminated five days ago when scientists brought up a watertight gold case containing what is believed to be the original Imperial Sword. (*Cut back to reporter.*) Although no photos of the sword have as yet been released, we are told it is in virtually mint condition. (*Glances down to read from press release.*) According to the ancient Japanese chronicles, this sword was given to Japan's first Emperor by the Sun Goddess Amaterasu-Omikami, some time around the year 600 BC, as a symbol of his divinity. Historians say it was later lost at sea in the 1185 Battle of Dan-no-ura. That bloody naval episode, the subject of much Japanese lore and tradition, marked the end of direct Imperial authority here and the rise of the first Shoguns, military governors who would rule in his name.

She rolled down the sound. Who needed some English press summary? She was watching the whole incredible event live as it unfolded. And her first thought was: Good God, that's like finding Excalibur, or maybe the Ark of the Covenant. Myth turned into reality. She glanced around the salon and already the electricity in the air was crackling. But what happened next turned out to be the real news, the hidden agenda.

After His Majesty finished reading the letter, he passed it to an underling and switched back to his ancient dialect. Now, though, his speech was being 'translated' across the bottom of the screen into modern Japanese.

He declared that since the Imperial Household, through the loyal services of Dai Nippon, International, had had restored to it that which it always possessed, namely the sword, he was pleased to honour the firm by allowing it to construct a new museum to house the sacred symbol at a site just outside Ise, home of the official shrine of the Sun Goddess. On his authority, ground-breaking for the museum would begin immediately. However, until such time as it was constructed and consecrated, the Imperial Household would make the sacred relic available under heavy guard for viewing by the Japanese people in a temporary showplace located at the Meiji Shrine in Tokyo . . .

By now shops had begun closing and the corridor outside was in tumult. An excited young clerk from the flower stall next door burst through the door and, bowing to everybody, lavished bouquets on all the girls. From the streets above came a cacophony of sirens.

But it still wasn't over. The most crucial part of all, totally missed by the Western news force, was yet to come. After His Majesty was bowed away from the microphone, another official stepped forward to elaborate on the Emperor's remarks (probably because His Majesty would not deign to mention anything so crass as money). As reward for restoring the sword to His Majesty, he said, Dai Nippon would be allowed to serve as trustee of an official, honorary investment instrument, to be known as the Eight-Hundred-Year Fund. Acting for His Majesty, DNI would direct those monies into endeavours 'commensurate with the nobility and ancient lineage of the Japanese people, as symbolised by the sword'. Then a telephone number flashed across the bottom of the screen. The current subscription would be closed after eight hundred billion yen were pledged. The president of Dai Nippon had asked His Majesty for the honour of contributing the first billion yen personally. Finally, in a quick aside, he added that interest paid by the fund would of course be tax-free, as was normally the case for savings accounts in Japan.

After a few closing formalities, interspersed with a photo session of the Emperor and the president of Dai Nippon, the historic occasion ended with a reverential shot of His Majesty being escorted to his limo.

Who was that silver-haired executive? Tam wondered. The man was audacious, and a genius. He'd just turned the Imperial Household into an accomplice in some kind of nationwide collection, using the Emperor for his own ends much the way Shoguns of old had done.

But she sensed he'd touched a nerve that went very deep. A fund in honour of the Emperor (that's already how everybody around her in the shop was describing it), something in which to take pride, not just a numbered savings account at the post office. Suddenly the girls and their Japanese customers were all talking money. Here was something *they* could do to show their regard for His Majesty.

A line was already forming at the phone. The way she heard sums being pledged, she calculated Dai Nippon would garner five million yen, more than thirty thousand dollars, right there amongst the shampoos and curlers. The typical Japanese, she recalled, banked over a quarter of his or her disposable income. Little wonder most of them had at least a year's salary in savings. At this rate Dai Nippon's 'Imperial Fund' would be over the top by nightfall.

That evening NHK newscasts claimed it had been fully subscribed in the first fifty-six minutes. After all, eight hundred billion yen was only about six billion dollars, scarcely more than loose change to a people saving tens of millions every day. It was, in fact, merely the beginning. The next day more 'Eight-Hundred-Year' funds were opened, by popular demand. Soon the pension funds started to feel the heat, and a lot of institutions began calling up. Yen flowed in a great river. All those homeless Japanese billions knocking around the world had at last found a guiding ideal. Some rumours even claimed the Emperor himself was actually going to manage the money.

Tam couldn't wait to get outside and see first-hand what was going on. This was something even Allan could never in his wildest dreams have predicted. As soon as she could get her hair dry she headed out; the girls didn't even bother to charge.

Tokyo, twelve million strong, was in the streets. Even in normal times the city could be overwhelming, but now ... It was in pandemonium, an advanced state of shock. As she struggled through the crowds a lot of men were waving sake flasks, already gleefully smashed. The sidewalks had become one vast *matsuri*, festival.

Something else, too. She found herself feeling a little uncomfortable. There were glares, and then as she passed a withered old man running a noodle stand, she heard him mutter *'gaijin'*. What did it mean?

What it 'meant', she reflected with alarm, was obvious. The world had just become a brand-new ball game. Japan's long-silent Emperor had once more spoken to his people, just as he had at the end of the war. Back then he had broken two thousand years of silence to inform his battered, starving subjects 'the war situation has developed not necessarily to Japan's advantage'. This time around he had confirmed Japan's long Imperial heritage. The 'meaning' was clear as day.

This wasn't a new direction. This was just getting back on track. Even though the Emperor had been humiliated and secularised after the Great War against the threatening *gaijin*, his people still thought of themselves as a single, pure family. For a time they merely had no focus for that identity. Now they had it again.

Well, she thought, why not? National pride. Not so long ago we Americans had the Soviets telling us we were second best, so we blew a few billion in tax money to plant a man on the moon and straighten them out. The space Super Bowl. Why should Japan be any different? For years now they've heard half the world claim they're just a bunch of hard-driving merchants with a bank-account soul, when they knew in their hearts it wasn't true. Now here's the proof, straight from the Sun Goddess. Time to get crazy awhile.

In the middle of all the bedlam and horns and sirens in the street, she yearned for somebody to talk with, somebody level-headed enough to put this frightening turnaround into some kind of perspective. That's when she thought of Ken.

Of course! He was Westernised; he took the longer view. Why hadn't she thought of him right away?

So off she went for a quick surprise visit with Kenji Asano at the Institute for New Generation Computer Technology, research headquarters for the Fifth Generation Systems Project. He and his staff would probably be in a holiday mood, just like everybody else. Maybe he'd loosen his tie and give her a little off-the-record rundown of what this was all about.

She knew the Institute operated out of the twenty-first floor of a downtown Tokyo skyscraper. She'd been there before. She still had the address, and the subways were clicking along right on time, though the fare machines were off now in celebration. Half an hour later she was there. She pushed her way through the milling lobby and grabbed an elevator.

As she rode, watching the lights tick off the floors, she found herself wondering again what Ken was really up to. And what had happened to Dr Yoshida? However, it was hard to think about something as boring as MITI and American defence vulnerability when people were whooping it up and passing around paper cups of sake right there in the elevator.

Well, don't jump to conclusions. This paranoia of Allan's is probably just a grotesque misreading. Dr Yoshida got promoted, and Ken's merely filling in for a while till the Institute can recruit a new director from some university. The work here's too important for politics. Intelligent computers are Japan's lifeline — the 'steam engine' of the next century.

How would Ken react to her just showing up? After all, Kyoto *was* two years ago. He'd claimed to be a widower, but was that merely conference fast talk?

Best thing is just to play it straight, she told herself. Strictly business. Let the rest fall out in time.

As she stepped off the elevator, she was relieved to see that the offices were still open. Well, she thought, my first finding is that Ken Asano runs this place with an iron hand, just the way Yoshida did. Total dedication. Through floor-to-ceiling glass doors she could see the receptionist at the desk, now excitedly chatting on the phone. Tam waved, and the smiling woman immediately buzzed her through. Just like that. No different from the last time.

Doesn't look to be any MITI conspiracy here, she thought. What exactly had made Allan so worried?

She bowed and handed over her *meishi*, her business card.

'Asano-san, onegai shimasu.'

SIX

'Matt, why don't you just send your action over to the 'bean pit, for chrissake?' The phone line from Chicago crackled. 'That's where the crapshooters are.'

'Jerry, I wouldn't know a soybean if I ate one.'

'Hell, half of those loonies over there buying and selling 'bean contracts wouldn't know one either. Come to think of it, I don't know anybody over on the Merc who's ever even *seen* a pork belly. Do they really exist?' He was yelling to make himself heard over the din of the floor of the Board of Trade. Futures on commodities were being bought and sold all around him. Just then he paused, followed by a louder yell. 'Right, I'll buy five, at the market. Yeah, I'm talkin' one and thirteen bid. What? You've got to be kidding. No way.' Pause. I could almost see the blue-jacketed floor traders frantically hand-signalling each other. Then he yelled again. 'Christ, Frank, I'm already long forty at sixteen. I'm getting murdered here. You guys are killing me . . . All right, all right, I'll pay fourteen for ten. Yeah . . . Shit. Hang on, Matt. I gotta write this down on a ticket . . . Jesus, I should be selling Hondas like my brother-in-law down in Quincy. Sits on his butt all day, screws his bookkeeper at lunch, and the man's making a bundle.' Pause. 'Hell, Matt, what'd I just say?'

'If I heard right, you just bought ten thirty-year Treasury contracts at one-oh-one and fourteen thirty-seconds. You just agreed to loan the US government a million dollars, Jerry. Very patriotic. Except you're probably going to turn around and unload the contracts in the next five minutes to somebody else.'

'Oh, yeah. Right. I should be so lucky. Christ, where's my pencil? This place is driving me nuts. I think my mind's going. I've gotta shorten up some here before the close. Hang on.' He yelled at a runner to take his buy slip, then came back to the phone. 'Matt, you're really shaking this place up, you know. Guys are starting to back away. And the people upstairs are beginning to wonder. You've gotta think about going off-exchange with some of this. Hit the market-maker banks. We can't keep up with you here. I could try to get the Exchange to waive their position limits, but don't hold your breath.'

'No problem, Jerry. My client's got plenty of other accounts. We'll roll the next thousand contracts through a different one.'

'Christ, whoever you're working for must have coconuts the size of King Kong. You realise you guys're naked here? You're getting short billions.'

'I just handle the orders, Jerry.'

'Your numbers scare the piss out of me just looking at them.' He sighed. 'Listen, Matt, take care. Get back to you tomorrow at the opening. Right now I've gotta find some greenhorn to take a few of these puppies off my hands or I'm gonna get blown out. Jesus, how'd I let myself get this long at sixteen? Forty fucking contracts. And I was sure ... Hey, gotta run. Think I see some idiot over there signalling a seventeen bid. Kid must be from Mars.'

'Good luck.'

'Right. Maybe I'll try prayer.' He was gone.

I'd known Jerry Brighton since we crossed professional swords once in the late sixties and I'd never seen the man actually sit down. He gave up law early, and these days he elbowed the mob in the Treasury bond futures pit with the grim determination of a horse addict shoving his way to the two-dollar window. If the bonds were sluggish, he'd roam the floor looking for action. Football, you name it. He'd *make up* bets. Rumour has it, one slow day he even set up a wager pool taking odds on which floor trader would be the next to go broke, 'tap out' in Exchange parlance. I'd guess Jerry's own number was pretty low. A reliable source once told me Jerry'd averaged a million a year for the past five, even while taking a hit year before last for over two million when a certain famous 'inside trader' sandbagged him with a phony merger rumour. Maybe it was worth the ulcers. Thing is, I know for a fact he'd have done it for nothing. A born market maker, right down to his rubber-soled Reeboks.

So when Jerry Brighton started complaining that Matsuo Noda's action was growing too rich for his blood, I knew we were in the big time. It took a lot to impress a pro such as him.

The thing was getting scary, but it was still perfectly legal. Let me summarise roughly what had happened over the three weeks since I had decided to play along with Matsuo Noda. First were the physical arrangements. To accommodate my new calling, I'd enlarged my operating space – the back room of the brownstone's parlour floor, looking out over the garden – into a makeshift brokerage office complete with a multilined telephone and quote services from S-tron and Telerate. I'd also installed a direct tie-line to the T-bill pit of the Chicago Mercantile Exchange, ditto the Note and Bond action at the Chicago Board of Trade. And because of all the computer hardware, I had to move Emma's desk out into the parlour. Consequently she could no longer listen in on my calls, which she did not take kindly. However, I was no longer forced to listen in on hers. I figure that sort of made us even.

In addition, I'd set up accounts at every futures brokerage house in the land, both coasts, to spread out the orders. We were moving a lot of contracts and the big-time outfits like Salomon Brothers were scrambling to make a market for us. Once again, therefore, nagging questions began to arise. Anybody who'd thought about it for more than a minute would have realised you can't make a play like Noda's without being noticed. There's no bigger rumour mill than the financial arena. The very idea of shorting the bond market to the tune of billions and remaining obscure and anonymous for any length of time was absurd. After all, there's two sides to every bet. But since I was supposed to be fronting his move specifically to throw sand in everybody's eyes, all this attention presented something of a quandary. Although we were trying to keep the lid on, buying small batches of Treasuries even as we were shorting them, the price was softening and margin calls were starting to loom on the horizon. None of this made any sense. Noda wasn't hedging or even speculating in the normal sense; he was playing a giant game of cat and mouse with the markets. This told me once again he wasn't showing all the cards in his hand. He had something major, and unexpected, in the pipeline.

Which brought forth the next insight: Matsuo Noda didn't hire me merely because he wanted some innocent-seeming outsider to do his bidding in the futures market; any number of players in this town could have handled that action as well or better. No, he'd sucked me into his operation for some entirely different purpose, at the moment known only to him.

But what? More to the point, why?

Welcome to Friday, and my rather disturbed life. Want to know what really disturbed me the most? Seeing my new employer on CNN's *Prime News*, standing there right next to the Emperor of Japan. Seemed as though I wasn't the only one now under Noda's spell. All of a sudden my mild-mannered client had become a world-class Japanese mover and shaker. And that made me very nervous.

Needing a little perspective, I decided to invite down Dr William J. Henderson, respected thinker and booze hound. As it happened, he had a little time to kill that Friday before his 'late date' with some advertising exec who was flying in from an assignment on the coast. Since three weeks had gone by since our talk up at Martell's, it seemed like a good occasion to get together and compare notes.

True to his word, he had formally resigned from the President's Council of Economic Advisers, though he'd reluctantly agreed to serve as a forecasting consultant for Wharton Econometrics. He'd also caused some unsettling rumours in the world markets by putting on some very heavy 'straddles' in December gold futures and oil. He called it insurance, predicting he'd be covered no matter what happened. Looked at another way, though, Bill Henderson was quietly shifting out of paper money and into commodities. And when Henderson started hedging, you knew the weather forecast was unsettled to stormy.

It turned out he'd also uncovered a few stray elements of what might well be a much bigger game. Nothing solid at that point, but enough to stir him up.

'Know who runs that outfit you've taken on as a client?' He leaned back in one of the leather chairs in the upstairs parlour, new pair of Gucci's glistening, and sampled his third drink. 'Guy by the name of Matsuo Noda.'

'Henderson, who do you think I was talking to up at Sotheby's the other night?'

'You check your wallet afterwards? We're talking heavy guns, my friend.' He snubbed out what must have been his tenth Dunhill in the last hour. 'You didn't tell me he was the honcho behind all this.'

'You didn't ask. Know anything about him?'

'Not till last week. I started to do a little checking and first thing I know I'm stumbling across his name everywhere I look.' He studied the glass in his hand. 'Tell you something about this Noda. The man drops a quarter, you let him pick it up himself. He'll nail you where the sun don't shine. Definitely a bad-news mother.'

'You mean that business with the sword?'

'Nah, what in hell do I know about swords? That's *your* toy box. I'm talking about the real world, friend. Turns out Matsuo Noda was the prime mover in one of the biggest takeover plays of the century.'

'What takeover? They don't screw around with corporate take-overs in Japan.'

'They don't take each other over. They take other businesses over. Washington may think that war back in the forties is over, but somebody neglected to pass the word to MITI. Seems they've got the idea it was just the opening skirmish – the only folks who surrendered were the army and navy.' Henderson grew ominously serious for a change. 'Question is, where's this thing headed? Is the idea of turning our industrial base into a packaging operation for imports some kind of conspiracy, or is it just nature takin' its course?'

Conspiracy? That wasn't a word Henderson threw around lightly. In fact, he tended to scoff at conspiracy theories, claiming they were a substitute for hardheaded analysis. I agreed. So what was he driving at? I pressed him.

He paused to light a cigarette. 'I bring up this unsavoury possibility because I'm beginning to detect a little operation code-named "eat an industry".'

'Henderson, that's my game. I pitch in to help the little fish fend off the big ones.'

'No offence, friend, but you probably couldn't even get into the ball park where Noda and his boys are playing. We're talking the very big leagues here.'

'Now hold on a second. Noda's not interested in companies. He's just shooting a little craps. From what I've seen so far, the guy seems to be completely on the up-and-up. In fact, looked at from the long view, you might even say he's putting money into this country, never mind it's just the Wall Street casino.'

'Sure he is. It's like he first kicks the shit out of you, then hands you a Coke so's you'll feel refreshed.'

'What in hell are you talking about?'

'Well, let's back up a notch. Since I don't want to bad-mouth your new client, why don't you let me give you what I'll call a purely hypothetical case.' He sipped at his Scotch. 'Let's suppose you were a Japanese guy, like Matsuo Noda for instance, and you wanted to take over some strategic American industry and ship it to Japan. How'd you go about it?'

'Well . . .'

'Have a drink, counsellor.' Bill plunged forward. 'And let me tell you a little fairy tale. About how Matsuo Noda ate the American semiconductor industry.'

'Noda?'

'It was MITI actually. But Noda was running the Ministry when they did it, and he was the guy who set up the play.'

'Noda ran MITI?' This was news to me.

'Yep. Vice-minister. Then he went on to greener pastures, being the Japan Development Bank, and left the details to another MITI honcho by the name of Kenji Asano. According to my sources, though, it was Noda who handled the tricky part, the money, after he went over to the bank. Got it together, laundered it and dispensed it.'

'Laundered it?'

'Can't think of a better word. MITI carefully made sure the kickoff funding from the Japan Development Bank got passed through a shell organisation called the Japan Electronic Computer Company, hoping nobody would trace it back to the government.'

'I think you're starting to see things, but I'd like to hear this little fantasy.'

'OK, off we go to the land of make-believe. Once upon a time not too long ago and not too far away, a few guys at Intel or Bell Labs or some damn place got the mind-boggling idea you could shrink down a computer's memory and put it on to a little sliver of silicon no bigger'n a horsefly's ass. Various outfits tinkered around with the concept and eventually it got commercialised. Lo and behold, Silicon Valley was born, where they start turning 'em out by the bucketful. By '78 we're talking a five-billion-dollar industry. Kids barely old enough to drink legal got so rich they just gave up counting the money.'

'The American dream, Herr Doktor.'

'That it was. Now, they were making a memory chip called a 16K RAM, that's sixteen thousand bits of Random Access Memory storage. Orders are pouring in, and they can't buy the BMWs fast enough out in Silicon Valley.'

'I know all about that.'

'Well, there's more. Seems Noda and Asano and their honchos at MITI had been watching this and thinking over the situation. They decided, probably rightly, that whoever's got the inside track on these computer chips has the future by the balls. Twenty years from now there's nothing gonna be made, except maybe wheelbarrows, that don't use these gadgets. So round about '75 they concluded they ought to be the ones in the driver's seat. MITI "targeted" integrated circuits.'

'Well, why not? We're the ones told them they were supposed to be capitalists.'

'In truth. But just like in fairyland, our princess had a problem.

See, these chips weren't as simple to copy as an internal combustion engine, or even a transistor. They're a heck of a lot more complicated. And to make things worse, back when America was inventin' these silicon marvels, nobody in Japan would've known one if it'd bit him on the butt. So it's a tall order.' He crumpled an empty cigarette pack and reached in his coat for another. 'Now, imagine you're these guys in MITI. You want to take over an industry you don't know the first thing about. How're you gonna start?'

'I'd probably begin by licensing the patents.'

'Nice try, but you don't want this job to be too straightforward. Then everybody'll suspect what's happening and, besides, it wouldn't be as much fun. So if you're this guy Noda, you decide to set up a sort of Manhattan Project, like America had to make the first A-bomb. You go over to see Nippon Telephone and Telegraph, their AT'n'T, and you say, "Boys, we just decided you're gonna pitch in with all you got." After that, you commandeer some labs at Toshiba and NEC. Then you get yourself a batch of these little American gizmos and start trying to figure out how the hell they work.'

Henderson poured himself another drink, then turned back. 'Now, since you need to catch up fast, you do a little "reverse engineering", which means you steal the other guy's R & D. You take a bunch apart and decide you'll go with the 16K RAM chip made by Mostek − a big outfit here that's since gone belly up, by the way, thanks to our friends at MITI. And by 1978 you've made yourself a Mostek clone. Bingo, you've got the technology.'

'I think I'm beginning to get the drift.'

'Whoa, buddy. You're just starting to get rolling.' He forged on. 'By this time everybody's wanting these chips, so all of a sudden Silicon Valley can't keep up. Now you and your boys at MITI are ready to move. You've got the know-how, so all you need to do is start turning them out by the truckload. Of course that takes millions and millions in plant investment, so you do what Asano did, bring your old pal Noda back into the picture. Since he's now running the Japan Development

Bank, he obligingly lines up a whole shit-load of cheap money for these outfits gearing up to chop America's nuts off. All in all, he gets together what amounts to a subsidy of low-interest bucks to the tune of about two billion dollars. All carefully laundered. Ready, set, go.

'Silicon Valley glances up from countin' its receipts and all of a sudden, from out of nowhere, here come your Japanese chips. Reeeal cheap, since you've got all these cheapo "loans" to capitalise your plants. Inside a year you've got nearly half the market.

'Now, you figure somebody's surely going to blow the whistle, so you can't believe your luck when Silicon Valley thinks you're some kind of joke. Come on in, they say, and sell as many of those crappy 16K models you can, since we've got ourselves a hot 64K version cooking, and that's where we're gonna make our real killing. When you hear this, you do a quick retool. And while the Valley is seeing how sexy and expensive a design they can come up with, your thrifty gang back home just sticks together a bigger version of that 16K chip you stole from Mostek in the first place – and you're up front with a 64K. Now it's time for hardball, so you flood America with these things. You drop the price of your 64K RAM chips from thirty dollars down to half a buck when they still cost over a dollar to make. Before you know it, you've got seventy per cent of the American market.'

'Selling at a loss. Dumping.'

'Exactly. 'Cause at this stage you don't care beans about profit. What you're going for is the big fish, market share.' Henderson lit yet another Dunhill. 'And sure enough, when it comes to the next generation, the 256K memory chip, you've got ninety per cent of the action. In very short order most of your American competition folds. You ate them. Matter of fact, Intel, which started it all, dropped out of RAM chips altogether – which is kind of like Xerox throwing in the towel on copiers. This is less than a decade after MITI's start-up, in an industry born in the USA. Hi ho, silicon, away.'

'Must have cost them a bundle.'

'Short term, sure, but now the future's wide open. You live happily ever after, my friend, just like in fairyland, because big bad America's dead and gone in the high-volume end of semi-conductors.'

'But MITI can't use dumping as a regular strategy. After all, it is illegal.'

'Well, now, ain't that a fact.' He exhaled a lungful of smoke, then coughed. 'So's selling your ass. But just take yourself a cruise down Eleventh Avenue and you'll meet up with a lot of entrepreneurial ladies who understand the reality of market forces. You've gotta get caught, tried, convicted. If it ever does get that far, the most that's gonna happen is a fine. A lot of folks claim MITI's dumped TVs, cars, steel, textiles, you name it. So when they decided to move on memory chips, Asano was given a free hand to do it the quickest way he knew how. And your buddy Noda ain't exactly a pussycat either, the way he laundered the Japanese taxpayer's money into them low-interest, *mañana* loans.'

As he returned to his Scotch, I sat there trying to think. What Henderson had just described was a fundamental insight into how high-tech industries operate.

'Henderson, do you realise what you're saying? That's a beautiful way to knock out a country's high-tech research capability. Take away the volume end of an operation and there goes your cash. Pretty soon you can't afford to finance any more R & D. Which means that sooner or later you're selling yesterday's news. You can kiss goodbye to your technological edge, right across the board.'

'Correct. America's semiconductor boys were figuring to use the profits from memory chips to pay for research in logic chips, where you put a whole computer's wiring on a chip. But now the money's gone. What it really means is, end of ball game in information processing. Maybe it won't happen tomorrow, but there's no doubt it's just a matter of time. You dominate semi-conductors, sooner or later you're just naturally gonna control computer technology and all that goes with it. I even met a guy a while back who claimed that whoever's ahead in computers is eventually going to have the say-so about who has advanced weapons technology.'

Could be, I thought. But that last extrapolation was a stretch. 'Bill, I think you're talking a pretty long line of dominoes. For one thing, we've still got plenty of computer research here. The US has a big lead in logic chips.'

'True, true. Who the hell can crystal-ball this one? All I know is, Intel was claiming exactly the same thing about memory chips a few years back, just before Asano and Noda and their pals chewed them up and spit them out. All I'm saying is, you'd better watch your backside.' He examined his drink and reached for the ice bucket.

About that time Ben came lumbering up the stairs to observe our maudlin ruminations. I watched as he settled himself near my feet with a grunt, then plopped his chin down on his paws.

'Well, your fairy tale about MITI may or may not be true. But that's water over the dam. Besides, who are we to be pointing a finger? The US has done its share of tinkering with foreign governments, making the world safe for American shareholders.'

'Hey, I make a profession of separating pious pronouncements from reality. I never take an official story at face value.'

'OK, so Noda says he's just playing the market. But if he's actually planning something else, then what is it?'

'Don't have the foggiest. Wish I did.' He glanced at his watch. 'But I do know duty's about to call. I'd better get uptown if I expect to have any female companionship for the apocalypse.'

'Take it easy. Nobody flies on schedule any more.' I settled back into my chair and glanced up at the large Japanese screen I had mounted on the wall opposite. It was Momoyama, around 1600, the time when the most recent crowd of Shoguns took over Japan. Against a gilded background was a fierce eagle, perched menacingly on a pine branch. The thing was so powerful I just kept the rest of the room bare; nothing else I owned could stand up to it. 'You know, Henderson, the trouble with your pattern is that it doesn't fit this time. Shorting Treasury futures is not exactly going after an industry. So what's the new angle?'

'Damned good question.' He stared at his glass, probably wondering if one more for the road would impair his performance later on. I guess he concluded yes because he didn't budge. 'Speaking of angles, what do you make of that sword business last week? Caused one hell of a flap in Japan, so I hear.'

'Major event. That sword should tell us a lot about early Japanese metal technology. I've been trying to find out more about it, but nobody's talking. No pictures, anything.' I reached over and gave Ben a pat. 'Curious though. I think I remember Noda's mentioning that sword the night I met him. Eight hundred years ago, the Emperor gets caught at sea and loses the Imperial symbol. But he didn't breathe a word about having a project underway to locate it.'

'Well, you're my Japan expert. What's it all about?'

'Never assume you understand the Japanese mind.' I pointed up at the wall. 'Take a good look at the eagle on that screen. You'd think it's just a picture, but actually it's an important subliminal message. The *diamyō* who commissioned this piece had that eagle put on it to let everybody know he was cock of the walk. Means you cross him and you're dead. Symbols are important in Japan. Noda and this woman Mori talked a lot about Shoguns and Emperors. Maybe they hope the sword will somehow bring back the good old days.'

'Well, he's got enough money to do it.'

'Looks that way.'

'Hope we're not about to get kamikazes with a chequebook. Thoughts like that could make a man real nervous.' Henderson rose and strolled to the fireplace. He examined his reflection in the large mirror over it, then set down his glass on the mantelpiece and turned back. 'You know, Walton, I think I'm starting to lose my touch. I don't believe anything I hear and only half of what I see.' He sighed. 'Been one hell of a day.'

'Pretty standard Friday, far as I could tell.'

'Well, a damned strange thing happened this afternoon.'

'Some woman turn you down? Maybe you ought to start working out, Henderson, trim that little spare tyre creeping in around the waistline.'

'Still no complaints in that department, friend. No, this actually goes back a ways, to a few months ago down in Washington, when I bumped into a long-haired professor coming out of a committee session. Guy I mentioned a minute ago.'

'The linkup between computers and weapons?'

'Him. We got to BS-ing in the men's room, and it turned out he was some computer hotshot from Stanford. He'd been testifying, I think, and he was still wound up. Probably I got to hear all the stuff he'd prepared and nobody'd asked.'

'What was the pitch?'

'Defence semiconductor dependency. Claimed that if we keep on the way we're going, relying more and more on foreigners for advanced chip technology, we may as well kiss the farm goodbye. I had a little time to kill, so I invited him to have a drink. He good as chewed my ear off. Finally had to fake a dinner date to get loose. Man had a bug six feet up his ass about the US buying half the latest chips for our hot-dog military hardware from Japan. Next war we fight, says he, we'll be buying high-tech weapons systems from the Far East. Problem with that is, anybody else could buy them too. And we'd get replacement parts whenever MITI feels like getting around to it. Today I happened to remember him, so I decided to give him a call, ask him if he still saw things the same way.'

'And?'

'No answer at his office, but since I had his home number, I decided to give that a try. Best I can tell, a lot of academics goof off half the time anyway.'

'You get him?'

'Some police detective answered, wanting to know who I was, what the hell I wanted, whole nine yards. Shook me up, don't mind telling you.'

'So what'd your pal do? Rob a bank?'

'I was about to start wondering. Finally, though, I got to ask some questions of my own, but it was a little hard to swallow the story. What I mean is, I don't necessarily buy what I heard.'

'Which was?'

'Well, seems he was supposed to meet the Senate's internal security committee this morning. Wife says she put him on the red-eye to Washington last night around ten. He was carrying some document he said he wanted to hand-deliver. Something about it had him scared shitless.' Henderson paused. 'Tell you, this is the kind of guy who takes security seriously. When *he's* worried, we all better be worried.'

'So what's the problem?'

'Cop claimed he's just disappeared. Not a trace.'

SEVEN

Ken looked terrific. That was Tam's first thought when he walked through the high-security inner doors to greet her. He was square-shouldered and sturdy, with high full cheeks, expensively trimmed dark hair, and a small delicate mouth. She figured him for late forties, early fifties. Funny, but he'd always reminded her of one of those steely-eyed, expensively dressed actors you saw playing executives on the Japanese soaps.

'Tamara!' He paused abruptly, then bowed. '*Ikaga desu ka?*'

'*Okagesama de genki desu. Anata wa?*'

'Doing well, thanks. You never cease to amaze me. What a marvellous surprise.' A smile attempted to break through his dark eyes. 'You've surfaced again, just like the sword.'

She'd forgotten how colloquial his English was. Then she recalled he'd told her once about doing his doctorate at MIT. Possibly because of that he could be either Japanese or Western, chameleonlike, as the backdrop required. He was every bit the charmer she remembered from Kyoto.

One thing was different, though. Kenji Asano was ill at ease. He was trying to mask it, but it was there. And that was very different from the old days.

As they passed the usual pleasantries, he led her down a hall, then through a room where intense young men in open shirts were now opening a case of Asahi beer. Computer terminals were in neat rows along the walls, beneath gleaming white 'blackboards' that sparkled with equations and quips. The place was so informal, so . . . American. There were plenty of jeans and frazzled sneakers among the forty or so young researchers, most of them in their late twenties or early thirties. Plastered across the low partitions were film posters and American countercultural bumper stickers ('Radio Already Stolen', 'Nuke a Commie for

Christ'); above a row of printers a blonde pin-up was unveiling her gynaecological mysteries to the movie still of a startled Godzilla; and a couple of rusty California vanity plates were hanging over one long-haired staffer's terminal like big-game trophies – one read 64K-1ST, the other EZ BKS. Probably commissioned by venture capitalists in Silicon Valley whose Porsches had since been repossessed, she thought. The rock and roll dissonance of Siouxsie and the Banshees sounded from a tiny stereo assembled out of computer hardware and a new Yamaha digital tape deck. Presumably as a stunt, the high end of the audio was being used to drive a garishly tinted computer graphics display that had been projected against one of the windows, creating a virtual image that seemed to dance amidst the Tokyo skyscrapers like a Martian *son et lumière*.

But she wasn't fooled by the frat-house trimmings. She realised these casually dressed young researchers were the pick of Japan's technical graduates. Making the Fifth Generation team these days was one of the highest honours in the land. After some initial scepticism the big corporations were now competing for the prestige of loaning their young stars to the project for a few years, since they hoped to reap enormous benefits down the road.

In fact, the youthful atmosphere was entirely intentional. That, she knew, had been the legacy of Ken's predecessor, Dr Yoshida, who had refused to let anyone over thirty-five on the project. Furthermore, since he believed the stuffed-shirt layout of most Japanese offices and labs stifled creativity, he had deliberately devised an un-Japanese work space to try to reproduce Western research environments.

Finally they reached a closed door. Metal. When she realised it was Ken's office, she almost remarked on this departure from what she remembered about Dr Yoshida's well-known attitude. He liked to be out on the floor, with just another low partition, right there interacting with his young staffers.

Without a word Ken inserted a magnetic card into the slot beside the door handle and then pushed it open. Not only a door, she thought, a locked door. Are they finally starting to worry about industrial espionage?

She wasn't surprised, however, to see that his office had a monastic spareness, with only his desk, a small but expensive leather couch, and a row of computer terminals along one wall. He was, she knew, a big believer in Zen philosophy. Maybe part of the reason for the door was just to shut all the madness outside and keep his own world serene.

Through the window behind him she could see Mount Fuji, outlined against a backdrop of autumn blue. He smiled and pointed it out, saying they were lucky to have a rare smogless day, then gestured her towards the couch.

'Welcome to my refuge.' He was cordial but entirely correct — right down to his conservative charcoal-grey suit. Not a glimmer of a hint about their brief Kyoto episode. 'Let me have tea sent in.' He leaned forward in his leather chair and punched the intercom on his desk.

'Ken, please, don't make a fuss. I know I hate it when people just drop by.' She glanced back at the locked door, wondering. 'Tell me if this is not a good time for you.'

'Tam, for you any time is a good time.' He buzzed again — there had been no response — then shrugged. 'I guess things are getting hectic out front just now.' He laughed resignedly, then turned to her. 'By the way, I saw your new book. Fine piece of work. I do hope somebody over there reads it. Are you still running your Center at NYU?'

'So far.' She decided to spare him the details.

'Well, it's a good school. Getting better all the time. You've got some first-rate supercomputer work at the Courant Institute, particularly with your IBM connection, but you should keep an eye on Columbia. Now that AT & T has joined with them to go after some of the Pentagon's AI contracts, they may finally start putting together a major computer science department up there too. In a few years Stanford and Carnegie-Mellon will have to step lively to stay out front.'

Hello, she thought. How come Ken suddenly knows so much scuttlebutt about US computer research? Nobody at home knows the first thing about what's going on in Japan.

'I was surprised to hear about this new appointment, Ken.' She settled back on the couch. 'I was guessing you had the inside track for MITI vice-minister in a few years.'

'Ah, well, for now my work is here.' He gestured uncomfortably about the room. 'Let me try once more for that tea.'

She realised he'd slipped deftly around her quick probe concerning MITI's new role in the lab. He knew how to be a team player, she thought. Very Japanese.

This time he raised a response. A female voice dripping with long-vowel honorifics announced his tea would be delivered immediately.

Next came a small, awkward lull as they both sat there remembering Kyoto and not sure how to get around that memory. She wondered if it was happening all over again.

Maybe it hadn't been just a fluke, a crazy one-night diversion. She was about to switch to Japanese, thinking that might provide the jolt needed to break the ice, but just as the silence swelled between them, there came a knock on the door and tea.

She was half annoyed, half relieved.

He rose to walk over and began chatting as though they'd been interrupted in the midst of some intense technical exchange.

'Are you scheduled to present a paper at that Kyoto conference coming up?' He pushed a button beside the door, and it swung wide. 'There's sure to be quite a crowd. Everybody here's excited about supercomputers these days.'

'No, this is strictly a pleasure trip. With maybe a few interviews thrown in to make it a tax write-off for a book I'm planning on robots.' She hesitated. 'Though I actually might go down and try to see a few people.'

'Then this could turn out to be a pleasant coincidence.' He took the tea, and the bowing girl vanished. Again the door clicked shut. 'I have to go too, but I'm hoping to steal a few moments of freedom.'

'You're chairing a session this year?'

'Absolutely not.' He turned serious. 'I'm not allowed time for anything like that any more, Tam. This new project is top priority.' He poured her a cup of the pale green liquid and passed it over, seemingly relieved that the tension had abated. 'There's a lot of work here at the Fifth Generation lab now that we're coordinating this programme with the supercomputer effort.'

'You mean with MITI's supercomputer project?' Caught your little slip, she told herself. You are still with MITI. Which means they *have* taken over this lab.

He didn't blink. 'As you probably know, MITI has the goal of creating a machine capable of a hundred billion computations a second, targeted just down the road. Which means we have to come up with entirely new computer languages and architecture.'

'Parallel processing.'

'Exactly. Handling multiple streams of information at once. Now that we finally understand what's required for a superfast computer, this work in AI just happens to be very relevant. It turns out we humans are already walking around with parallel processing in our heads, able to handle words, images, ideas, all at the same time. So if we want to create machines that operate as fast as possible, then it's crucial to understand how our brain manages things like recognition, learning, inference. Our hope is that by utilising the studies here in those areas, incorporating them into our supercomputer work, we might be able to put ourselves a major step ahead . . .'

Good God, Tam thought, it's elegantly simple. That's why MITI has taken over the Fifth Generation Project. They're going to use this research in artificial intelligence to come up with a computer more powerful than anything the world has yet imagined. Their silicon monsters are about to start replicating themselves, getting smarter as they go, like in some bad fifties horror flick. The difference is, this isn't make-believe.

'So you're here on behalf of MITI.'

He paused. 'For coordination. As I said, MITI needs the Fifth Generation work to be accelerated.' He still hadn't exactly answered the question. 'As part of our supercomputer effort.'

Tam knew that Hitachi and NEC were both already claiming they had the world's most powerful machines, faster even than Cray's entry, the best American computer. What did MITI want?

He continued. 'With 16-megabit chip production already going strong and 64-megabit commercialisation in the wings, it did seem the right time to pull all our work together. If you think about it, computer speed and computer intelligence go hand in hand. I'll show you in a second what I mean.'

Not kilobit. *Mega*bit. MITI was going for the kill. This was a crash programme. Why?

'Does this mean you plan to increase your funding for the Fifth Generation effort?'

'Whatever it takes to do the job,' he replied after a moment's hesitation. 'I suppose there's never enough money, is there?'

'Ken, why the rush? This sudden drive?'

'It depends on whom you ask.' He leaned back and looked at the ceiling. 'Some call it survival, Tamara. Maybe it is that simple. Japan is at a crossroads; we're rapidly losing our edge in the cost of labour. The only possible way to counter that is to step up our use of smart machines.'

'Well, it looks as if I came to the right place. I'd like to add your name to my interview list.'

His look darkened a moment. 'Strictly off the record.' Then he smiled. 'And only if we can do it over dinner.'

'That sounds like a bribe.'

'Call it an offering from an old admirer.' He smiled, attempting to ease the tension. 'The most I can do, for now at least, is just give you a small peek at a few of our experimental gadgets. Details are strictly proprietary. At the moment we're concentrating on computer vision and voice access. And on that last, by the way, I think we've just about reached AI's Holy Grail, natural language comprehension.'

'Good luck.' That was one of the mythical dreams of AI research, a computer that could understand the speech of anybody who happened along. Even though millions had been invested in the US, nobody was anywhere close yet.

'I think we're getting there. Enough so in fact that we're starting to look at applications. Expect commercialisation in, oh, say a year, two at most.'

Look out IBM, she found herself thinking.

'I probably shouldn't be showing you this, Tamara. So let's just keep this informal. No notes. But here, have a look at one of MITI's new toys. Can you guess what this is?' He passed over a small device that had been sitting on his desk, his hand lingering on hers a moment longer than absolutely necessary.

She stared down at what appeared to be some kind of calculator-watch, except there was no face, merely a small speaker and two buttons.

'That uses advanced versions of MITI's new 64-megabit memory chips. There's nothing like it anywhere in the world. Without ever having heard the speaker's voice before, no calibration, it can translate ordinary spoken English into Japanese.' He pointed to one of the buttons. 'Just press there and talk. When you finish, push the other button for the translation.'

She did, testing it with the opening paragraph of *Pride and Prejudice,* her favourite novel. A simulated voice emerged from the small speaker on the face of the device and gave it back . . . in flawless Japanese.

'Not bad.' She set it carefully on to the desk. The thing was actually almost frightening.

'Using this, linked to our new high-definition video and satellite, you could punch a button in your living room and bring up people on a wall-size screen from anywhere in the world, then talk to them in your language and be understood in theirs. It's a quantum advance over current technology.' He retrieved the device, dropping it into a desk drawer.

'I must admit I'm very impressed.'

'Truthfully, so am I. Where's this programme of MITI's taking us?' He looked up. 'But let me show you something else, which I think is even more astonishing. Of course you're aware that speech comprehension is easy compared to the really tough nut, duplicating the human eye. Since a visual image can contain billions of pieces of information, it can be very time-consuming for a computer to analyse all those at once and figure out what it's looking at. I've heard people at IBM claim that for a computer to recognise something even as simple as an odd-shaped coffee cup would still require almost an hour of processing, that to match the human eye and brain could take a computer the size of a building. But watch.'

He walked over to a black metal installation attached to the wall and held up three fingers before its small lens. Then he pushed a button and spoke into a built-in microphone.

'What do you see?'

She started to reply herself, then realised he was talking to the lens.

This time the answer took about ten seconds. Finally a voice in passable simulation of the Tokyo dialect emerged from a grey speaker beneath the lens. *'That is a human hand.'*

'How many fingers does this hand have?' he continued.

Again the eerie, disembodied voice. *'The normal human hand has five fingers. This appears to have only three.'*

'Thank you.' He punched a button and turned back. 'That came off the mainframe here. Can you imagine the amount of memory and logic processing required to achieve what you've just witnessed: the data base and the computational power and speed? Not to mention the recognition of my voice commands.'

'How does it do it?'

He paused. 'Tam, this is proprietary, top secret, but what you've just witnessed is an example of parallel processing with MITI's new, still classified 256-megabit dynamic RAMs.'

'A quarter of a billion bits of data on a chip.' She just stared. 'Are they writable?'

'Of course.' He again settled himself behind his desk. 'The test versions have circuits only a hundred or so atoms wide. And this is only the beginning. Within five years, maybe no more than three, MITI fully expects to have a desktop machine that will pass the Turing test.'

'Three years?' It was almost unbelievable. Passing the 'Turing test' meant the computer's 'thoughts' and 'speech' would be so lifelike you'd be able to talk with it and not realise it wasn't human. AI's end-of-the-rainbow.

'As you can see, the project is getting close.' He looked pensive, like some Zen monk. 'Strictly off the record – and I mean that – what MITI is working toward is total automation. Factories run by machines with human skills, intelligence, manual dexterity. In fact, several of the robotics labs at Tsukuba Science City already have prototypes in advanced stages of development.'

She was stunned. This was the kind of futuristic talk you heard from all the AI buffs, but it was still mostly speculation in the US and Europe. Japan, though, was taking it straight to commercialisation.

'Why are you telling me all this?'

He sat silent for a moment. Then he looked at her. 'Because it's time the world understood something very important about this country. There are people here . . . with an agenda. And resources.'

'What do you mean?'

'Tam, there are people, important people, who are getting fed up. Know what they're saying? Try this. Our country has a monarchy older than Rome, a heritage of literature, art, aesthetics, equal to anything in the West. We've never had any colonies, any raw materials besides air and water. All we do have is a willingness to work and save – the one natural resource running short in the West. In less than half a century we've risen from the most total devastation any country has ever experienced, and achieved technological parity with both the US and the Soviets. We launch satellites, split atoms, splice genes. But still a lot of foreigners claim all this country can do is copy from the West, steal and commercialise other nations' inventions. Only a short time back the leader of France called our Prime Minister a "transistor salesman". That's right. A "transistor salesman".'

'Ken, that stupid crack was by de Gaulle. Years ago. It's—'

'Tam, look around you. This is an old country. And a lot of influential people have long memories.'

'You're getting melodramatic.'

He shifted in his chair and studied the white peak of Fuji. 'Think so? Don't delude yourself. Believe me, the West is about to dig its own grave.'

'What are you trying to tell me?'

'Nothing you can't see with your own eyes.' He turned back. 'MITI is now ready to move into the next phase. Finally here's a project that's as strategic, in its own way, as the bomb. If Japan can succeed in creating a machine capable of humanlike thinking, it will be the most profound achievement in the history of mankind. And this project is well on its way. There may be nothing that can stop the events that lie ahead.'

'Stop what? What events?'

'That's not a simple question.' He caught himself and eased up, smiling uncomfortably once again. 'Forgive me. None of this is for publication.' He hesitated. 'Your work is well known here in Japan, Tam. You are one of the few Americans our industrialists respect unreservedly. Maybe you weren't aware of that. Your books are highly regarded; in fact, I read the new one in manuscript.' A long pause, then, 'Would you ever consider working with me for a while? Come back home, so to speak? You can see the implications of this project.'

'I see the implications all right.' She didn't know what to say. Why a sudden job offer from Ken? Or was it from MITI? 'But where is this headed? If Japan achieves this technological supremacy, what then?'

'Before the flowers bloom, MITI must tend the garden.' He rose and poured more tea into her cup. 'But enough. You know, I've thought about you a lot. Tell me how you've been. What've you been doing?'

'Teaching, writing, you know. Everything and nothing.'

He smiled, then brushed an imaginary fleck of lint off his tailored woollen cuff. 'Well, perhaps we'll have some time to talk.'

What was he driving at? Was there more? Something going on he didn't want to broach here in the lab?

'Tam, it is so good to see you once more.' He looked up again. 'Would you be interested in going down to Kyoto with me day after tomorrow? There are some things . . .' He sipped at his tea. 'As I said, I'm scheduled to look in on the conference and see a few people, but I should have some free time.'

'That conference doesn't start till next week.'

'Actually I need to be down a few days early.'

'Oh. Why?'

He measured his words. 'Oddly enough it has to do with the

sword. Things have started moving pretty fast since those archaeologists working for Dai Nippon recovered the Sacred Sword of the Emperor Antoku.'

'I saw the Emperor on TV. Try going outside now.'

'Well, I think I'll close here a little early and let my people go on home. It sounds like their celebration has already started anyway.' He gestured towards the music and noise filtering through the door. 'But the reason I need to be in Kyoto a few days in advance is to see the president of Dai Nippon.'

'The firm that—'

'That's right. His name is Matsuo Noda. I've known him for some years actually. He contacted me a couple of days ago about a meeting. I'm not sure what he has in mind precisely, but I have to find out. He's just become one of the most influential people in the country, not that he wasn't already. And now with all the money he's about to have in his new Imperial fund . . .'

'The one mentioned at the Emperor's news conference?'

'Exactly. As you might suspect, that was merely the formal announcement. Some of us at MITI heard about it several days ago. My private hunch is that in a few days Matsuo Noda could well have more resources at his fingertips than any one man in the history of the world.' He looked at her. 'It's almost frightening when you think of the power he'll soon have.'

'Ken, I think I *would* like to come along with you.' What was going on? MITI's plans already were pretty astonishing. And now this new national hero, the president of Dai Nippon, was about to get involved.

More than that, she'd half forgotten how interesting Kenji Asano really could be. Her trip was taking a lot of unexpected turns.

'Well, then, in that famous American phrase, "Why not?" ' He smiled, the mask firmly back in place. 'In fact, I'll try and arrange for you to meet Matsuo Noda while we're there.' A conspiratorial wink. 'Maybe he'll even give us a glimpse of the sword.'

Tokyo was one big party that night, the streets mobbed. They eventually found themselves in Shinjuku, in a high-tech new restaurant all chrome and glass and New Age prices. The tuna *sashimi* seemed only minutes from the sea, and the aged sake was smooth as a flawless white Bordeaux. Afterwards they grabbed a taxi over to the Ginza, where Ken got seats on the *tatami* straw mats down in the orchestra of the Kabukiza, and they took in the last act of a Kabuki play (featuring the famous Ennosuke III) that had been underway since late afternoon. The evening ended up in the art-deco mezzanine bar at the Imperial, the part salvaged from the old Frank Lloyd Wright structure, where she kicked off her shoes, ordered a $20.00 cognac, and nestled against his elegant shoulder.

What was that he'd said about coming back home? Her books being circulated here in manuscript? What was he hinting at?

Finally around two a.m. he called for the bill and neither said a word as they headed for the elevator.

She thought one last time about Allan's warning as she watched the floors flash above the door and searched for her key. But this was no time to brood about conspiracies. Ken made her feel good. Which was a hell of a lot more than Dave Mason had done. Besides, Ken had some style; all Dave did was mope around in a pair of baggy chinos and whine about his department. Ken was upbeat, alive, aware.

What's more, she was enjoying being with him, feeling the heat of his cheek against hers. As the elevator doors opened, he slipped an arm about her waist and nuzzled her hair. Then their lips met.

He was just as she remembered. His touch, his taste, his body. Still, something about him was definitely changed.

Then he reached for her key and opened the door. The minute they entered the sitting room of her suite, he took her in his arms.

'Tam, let's not talk any more about business, no more swords. I'm already bored hearing about it. Just us. What do you say?'

'Agreed.' She looked at him and suddenly realised something. Ken Asano was beautiful, *kirei*. Not handsome, beautiful. *Anata wa kirei desu*, Kenji Asano. 'Want a nightcap? There's some airport Remy in my—'

'Who could even think about another cognac? I just want to

think about us.' He stood back. 'Well, all right, maybe if you insist. For old times' sake.'

' "Old times" is right, Ken. It's been a very long time since Kyoto.' She located the dark Remy bottle, still packed in her leather flight bag. A nice inauguration, she told herself. 'What was that all about? Was it real? Or did I just imagine it all?'

'The heart never lies.' He settled on the couch. 'Do you really remember?'

'Vividly.' She laughed as she poured an inch into each of two thin hotel tumblers. 'Including that dreadful bar you took us all to.'

'A glimpse of the real Japan, Tam, for our tourist friends. Show them it's not all *ikebana* and haiku. Believe me, it's not.' He clicked her glass. 'Do try to forgive me. And here's to us.'

'To us.'

'And to the slightly scary world we're stumbling into. Japan needs you here.' He pulled her next to him and brushed her cheek lightly with his fingertips. Then he kissed her deeply on the mouth, and again. '*I* need you here, Tam. Somebody like you. There's . . . well, there's a lot we could do together.'

She reached up and loosened his tie, then began unbuttoning his shirt. His chest was firm, smooth, scented. She wanted him. 'Let's just remember Kyoto for a while.'

'I've never forgotten it.'

Some time around four a.m., more content than she had been in a long, long time, Tam Richardson lay awake on the cool sheets, Ken's trim body beside her, and wondered how it would end this time around.

Or possibly, just possibly, it wouldn't.

EIGHT

Back in New York, optimism was in increasingly short supply. What do you do if you think you're being set up? One thing, you may have occasion to muse long and hard about the consequences, personal and otherwise. You also may choose to ponder the larger motives of the individual behind it all.

So far, what had happened? Matsuo Noda had hired Matt Walton, corporate attorney-at-law, to begin shorting the American Treasury market, then proceeded to make himself a bona fide hero back home, in the process of which he acquired access to the biggest chunk of savings in the world, presumably the 'financial arrangements' he once alluded to. Using that money as margin, Noda was ready to shift his play into high gear. My latest telexed instructions indicated he was poised to accelerate dramatically, 'borrowing' bonds and selling them for whatever the market would pay. Of course, if the price went down any time soon, he could then replace those borrowed instruments at some fraction of what he'd sold them for. The man was gambling, for God's sake. With the 'Emperor's' fund.

Or was he? Therein, as somebody once said, lies the rub. Short selling has always been a reasonably good definition of gambling, except ... except you are gambling only if you are wagering money on an event whose outcome is not precisely known. If you do know it, you are not gambling. You are taking prudent steps that will allow you to benefit from prior knowledge of said, etc.

Enough airy semantics. The big question: Why me? Now, I've been set up a few times before in my life. Everybody has. I even wonder in darker moments if the reason Joanna demanded a champagne lifestyle wasn't to make sure I spent all my time supporting it, thereby rendering me exactly what she eventually accused me of being — an absentee husband and father. That is a no-win situation.

The undertaking at hand, however, could have a very obvious beneficiary. Matsuo Noda. The only problem was that in order for Noda to win, America had to lose. Massively. The old zero-sum game: for every winner there has to be an equal and opposite sucker.

After that Friday evening with Henderson, I spent the next week mulling over the complexities of the situation. The whole thing boiled down to two very strong presumptions: one, I was indeed being set up, being told one scenario while the truth lay in quite another direction; and two, my employer had something very lethal to America's financial health up his sleeve. Still, these were merely presumptions, nothing more. The only thing I was sure about was that I had a very unpredictable tiger by its posterior handle. Time to find out a little more about our pussycat.

I hadn't actually seen Dai Nippon's midtown office, but I talked to the manager almost every day on the phone, and he occasionally shipped materials down to my place in the Village. I knew they'd taken over the building, installed a new security staff, moved into the vacant floor and were doing something. However, I hadn't been invited up to see what that something was. I concluded the time was at hand.

As I understood it, Dai Nippon's purpose in life was to oversee the use of investment capital. Well and good. As it happens, Japanese business tends to be funded a little differently from our own. Instead of selling off stock to the public, Japanese industry relies much more heavily on bank financing. In fact, less than twenty per cent of Japan's industrial assets are publicly traded. Consequently the rules of the game are changed. If your company is beholden to a financial institution instead of a lot of nervous stockholders and fund managers, you're partner with somebody less interested in next quarter's profits than in the larger matter of your still being around ten years hence to pay off its paper. That lender naturally rides herd very closely on your long-term planning.

As best I could tell, DNI was one of the herd-riders, a sort of hired gun that monitored various companies' operations to make sure they were managing their loans prudently. Again, since the prospectus emphasised they were specialists in overseas investment, I assumed that maybe part of the reason they were coming to the US was to oversee the Japanese companies doing business here with money borrowed from back home.

Nobody had actually told me this. In fact nobody had told me anything. That was merely what I considered to be an educated guess. It was the only thing I could think of that made the slightest sense.

The following Monday morning I told myself the guesswork was over. It was high time I went up and saw for myself what they were doing. All I needed was an excuse.

Then the phone rang. I was in the garden out back, skimming the *Times* and working on a pot of fresh coffee while waiting for the Chicago exchanges to open. Ben was cruising the fence line, sniffing for cats.

When I picked up the receiver, waiting at the other end was Mr Yasuhiro Tanaka, office manager for the New York operation. He chatted a bit about the weather, how nice it was to be working in the US, the usual. Finally he mentioned that he needed to meet with me to discuss, among other matters, certain legal questions concerning one of the other leases in their building. Would it be convenient if he came to my place and we went over the paperwork?

Not necessary, I replied. I just happened to be headed for midtown in the next few minutes. I'd throw a copy of the leases into my briefcase and drop by to see *him*. Then before he could protest, I mumbled something about the doorbell and hung up. The phone rang again immediately, but I didn't answer it. I was already putting on my jacket.

I scribbled a few notes for Emma, taped them to her word processor, and headed out the door. Minutes later I was in their Third Avenue lobby, greeting the new security staff, several of whom, as a favour to Tanaka, I'd interviewed for their jobs.

Then I took the elevator up to DNI's offices on the eleventh floor and proceeded to have my argyle socks blown away.

First off, top security. The entryway just off the elevator bank had been completely transformed. TV intercom, steel doors, it could have been the vault at Chase. I told the camera's eye who I was and then waited while a computer somewhere gave me a voice-ID check. How they managed to have me in the system already I wasn't exactly sure ... maybe they'd taken it off the phone?

After I'd cleared that, the doors slid open and I entered the first chamber of a two-room security check. An electronic voice ordered me to put my briefcase into the X-ray machine while I proceeded through the metal detector.

That cleared, the set of steel panels leading into the next room slid open and I went in ... to be confronted by two crew-cut guards who could have been retired sumo wrestlers. As the doors clicked behind me, I took one look at DNI's welcoming committee and realised they were packing Uzis, those Israeli automatics that could probably cut down a tree in about two seconds. No candy-ass .38's for Dai Nippon. Without ceremony they commenced a body search. It was all very polite, but it sure as hell wasn't perfunctory. I just stood there in astonishment while this gorilla roughly twice my size felt me up.

That indignity completed, I was now in line for the real surprise. Yet another set of steel doors opened, and there awaited the man I'd been dealing with over the phone, Yasuhiro Tanaka. Medium build, late forties, cropped hair, automatic smile – he was Noda's chief of operations for New York. He didn't say much, just led me on to the floor, heading for his office. But he was clearly the on-site *daimyō*: lots of heavy bowing from the young, white-shirted Japanese staff as we headed for the corner suite.

Which brings us to the real shocker. Dai Nippon's floor operation looked like the flight deck of the *Starship Enterprise*. Let me attempt a brief description. In the far back was a massive NEC augmented supercomputer – a half dozen off-white octagonal units about head high, one the mainframe and the others storage modules arranged alongside in a neat row. Pure power. The whole thing was encased in a glassed room with (I assumed) critical temperature and humidity control. Then out on the floor were lines and lines of workstations. Computer screens everywhere, printers running, stacks of colour hard copy – pie charts, bar graphs, spreads – plus terminals carrying every financial service offered by cable or satellite.

This was just the first, five-second glance. Incredible, I thought. There must be a heck of a lot more Japanese investment in the US than anybody realises.

But something had to be wrong here. Why should . . .? Finally I slowed down – Tanaka was hurrying me along, clearly annoyed that I'd appeared uninvited. That's when I noticed the rest. Across one wall was a line of projection TVs, on which computer data was being scrolled. As we walked past, I noticed that each screen seemed to be under the scrutiny of a team of analysts, who were intently studying the numbers, comparing notes, running calculations on their individual terminals.

What's this all about?

I stopped before one screen and studied it a second. Beneath it a small sign said simply 'Electronics'. The one next to it read 'Biotechnology'. Then I glanced at a couple of others. Each one covered a different industrial sector. Gee, I thought, you're really out of touch, Walton. Who would have guessed Japan has so much investment in manufacturing here? I didn't remember much going on besides a few joint ventures. Sure, they've got a few auto assembly plants, that steel plant they'd bought out on the coast, some TV-tube production, chips, VCRs. But mostly it represented entries into sectors where they're trying to get the jump on protectionism, start a token manufacturing operation here before they get shut out.

'If you have any questions, I'm sure we can discuss them later.' Tanaka had taken my arm and was urging me politely towards his office. The whines and hums of laser printers and the beep of computers made conversation all but impossible.

'Well, I was merely interested . . .' Then I stopped.

Know that test psychologists have, the one where you look at a couple of silhouettes and describe what you see? If you think you're supposed to look at the white part in the middle, then you see one thing – I think it's a vase. But if you concentrate on the black instead, you see something else entirely, maybe the profiles of two human faces opposite each other. Thus what you see is largely a product of your prior assumptions concerning what you're supposed to be looking for. Or maybe it measures whether you view the world as a positive or a negative image, something like that. I don't recall exactly. I do remember receiving B— in Psych 101, which was generous.

The point is, what I first thought I saw was actually the inverse of what was really there. I'd told myself what it was, rather than believing my eyes.

Dai Nippon was running analyses, bet your ass, but the industries under their silicon microscope weren't Japanese. They'd computerised the financial report of every American company traded publicly and were now in the process of taking those outfits apart.

And I can assure you it was cold-eyed in the extreme, strictly hard numbers: quarterly earnings, long-term debt, inventory, stock outstanding, CEO bonuses. As any professional analyst would do, they'd cut right through a company's glossed-over excuses, phrases such as strategic retrenchment, aimed at the dividend-nervous retirees in Cedar Rapids. They were putting together the real story.

Same with the financial markets. Screens were scrolling up-to-the-second quotes on everything from three-month T-bills to thirty-year Treasury bonds. Computers were running arbitrage spreads on every issue. They knew exactly where they stood with all their futures contracts. I realised my little telephone boiler room had merely been the tip of some awesome iceberg.

'Mr Walton, it is a pleasure to meet you in person.' Tanaka was ushering me into the corner office after our pass through the floor. Unlike most executive suites in New York, its windows were sealed with heavy drapes. Again, total security. 'Let me order tea.' He waved at somebody out on the floor.

I nodded, still chewing over the set-up and trying to understand what in good Christ was underway.

'I'm sure you are a busy man, so perhaps we should proceed directly to my concerns. As you may have guessed, we are almost ready to move into a new phase of our operation.'

'Oh.' I guess it must have sounded dumb, but I honestly couldn't manage a full sentence. Finally I recovered slightly. 'I'm a little surprised by the scope of all this. What's the purpose?'

'Our president, Noda-san, should be arriving in a few days. I'm sure he will be happy to address your questions in detail.' Tanaka paused for the green tea, delivered by a silent girl – the young smiling uniformed Japanese 'office lady' – who scarcely looked up as she settled the tray on the desk. After she was gone, he continued. 'This, of course, is only the financial nerve centre for our operation. Our technical staff will begin arriving soon.'

Technical staff? Then who were those grim-faced minions out there punching computers?

'You're bringing in more people?'

'Correct. Which is why I needed to see you. I understand that the lease on the floor above is due for renewal at the end of this month. We would like to acquire that space. We will need to convert it as quickly as possible.'

'What about the current tenants?'

'There is a rider in their lease, Mr Walton, that permits the owner of the building to reclaim the space for his own use at the time of a renewal. We fully intend to make use of it. Consequently as our American attorney you are hereby authorised to inform them that their lease will not be automatically extended, that they will be expected to vacate. In accordance with the legal and binding terms of their lease. Advise them also that there can be no grace period. We will require the floor immediately.'

I looked at him. So much for the current tenants. 'What will these new offices be used for?'

Tanaka sipped his tea. 'That section will have another managing director. Our range of operations here brings other responsibilities.'

'What section, what range of operations?'

'I am regrettably not at liberty to discuss the specific extent of DNI's interests.'

'Well, let me break some news to you. I like to know who I'm working for. So you'd better start discussing specifics and fast.'

Tanaka seemed to be having trouble meeting my eye. The skull beneath his short-cropped hair glistened under the harsh neon lighting.

'Mr Walton, you are now part of the DNI team. That position includes obligations I am sure you would not wish to take lightly.'

'Hold on.' The hell with politeness. 'I'm not part of your "team" or anybody's. I came on board with the explicit understanding that . . .'

'Mr Walton, kindly sit down.' He pointed, without ceremony, to a chair. I looked at it, then back at him.

'As you are a scholar of Japan,' he continued, 'I'm sure you are aware that an employee's loyalty to his company is considered to be a gauge of his character. A company is a family, and one considers its interests in that spirit.'

'Maybe you didn't notice, but I'm not Japanese. "*Nihon-jin*" as you'd probably put it. I'm a *gaijin*. We usually work for number one.'

'At the moment, Mr Walton, you work for Dai Nippon. There is an assigned role for you, one that Noda-san expects you to fulfil.'

'Maybe I just handed in my resignation.'

'I do not really think you would wish to do that.' Deadpan. The confidence with which he made that statement told me this guy could make a killing at poker. Unless he had a few cards in the hole I didn't know about. 'It would hardly be in your best interest. We expect your contribution to be crucial.'

'What contribution?'

'That will become plain in due time, Mr Walton.' He was measuring his words as he continued, maybe easing up a bit. 'For now, let me merely say we know you to be a man with substantial curiosity. Consequently we believe that what lies ahead will be of considerable interest to you.'

What was this *samurai* up to?

'Maybe it's time everybody put their cards on the table. And why don't we begin with you?' I thumbed at the floor outside. 'What the hell's going on out there?'

'At the moment nothing in this office need concern you. But perhaps I can tell you this. Now that you are serving as our corporate attorney, you are in a position to help us pursue other avenues.'

I looked him over. Tanaka was beating about the bush. Why? Maybe it was merely the Japanese style, but he also seemed to know exactly what not to say.

'I'm still waiting to hear what's next.'

'Very well. As long as you're here ...' He sipped calmly from his cup. 'It is common knowledge that Japanese savers have become the world's largest lenders, with overseas investment that now exceeds, by the way, the greatest rate of lending by OPEC even at its peak. The Japanese people will have over a trillion dollars in overseas assets within the next few years.'

'I'm familiar with the numbers.' I also knew that with several trillion dollars in spare change sloshing around back home, they were sending abroad a mere dribble of what they had.

'Were you also aware that over four fifths of our overseas investment is currently in dollar-denominated instruments?'

'No surprise. The dollar's still the name of the game, worldwide.'

'True enough, but we at Dai Nippon are concerned that so many of our institutions have such heavy exposure in a single currency. Accordingly, in addition to our programme with interest-rate futures, we also feel it would be prudent to provide some protection for this currency risk. In the same manner, I might add, that American investors often do.'

'You mean some downside protection? On the dollar?'

'That is correct. A devaluation or a sudden drop in exchange rates would jeopardise much Japanese capital. Therefore we feel it would be prudent to enter the currency-futures markets to cover at least some of the dollar exposure of our investors.'

Jesus! I suddenly needed a Valium. In addition to Treasuries, now Dai Nippon was about to short the dollar, presell it in advance of . . . of what?

Had Noda been lying to me right down the line? Setting up a cockamamy cover with interest futures while all along he was setting up an international currency swindle?

Or were we about to get down to the real action? He'd scheduled his curtain raiser, whatever it was, then realised he might accidentally pull the plug on the US greenback? So he'd decided to arrange a little currency insurance for everybody back at the ranch, just in case.

Don't ask me why, but I was drawn to this pending nightmare like a moth to flame. This was a ringside seat at . . .

All right, who am I trying to kid? That was the moment when I finally, *finally* grasped what our meeting was all about. It was to formally announce the tidal wave that would soon engulf America. And now Matsuo Noda – or maybe I should say Noah – was, in his oblique Japanese way, handing me a pair of tickets good for one round-trip passage on his ark. The only thing missing was the schedule.

By then I didn't care whether I was on board or not; I figured I'd just as soon try swimming on my own. But I had one very good reason to play along.

'OK, what's the game? Want to sell some dollars for delivery down the road?'

'We assume you are familiar with the markets.'

'I stay in touch. How would you like to go? If you want currency futures, there're the exchanges. Or you can buy forwards, which are more or less the same thing, from any number of banks around town. Futures only go out for a year, maximum, but I can probably get you forwards out to three. Come to think of it, Citibank will quote you ten-year forwards.'

'We would be looking at shorter terms.'

'No problem. Currency futures are quoted for March, June, September and December. That's on the Chicago Mercantile

Exchange's IMM. But if three months are too far out, then you can get options on spot currency contracts down at the Philadelphia exchange, which allows early exercise. Or if you want, I think you can get off-exchange bank quotes as short as one month. Citibank has a big FOREX desk. And Bankers Trust, and First Boston, or even Banque Indosuez. Of course, if you really want to get serious, there's the currency trading floor at Barclays Bank in London . . .'

'We expect to be active in all markets, worldwide. That seems best,' Tanaka continued. 'However, we are only interested in December futures and one-month contracts in the forwards. After that, we may choose to . . . make other arrangements.'

Hang on, America.

'Right. And what are we talking here in terms of amount?'

He handed me a sheet of paper.

It was like he was ordering up sandwiches from the deli. Corned beef on rye, lean, with extra mustard and a slice of pickle. How many? Let me check. Oh, say a few hundred billion.

'This is going to take a few days.' I passed it back, calmly as I could manage. 'Why don't you send a schedule down to my place late this afternoon? My secretary will be there. I'll get started in the morning.' I rose. 'In the meantime, you'll understand if I take today off and catch up a little on other work.'

'Of course.' Tanaka bowed, head still glistening.

'Be in touch tomorrow.' I nodded farewell.

'Until then, Mr Walton.' Another bow as I turned to leave.

I walked back through the floor, again trying to digest the spectacle. This was undoubtedly the most comprehensive operation I'd ever witnessed. What in hell did all this analysis of industrial sectors have to do with currency hedging?

Not a lot of time to reflect on the question, however, since I was summarily being ushered towards the steel security doors by one of Tanaka's flunkies, a young tough who seemed to speak no English, but who could strong-arm very eloquently.

In moments I was outside, facing the bank of elevators. That was when I remembered the upstairs tenant, a big public relations outfit. Better take a couple of minutes and give them the word.

Rausch, McKinley and Stein were in the middle of proving conclusively that our Mayor knew nothing about contract kickbacks, that he was in fact the closest equivalent New York had to driven snow. His Honour, in the meantime, was hastily returning the campaign contributions of all the real estate executives who, flanked by their lawyers, were now being featured on the front page of the *Daily News*.

Since RM & S had their hands full and also had expected an automatic renewal of their lease, there weren't too many politic smiles when I broke the news. Fact is, it was a very unpleasant scene. Finally I called for their lease and showed them the rider. They'd signed the damn thing, not me.

'Sorry, fellows, all I can do is maybe drag this out a little for you, mislay the paperwork or something. Have one of your attorneys give me a call, off the record. But I'd also advise you to start looking for space.'

Then I headed downtown, a man with a mission.

Dai Nippon had to be getting ready to kick hell out of something or somebody. Trouble was, I had no idea who or what. But I'd had plenty of hints it wasn't going to do great things for the dollar. I briefly toyed with alerting Jack O'Donnell and telling him to leak some anonymous storm signals. But what storm? He wouldn't put his senate reputation on the line to peddle guesswork, and all I had to offer was — what? — circumstantial premonitions.

Where to begin? Henderson was in London and unreachable, meaning there was no chance of getting him and his less reputable Washington connections to start shouting 'fire' from the rooftops. That left the press. Right. What I needed was the *media*. Think. Somebody who, if the whole thing proved to be smoke and mirrors, could shrug it off; *but*, a comer who would be intrigued by the possible broadcasting coup of the century. It had to be somebody with ready-made exposure, yet a personality with little to lose and a lot to gain. That brought to mind the perfect candidate, a former, well, acquaintance.

When I got home, I went straight to the office upstairs, looked up a number I hadn't used in a long time, and dialled it. It felt very familiar.

'Channel Eight. "The freshest news in New York." May we help you?'

I always loved the way they peddled information as though it were Wonder Bread.

'Donna Austen, please.'

'One moment please.' There was a click, then another voice. 'Channel Eight news desk.'

'Donna Austen, please.'

'Who's calling, please?'

'Matthew Walton. Tell her it's business, not personal.' Enough *please*'s.

'Thank you, Mr Walcan.'

'Walton.'

'Thank you.' On came the Muzak.

Would she do it? She used to complain how fed up she was interviewing witnesses to car crashes. Her career needed a transfusion of hard news so the station management would start taking her seriously. Well, here was her shot. And since she was roughly tenth in line for the 'anchor' spot, she had no reputation of noticeable proportions to jeopardise by leaking an anonymous rumour the US was about to be shelled by an offshore battery of financial guns.

'Ms Austen said to tell you she's in a meeting and can't be disturbed.'

Why is it some women can't just let bygones be bygones? Give me a break, Donna. I was ready for anything, except her little bedroom games. 'How about advising Ms Austen I'm sorry I called at such an important time, but I have some information that might just save her and everybody else from total ruin.'

'I'm very sorry, but . . .'

'Just tell her, goddammit.'

'One moment.' No please this time.

Another very long pause. Finally I heard Donna's broadcast neutral diphthongs, those lower-register reverberations she'd worked so long to perfect.

'Matt, you've got your nerve. This damned well better be quick.'

'Sorry I yelled at the messenger. I'm sorry about a lot of things, but that's not the reason I called. Donna, how'd you like an exclusive? The world as we know it is about to end. Inside a month.'

'Matt, have you been drinking?'

'No, but that's not a bad idea.'

'Well, what is it you want?'

'A small favour.'

'You have *got* to be kidding.'

'Not for me. It's the country I'm concerned about. That includes you. How about doing the US a favour and leak a heavy rumour from the world of high finance. The American dollar, dear to us all, may be about to go the way of Confederate mustard plasters. I'll even dictate the statement for you.'

'Matt, why don't you give this earth-shaking scoop to one of your bigshot connections down at the *Wall Street Journal*, assuming it's such hot news?'

Good question. The answer, sadly, was that nobody *inside* the system would want to even hear this kind of talk, let alone spread it. Everybody in the financial community was already whistling in the dark, terrified those Latin debt dominoes might start to tumble, taking a few of our flagship banks along with them. And now this? No way.

'Donna, I need somebody willing to go out on a limb.'

'You shit.' She gave a snort. 'I let you mortify me once. And believe me that's the last . . .'

'Will you listen, for chrissake. I know it sounds crazy, but this is dead serious. I've taken on a foreign investment firm as a client. I can't tell you the name, but I'm absolutely sure the guy running it is about to screw this country somehow. He's been shorting the bond market, and now he's going to start dumping dollars. Billions and billions. I want to blow the whistle. Get something on the air that'll cause a few bankers and traders to look up from their computer terminals and—'

'Matthew, darling, how about your doing *me* a favour?'

'Name it.'

'Simple. Don't ever call me here again. And while you're at it, tell that asshole friend of yours, Bill Henderson, I think he's the biggest—'

'Look, I'm genuinely contrite about the scene he caused at your place. If—'

'*Good.*' Click, then the hum of a New York Tel dial tone.

Maybe she was right. Maybe I *was* seeing things. In any case, that aborted Monday's attempted guerrilla war against Matsuo Noda. Now to man *my* barricades.

Which moment coincided with the sound of Emma Epstein's key in the front-door lock. The time, obviously, was exactly 1.30 p.m. Exactly. I waited till she'd settled in before taking the fatal step.

'Emma, how about bringing me that file in your left-hand desk drawer? The one marked "Trust Account".'

'The blue one?'

'Right. Amy's. You know it. You updated the thing about a month ago when I switched all her money out of stocks and into money-market funds.' That move had been my one small attempt to ride Noda's horse in the direction I suspected it was headed.

'I remember.' She glanced at me disdainfully. 'I also remember you predicted interest rates were about to go up.'

Which, she was tactful enough not to add, they hadn't. She also didn't mention she had greeted my market prognosis with open scepticism. As usual.

'Well, for what it's worth, I still think rates are headed up soon. And Emma . . .'

'What?' She was grimly digging through the files.

'Ever think about some gold stocks for your retirement investments? There're some mining issues I hear look good. Golden Sceptre, Golaith, Vanderbilt . . .'

'That's Amy's portfolio you wanted, correct?' She didn't miss a beat.

'Right.'

She doted on Amy and always got very testy whenever I dabbled in the management of my daughter's little nest egg. It's galling to admit Emma's market instincts did at times seem superior to mine. John Maynard Keynes once said there's nothing so disastrous as a rational investment policy in an irrational world. Maybe he was right: could be I was shackled by too much logical introspection. Never a problem for Emma. All I know is, if her daughter-in-law in Jersey phoned in (on my line) that she'd just baked a terrific cherry pie using 'New Improved!' Crisco, Emma marched out and loaded up on Procter & Gamble. And the damn thing automatically went up ten points.

'Here it is.' She placed it on my desk with a decidedly disapproving sniff.

'Thanks.'

Dear Lord, I thought, stand by us sinners now and at the hour of our death. I went over it quickly with a hand calculator. About ninety-four thousand. Which I figured would pay for roughly a year and a half of college the way those already inflated costs were skyrocketing. But by the time Noda got finished with the dollar, it probably wouldn't cover a weekend seminar.

Maybe I couldn't save the US, but I was damned well going to get my daughter through school. With fear and trembling I started calling banks. Naturally I spread the action around town, BS-ing a lot of currency traders and bank FOREX (foreign exchange) departments in the process. I'd buy some pounds sterling, then ... by the way, long as we're on the phone, Mort, I think I might need a few million yen in, oh, say about a month. Why don't we just save time and write some contracts now? Besides, bird in the hand, you know. Then I'd take those pounds I'd just acquired and use them to buy several million Deutsche-mark forwards from the next dealer I knew.

How much did I go out, total? Remember, currency forwards run around a penny on the dollar, so I effectively 'sold' something like ten million greenbacks, deliverable in one month, when I figured they'd be worth . . . it was hard even to imagine. Most likely zilch. Since I was flying blind, Amy's college fund bought *everything*. You name it, I went long. She ended up owning forwards on Swiss francs, German marks, yen, lira, pounds sterling, Canadian dollars, even French francs. I was actually tempted, briefly, by the peso (well, she loved her trip to Mexico last summer), a sentimental gesture I sternly resisted.

By the time I'd finished it was 4.45 p.m., meaning my new ninth-grade owner of a United Nations basket of foreign currencies had just arrived home from her West Side private school. She always charged in at 4.30. I called Joanna and asked to speak to my daughter. Jo's response to the sound of my voice was only slightly less fulsome than Donna Austen's. Finally Amy appeared at my ear.

'Dad, how come you're calling on the downstairs phone? You're supposed to always use the one in my room. Mom hates it when—'

'Sweetie, that line is in constant and uninterrupted engagement between the hours of 4.31 and 8.15. It's *never* possible to reach you there at this time.'

'OK, so what's up?'

'Nothing much. How about if you and I caught up on things a bit? What do you say to dinner tonight? Just the two of us? We might even consider a real grown-up meal for a change, no alfalfa sprouts.'

'Where?' She was immediately on guard. What if she ended up confronted with a red-tinged steak, sliced off one of the living mammals of the earth?

'Anywhere. Someplace you've always wanted to go. My treat.'

'Wow! Anywhere?'

'Your pick.'

Long pause, then, 'How about Windows on the World?'

'Sounds good.' I guessed one of her school friends had just been. Meaning prestige was on the line. I was right.

'Sharon's dad took her there last weekend for her birthday and it sounded really neat. She said you can see everything. It's probably a *lot* nicer than Top of the Six's.'

Where, in case you hadn't guessed, I'd taken her on *her* birthday.

'Food's standard, but I think we can piece together a spread that'll meet your guidelines. Will your mother let you go?' Joanna had total weekday custody and she played it for all it was worth.

'She's got a big date tonight. That creepy real estate guy I told you about. The one with the new silver Saab he thinks is so hot.'

'Don't tell me about it. And don't call your mother's friends creeps. I'm sure they're all very nice.'

'Want to bet? This guy is total weirdness. But she'll let me go. No sweat. What time?'

When I was a youth, I don't remember young ladies using phrases such as 'no sweat'. Probably an imperfection of memory, one of many.

'Pick you up at 7.30 sharp. Call me if there's a problem.'

'OK.'

'And Amy . . .'

'Yeah.'

'Uh, think about wearing an actual dress. Not one of those experimental East Village—'

'Daaad. I'm gonna look so straight. You'll see.'

'Never doubted it for an instant.'

That night I'd intended to explain that her college fund was currently being hedged via a comparatively unorthodox investment scenario. However, she was too busy marvelling over the lights of Manhattan a hundred storeys down to give me much time to talk.

What I really wanted to tell her but somehow didn't was that I'd had this spiritualist vision we'd been reincarnated as a couple of those crazy sheiks at Monte Carlo – when I'm the guy who never ventures past the quarter slots next to the door. It was as though I'd pillaged the hundred grand carefully hoarded for her future and spread it over a giant roulette play, stacking chips on every number on the board. Who knew where Dai Nippon's wheel would stop, but when it did, one of them *had* to pay off a hundred to one. Noda couldn't touch us. Right?

No sweat.

NINE

Tam was headed east in the black Nissan limo, listening to the talk. And thinking. Seated alongside was Kenji Asano, wearing a light tan suit and gold cufflinks, while the space opposite was occupied by two individuals who made her very uneasy. One was the instantly famous Matsuo Noda, the other his niece, talk-show economist Akira Mori. Noda was wearing a black three-piece banker's suit, the perfect accompaniment to his silver hair, and small wireless spectacles that magnified his penetrating eyes. Mori, in designer beige, looked as if she'd just stepped from the NHK studios, which in fact she had only a few hours earlier.

Three days had passed since Noda's Imperial press conference, four counting today, with this sudden trip being only the latest in a series of unexpected events. The major new twist: getting her interviews rolling was turning out to be a lot harder than it should have been. Before leaving New York, she'd arranged for a day with Dr Noburu Matsugami of the Electrotechnical Institute at Tsukuba Science City to go over the latest progress of MITI's Advanced Robot Technology Project, now the world leader, the undisputed state of the art in robotics. Matsugami had even volunteered to supply introductions to the other MITI labs at Tsukuba. Everything was set.

Except now it wasn't. When she called Friday to confirm their meeting, Dr Matsugami advised her that some unexpected schedule conflicts had come up. Most apologetic. Perhaps they could try again week after next.

What's more, that was her last call for the day, because immediately afterwards her hotel phone had gone dead for five hours. Management was strangely evasive about the problem. When a temporary line was finally installed, it had a curious whine that made conversation all but impossible.

My luck, she thought. Japanese technology, the best in the world, breaks down on me.

Consequently it was almost a relief to get out of town. Not the least of reasons being Tokyo still had a hangover from all the sword celebrations. Its streets were strewn with debris and services remained haphazard. As planned, she and Ken departed the next afternoon on the Shinkansen 'bullet train' – first class, where the porters wear white gloves and bow after making an announcement to the car. The only way to travel. Finally some peace and quiet after the madness of Tokyo, she'd told herself. It felt like the Concorde, except with legroom. She leaned back to watch as the white peak of Mount Fuji flashed by at 140 m.p.h. and chatted with Ken, who was sitting next to her, glancing through some MITI memos he'd brought along.

The trip down, zipping through industrial Nagoya, had helped to settle her mind. Kyoto. For her there was nowhere else quite like it in the world. If you knew the byways, it could be a universe away from the mania of Tokyo. Time to lighten up. At least she had no reason to suspect Ken was giving her the runaround. He'd seemed genuinely disturbed when she told him about Matsugami's polite refusal to talk. Didn't say much: just frowned, was strangely silent for a moment, then declared he'd make a few phone calls and check into it when there was time.

Kenji Asano, she noticed, seemed to have a split personality: one for her and one for the rest of the world. In public he was all Japanese, striding ahead and ostentatiously barking opinions. But that, she knew, was merely for appearances; he'd have been the object of silent derision by elders if he'd displayed the slightest consideration for his female companion. (She recalled that famous Japanese proverb: The man who falls in love with his wife merely spoils his mother's servant.) OK, she told herself as she trailed along, when in Rome. . . . Japanese men need to strut and bully their women in public; it's the only chance they get. Everybody knows the obedient little helpmate dutifully pacing behind garnishes his paycheque and doles back whatever she likes.

Ken's stern traditional public face, however, was merely one of his many personas. Alone with her he could be as Western as any Japanese man would permit himself. For a Japanese, of course, 'Western' doesn't mean all the glad-handing *bonhomie* of an American; there's always an element of reserve. Just the same, he was nothing like the typical sexless, oblique Japanese business-man. He had a superb body, taut and athletic, which he knew better than to bury in some cheap off-the-rack Japanese suit. No polyester; strictly silk and finest wool. He had a sense of style: the power look. And he really was a widower, whose wife had died in a freak auto crash soon after their marriage.

In short, Kenji Asano was complex, not easy to categorise.

The same went for Matsuo Noda. As she and Ken were coming down on the train, a porter had come through the car announcing '*denwa*', a call for Dr Asano. When he returned, he reported that Matsuo Noda needed to make a quick trip down to the famous Shinto shrine at Ise tomorrow morning, to review the site for the new museum Dai Nippon, International would build to house the sword, and wanted him to come along, a good time to discuss their mutual interests.

'He always seems to know everything that goes on.' Ken smiled wistfully. 'He also "suggested" that perhaps my visiting American colleague would like to make the trip too.'

Oh, Tam thought, why me? That's not the way Japanese executives go about things. Women aren't part of their high-level conferences.

'I don't understand this, Ken.' She'd been half dozing, but now she was coming awake very rapidly. 'Seems a little strange, don't you think?'

Asano shrugged. 'He just said he'd like to meet you.'

'But why? What did you tell him about me?'

'Nothing, really . . .' He glanced away.

'Curious.' She was fully alert now. 'Then how did he . . .?'

'Tam, don't be naive. Matsuo Noda knows who you are, believe me.' He shot her an admiring glance. 'Why are you frowning? It's true. He knows all about your work. He practically demanded you come along. He called you — what was it? — "that brilliant American professor".'

'You know, something about this doesn't add up.' She was

having her first experience of Matsuo Noda's long arm, and she found it unsettling.

'Why not? Tamara, you of all people should know we Japanese have a national tradition of honouring guests. Noda-san is old school, through and through.' He leaned back. 'Besides, he's bringing somebody else along to meet you. Could be very interesting.'

'Who?'

He told her.

So here they were in the Dai Nippon limo, a stretch, with acres of room and green tea that flowed till she thought she would burst. What was that old line about the roomful of *zaibatsu* negotiators: the one with the toughest bladder prevails.

Seeing Matsuo Noda in person confirmed everything she'd sensed about him on the TV. He was a genius. Still, something about him told you that when you sat down to cards with this man, you'd do well to cut the deck. What really took her aback, though, was the woman alongside him, Akira Mori.

Could be it was just her style. Tam was definitely overwhelmed. For the trip she'd worn her softly tailored Calvin Klein suit (her only one), in shades of pale, warm grey, and set off with some simple, stark silver picked up on a trip to Morocco. Perfect pitch. She looked smashing, feminine yet all business, and Ken had told her so at least three times. All the same she wasn't prepared for Mori's ostentatious fashion statement.

When the DNI limo appeared at their hotel, the International, Japan's favourite TV money guru was wearing one of her severe Rei Kawakubo ensembles, a small ransom in gold accessories, and enough make-up for an haute couture ramp model. It turned out she'd taped an early-morning interview show at NHK's Tokyo studios for broadcast that night, then come down directly on the Shinkansen. She greeted Tam and Ken with scarcely more than a frosty nod. Tam found this stand-offish manner puzzling.

On the other hand it did fit perfectly with Ken's quick morning briefing on Noda's famous niece. Quite a story. According to him, her father, Dr Toshi Noda, had been a celebrated figure in years past. An honours graduate of Tokyo University, he'd been the star mathematics professor of Kyoto University when he was summarily conscripted by Prime Minister Tojo to take charge of wartime cryptography, codes. Tojo wanted the best, and he got it. Consequently mild-mannered Toshi Noda had been one of the minds behind the famous Purple Machine, used for Japanese ciphers during the early part of the war.

Eventually, however, the project became redundant. After a time Tojo ceased to trust the Purple Machine and decided to replace it with that famous Nazi invention, the Enigma Machine. (On that one, Ken had added with a touch of irony, Toshi Noda was well vindicated. The Enigma Machine code had already been cracked by the Allies long before Hitler – declaring it unbreakable – delivered it to Tokyo.)

Toshi Noda resembled his older brother Matsuo physically, but he differed radically in outlook, being a devout Buddhist and a pacifist. After the stunning Japanese bloodbath at Saipan, which demonstrated the war was clearly lost, he'd been one of those imprudent citizens who'd spoken out publicly for peace. Not surprisingly, he was immediately placed under surveillance by the Kempei Tai, Japan's secret police, and shortly thereafter jailed.

After three months internment he was released a broken man. A week later he committed ritual *seppuku*, disembowelling himself for the crime of having disgraced the family.

Toshi Noda's diaries, published posthumously and read widely in Japan, revealed his deep repugnance for the wartime government. He believed that Prime Minister Tojo had become, in effect, a neo-Shogun. Although the Shogunate supposedly had been abolished when Emperor Meiji took control and opened Japan in 1867, Toshi Noda saw it restored with Tojo, another 'Shogun' who had come along and isolated the country once again. Nonetheless, he'd been a man of few words. His death poem, written only moments before he put the knife to his stomach, was as simple and intense as his life.

> Darkness upon Yamato,
> Land of the gods,

Awaits the new dawn —
Ten-no-Heika.

That last was a traditional phrase which, simply translated, meant 'Son of Heaven'. For a Japanese, though, the overtones are more; they say 'the way of the Emperor'.

Subsequent history proved him prescient on several points — the main one being that militarism was a disaster for Japan. Also, he had rightly feared that the monarchy would become an empty symbol in the ruins of Tojo's hopeless war. Although he hadn't lived to see Tojo tried and hanged as a criminal, he had predicted the outcome of the war unerringly — and he'd insisted that his infant daughter be evacuated to Sasayama just before the Allies moved in for the kill. Because of his foresight she escaped the first firebombing of Tokyo, which converted the city into a giant death oven for 80,000 innocent Japanese civilians too old or young to escape. America's pragmatic 'final solution': Auschwitz with airborne incendiaries. The rest of Toshi Noda's family was burned alive.

Afterwards Matsuo Noda had complied with another of Toshi Noda's wishes and made certain his daughter received a first-class education. Since she had a natural instinct for economics he'd encouraged her, rightly foreseeing it as a discipline vital to Japan in the twenty-first century. She had excelled beyond his fondest expectations; she was in fact brilliant. As a result he grew to dote on her, to an extent that eventually grew almost obsessive. He'd even made her his heir since he had none of his own. His fortune was rumoured to be in the tens of millions.

Probably the most important thing to keep in mind about Akira Mori, Ken had concluded, was that she merely looked avant-garde. Inside, she lived in another age. In fact he suspected the reason she'd never married had something to do with the fact she was already wed: to the vision of Japan's powerful sacred Imperial past.

On the trip down to Ise, Mori had silently sipped her green tea while Noda chatted with Asano about the costs and timing of commercialising the intelligent machines that would come out of the Fifth Generation Project. Although Noda stuck to generalities, it was clear he was totally conversant with the latest developments in the field. In fact, Tam found herself thinking, he seemed to know anything there was to know about just about everything. He displayed the same obsession with Japan's technological future that the old-time Shoguns must have had about the goings-on of their vassals.

She also sensed that he and Asano were doing a lot of their communicating in a verbal shorthand, enough so that she began to suspect they had worked together before: they were like father and son, each anticipating the other's thoughts and conclusions.

By the time they reached Ise it was already late afternoon, but Noda's driver had phoned ahead from the car and arranged rooms for the night at the local spa, so they wouldn't have to go back late. She noticed there hadn't been any talk about the famous sword, but she figured maybe he was saving that for dinner.

The museum Noda planned was to be built outside the shrine proper, just before you crossed the wide, arched Uji Bridge spanning the Isuzu River that separated Shinto's holy ground from the ordinary world. The shrine itself, a collection of thatched-roof buildings in severe traditional style, was hidden down a long trail among giant cryptomeria trees that towered hundreds of feet into the pale afternoon sky.

Attesting to the speed with which things can happen in Japan when there's the go-ahead from above, the location had already been staked and the trees cleared. Excavation for the foundation merely awaited Noda's approval. While everybody else stood around and waited, he consulted with the site engineer, checked over the plans, and made a few final changes. All the while, onlookers were bowing to him right and left. He'd become, overnight, an authentic Japanese legend.

After finishing with the engineer, he suggested they stroll on down to pay respects at the shrine itself, since they'd come all this way. Their burly chauffeur suddenly became a bodyguard, clearing the path ahead. Noda was expansive now, presumably confident his niche in history was secure. As they were crossing the wooden bridge, he casually asked Tam what she knew about the sword.

A one-of-a-kind historical find, she replied. Important and fascinating. She'd seen the Emperor on TV . . .

'I assumed you would understand its significance.' He was leading the way down the path. 'Perhaps then you'll indulge me a moment for an ancient tale about it.'

By now the entire shrine had been cleared of tourists and they were surrounded only by bowing and smiling priests in white robes: the VIP treatment. 'The Imperial Sword harkens back in a way to our version of Adam and Eve. Except, according to our own creation story, they were also the ones who created Japan; they were the original *kami*.'

'The original Japanese gods.'

'Well, perhaps "god" is too strong a term, Dr Richardson. I prefer to think of our *kami* as merely spirits of life.' Noda shrugged, then continued. 'According to the myth, the first male and female *kami* stirred the sea with a long spear, then lifted it, and the brine that dropped from its tip piled up and became Japan.'

She caught herself smiling. 'I've always wondered what Freud would have thought of that.'

Mori glared at her in a way that suggested some offence at her irreverence, while MIT-educated Ken merely stifled a grin. Noda, however, took the quip in his stride.

'Freud? Ah yes, your philosopher. I seem to recall he's the one who regarded almost everything as some manifestation of our sexual appetite. Well, these are primitive stories, Dr Richardson, that describe the beginning of life. I suppose they should be somewhat earthy, wouldn't you agree?' He chuckled. 'Nonetheless, according to our early tales, the Sun Goddess — whose shrine this is — was created out of the left eye, the side of honour, of the first male *kami*, and the Moon God was created out of his right. Then they ascended into the skies.'

She glanced up. The Sun Goddess appeared to be headed for bed, the sky itself barely light through the cryptomeria. The air was beginning to grow slightly crisp.

'Now we come to the sword. When the Sun Goddess finally sent her grandson down to rule over the mortals below, he brought with him the three items that became the emblems of Imperial rule. They were the sacred mirror, signifying purity, a curved bead necklace, used to ward off evil spirits, and the sword, standing for courage. The great-grandson of that first earthbound immortal extended his dominion over all of Japan and became the first Emperor. We are told his name was Jimmu, and the legends say that was around 660 BC.'

'Sō desu,' Miss Mori interjected abruptly, startling even Ken. She seemed to be lecturing directly to Tam. 'We all know our Emperor today is directly descended from Him. In fact, He is precisely the 124th Emperor after Jimmu. Japan and the Imperial line were born simultaneously, and every Japanese is related to Him. We are a monoracial state.'

Tam glanced at her. By God, she wasn't kidding.

'Well, it's possible the traditional account has reworked historical facts a trifle,' Noda continued smoothly. 'Actually the peoples who became our modern Japanese seem to have made their way here to the main island from somewhere in the South Pacific and settled in this area around Ise. Near here we still find burial mounds that contain replicas of their early symbols of Imperial authority — mirrors, gems, swords.'

'But the sword you found? Did it really come down from on high?' Tam asked, half hoping to rankle Akira Mori.

'You mean was it that very first one?' Noda shrugged. 'Who could locate the original Garden of Eden? Please, we all must allow for a certain element of poetic licence in our myths. But it is unquestionably the sword referred to in the ancient chronicles such as the *Heike Monogatari*, which dates from the Heian era, the ninth through twelfth centuries. That sword was lost in 1185, and now it's been recovered. That's all we know for sure.'

Mori, walking along in her quick, Japanese-woman pace,

131

obviously was not satisfied with Noda's rationalist version of history.

'Dr Richardson,' she cut in again, 'what the recovery of the sword has achieved is to remind the Japanese people that we are unique. We Japanese have a special soul, a Yamato *minzoku* of pure blood and spiritual unity. All Japanese are related to each other and to the Emperor, so there is a oneness of spirit, a blood-and-soul relation, between the Emperor and his people. Yamatoists believe, rightly, that a temporary eclipse of our Japanese *minzoku* was brought about by the American occupation, whose imposed constitution and educational system were acts of racial revenge against Japan. Our postwar identity crisis, our negative image of ourselves, was created by Americans. But that time is over. Although we have no single God, as in the Judaeo-Christian tradition, we have something even more powerful. Through our Emperor we have a line of descent that harkens back to the beginning of our world. Perhaps we no longer choose to claim he is divine, but that makes him no less an embodiment of Japan's special place.'

Akira Mori, Tam suddenly realised, was a closet Yamatoist, those new right-wing racist firebrands of modern Japan. Time to give her a little heat.

'Surely nobody today seriously thinks the Emperor's forefather came down from the skies?' She turned back to Noda. 'You don't believe it, do you?'

He shrugged. 'Ours is a sceptical world, Dr Richardson. Is your Pope really infallible, or did he acquire his right to be divine spokesman by winning a small election? Nonetheless, popes and kings are like ancient tribal leaders. Despite all our modern democracy, we still yearn for a figure to embody our identity. For the Japanese to have an Emperor who, if only in legend, has blood kinship with the gods who created our homeland – what could be more important?'

About that time Tam glanced up and realised they were passing under a large *torii* gate, entryway to a place that seemingly had nothing to do with the real world. Just beyond were the shrines, reminding her somewhat of a sanitised tropical village as imagined by Hollywood. Each of the cypress-wood buildings, set above the ground on stilts, was architecture at its most primal, a study in simplicity. Their polished wood was untouched by a speck of paint, while the foot-thick blanket of woven straw comprising their roofs had a creamy texture that looked like cheesecake. There was nothing in the world to compare.

What really made them unique, though, was something else entirely. Although the shrines were merely straw and natural wood, possessing none of the centuries-old authority of the cathedrals of Europe, in a curious way they were actually older, for they had been rebuilt anew every twenty years since time immemorial.

Suddenly the real significance of that struck her. What other people had kept alive such a powerful symbol of their common heritage for centuries and centuries? Westerners had difficulty grasping the continuity this shrine represented. Little wonder Noda could galvanise his clan with some powerful new reminder of who they were. Shinto wasn't a religion; there were few rules and no payoff in the sky. Instead it was the mortar binding a race.

'The main shrines over there,' he continued, pointing to a collection of buildings in an area enclosed by a high wooden fence, 'are off limits to all save the Emperor himself and certain of the priests. That ground is the sacred link between our Emperor living now and those of times past. Even photographs are forbidden.'

Tam noticed that many of the gables of the buildings were tipped in gold, burning amber when an occasional shaft of late sunlight reflected off them. Dusk was starting to settle in and the evening birds and crickets had begun to add their eerie sound effects. She found herself deeply touched. What was it about the place that inspired such reverence? Was it the serenity? The purity?

Yes, this Shinto holy of holies possessed a secret power, the unassailable strength of nature. It moved her; how could it not? Somewhere inside she felt envy of them all, felt a yearning to share their absolute sense of who they were.

While she reflected on that, surrounded by the white gravel and golden woods, she found herself looking anew at Ken. Being here with him at Ise made her question once again whether in his world, his austere yet deeply passionate world, she could ever be anything but a *gaijin*, an outsider.

TEN

It was almost dark when they reached the spa, one of those vast Japanese resort hotels catering to the middle class. It had a fake-traditional exterior and hundreds of rooms inside, as though the Temple of the Golden Pavilion had somehow been hollowed out and enlarged to encompass a health club. Strangely, though, it had been completely cleared, guests sent on their way; it was totally, absolutely empty. The parking lot was cordoned off, and gardeners were busily clipping and manicuring the grounds. Tam was impressed. Dai Nippon must have plenty of clout, she told herself, to be able to commandeer an entire hotel.

The manager came out to meet Noda, deferentially bowing and sucking in his breath, after which their few bags were summarily swept away. When Noda returned he said nothing, merely smiled and suggested they all retire to the big public baths on the lower level. Since the hotel was a vacation retreat, the basement was almost entirely devoted to the one universal love of the Japanese public — scalding water.

Down they went through the concrete hallways, attendants and staff bobbing. The saunalike baths, like the hotel, seemed to be theirs alone. While Noda and Ken retired to the men's section down the corridor, Tam and Mori entered the women's side, a cavernous tile-floored room with a steaming pool at one end. Local women in white head-kerchiefs immediately appeared and began to fuss over their guests, scrubbing and rinsing them while praising the famous Noda-san. Then, as Mori's towel dropped away, Tam looked her over.

Good figure. She had always believed that, judged by Western standards, Japanese women tended to be somewhat flat-chested and to have shortish calves, characteristics the high-waisted kimono was well designed to disguise — which also explained why a Western woman wearing one could easily look like a buxom stork. Mori, however, had a lithe well-proportioned shape and her breasts were positively generous.

The intimacy of the bath didn't noticeably humanise her, however. While they soaked and steamed, she volunteered nothing beyond a few routine pleasantries. No more tirades about Yamatoism and American treachery, but no informal talk either. After a polite interval Tam excused herself to go upstairs to her room and freshen up for dinner. Mori's agenda clearly differed from Noda's; this woman, she concluded, had a game plan all her own. But what?

Not long afterwards she heard Ken tapping lightly on the door. Just as she'd hoped. After the hot steamy bath, he couldn't have been more welcome. In fact she took one look at him, pristine and elegant in his blue silk *yukata*, and briefly considered undressing him right there in the doorway — with her teeth.

He was a wonderful lover, by turns gentle and forceful, as though their being together were some exquisite ceremony. Their lovemaking always had a particularly Japanese quality, a heightened appreciation of the erotic, derived no doubt from a tradition that values subtlety and sensual satisfaction. Afterwards they shared a brief soak in the little redwood tub there in her room, then he headed down the hall to change.

Well, she told herself, coming down to Ise has been well worth the trip. Matsuo Noda is definitely eccentric, but all the same he's a Renaissance man by any gauge. Still, why did he want to meet me? Just to tell me ancient fables? No, that's some kind of prelude. The real theme is yet to be announced.

As she started putting her hair up in some quick curlers to try to recover from the steam, she pushed aside her misgivings. Although she only had the suit she'd worn down, intended for business, she decided it didn't matter. Surely tonight would be informal.

She was just finishing up with her hair when she heard a frantic pounding on the door. Very un-Japanese. Puzzling, she cracked it open.

Ken was standing there, no slippers, still in his *yukata*, which he hadn't bothered to tie, all the colour gone from his face. Behind him were two uniformed hotel maids, bearing what was surely the most gorgeous kimono she had ever seen, heavy silk with a hand-painted landscape, edged in gold brocade.

'Tamara, I had no idea, honestly. Noda-sama only found out when we got here, and he couldn't say anything. It was all top secret, heavy security. They only just arrived a few minutes ago and he's asked Noda to dine with him.' He paused for breath. 'We're invited too.'

'Who's just arrived?'

Asano was so nonplussed he didn't hear her. 'Apparently he wanted to review the site plans personally, tomorrow, to see where the museum will be. I hear the Imperial Household was set against it, but he insisted.'

'Who, for God's sake?' The impossible answer was rapidly dawning.

Abruptly he paused, embarrassed by his own mental disarray.

'His Majesty. Tam, we're about to meet the Emperor of Japan.'

In marched the bowing maids, lots of long-vowel honorifics — they apparently assumed the honourable Richardson-san must be America's First Lady — and took over.

Tam knew full well that donning a formal kimono was no small undertaking, but she'd forgotten what a major task it really could be. First came the undergarments: cotton vest and silk underkimono, secured twice, once with a cord and then with an undersash. Next was the kimono itself, right side folded under the left and then bound at the waist with a cord, the excess length being pulled up and folded over so that the hem just cleared the toes. That fold was in turn secured by another waist cord, after which came yet another undersash. Now it was ready for the all-important outer sash, the *obi*, a heavy silk strip wound around the waist twice, cinched hard and knotted at the back, long end up, short end down. Then the long end was folded into a sort of cloth *origami*, this one a butterfly, after which it was rolled into a makeshift tube, into which the short end was stuffed. Finally this *obi* sculpture was secured with yet another waist cord, knotted in front.

It was all done with minute precision, including the rakish display of a prescribed few millimetres of silk underkimono at the neck, an erotic touch for traditionalists. Finally she put on special *tabi* stockings, bifurcated at the big toe to accommodate her thonged slippers.

Then they attacked her hair, brushing, spraying, adding ornaments. The makeover took a good three quarters of an hour and even so it was a rush job.

As the sashes and cords and cinches got ever tighter and more suffocating, she remembered what wearing a kimono can do to your psyche. The *obi* seemed designed to demolish breasts, the multiple waist sashes and cords to totally immobilise the torso from rib cage to thigh. When Ken finally escorted her in to the elevator she felt like a walking mummy . . . *this*, she remembered, is why a lifelong kimono wearer minces along in short, pigeon-toed steps that suggest she's been shackled at the knees.

Downstairs the kitchen had been placed on war footing, and what awaited when they entered the *tatami* banquet room was the tableau for a full-scale feast. The lacquer table was dotted with delicate rice-straw mats, on which was marshalled an array of ancient stoneware plates and cups – rugged black Raku, creamy white Shino, green-tipped Oribe. The *kakemono* picture-scroll hanging in the *tokonoma* was a severe monochrome landscape in the angular ink style of the great master Sesshu. Was it authentic? she wondered. Where'd they get it?

After a few minutes' wait the stately man she'd first seen on TV appeared in the doorway and began removing his shoes, surprisingly relaxed and informal despite the Household guards standing just outside for security. While everybody bowed to the floor, he greeted Noda – she remembered they'd met when Noda presented the sword – and exchanged a few pleasantries. His speech was now ordinary Japanese, not the archaic court dialect of the news conference. This was the real man. Noda bowed politely from time to time, then turned and introduced his party.

The Emperor of Japan, Tam noticed, seemed to have an eye for the ladies. When her turn came, he was all easy smiles, saying something about how pleasant it was to meet such a charming American, since he rarely had the honour. He then complimented her kimono.

After that, His Majesty took the place of highest status, his back to the *tokonoma* alcove (traditionally the safest spot to be, since it was the one location in a room sure to be backed by a solid wall), and motioned for Noda to sit next to him on the left, the second highest place of honour.

Then he nodded towards Tam, calling her his honourable foreign guest, and asked if she would indulge him by sitting on his right. She bowed back and took her place. Mori, whose own kimono was a pattern of delicately shaded autumn leaves, was seated alongside Noda, while Ken was placed next to Tam. As he was settling everybody, an important ritual of prestige, the Emperor kept repeating how delighted he was to meet a real American – his exposure to the outside world these days apparently consisted mainly of television.

He started things off by toasting Dai Nippon, International with a saucer of sake, after which he asked Noda to repeat for him again exactly how the sword had been recovered. Since his late father had been an ardent marine biologist, he loved the part about the computerised magnetometer and pressed for all the details.

Finally the banquet got underway, course after course of a little sliver of local seafood and an ornamental portion of seasonal vegetable, everything on some unexpected serving piece. It was a feast of sight as much as taste. A delicacy called *mukozuke* came in a black lacquer bowl, *hassun* on a bamboo tray, *hashiarai* in a brown Raku cup, *konomono* in a weathered earthen dish, *yakimono* on a grey Oribe platter tipped with green. The sake pot was cast-iron, sixteenth-century, with a pale turquoise porcelain top. They all drank from saucers of crusty white Shino ware – the Emperor's tipped in gold.

By then Tam's legs had begun to ache. She knew that sitting in formal Japanese style, on the heels, can eventually induce what seems like semi-paralysis of the lower extremities. As she glanced around, she decided that only Ken, who'd told her he was accustomed to kneeling traditional style for hours practising the tea ceremony, actually seemed comfortable.

Finally the table was cleared for the famous speciality of the spa, which His Majesty had specifically requested. It was an ornate *yosenabe*, a lusty Japanese bouillabaisse of artfully sculptured components, each of which signified some episode in the fateful battle of Dan-no-ura — in fact, the very engagement in which the sword was lost. That was eight hundred years ago, Tam reminded herself, yet you'd think it was only last week.

They were just concluding the meal with the traditional serving of *gohan* or rice when the manager of the spa entered and announced that their special entertainer was now ready. He apologised that, although he could offer nothing truly worthy of His Majesty, his humble spa had brought from Kyoto a performer he hoped would not be judged too harshly. He then ordered more sake sent in.

Although drinking more sake after a banquet's closing round of *gohan* is normally judged impolite, His Majesty just smiled and thanked their flustered host. Around went the small flagons once more, maids scraping the *tatami* with their foreheads as they refilled the Emperor's gold-trimmed saucer.

Then the *fusuma* parted and the evening's surprise swept into the room, wearing an austere autumn kimono of finest silk and holding a *shamisen*, a three-stringed instrument with a cat-skin face and gold fittings. Her lips were vermilion, her lacquered wig coal-black, her face chalk. As she bowed low before His Majesty, only one visage in the room was paler than hers.

She was, Ken whispered to Tam with great delight, none other than Matsuo Noda's former 'protégée', Koriko.

After she had bowed low before the Emperor, she greeted the president and CEO of Dai Nippon as though he were merely another guest. He nodded and mumbled back a reply both curt and incomprehensible. Next she tossed mildly flirtatious acknowledgment to Ken, who returned her wink and toasted her with his sake saucer.

That ended the formalities, since she treated the women in the room as though they were composed of thin air. Their presence violated all tradition, an embarrassment that could be papered over, Japanese style, simply by pretending they didn't exist. Tam couldn't have cared less, while the pained face of Akira Mori indicated she was positively relieved.

Koriko took immediate command of the room with an easy poise that confirmed her professionalism. Tam guessed she was pushing forty but knew that aficionados of *geisha* prefer talent over youth. Using a large ivory plectrum, Koriko strummed her *shamisen* twice, its wound-silk strings piercing and whiny, then began a high-pitched song from her ancient repertoire. Tam couldn't follow the words and doubted if anybody else could either. However, she knew it was the convention that counted. Then at a dramatic moment two more *geisha* entered with a flourish and began a classical dance, all fans and rustling silk. It was a stunning floor show for those who appreciate slow-motion poses and flirtatiously exposed napes of neck. Between dances Koriko urged more sake on the men, joked with His Majesty and with Ken, and induced them both to sing a racy song. Noda, who sat there glaring, was diplomatically ignored.

For her own part, Tam was finding this traditional '*geisha* party' extremely juvenile and silly. Was this what supposedly intelligent Japanese businessmen consider the height of refined amusement, all this fake flattery and cajoling, mixed with not a few ribald *double entendres*? How depressing.

After a few more songs and dances Koriko and her ensemble began preparing to depart, whereupon His Majesty presented her with a small gift, or perhaps an honorarium, wrapped in gold paper and tied with an elaborate purple bow. In keeping with etiquette she didn't open it, merely thanked him graciously and tucked it into her *obi*. She then caressed the ivory pegs of her *shamisen* with reverence, saying she would treasure it forever as the unworthy instrument that had solaced the ears of His Imperial Majesty.

With a final bow to Noda, never hinting she knew him, she backed out the door and was gone, followed by the others. His look of relief reminded Tam of a man who'd just walked away from a collapsing building.

Whatever may have been Tam's, or Matsuo Noda's, secret thoughts about Koriko, the Emperor clearly had had a rollicking time. Presumably he didn't have all that many occasions to flirt with *geisha*. Now slightly the worse for sake, he began to wax pensive, turning to his American guest and offering to provide an account of the battle of Dan-no-ura. It was a definite switch of mood, but Koriko's traditional songs seemed to have struck a nostalgic nerve. Or perhaps the sword had brought him a new enthusiasm for the past he wanted to share. As he started recounting the battle, Tam smiled to think it was like having the Queen herself brief you on that family squabble of yesteryear called the Wars of the Roses.

'That battle, Richardson-san, between the Heike and Genji clans, was a turning point in the long history of our country; it represented the rise to power of the warriors. The Shogunate.' He smiled politely. 'I'm afraid the Monarchy never quite recovered.

'In fact, today the crabs in the Inland Sea have a mark on the back of their shells that people say is like the insignia of the Heike, that they represent the fallen banners of the Heike nobles.' He paused while a maid topped off his tiny cup with more hot sake. 'I suppose you've seen them?'

'*Hai, miraremashita.*' Of course, she nodded, stretching out her vowels to maximum politeness. She wasn't sure she had actually, but this was no time to appear like a dumb *gaijin*.

'Well, after many years of fighting the Heike nobles and the boy Emperor they were defending fled to an island across the Inland Sea. But the Genji forces pursued them and eventually they were forced to take to their boats once more. Finally the battle was joined. Since the Heike were experienced sailors, they assumed they would prevail in a naval encounter, and thus their commander unwisely elected to make his stand in the straits, where the riptide was as quick and treacherous then as it is today. At first he had the tide in his favour and they held the enemy, but around noon the tide changed and was against them. Gradually the forces of the Genji surrounded the ship bearing the Emperor and the court.'

His voice faltered slightly, and she realised the story was still as fresh for him as if it had happened yesterday. Finally he continued.

'As the sad story is told in the *Heike Monogatari*, the court nobles saw a school of dolphins coming towards them. They said, "If these turn back, the Genji will be destroyed and we will triumph. If they proceed, it will be a bad omen." When the dolphins continued on, even diving under their ships, the Heike realised they were lost. And sure enough, at that moment the Genji ships began closing in.

'Now the tragic part. The nurse of the boy Emperor – Antoku was only eight – resolved what she would do. She donned a double outer dress of dark grey, the colour of mourning, tucked up the long skirts of her heavy silk *hakama* robe, and wrapped the Sacred Sword in her girdle. Then, taking young Antoku in her arms, she moved to the gunwale of the vessel and looked down at the waves. Finally she said to the men of the court, "Though I am only a woman, I will not surrender myself to our enemies. I will accompany our Sovereign Emperor on his journey."

'At that moment little Antoku looked up, his long black hair streaming down his back, and asked, "Where are you taking me?"

'Tears began to flow down her cheeks. She said to him, "Bow to the east and bid your farewell to the Great Shrine at Ise. Our capital will no longer be Kyoto but a place beneath the seas, where there is no sorrow."

'So the young Antoku, his white robes the colour of the dove, bowed east to Ise – whereupon the nurse, holding him in one arm and the Sacred Sword in the other, leapt into the waves.

'Next, another woman tried to jump overboard with the casket holding the Sacred Mirror, but an arrow pinned her *hakama* to the gunwales, and the Genji soldiers retrieved it. All we know of what happened next is the dispatch they sent back to the new rulers in Kyoto, which declared, "The former Emperor is at the bottom of the sea, and the Sacred Mirror has been recovered. But the Sword is lost and a search is being made."' He turned and nodded towards Noda. 'Only tonight, eight centuries later, can the rest be told. At last, the Sword has been restored to Us.'

Noda bowed low and offered a toast to the Imperial line.

It was then that Akira Mori first spoke. Although she addressed her words to Tam, they were obviously meant for His Majesty. 'Richardson-san, recovering the sword is a more important historical event than many realise. Its loss coincided with the end of Imperial power in Japan. After that, the Emperor became a figurehead, a captive of the Shoguns.' She shot a quick glance at Noda. 'If the sword means nothing else, it should remind us all that no Shogun must ever be allowed to rise again.'

What's she driving at? Tam wondered.

'Of course.' His Majesty took up the theme. 'Although there was a time in this century when the militarists once again made a tool of the Emperor of Japan, I agree it was wrong.' He looked at Mori with admiration. 'The respect your words show for the Imperial house of Yamato touches me deeply.'

While she bowed in acknowledgment, he turned to Noda. 'In the same manner, Noda-san, Japan's important place in the modern world brings special respect to Us as well. For that We must thank you and all those helping to fashion the new Japan.'

Tam watched Noda, puzzling. Something was going on, some kind of coded cross-talk she didn't fully comprehend. Shogun. Emperor. What was everybody's unspoken agenda?

At that point His Majesty rose unsteadily and announced he had a heavy day ahead, whereupon he summarily bade everyone good evening and exited, Imperial Household guards in attendance. Tam noticed that Mori watched his departure with a wistful . . . worshipful, gaze.

After he was gone, a reverent stillness settled around them. Even Ken, normally talkative, was subdued. What's going on here? she puzzled. One thing was sure: Japan was like a magical onion, with layers to be peeled away slowly. Each time you learn something new, yet you never really get to the core.

When the last dishes had been cleared and nothing remained on their low table except fresh kettles of sake, Noda leaned back and broke the silence. She realised he was speaking to her. Matsuo Noda, it quickly came to light, was fully familiar with her books.

But that was merely the beginning. Next, Akira Mori, who'd been quietly waiting her turn, joined in.

'Were you moved by the story of the nurse who threw herself into the waves, Richardson-san? The one who sacrificed her own life to honour her ideals?'

'It was a very touching account.' Tam looked at her, surprised by the sudden friendliness. 'I understand even more now why everybody's so excited about the sword.'

'Presumably you know,' Mori continued evenly, 'that the young Emperor's nurse was undoubtedly Fujiwara. Perhaps of low rank, but nonetheless a member of the family that historically has been closest to the throne.'

'Of course, the Fujiwara were always Imperial retainers—'

'Have you taken no interest in that family?' Mori continued, her face still revealing nothing.

'I . . . no, not really.' Tam studied her.

'Perhaps you should, Dr Richardson.' She switched to flawless English. 'Are you aware that your own mother was Fujiwara? In fact, it is possible that in your veins runs the same blood as in the nurse who gave her life for the Emperor that April day eight hundred years ago.'

Tam felt a numbness sweep over her. She'd never thought much about her real mother, or father. Naturally there would have been no way of tracing him, at least none she knew. But of course there'd be full records of the woman who bore her, then put her up for adoption. For some reason Mori – or was it Noda himself? – had had them looked up. They'd uncovered something about her that she herself had never wanted, for well-examined reasons, to explore. Her adoptive parents had been all anybody could desire. Why stir up unknowns? Besides, she believed in nurture, not nature.

'You both seem to know a great many things about me.' Her glance shifted back and forth between them. She was surprised, yes, but if they'd assumed she'd be stunned, they were wrong. She'd decided long ago not to let herself care.

'Although your true mother no longer lives, you are most certainly Fujiwara,' Mori went on. 'You have blood ties with the family that once stood ready to give its life for the Emperor. Therefore you may even have a connection with the sword itself.'

Noda moved in. 'We also believe, Dr Richardson, that you, because of your work, could have a vital role in the endeavour Dai Nippon will soon undertake. That is the reason we want to speak with you tonight.'

At last, Tam thought. I'm finally going to find out why Matsuo Noda 'accidentally' happened to ask me along.

'I've been waiting to hear this.'

Since the *fusuma* sliding doors were drawn closed, shutting out the serving women, Noda breached conventional etiquette and reached across the table to pour more sake into Tam's tiny Shino dish himself. Ken merely looked on silently as Mori took up Noda's theme.

'We would like you to be part of something that would do honour to your Fujiwara heritage, Dr Richardson, the noble family that so long served the Emperor.'

'I may or may not be Fujiwara, Mori-san, but I already have my work.'

'Dr Richardson, do hear us out,' Noda interjected, pressing. 'We wish to advise you that important, even potentially disruptive events, lie ahead for America. Very soon. And we would like very much for someone such as yourself, a pragmatist, to be involved. Especially since, in addition to your professional skills, you are in a position to understand the cultures, the attitudes, of both Americans and Japanese. Your assistance could be invaluable.'

'Invaluable for what purpose?'

'A worthy undertaking, we assure you. Think of it if you will as an attempt to prevent Japan and the West from going to war with each other again.'

She looked back and forth between the two of them, trying to fathom what they were driving at. Then Noda continued, revealing again that nothing had happened by chance.

'We brought you here today to Ise to remind you of the importance of your Japanese heritage. A heritage whose sole purpose is, like Shinto itself, the peace and ordering of the world.'

'What's this all about?' She looked at Ken, in a black silk kimono, serenely sipping his sake and looking the essence of cultivated, tantalising otherness. 'Did you have anything to do with this?'

He carefully set down his Shino dish and smoothed his long sleeve. 'I did have occasion to remind Noda-sama that you have a unique combination of background and expertise, Tamara, that could be very instrumental in the realisation of his objectives.'

'And what are his objectives?' She looked back at Noda. 'Your objectives?'

'You, Dr Richardson, should appreciate this better than anyone.' He studied his sake saucer. 'There are things the West excels at doing and there are areas, I trust it is not improper to say, in which we Japanese have demonstrated aptitude. Why should we compete in each other's spheres? It leads only to divisiveness. We open ourselves to predators — from the steppes of the Caucasus to the oil-rich deserts of Araby. But if we join together, the peoples of Japan and America can achieve insurmountable strength.'

'You're talking about something that would more properly be in the realm of diplomacy, Noda-san.'

He laughed. 'Pardon me, Dr Richardson, but diplomacy is merely the window dressing for reality. The world cares not a penny for diplomacy, only for power. No one troubled about the Persian Gulf states until they had OPEC and the rest of us had no petroleum. Then suddenly they were toasted worldwide as men of great moment. That is the meaning of "diplomacy".

'The reason I knew you would understand the importance of Ise,' he went on, 'is that, in your genes, you are part of us. You appreciate the value of harmony, one of the first teachings of our philosophy. There must be harmony between man and his world.'

'What does that—'

'Please, just allow me to finish. In like manner, there must also be harmony between nations. Yet all we hear about today is friction. Usually trade friction. Between our nations. But what can be done? The solutions we hear talked of seem, for reasons political and otherwise, impossible to implement. So what course does that leave? You speak of diplomacy, but already diplomacy has been shown inadequate. Why, we might ask, is that so? Because, as your Thomas Jefferson observed many years ago, *money* is the principal exchange of civilised nations. Diplomacy comes out of economic power. It was trade that estranged our two nations once before in this century, leading to a conflict neither of us desired, and it is money that creates these "frictions" we hear about so much today. Since diplomacy has failed, we must now find other means to bring stability and thus harmony to both our nations.'

She was tempted to ask him how all the right-wing, nationalistic fervour he was churning up with the sword would contribute to this so-called harmony, but instead she inquired what, specifically, he was proposing.

'The most pressing problem America has today, Dr Richardson, is the growing inability of your industries to compete. If I may be allowed to generalise: America's strength has long been in innovation, but I think it is reasonable to suggest that Japanese management has had a commensurate share of success. So much so that we have been the subject of a flurry of books in your country.' He smiled. 'Even, I should add, several very insightful volumes written by you yourself. Also, Japanese industry has already been part of a number of joint ventures, instituting our management techniques in the service of America's business.'

'Well, unquestionably we do have problems in our industrial sector just now,' Tam interjected. 'But Japan has plenty of difficulties of its own.'

'Most assuredly.' He nodded. 'However, as some might put it, "the proof is in the pudding." I merely ask you to compare your, and our, balance of trade, or productivity. Surely these both suggest there is truth in what I say.'

At that point Akira Mori abruptly seized the floor. 'You know,

Dr Richardson, there are those in your country who are now saying your trade problems are caused by Japan. That we should work less, save less, squander more, just as you do. Perhaps so we will self-destruct economically as America is now doing and no longer be an embarrassment to you.'

'That is hardly—' Noda tried to break in, but she waved him aside.

'No, this needs to be said. I am tired of hearing Americans tell us to follow their example.' She turned back. 'Your media chastise us for our thrift and hard work, while your businessmen, who are happy enough to grow rich retailing the superior goods we make, refuse to invest their profits in modernising their own factories. Instead they give themselves bonuses and Japan lectures.'

At that she wound down, to the obvious relief of Noda and Ken. The outburst seemed to pass as quickly as it had come, but it succeeded in reinforcing Tam's reservations about Akira Mori.

'So what exactly do you have in mind?' She looked back at Noda.

'Dr Richardson, no one in Japan desires to see America's industrial base disintegrate. That is dangerous for the future, both yours and ours. Yet joint ventures and management seminars are too little, too late. We, and by "we" I mean Dai Nippon, are determined to make a more structured contribution.'

As he laid out his plan, she realised that Matsuo Noda had decided to play God. Still, in this world such things were possible; all it took was enough financial clout. If anybody doubted that, just remember OPEC.

But that was the last time around. Now Japan had the money. Maybe the oil billionaires of years past had no good idea what to do with their winnings, but Matsuo Noda had a very precise idea indeed.

The one remaining problem: he needed Tamara Richardson.

ELEVEN

In the aftermath of that evening down in Ise, Tam was convinced of only one fact. Nobody was giving her the straight story. Not Noda, not Mori, not Ken. And when she tried to talk super-computers with MITI officials at the Kyoto conference, she again sensed she was hearing a runaround. Suddenly all she could get was Japan's public face, that version of reality Japanese executives call *tatemae*, superficial and soothing assurances, intended to pro-mote the *wa*, harmony, so desirable in human affairs. When Japan doesn't care to give answers, *hai* no longer translates as 'yes'. It just means 'I heard you.'

Even more troublesome was the question of Ken. As best she could tell, he was merely a reluctant accomplice in Noda's grand design. But why was he going along with Dai Nippon if he was as apprehensive as he seemed? Ken, she concluded, knew a lot more about Matsuo Noda than he was saying.

So instead of giving them all an answer outright, she decided to spend a few days analysing what she'd managed to piece together so far. As Noda had couched his proposition, it was simple: he was offering her a chance to do more than merely write prescriptions for America's economic recovery. She would guide it.

One thing, Matsuo Noda was no proponent of half measures. The way he laid out his scenario, it was visionary ... no, rev-olutionary. After thinking over his proposal for a week, she still wasn't sure whether he was brilliant or a megalomaniac. Dai Nippon's programme could conceivably change the course of world history and the prospect of being at the helm of its jug-gernaut was seductive. All the same, what if Ken's hints were right? What if Noda did have something much grander in mind, something impossible even to imagine. When you ride the whirlwind, who's really in charge?

In between her visits to the conference she spent some time at DNI's Kyoto offices getting acquainted with Noda's operation – the computers, fibre-optic links, analysts. Very impressive. Although Dai Nippon was technically only a shell corporation, all Matsuo Noda had to do was pick up a phone to have at his disposal the expertise of any one of a hundred Japanese corporate brain trusts. Half of Japan's new high-tech movers, it seemed, owed him some kind of 'obligation'. Given that, and all the money, he could well be unstoppable.

Also, the austerity of Dai Nippon's offices reminded her once again that none of Japan's new power was accidental. The discipline of the *samurai*. It was almost as though this country had been in training for centuries, toughening itself through self-denial and work-as-duty to be ready for an all-out economic blitz. Now, finally, Japan had an edge on the entire world. More technology *and* more money.

Was Noda about to just give away that edge? The implausibility made her certain something was missing.

Late that Friday, the conference over, she and Ken packed their bags and checked out of the International. But after they'd shoved their way through the usual pandemonium in the lobby and hailed a cab, he gave the driver the name of a place on Shinmonzen Street, the antique district. Not the train station. When she tried to correct him, he waved his hand and said he'd arranged for a surprise.

'Tam, the International always leaves a bad taste in my mouth. It has nothing to do with Japan. It could be anywhere, just like some Hilton next to a freeway.' He smiled and lightly patted her hand. 'Let's not go back to Tokyo just yet. Please. This weekend let's stay at a place where nothing will exist but you and me, not even time.'

'Just turn off the clocks?' Sounded like a great idea.

'Well, now and then it's nice to turn them down a bit, don't you think?' He laughed self-consciously. 'That's a contradiction about me you'll some day have to get used to. I like a high-tech office, but when I'm away I prefer to be surrounded by things that are very, very old.' He leaned back. 'Indulge me.

Let me show you my favourite spot in all of Kyoto. A place time forgot.'

This is going to be quite a trick, she told herself. Very little was left from years past. Maybe the city hadn't been bombed out during the war, but the blitz of urban renewal was rapidly accomplishing much the same result. Through the light of dusk, construction cranes loomed above the few remaining thatched roofs of neighbourhoods about to be overwhelmed by steel, glass, cinder block.

Kenji Asano, it turned out, deplored this immensely. As they rode along, he pointed out the latest construction sites with the sorrow of a man documenting the end of civilisation.

'This, we hear, is the price of progress. I'm always tempted to ask, progress towards what?' He leaned back with a sigh and lit a Peace cigarette, nonfilter. 'Someday I think we may have to ask ourselves if this modern world we've created for ourselves was actually worth the toll it's taken on our sensibilities.'

Eventually their taxi pulled into a narrow side street, edging past a few women carrying small bundles of groceries bound in scarves, then easing to a stop before the ramshackle bamboo gates of a place that seemed abandoned to foliage and vines.

The driver helped carry their bags in through the gates and up the rocky, hedge-lined pathway leading to a wooden veranda. Ahead was a thatch-roofed, weathered house shrouded by towering elms. As they approached, an elderly woman in a dark kimono emerged from the recesses of the interior. She sang out a welcome, bowed deeply, and produced two pairs of leather slippers with an air of ritual solemnity. They were expected.

Off went the street shoes, on went the slippers as they melted into a world that would have been perfectly natural four centuries ago. When they passed the 'lobby' — off to the side, *tatami*-floored, with a few ancient screens scattered about — Tam noticed that there appeared to be no 'desk'. But there was also no 'check-in'; the proprietress clearly knew the honourable Asano-san. She also must have known he was MITI, since her honorifics soared into the upper reaches of politeness as she guided them along the interior hallway.

Tam realised they were in a traditional Japanese inn, *ryokan*, surely the last vestige of classical Japan. As they moved out on to another veranda, this one circling a central garden and pond, the place appeared to be totally empty. The woodland vista in the centre hinted of infinity, with stone paths and a wide pool dotted with shapely rocks. Although there were a dozen or so closed doors along the wooden platform, the inn seemed to be there solely for them. In the cool dusk clumps of willows across the pond masked the view of the other side, furthering the illusion that they had the place all to themselves. It couldn't be true, though, since chambermaids in kimonos darted here and there balancing lacquered dinner trays.

When they reached the end of the veranda, their hostess paused before a set of *shōji* screens, knelt, and pushed aside the rice-paper-covered frames to reveal a room entirely bare except for a low lacquer table. Well, not quite: on the back wall was the traditional picture alcove, *tokonama*, in which a seventeenth-century ink-wash scroll hung above a weathered vase holding three spare blossoms. Their room had no keys, no clocks, no television. It was a cocoon for the spirit, a place of textured woods, crisp straw, lacquer, and rice-paper.

The woman deposited their bags on the black-bordered *tatami*, consulted briefly with Ken concerning dinner, then backed, bowing, out of the room, leaving them alone together in another time.

'Ken, this is perfect. I needed someplace like this.'

'We both did.' He embraced her. 'They're running our tub now. Afterwards I have another surprise for you.'

'What?'

'Allow me some mystery.'

Whatever he had planned, she couldn't wait to throw off her clothes, don a loose cotton *yukata* robe, and pad with him down to the little wood-lined room where their steaming bath awaited. The floor was red tile, the walls scented Chinese black pine, the massive tub cedar with rivulets of steam escaping through cracks in its cypress cover.

While they perched on little stools beside the tub, he soaped her back, occasionally dousing her with the bucket of lukewarm water. Then she did the same for him, watching half mesmerised as the soapy bubbles flowed off his shoulders, broad and strong. Almost like an athlete's. Finally they climbed in, and amidst the cloud of vapour her last remaining tensions melted away.

'You know, I think of you every time I come to Kyoto, wanting to lure you back.' He reached for the brush and began to gently massage her neck. 'I honestly never dreamed Matsuo Noda would come along and try to hire you.' He paused. 'I wish I could help you make your decision. But the most I can do is warn you to be careful.'

What are you telling me? she wondered.

'Ken, you seem troubled about something. What is it?'

'Tamara, powerful forces are at play here, beyond the control of either of us. Things may not always be what they seem. Just be aware of that. But please don't ask me any more. Just look out for yourself.'

'I've had a lifetime of looking out for myself. I can handle Matsuo Noda.'

'Just don't underestimate him. He's not like anyone you've ever known before. The man is pure genius, probably the most visionary, powerful mind in the history of this country. You've met your match.'

'That remains to be seen.' She leaned back. Ken was challenging her now. On purpose? Maybe he figured that was the only bait she would rise to. He wanted her to play along with Noda, but he wouldn't tell her why.

After they'd simmered to medium rare, heading for well done, they climbed out, towelled each other off, slipped back into their *yukatas* once again, and glided back to the room. She noticed that an interior screen had been pushed aside, opening on to another *tatami* room where a thin *futon* mattress had already been unrolled and prepared with white sheets and a thick brocade coverlet. Hot tea waited on their little lacquer table, but their bags had disappeared. She checked behind a pair of sliding doors and saw that all her things had been neatly shelved by some invisible caretaker. Even the clothes she'd been wearing were already hung in the closet.

'Now for my surprise.' He was slipping on a black silk kimono. 'They have a special little garden here that only a few people know about. I've arranged everything.'

'Shouldn't I change too for whatever it is we're doing?'

'Theoretically, yes. But formality doesn't suit you.' He cinched his *obi*. 'Come on. You can be formally informal.'

He led the way to the end of the veranda where they each put on the wooden clogs that were waiting. Then they passed through a bamboo gate into yet another landscape, this one lit by candles set in stone lanterns. At the back stood a small one-room structure of thatch, reed and unfinished wood. A teahouse.

'Tam, can you sit here for a second, in the waiting shelter?' He indicated a bench just inside the gate under a thatch overhang. 'I'll only need a few minutes to prepare.'

Off he went, clogs clicking along a string of stones nestled in among the mossy floor of the garden. He was following the *roji*, the 'dewy path' that led to the teahouse half hidden among the trees at the back.

Unlike the *ryokan*'s larger garden, this one had no water; it was meant to recall a mountain walk. The space was small, with natural trees, offering no illusion of being more than it was. But it was a classic setting for tea, a kind of deliberate 'poverty'. While she watched the flickering stone lanterns and listened to the night crickets, the cacophony of Kyoto could have been aeons away.

Finally Ken appeared beside the doorway of the teahouse and signalled her forwards. As she moved along the stepping stones, she noticed that the pathway had been swept clean of falling leaves, after which the gardener had strewn a few back to give it *wabi*, an unaffected natural look. The art of artlessness, she thought, as she paused at a stone water basin to rinse her mouth from its bamboo dipper, part of the preparatory ritual.

The *cha-no-yu* or 'tea ceremony', she knew, required almost a lifetime to master completely. It was a seated ballet of nuance and perfect clarity of motion. One awkward gesture and its carefully orchestrated perfection could be spoiled. She hoped she could remember the rules well enough to get it right.

Ken was already seated across from her, tending a small charcoal brazier sunk into the *tatami*-matted floor. From its light she could just make out the room's rough-hewn timbers, the straw and mud walls, bark and bamboo ceiling. A small calligraphy scroll hung in the *tokonoma* alcove. As he beckoned her formally to sit, the room was caught in an unearthly silence, the only sound the sonorous boiling of the kettle.

Ken was profoundly transformed, almost like another being. Warm and attentive only minutes before, now he was part of a different world, solemn and remote. The black silk of his kimono seemed to enforce the seriousness in his dark eyes.

She watched as he ritually wiped a thin, delicately curved bamboo scoop with a folded cloth, first touching the handle, then the uptilted end, after which he balanced it atop the lacquer tea caddy. Next he lifted the tea bowl, an earth-tone glaze that shifted from mauve to brown as he rotated it in his hand and wiped the rim. Finally he swabbed the bottom and positioned the bowl on the *tatami* in front of him. Now the utensils had been formally cleansed. He was ready. From the tea caddy he spooned a mound of jade-green powdered tea and tapped it into the bowl. Then another, this last with a carefully prescribed twist of the scoop.

Next he extracted a dipperful of boiling water from the iron kettle and measured a portion into the bowl, lifted the bamboo whisk sitting inverted beside the bowl, and commenced a vigorous blending. The tea immediately began to resemble a pale green lather. Still no words, no sound save the whirr of his whisk intruded upon the quiet of the room. It was a moment hundreds of years old, framed in silence.

The economy of ideal form. That, she found herself thinking, was what this was all about: how flawlessly you could perform what seemed the most simple, humble act. And he was good. Whereas the mastery in his hands revealed itself by the control with which he whipped the tea, the rest of his body remained taut as a spring. Total discipline. Each tiny motion was distilled to its crystalline essence.

At last, when the green froth was ready, he gave the whisk a final half-turn, then set it aside. Next he lifted the bowl, rotated it in his hand, and placed it on the mat beside the open charcoal fire.

His part was over. It was as though the authority had been passed. Ken had prepared the work; now it was her turn to take up and finish it. Her role was different yet required its own kind of skill.

She bent forward and ceremonially shifted the bowl a short distance towards her. Then she scooted backwards on the *tatami* and again moved the bowl closer. Was she doing it right? The flicker in Ken's eyes said yes.

Finally, with a bow of acknowledgment, she raised the bowl in both hands and brought it to her lips. After the first sip she bowed again, then drank it down as he watched in silent approval. The powdered green tea was harsh and bitter, just as she remembered from times past. Even for a Japanese it was difficult to feign appreciation of the musky beverage produced in the *cha-no-yu*.

She recalled what was next. With deliberate dignity she extracted a small napkin from the *obi* of her loose *yukata*, wiped the rim of the bowl, and placed it carefully on to the *tatami* in front of her. The motion had to be quick, spare. Ken didn't try to disguise his pleasure; she had passed some sort of crucial test.

And, she told herself, he had too.

Together they had joined in one of the most demanding yet exquisite bonds two people can share. At that moment she felt — was it imagination? — like an ancient Fujiwara, celebrating some age-old tradition . . .

The ceremony was over now. She bowed again, then lifted the bowl to admire the light crackle in the glaze, the slightly inturned lip.

'It's Raku. I think it's the finest I've ever seen.'

'From my collection. It's by the hand of Chojiro, the seventeenth-century Korean who was in the employ of the Shogun Hideyoshi.' He smiled. 'I had it brought down to Kyoto especially for tonight. For you.'

'I'm honoured.' She was.

After she had admired the rest of the utensils — the remaining formality of *cha-no-yu* — they both relaxed, their minds purged, their spirits attuned. Like the ceremony itself, the moment was aesthetic and sensual.

'Tam, this has been a wonderful rebirth for me, being with you again. You've helped revive in me so many feelings I'd almost forgotten. The joy of it all. Who could have known?' He leaned back and reached for a flask of plum wine. Formalities were definitely over. 'As someone once wrote, "Love. Its roots are deep. Its source unknowable."' He was pouring two small glasses.

'That's from the *Tsurezuregusa*, fourteenth century. Right?'

'Again you amaze me. You really *are* Japanese.'

'I like the poetry.'

'Then you know, Tam, our poets excel in *feeling*. We've always celebrated emotion over logic.' He smiled. 'Which one said, "Love is the passion in the heart of man — those who will not listen to reason"?'

'What does reason have to do with love?' She took a glass. 'Didn't Shakespeare say "love and reason keep little company together"?'

'My turn. *That's* from *Midsummer Night's Dream*, which was . . . sixteenth century. You're pulling out the moderns in me.' He laughed with delight. 'You know, in Heian times, eight hundred years ago here in Kyoto, I'd be expected to make a linked verse about the night now.' He looked out of the doorway, then back. 'How about . . .

> The moon in veil,
> Perfumed with night,
> Who can deny love
> At a time like this?'

Then his visage quickened, another mood switch. His eyes mellowed as he turned and carefully lifted the bud from the vase behind him. It was a camellia, purest white. He held it before him as he turned back, its long stem still dripping.

'You know, there's a haiku by Basho I love very much. Let me give it in Japanese . . . a haiku only sounds right in the original.

Ume ga ka ni
notto hi no deru
yama ji kana.'

She paused to let the meaning sink in, to feel that open-ended sensation a good haiku always sends your imagination spinning off into. 'How's this for the English?

With the scent of plums
on the mountain road — suddenly,
sunrise comes.'

'Not bad.' He glanced at the blossom in his hand. 'I don't know why, but the camellia makes me think of you.' He rotated it carefully, then looked back. 'Let's dedicate tonight to our own sunrise.'

He inspected the flower again, then impulsively leaned forward and placed it on to the *tatami* in front of her. Next, with the same control in his powerful hands that had touched the glaze of the tea bowl, he gently gripped the shoulders of her loose *yukata*. She felt her body flush with warmth as slowly, gently, his strength once more held in check, he carefully slid back the cloth off her shoulders until her breasts were free. Then plucking a petal from the bud, he reverently brushed one nipple, then the other.

It was an erotic game she knew he loved, one of many. Games. Sometimes she had imagined them inhabiting an eighteenth-century *shunga*, those woodblock prints picturing lovers in what she had once thought impossible embraces.

He'd once declared that the kimono was actually the most sensual garment in the world. Take a look at some of the *shunga*, he said, and the possibilities become obvious. Though it seems cumbersome, entangling, yet it lifts away like a stage curtain to invite all sorts of dramatic possibilities. The human nude is only interesting when half concealed.

Games. She reached and took the petal from him, then ran it

along the silk of his own kimono, over his muscular thighs as he sat, Japanese-style, feet back. Next she lifted away the silk from the flawless ivory skin she knew so well. She drew it along his thighs to tease him.

'Tam . . .' He reached to slip away her *yukata*, but she caught his hand. Then she touched his lips with her fingers, silencing his protest. She pushed away his kimono and trailed the petal upwards, lightly brushing his own nipples. Finally she pushed him gently backwards and smoothed her cheek against his thigh, drawing back his kimono even more.

The glow of the coals was dying now. As the last shadows played against his face, she laid the petal on the *tatami* and moved across him . . .

They lingered till the moon was up, then strolled back through the garden wearing their antique wooden clogs. The air was scented, musical with the sounds of night. Later that evening they downed an eight-course meal off antique stoneware plates, drank steaming sake on the veranda, then made love for hours on the *futon*.

Around midnight he ordered one more small bottle of sake, a *go*, and suggested they move out on to the veranda again, this time to watch the moon break over the trees. She slipped on her *yukata* and padded out. She'd just decided.

'Tamara, I want to tell you something.' He poured her small porcelain cup to the brim. 'You are everything Matsuo Noda is seeking. The way you held the tea bowl tonight, tasted the tea. The *cha-no-yu* doesn't lie. You have discipline, our discipline. That's very, very rare.'

'You mean, "for a *gaijin*"?'

'For anyone. Besides, I don't think of you that way. You are one of us now.'

She looked into his eyes, dark in the moonlight. Then she remembered the *tokonoma* alcove in the teahouse where a rugged vase had held the single white bud, its few petals moist as though from dew. Not a bouquet, a single bud – all the flowers in the world distilled into that one now poised to burst open.

Kenji Asano lived that special intensity, that passion, which set Japan apart from the rest of the world.

'Ken.' Her voice was quiet. 'I'll do it.'

'You mean Noda?'

'Noda.'

He said nothing for a moment, then finally he spoke.

'The game begins.'

TWELVE

Over the last three weeks I'd spent long hours on the phone handling Matsuo Noda's new hedging in the currency markets. The play started out modestly, but as his Eight-Hundred-Year funds became bloated with cash, it grew into an avalanche of speculative positions.

His guiding principle was to keep a low profile in order not to spook the markets, same as any good trader would do. Whenever the FOREX desk of one market-maker bank on his list would start getting nervous, I'd just hit the next place in line. Finally after everybody on this side of the ocean began backing away, he went international. Zurich, in particular, loved the action and took everything he threw in its direction. I guess the Swiss are used to high rollers, since their financial casino never got cold feet and invented a house limit.

Somewhere along the way I also came to realise I couldn't possibly be the only agent in his employ; there was far too much money to move. Also my list of contracts eventually got pared to manageable levels, so somebody else had to be picking up the slack. It appeared that just as I was spreading the action he'd assigned to me all over the globe, he was spreading his own assignments worldwide. The man had to be covering a major chunk of the world market in interest-rate futures and currency forwards, but not a penny of it was traceable to Japan. Or to Matsuo Noda.

How, I kept marvelling, could this be happening right under the nose of all our supposed geniuses of world finance? One thing, Noda had all his moves down pat. My hunch was he'd started routeing a lot of short selling through Sidney and Hong Kong, and also was hitting the off-exchange 'third market', any-place he could find somebody to take his bets. If you remember how the dollar plunged in the mid-eighties, you'll also recall that anybody who'd had the foresight to dump it in advance would have been sitting pretty. Plenty of traders did, but none of them received any particular attention, since the pond is so huge. In cumulative totals the currency exchanges worldwide easily handle as much as two hundred billion dollars a day. Although DNI's massive short position clearly signalled that somebody major was anticipating a crash of the dollar, Noda realised that all he had to do was keep moving and nobody would put it together.

Need I add that my own little dollar hedge for Amy was peanuts compared to what was going on now. Dai Nippon through its anonymous agents was dumping American currency in the multi-billions worldwide, but since Noda kept the action spread out, nobody bothered to notice the pattern. Ditto his awesome 'naked' shorting of Treasury futures. I mean, anybody who'd troubled to assemble the numbers could have predicted somebody up on the bridge must have sighted a reef dead ahead. I kept trying to warn traders I knew, both on and off the exchanges, but nobody wanted to hear downbeat speculation from some Cassandra. They were all too busy pocketing commissions and ordering more champagne.

And then it happened. In broad daylight. I'll explain the operative details shortly, but if you were there, that could be a little like reviewing the theory underlying nuclear fission for somebody standing at ground zero when the bomb hit. So first let me recollect how it felt down in the trenches.

I was breakfasting at the dining-room table downstairs that particular Monday morning — 7 November, as we all remember so vividly — when Matsuo Noda dropped the first shoe, or maybe it's more accurate to say he began loosening the laces. I'd just finished squeezing some orange juice when I punched in the number of a financial update service on my trusty cordless phone, mainly to hear the (recorded) sound of a human voice. I'd totally forgotten the US Treasury was holding its quarterly refunding that day.

Newsbreak. Dealer banks were reporting that demand for the

long bond, the thirty-year, was extremely soft to non-existent. Equally unnerving, there wasn't any noticeable interest in Treasury's ten-year notes either. The reason seemed to be that the usual heavy participation by major Japanese investment houses (typically twenty to forty per cent of the total) had inexplicably evaporated. In fact, a rumour currently flying across the floor of the Chicago Board of Trade said a number of Japanese securities houses and banks in New York had begun what appeared to be a programme to divest their current Treasury holdings massively. Since spokespersons at Japanese outfits like Nomura and Daiwa Securities had clammed up, refusing to deny that rumour, the usual institutional buyers like Oppenheimer and Goldman, Sachs were holding back, nervous.

Hang on, I said to myself. Can this mean we're about to test out Henderson's 'worst-case' scenario, that Japanese pullout all the analysts say could never happen? But there's no reason. No sudden icebergs out ahead . . .

Noda. I said the word out loud. Noda's kicked off his play.

I almost laughed at the thought of his naivety. Was this going to be his game? Who was he planning to fool? For once, you've got a little surprise in store, chum. Treasury may have to sweeten the pot, but there's a lot of money in the world. The United States of America can't be blackmailed.

Then I glanced out at the blue morning sky, empty except for a single swooping sparrow, and had a strange premonition, one of those mystical moments when everything sparkles with crystalline clarity. I had this feeling I can't explain. Still in a reverie I carefully set down my orange-juice glass, walked upstairs to the 'office', and dialled one of the computers into Reuters's Wall Street service. How were the securities markets taking the news? It was already 10.30 a.m., time enough for some initial response.

Dear God. For a second or so I just stared at the numbers in disbelief. What was happening? Noda hadn't gone near the stock market.

I quickly switched on the TV and located CNN, which was already carrying a special report live from the floor of the New York Stock Exchange. There stood a badly shaken Lou Dobbs, minus his tie. Minus, in fact, his jacket. The scene around him was pandemonium.

'. . . and the Dow Jones average . . .' – he glanced down at a monitor – '. . . has dropped a hundred and eighty points in the last fifteen minutes . . .' At that moment somebody jostled against the cameraman, giving us a momentary view of the ocean of paper buy-and-sell slips littering the floor. 'A hundred and ninety million shares have already changed hands in the first half hour of trading this morning . . .'

My God, I thought, the market is in free-fall. Was Meltdown Monday in '87 just the warm-up?

'As yet unconfirmed rumours concerning a slow foreign response to today's Treasury auction . . .' – although he was weighing his words carefully to give the appearance of calm, the hasty make-up on his forehead was already beginning to bubble with perspiration – '. . . seem to be responsible for what most analysts are describing as an entirely inappropriate overreaction in securities prices here this morning. . . .'

What else could he say? It was as though everybody's gnawing, primal fear had just been confirmed. There really was a hairy beast lurking in the bedroom closet, whetting to jump out and eat us in our sleep. The market was running to mommy: safe and soothing cash.

Next he made the tactical error of buttonholing a couple of floor traders and specialists for comments. They didn't bother to mince words. Their one, terrified question: Had Japan finally decided to let the US and its towering debt just twist slowly in the wind? If that happened, US capital would simply dry up, sucked in by Treasury's massive money-sponge: interest rates would soar, murdering the US economy. The Great Depression of the nineties.

As I watched, a bulletin started running across the bottom of the screen: bids on the new issue of thirty-year bonds had now dropped an amount equivalent to raising their return almost two full interest points. I zeroed in as the text continued. Worse news. The 'coverage ratio', which measures how many more bidders there are than necessary, had plummeted from 2.7 to 1.3.

And still dropping. More and more potential buyers were running for cover.

Lou, who was now surrounded by traders in blue jackets and couldn't see his own monitor, was assuring his viewers that experienced market analysts were all saying the slowdown in Treasury action did not accurately reflect worldwide demand, that Deutsche marks and pounds sterling undoubtedly were already winging westward to take advantage of the new higher rates.

Sweating there in his melting pancake, the poor guy had no inkling the patient was slipping into a coma just as he'd forecast full recovery.

Well, I thought, there's always prayer. Anything's possible. But . . . as Henderson used to say, if frogs had wings, they wouldn't bump their ass.

I got up to go downstairs and pour another cup of coffee. Coming back, I decided to forget about the stock market for a moment and just focus on Treasury, so I clicked on my Telerate service and scrolled through the financial quotes.

Friends, by that time there was no, repeat no, market out there for Treasury paper. Now that the Japanese dealers appeared to be dumping everything, European banks had hit the sidelines, waiting to see what transpired. Would rates continue to move up? Would Treasury be forced to withdraw the issue? Should everybody be bailing out now before bond prices went through the deck and demolished years of interest earnings? Looming over it all was that standing terror of the bond markets: no liquidity.

Back to Cable News Network. An officer from one of the dealer banks (which bid on big chunks of Treasury paper, then retail it) had rushed over to CNN's midtown studios and was explaining to us all it was clearly nothing more than some minor trans-Pacific communications snarl. The problem, obviously, was simple: Japanese securities firms here just hadn't received authorisation from their head office in Tokyo, where it was after business hours. A clarification would be forthcoming any minute now.

Well, if you've ever been turned down for a mortgage and you fantasised a day when you'd see that high-and-mighty clerk behind the desk have to ask *you* for a loan, I hope you caught that one. This paper-shuffler whose secretary had a secretary had agreed a week earlier to take on three billion dollars of Treasury's new debt issues – paper he now couldn't give away, let alone resell – and he was practically on his knees begging America to save his bank.

What the hell was going on? My mild-mannered friend Matsuo Noda had inadvertently (I assumed) kicked off a major financial panic.

I clicked the dial over to Financial News Network, FNN, which had momentarily interrupted its heavy midday fare of California snake-oil-and-options hucksters. Now a decidedly pale investment banker, this one an unindicted employee of Drexel Burnham, was declaring it was all merely a little 'tempest in a teapot'. His precise words. The Japanese securities houses wouldn't dare pull out their funds and kill the market, he explained. It was absurd. If they did that, their investors would lose a fortune, since any big sell-off would automatically drive down the value of their own massive portfolio. Ergo, Japan's funds had no choice but to stay invested. No problem.

My friend, I thought, where have America's bankers been? Out repossessing some widow's Chevy? As a matter of fact the Japanese outfits here don't give a flying fig what happens to our debt market. If you'd been doing your job, you'd know that Matsuo Noda had already sold Treasury futures far in excess of Japan's portfolio back when values were still high. Now he can go out and pick up all the notes and bonds he wants, costing approximately nothing, and turn around and deliver them at yesterday's full price. The man must feel like a riverboat cardsharp who's lucked into a saloon full of Huck Finns on payday. Don't you realise he's just cleaned you out, right down to the fillings in your teeth? And now he's got his team on the bus ready to roll.

Over to CBS, a Special Report underway. It featured a stream of well-meaning and incoherent Treasury officials, none of whom had the slightest inkling what to say. Then Jack O'Donnell came on from the Senate pressroom, breathing fire. The Administration's 'light at the end of the deficit tunnel' had turned out to be a freight train heading our way, just as he'd predicted. America's debt chickens were coming home to roost. He was demanding that the Speaker call a joint session of Congress this very day and by God do something.

Right, Jack. What? Looks like our pal Matsuo Noda is about to have the US of A exactly where he wants us. By the balls.

I guess I must have been operating solely on instinct by then, because a phone number popped into my head that I hadn't recalled in years. Sam Kline, my old broker at Merrill Lynch. I hadn't talked to Sam in ages, but his number used to come to my fingers whenever the market started acting up. Maybe he was sort of a father figure. Truth is, I'd first learned what little I know about the market watching that giant ticker ML had up at one end of the office just above Sam's desk – and long gone in this age of computers. I remembered how heavy trades – over ten thousand shares – were marked with stars, always fun to watch.

Forget the 'financial experts'. They were reduced to spouting pure gibberish. Time to check in at the real front line. Sam Kline.

Maybe I just wanted to have Sam to soothe me like in the old days, pour some of that dreadful coffee he had in his Thermos, tug down the cuffs of his trousers, and say not to worry, there's always tomorrow, the disaster in my portfolio merely reflected a long-overdue and healthy 'correction' in the market. (Only years later did I finally realise that 'correction' was a special Wall Street expression meaning all the stocks *you* own just tanked.)

When Sam finally got around to my call, he was barely coherent but still trying.

'Matt, what's new?' There was turmoil and yelling behind him, as though the office was about to go under a wrecking ball.

'You tell me.'

'Well, at the moment it's something of a downside morning, but—'

'Sam,' I snapped, 'this is me, Matt, save the Pollyanna.'

A short pause, and then he crumbled. 'Matthew, want the truth? The Monday Massacre of '87 was a rally compared to this.

That crash was just stocks. This time it's US bonds, the dollar, everything. The market's falling apart. Right this minute the trust departments at First Boston and Morgan are dumping weak sectors like they were some nervous greenhorn in Oshkosh. Pension fund managers I've known for years are liquidating whole blocks "at the market", for whatever they can get. One specialist downtown just told me he had to eat a hundred thousand shares of, Christ, General Dynamics. You can't give away Northrop. And Lockheed, forget it . . .' Another pause. 'God Almighty, Matt, we need a market up here. How about—'

'Not now, Sam.' It was like hanging up on my own father. A knife in my heart. 'Look, I'll get back to you. Best to Naomi.'

Good God. I wanted to hire an airplane and skywrite a big sign over downtown: WAIT. Trouble was, I wasn't sure myself what it was all about.

However, there was one thing I could do. I punched in the contact number for Dai Nippon, uptown, and told the polite little lady who answered the phone to get Tanaka on the line this goddamn minute. About ten seconds later he was there.

'Are you guys nuts?' I yelled. 'Doesn't anybody up there know what's happening?'

'We are well aware of the situation, Mr Walton.'

'Well, then, do something, for chrissake!'

'Our securities dealers here are in contact with the appropriate officials. Nothing is to be done without explicit instructions from Noda-san. He has not yet been in communication.'

'Well, get him in communication.'

'There is no cause for alarm, Mr Walton.' He continued calmly. 'Noda-san has made sure that our dealers' exposure in Treasuries is covered by the futures contracts DNI has acquired. Japanese investors are sheltered from price fluctuations. Noda-san is most grateful for your—'

'Listen carefully,' I said. 'Fuck Noda.'

I hung up.

The rest of the morning I just sat there and watched the market crater. After bond futures prices on the Chicago exchanges had sunk the daily limit, as far as they could drop in a single session, the action merely moved elsewhere. A cash market developed off-exchange worldwide and was going crazy, with spot quotes nosediving. Prices now were only rumours, but the satellite services were still trying to track them. At exactly 12.37 p.m., the President finally got around to issuing an Executive Order suspending all trading at the exchanges in government bills, notes and bonds, including futures contracts, until further notice. It turned out to have been about as effective as Prohibition. Besides, by that time I figured Noda had already cleared at least fifty billion.

Enough. I couldn't watch any more. All of a sudden I felt like a guy who'd bailed out of his flaming F-16 only to see it total a schoolhouse. I kicked off the computer, slipped on a suede jacket, and headed for Bleecker Street to fortify myself with mussels marinara and a stiff Bloody Mary. The early *Post* at the corner newsstand proclaimed with characteristic understatement the imminent passing of the civilised world.

Over cappuccino I finally started to think rationally. Nothing anybody was saying added up to a full picture. There had to be more, or less, to the story . . .

Then the truth glimmered before my eyes, yet another transcendental moment. What Noda was planning was *obvious*. At last I realised why he'd hired me. Like a great chess player, he could see about ten moves ahead. The question now was no longer what his next move would be. It was when.

You want to win World War III with a quick blitzkrieg, knock America to its knees? Simple. Go for the blind side. First you short a piece of the debt market, then for fun you dump the currency in advance (since it's just naturally gonna go the way of the peso when you make your opening move, and you might as well squeeze the orange if it's just lying there anyway). Next you kick things off by giving everybody the *impression* you're divesting all Treasury paper, which causes the dollar to predictably plummet . . .

Christ! What about Amy's currency hedge! Three weeks ago I'd contracted to sell the banks of New York ten million dollars she didn't own. In all the pandemonium, I'd completely forgotten.

I threw down a twenty for the lunch and literally raced around the corner to look for a pay phone on MacDougal. When I finally found one that worked, I shoved in a quarter and dialled the FOREX desk at Citibank for a dollar quote.

Henderson was right. Paper money is predicated on trust. It seems that when the second largest industrial nation in the world apparently doesn't think enough of the credit rating of the first largest industrial nation in the world to loan it two cents, then talk about the full faith and credit of said first largest etc. doesn't cut much ice. The Fed was out there buying dollars and dumping marks and yen and pounds in the billions to try to keep the dollar afloat, but nobody else in the Group of Five – those countries supposed to step in and buy each other's faltering currencies to prop them up – was lifting a finger. In spite of our Treasury Secretary yelling fire and damnation, all they'd done was announce an evening meeting in Paris. Period. What, they inquired, had the US done lately to help out France, West Germany, Britain, or Japan?

Behind our allies' diplomatic and not-so-diplomatic posturing lay a simple, rhetorical question: Who needed passage on a sinking ship? At the moment the only thing governments around the world wanted less than US Treasury debt was US greenbacks. I'd contracted to swap ten million of them for other currencies back when they were worth a dollar. That afternoon I settled with bills worth eighty cents and sinking. That's right. Amy's college-fund hedge cleared two mil.

And if you think Miss Amy Walton survived the dollar's crash intact, what about Matsuo Noda, now holding tens and tens of billions in world currency forwards?

What didn't prosper that Monday was a state of mind called Wall Street. By mid-afternoon all the market indexes were down by half; exchange trading had been halted in a good two-thirds of the Dow stocks; a major brokerage house had frozen accounts and announced Chapter 11; and gold futures were soaring. The October crash of '87 was now a nostalgia item, remembered as a few sessions of light trading with a hint of downside bias.

A lot of investors went to cash, but most switched into money funds (what else could they do?). While sophisticated players were shorting the stock indexes and futures, the newsletter gurus — which charged two hundred dollars a year for stock tips about equal in worth to those of a New York cabbie — were calling their major clients. A big sell signal was emblazoned in the streets of lower Manhattan. Everybody assumed the situation was temporary, but nobody needed to ride the ship down. By the closing bell the Dow had sunk over eleven hundred and fifty points. And don't forget, the DJ Average represents blue chips; prices for over-the-counter outfits like Widget-tronics, Inc. just packed up and headed south for the winter.

The way I figured it, Noda was probably more or less on schedule. By nightfall the stock exchanges had blood on the floor, a dollar was worth roughly two-thirds what it had been at sun-up, and the US Treasury couldn't have panhandled a nickel anywhere in the Free World.

I've mentioned Jack O'Donnell a time or so previously, the Columbia University professor turned politico. Jack was the junior Senator from New York: Irish idealism goes to Washington. I'd gotten to know him reasonably well, thanks mainly to a series of rubber-chicken dinners I'd pitched in to help him with.

Needless to say, O'Donnell's well-known attitude towards fiscal sleight-of-hand in the corporate sector had made raising money on Wall Street a decidedly uphill endeavour. His Insider of the Month award was especially unpopular. That was a large gold-plated screw, suitable for mounting, which he regularly bestowed on any corporate board members who'd just happened to dump big blocks of their personal holdings about a week before a disappointing quarterly report sent their company's stock price through the floor. For some reason Jack never seemed to buy their collective 'Gee, we had no idea' explanation.

Jack always assumed that corporate managements would walk off with anything not securely riveted to the floor. He also believed most of the corporate takeovers these days were about as helpful to America's competitiveness as masturbation was to population growth, a viewpoint I tended to share — which is one reason why I helped him raise money from time to time. More than that, though, I admired him immensely. The man was a *real* samurai. Unfortunately, however, he was his own worst enemy half the time when it came to soliciting campaign cheques; he could never understand why executive dining rooms weren't necessarily the optimum terrain to start raising hell about shareholders' rights. I once sent him a dog muzzle for Christmas after he pulled just that trick at a CEO fundraiser I'd carefully set up in one of those private suites atop the World Trade Center.

He'd been especially busy this session. When he did come to New York, he spent most of his time up at the West Side apartment of a female aide of his, where they reportedly were polishing a lot of position papers these days. Monday, however, he had only one thing on his mind: how to keep the US monetary system from going belly up. Trouble was, he had no idea what to do. Naturally he immediately cancelled his subcommittee hearings for the day – an inquiry into how charge cards and the banks touting them (loving those wonderful loan-shark rates) were lofting consumer debt to dizzying heights. That afternoon he began working on a speech for the Senate floor, a hellfire preachment intended to shame the Administration into some kind of action.

After thinking about it awhile, he'd decided that, since all the nervousness in the market was traceable to an apparently total Japanese loss of confidence in US government obligations, he'd have his staff call around concerning what other Japanese moves were underway. He had questions such as: If they're pulling out of Treasuries, are they dumping corporate bonds too? Real estate? Where in blazes is it going to stop?

Simple questions, maybe, but tough ones to attack on short notice, given the clampdown at the source. So his people started making calls, and finally one of them got hold of Charlie Mercer, an executive VP at Shearson. Purely chance. Did Charlie happen to know any big Japanese players in town?

Well, yes and no, replied Charlie. Strictly off the record, one of his biggest personal clients lately was an attorney here in New York, who always paid with corporate cheques bearing the logo of a Japanese-sounding outfit. But it was a purely private arrangement and he was sure . . .

The staffer immediately told him to please hold while she switched the call to Senator O'Donnell.

Actually I'd known Charlie for years, and I also knew the poor guy's wife had some kind of esoteric bone cancer that meant ten thou a month in radiation therapy. So I'd let him set up an account on the side and do some full commission churning in the name of one of Dai Nippon's dummy fronts. Why not?

Then Jack came on the line. 'Mr Mercer, am I to understand you've been handling heavy trades for a Japanese firm?'

'Nothing illegal about that, is there, Senator?' Charlie was growing nervous, suddenly seeing himself under the hot glare of TV lights in Jack's finance committee. 'Truthfully, the man I actually deal with is an American attorney here, named Walton.'

'*Matt* Walton?' roared Jack.

'You know Matthew, Senator?' inquired Charlie, stunned by the sound of the august public figure abruptly bellowing in his ear.

'Know him? I may kill the prick for not talking to me sooner.'

Approximately five seconds after this conversation my phone erupted.

'Tell me, Judas,' he yelled, 'is it true you're helping them out? I want the goddamn truth and I want it now.'

'Jack?' I finally recognised the voice. 'Helping who?'

'You know who, you fucker. Our good friends the goddamn Japs, that's who. They're—'

'Jack, calm down a second,' I interrupted. 'It's just possible this whole thing is some kind of scam. Not at all what it seems.'

'Talk to me.'

'Not over the phone. Client confidentiality. But if you're coming up any time soon, I'm mad enough to give you a full rundown of all I know, strictly off the record.'

'I'm scheduled in on the six o'clock shuttle. Where can we meet?'

'How about the club? I promise you an earful.'

'The Centurion?' He inquired sourly. I knew how he hated it.

'Jack, wouldn't kill you to rub elbows now and then with an actual capitalist. Don't worry. There won't be any photos to sully your reputation.'

I suggested the place partly to pay my respects to a wounded ward after the day's carnage and partly for Jack's convenience. It was a combined press hangout and 'new money' convocation, located just around the corner from his New York office in one of those old mansions right off Fifth, midtown. They'd just begun allowing the fair sex to cross their hallowed doorstep (after a lawsuit), a move certain diehards felt signalled the curtain raiser on the West's Decline. For my own part I'd actually put up Donna for membership as part of the test case. We eventually established that the Centurion's unwritten membership criteria were actually pretty simple: in addition to being white and male, you also needed to be either rich or well-known. Being all four made you a shoo-in.

A couple of us fortunate enough to have friends on the circuit bench called in a few favours and arranged for a black female judge to hear the case. The proceeding was over in time for lunch.

'Is eight OK?'

'Done,' he said. 'I'll be there on the dot.'

He was late as usual, but I managed to pass the time. It was enough just to sip a Perrier and observe the shell-shocked faces of golden-boy brokers presently mainlining martinis down the bar. Fortunately the place was on the ground floor so nobody could take a dive out a high window, but the crowd had all the insouciance of hookers working a Salvation Army convention. I checked over the room – lots of designer suits topped off by long faces – and wondered how many millions had been dropped that day by those present. Booze was flowing across the mahogany bar as if there were no tomorrow. Maybe there wasn't.

At a quarter to nine Jack O'Donnell marched up the blue marble steps, a man in from the war front.

O'Donnell was a big guy who looked every inch a senator, right down to the thirty-dollar haircut and the eight-hundred-dollar suit. I think it was his overcompensation for being Irish and being crapped on by the Columbia University administration most of his days. A so-so academic, he'd blossomed as a politician – firm handshake and steel eye – and had easily devastated the smooth-talking Long Island party hack the big money had thrown against him. The man was a straight shooter who believed the purpose of capitalism was to make a better place for all Americans, not merely enrich the unscrupulous or crafty few. As a result, his Senate harangues were a lonesome cry in the takeover/arbitrage/leveraging/executive-perk wilderness. His contempt for overpaid investment bankers was exceeded only by his disdain for overpaid corporate CEOs.

Anyway, we settled into the leather chairs of the back room while he ordered a medicinal Scotch, double. After his nerves stabilised a bit, I suggested he let me give him an informal rundown of what little I knew.

'High goddamn time.' He grimly extracted a notebook.

'Jack, here's the *mea culpa*. I now confess before God and you that I've been a very uneasy point man for an outfit that calls itself Dai Nippon, International. They have been playing a little game with interest-rate futures and currency forwards in quantities that stagger the mind. Thus far, however, their activity has been strictly legal and right out there for everybody to watch. I also tried to warn anybody who would listen. Consequently any of our financial analysts who didn't see this brouhaha coming a mile away has been suffering a severe rectal-cranial inversion.'

He snorted and pulled at his drink. 'OK, since you seem to know so much about this Dai Nippon outfit, care to clue me in on what's down the road?'

'Jack, I think the answer is one nobody's figured.' Then I delivered my brand-new theory.

He stared at me sceptically, sipping at his drink. 'Good God, you've gone off the deep end, Walton. I always assumed it would happen some day.'

'Jack, from what I hear, none of the big Japanese securities dealers here will even pick up their phone. What does that tell you? They're softening us up using the weapon the market dreads the most. Uncertainty. What better way to terrify the Street?

Christ, let somebody start a rumour the President has a toothache, and they practically have to shut down trading.'

'Matt, nobody's going to believe your crazy scenario. Matter of fact, I don't either. It's too wild. I'll tell you what most people are saying. All the news shows tonight hauled out our doomsday economists, Lester Thurow and his ilk, to declare we had this one coming. The consensus going around is the Japanese are finally fed up hearing us bellyache about trade barriers, so they've decided to treat us to a point demonstration concerning exactly who needs who. That's all. Japan now controls America's destiny. But since a few people here still have the idea we won the last war, Tokyo just wants to make sure we get our history straightened out.'

Could be, I answered. But I still thought everybody was missing the forest for the trees. Then I went on to describe Noda's building, his high-security computer set-up. Nobody would install an elaborate headquarters like that merely to get your attention.

He listened in uncharacteristic silence, beginning to appear a little more convinced. 'Well, let's run with your cockamamy theory a second.' He rattled his ice cubes, a habit of his I always found distracting. 'Say something bigger *is* coming up, and this is just the pre-game warm-up. What can we do?'

My suggestion, that the President close down all our financial markets immediately to keep Noda's hands off them, was not received enthusiastically.

'You want me to stand up in the Senate and propose that?' His already ruddy cheeks were beginning to redden even more as he glared around the panelled room. 'Matt, I'd be tarred and feathered by every stockholder in the country.'

Maybe so, I said. But what about Noda's vast Third Avenue nerve centre? His supercomputer? The Uzis? It had ominous portent. 'Tell you the truth, Jack, I'm not even sure I should be talking to you. After what happened today, that guy scares hell out of me.'

We ran through the known facts a couple of times more, not getting any closer to agreeing on the big picture. Finally he summed up his own fears: 'In my view, we weathered the October

'87 crash because the Fed still had some control over liquidity. When money started disappearing out of the market, they just printed more. They countered deflation with inflation, kept the dollar in balance. This time, though, we've lost all three pillars under our financial house – stocks, bonds, *and* the dollar. There's nothing the government can do to stop this one.'

At that moment there was a tap on my shoulder, and I looked up to see Eduardo, the club's recent attempt at Hispanic affirmative action, handing me a cordless phone. Then I remembered I'd set up things downtown to forward calls to the bar. The next sounds in my ear were the mellifluous profanities of Dr William Henderson.

Bill had just gotten off a plane after spending a few days loosening up at the Sandy Lane in Barbados, assaulting its reserves of Sugar Cane Brandy, and he was mad as hell. His 'Georgia Mafia' had been caught flat-footed. Why hadn't I warned him that the Japs had scheduled this move? Surely I must have had an inkling. He would have shorted the market and scored a pile.

I suggested he calm down, that nobody, me included, had seen it coming. What's more, I had a strong feeling it was all—

'What the hell's next?' Bill continued, oblivious. 'What's Noda saying?'

'Nothing here but speculation. He's probably getting his beauty sleep at the moment. But take some of your own advice, friend, and stand clear. I've got a feeling there's less here, and more, than meets the eye. Don't, repeat, don't get the idea you can outguess Matsuo Noda. I think he's pulling a number, but—'

Bill interjected something brief and unrepeatable and rang off, undoubtedly headed for consolation.

'Was that Henderson?' Jack asked, then watched me nod. Bill had pitched in to help Jack out of a few tight spots on the money front, in appreciation of which O'Donnell had proposed him for the Council of Economic Advisers – and shortly thereafter forfeited all credibility with the Administration. These days he couldn't have gotten into the White House on a VFW tour. 'Well, the man's got no idea when to keep his mouth shut with the press, but he's nobody's idea of a fool. What does *he* think this is all about?'

'Sounds like he's just studying the tea leaves like everybody else.'

Jack sighed, then rattled his cubes some more. 'Well, if Henderson can't figure out what's going on, then nobody can. That in itself ought to tell us there's a patch of slippery ice down the road. My own guess is the Japanese have decided to play a little poker with the American markets without having the damnedest idea of the consequences.'

'Jack, what if they *do*?'

After we sat there gazing at the gilded plasterwork ceiling for a while, we started getting caught up on old times. He inquired what I thought the press would do to him if he married one of his staffers. My guess was that a photo of Washington's most eligible divorce veteran at the altar once more would probably make the cover of *People*. Everybody loves a lover. That possibility seemed to cheer him up a bit.

It was round about then, probably close to 10.30 p.m., that another call came through. This time I already had a feeling who it was, and I momentarily considered not taking it. But then, why not let O'Donnell have the story straight from the source.

The caller was, of course, Matsuo Noda. It must have been late morning, Japan time, after a very long night.

What, he inquired, was my on-the-spot reading of the scene?

'I don't know.' The phone had that same funny whine I remembered, as though he had a private phone system worldwide. 'Maybe you should be telling me.'

Noda-san, no surprise, didn't seem particularly unsettled by the developments. 'I assure you there is no cause for alarm, Mr Walton. The situation may seem temporarily unfortunate, but I have long believed all things turn out for the best.'

'Could have fooled me. But while we're all waiting for the silver lining to this cloud, you might do everybody a favour and get your goddamn securities dealers here to issue a statement clarifying their intentions.'

'Mr Walton' – he chuckled – 'you ascribe far too much

influence to me. I am merely a banker, one of many in Japan. I have no control over what our institutions choose to do or not do.'

'I wish I could believe that.'

'Well, I suppose there are many things about Dai Nippon that need to be explained more fully. I look forward to seeing you next week. We can talk then.'

Upon which he advised me just to sit tight. All further communications would be routed through their office uptown. And with that dictum in place, he suddenly had better things to do and said thanks for all my help. There was the sound of some satellite bleeps, then silence.

Welcome to the Brave New World, I thought. Again I had this definite feeling the DNI rodeo had just begun.

By then Jack was nearing terminal exhaustion. I passed along Noda's cryptic refusal to lift a hand, advised him to make a statement tomorrow that the US financial markets could be dangerous to everybody's health and helped him into a cab for his aide's place uptown. The evening was fizzling out with nobody left at the bar but regulars. Thus I went home alone to check in with Amy and then drift off into a very unsettling dream.

My nightmare was over by morning. America's was just beginning.

THIRTEEN

Funny thing about investor confidence: often as not it relies more on faith than facts. Give it a little unsettling heat and it can just melt away. Belief turns to fear, then blind panic.

Insight number two: the bigger you are, the scareder you tend to get. So what appeared to be a sudden Japanese loss of conviction regarding the US Treasury's ability to meet its standing obligations received close attention from the world's bankers, from Zurich to Hong Kong. The Japanese securities outfits just kept dumping and nervous phone inquirers from locales as diverse as the White House and Red Square were all advised that everybody was 'in a meeting and will get back to you'. As a natural consequence the world's major financial players succumbed to a terminal case of nerves.

When the bond markets finally reopened on Wednesday, Treasury's thirty-year issue had scooted up four full interest points. There was still a market for Uncle Sam's IOUs – everything on this planet will move for a price – but buyers were wary. They wanted their newly perceived risk sweetened considerably.

Predictably, rates on corporate and municipal bonds did a similar tango north, leaving America's conservative investors wondering what hit them. In fact, a lot of scheduled corporate debt offerings were scuttled to await more settled times and lower rates.

The dollar also stayed on the critical list. Everybody was worried the US Treasury might just rev up the printing presses to produce enough greenbacks to pay off all the foreigners who wanted their money back. Since Paul 'tight money' Volcker – who probably would have thrown his robust torso on to the ink to prevent that from happening – was now gone, there was nobody at the Fed with a real commitment to holding back the flood.

And the stock market. People weren't starting to call this Black November for nothing. A lot of players feared that the higher rates would hobble the economy, a perfect excuse to head for the exits while the getting was good. As Henderson liked to observe: psychology is a fundamental too. The next day the Dow sank another two hundred points; the day after that a hundred more. (Where had *those* sellers been two days before?) The fourth and fifth days it slowed, heaved a sigh of exhaustion and sort of peered up out of the bunker to see if the bombing runs had let up. The downward pressure was still evident, but it was finally losing some of its steam.

Yours truly did a lot of thinking as the week wore on, while the country appeared to wobble on the brink of unprecedented disaster. I also conferred now and then with Jack O'Donnell and with Henderson in between their appearances on TV chat shows. Although Bill's bearish reading of the nation's estate had been vindicated well beyond what even he had envisioned, I can report he took small pleasure in his newfound celebrity; he was increasingly miserable over his own missed opportunities in the financial casino. Jack, for his part, had gained a profound appreciation of the helplessness of government to intervene when fear and greed seize the marketplace.

My personal ruminations on the situation turned out to be too Machiavellian for anybody to entertain seriously. Question: If you wanted to pull all your money out of the US, is this how you'd do it? Answer: No way. Instead you'd go about it gradually, a little at a time, in order not to stampede the markets and cause exactly what was happening now.

Ergo, I concluded, this isn't real. Noda just wants every investor in the world to *assume* there's a Japanese pullout underway.

But why the grandstand play? Sure, he'd made a pile, but he didn't seem like a guy who had to sweat his mortgage payments. Nor did this kind of market manipulation require a building in midtown Manhattan and a computer set-up to rival NORAD headquarters. Something more had to be coming. And the only thing I could think of was that Noda's something had a lot to do with my profession.

This was not a welcome piece of prognostication to loose upon the world. Since the financial markets already had plenty of problems on their plate, there wasn't all that much interest in speculating about the next course. Consequently nobody made the slightest attempt to man the ramparts for what was ahead. Our financial battleship had been stopped dead in the water and its engines disabled, but nobody was even bothering to prime the guns. This couldn't be an all-out attack. Right?

Wrong. The stage was now set for Noda's real move. The following Saturday I was summoned to Dai Nippon's midtown fortress where I watched my crazy theory become reality. Before anybody in our shell-shocked financial centres had time to digest what had happened, Matsuo Noda — his Dai Nippon Eight-Hundred-Year funds underwritten through a syndicate of Japanese banks and insurance companies led by the Dai-Ichi Credit Corporation, Ltd. of Tokyo — hit the beach.

In the days to come I did manage to assemble a rough outline of how Noda pulled off his brilliant opening feint. It was elegant, and to savour it fully requires a quick peek at his reserves — Japan's bankbook.

Start with personal savings, the hundreds of billions being squirrelled away by individual Japanese. Then add to those monies the assets of Japanese pension funds, private savings organisations with several hundred billion dollars to lend out. Next come insurance companies and corporations, similarly awash in loose cash. Taken together, the total amount of excess capital in Japan is now well over five trillion dollars.

If all those zeros befuddle you as much as they do me, try thinking of it like this: a trillion dollars is the size of the annual US budget. So if the Japanese regulators open the floodgates and let all that money roll, its citizens have the ready bucks to finance our government's entire budget — Lockheed, stockpiles and pork barrel – for at least five years using just what's in their mattresses.

As it happens, all this Japanese cash has become an important, nay, indispensable, component of the American financial scene. We and the Japanese are like an old married couple: they're the wife who scrimps and saves, we're the husband who borrows and squanders. The middlemen who rifle her purse and ship the proceeds to us are, increasingly, Japanese investment firms.

At least half a dozen major Japanese securities dealers with offices in New York run big bond departments. The foremost of these is, of course, Nomura Securities International, the world's largest brokerage house. With over two hundred billion dollars in customer accounts, Nomura is now a primary dealer in US Treasury issues, meaning they can buy directly from the government and sell to their clients. And since Treasuries pay several interest points better in return than Japan's miserly savings accounts, their customers back home think they're getting a terrific deal. Little wonder Japanese investors finance a full third of America's budget overdrafts these days.

Another major player is Daiwa Securities America, which also underwrites federal paper on its own. Nor should we overlook Nikko Securities and Yamaichi Securities, both handling money in the tens of billions. These outfits and others are well past the beachhead stage of entry into the world capital markets. They're entrenched; they're big; and they know how to play hardball. Were they involved in Noda's assault? Nobody ever knew for sure. But you figure it out.

Banks. As it happens, the biggest one in the world is Japanese. The Dai-Ichi Kangyo Bank, Ltd. of Tokyo has unceremoniously reduced Citicorp to second banana. Rounding out the top five worldwide are Fuji, Sumitomo and Mitsubishi. And worldwide means everywhere. Japan controls ten per cent of the US banking business, a quarter of all British banking. Of the ten largest banks in the sovereign state of California, four are Japanese. Japan in brief is rapidly becoming banker to the planet, with more ready money than anybody else and a battalion of financial *samurai* who know the game.

What makes these Japanese players especially powerful is the kind of bucks they represent. It's called hot money — cash lent out short-term and therefore subject to immediate withdrawal. Instead of tying up their overseas bankroll for years, they stick to offshore investments that can be called in tomorrow. At home Japan invests for the long horizon, but abroad the bulk of the money is short. Hot money.

Since foreign investors normally pick up well over half of a given Treasury refunding, the paralysis when Japan began re-calling its hot money, thereby spooking buyers worldwide, was as predictable as the sunrise. Matsuo Noda didn't have to be a Rhodes Scholar to realise how much mileage there'd be in a big Japanese sell-off programme and a 'no comment' from his dealers.

Here's how he orchestrated the details. Apparently it had all been very Japanese, very consensus. A few phone calls, then a lot of meetings over green tea. Later on, some late nights with sake. Noda, thanks to his new clout, had been in the driver's seat from the start. The money managers in Tokyo were all feeling the heat over demands by investors that they participate in the multiple Eight-Hundred-Year funds he'd floated. All across Japan people were starting to ask whether *their* savings were out there waving the flag too. A lot of those managers were starting to get edgy, so Noda obligingly struck a deal, a little consensus.

OK, hold your monies, but let's get organised. When the next Treasury collection plate comes by, don't roll over any more short-term US T-bills, and don't take a piece of the next sale of long bonds. In fact, that's the day you begin to divest. Staggering losses? No problem. I just happen to have everybody's portfolio insulated with futures contracts. Sell away, and even when the price plummets, nobody's gonna lose a yen. In fact, you can have a piece of the currency windfall I've set up. Apparently everybody shook hands on it, or whatever they do in Japan nowadays.

Consequently none of the big Japanese houses in New York had to take a lot of risk. The sellers were covered by Noda's rate contracts, which I later discovered he'd passed along (at cost) to anybody who needed them. The rest he sold himself for a hefty profit. So in the course of his play, he incidentally raised several billions in additional operating capital for Dai Nippon while fully protecting the home team.

When the dust had finally settled, it turned out he didn't actually liquidate very much Treasury paper after all. He didn't need to. In fact Japan dumped only about eight per cent of its holdings. If you think about it a minute you realise they couldn't possibly have hoped to divest everything they had in dollars. What would they do with all that cash? Loan it to Brazil?

Veterans of world finance will tell you there were already precedents for this kind of Japanese muscle. Back in the mid-eighties, Nomura Securities had unsheathed its financial sword and totally controlled the Eurobond markets for about a fortnight. They were just letting everybody know they were in town. So there was nothing particularly unprecedented about a little number whereby a handful of Japanese banks and securities firms could, by concerted action, bring the US financial system to its knees.

Although I'd been convinced from the very first that Matsuo Noda had engineered the whole move, I had no hard proof. Besides, what was I supposed to do? No laws were broken. He was playing strictly by the rules. So I just took cover like everybody else and watched the marketplace disintegrate. My main preoccupation was a growing suspicion that Noda was now moving up his battery of guns for the next round of shelling.

I was right. His Treasury sell-off had merely been a demonstration of firepower. Its effectiveness must have given confidence that his beachhead was secured, since he came ashore at the end of the week to take personal command of the real landing.

He and his general staff hit town quietly and with no fanfare on Thursday, spent Friday in a strategy session, and on Saturday took over the computerised command HQ on Third Avenue. That afternoon Tanaka called and ordered me (very politely but curtly) to assemble my records and come uptown. The operation was being consolidated and Noda-san wanted me coordinated. From now on I would be working out of their offices.

This was it. Just what I'd been waiting for. At last I could confront the bastard, one-to-one. No way was I going to be part of the big assault I saw directly ahead.

My first look at the revised operation uptown confirmed my worst fears. The technical analysts had been replaced by a new set of troops: money men. Open collars were gone, supplanted by a lot of business-school types wearing thin black ties. Tanaka's office had been moved off to the side; the corner office now belonged to Dai Nippon's four-star commanding general: Matsuo Noda. After I'd cleared security, that's where I was led.

'Mr Walton, how good to see you again.' He looked up from a printout, his silver hair perfectly groomed. 'I trust today is convenient for you.'

'This is going to be brief.' I ignored the chair he rose to adjust for me. 'I'm only here to advise you that my participation is officially terminated as of this moment. I'll be sending you a final invoice next week. You can find yourself another attorney.'

'But your work has scarcely begun.' He appeared to be mildly puzzled, as though I'd just made a small misstatement about the weather or some such. 'We expect your participation to be crucial.'

'Surely you're joking.' I was turning to leave.

'Mr Walton.' He shifted the printout around and shoved it across the desk. 'Contrary to what you may presume, we are here to help this country. You might wish to look over our programme for the near term.'

'This I've got to see.' I came back and studied it for a few seconds . . . then stared back at him.

'Impossible.' I finally realised he was serious. 'Whatever you're thinking, I'll tell you right now you don't have a chance. These outfits have lawyers. Hundreds of them.'

'Ah, but that's why you are on our staff. This is your speciality.' He smiled. 'Remember the *Book of Five Rings* by the swordsman Miyamoto Musashi? In it he describes the three kinds of attack. There is the *Ken no Sen*, where you move first and catch your opponent unprepared; next is the *Tai no Sen*, whereby your initial move occurs a split second after your opponent's; and finally there is the *Taitai no Sen*, in which you and he attack at the same instant. What has happened up until today might be likened to the *Ken no Sen*. We have made sure that nothing was anticipated. Very soon, however, we will have to move to the *Tai no Sen*, responding with lightning speed to the moves of those who would thwart us. Miyamoto Musashi declared correctly that if you are attacked with force, you must counterattack with even greater force and thereby upset momentarily your opponent's rhythm. That moment can mean victory, but only if you are totally prepared.' He leaned back. '*We* must be totally prepared.'

'Why in *hell* would I want to help you? I guess you didn't hear me. I've just resigned.' I turned for the door. 'Besides, nobody could pull off what you're planning. You're going to have battalions of attorneys moving against you.'

'I expect that.' He stopped smiling. 'But that area is your responsibility now, Mr Walton. A good swordsman does not think, he acts. Intuitively.'

'And if I refuse?'

'You cannot possibly.'

'Try me.'

'Only you can handle this, Mr Walton. Betray us, and you may well witness the disappearance of America as an industrial nation. The time is now or never.'

That zinger gave me pause. He meant it. But before I had a chance to tell him he was completely crazy, he went on to sketch out what he claimed was his objective. How he planned to address the American 'crisis' and resolve it.

Let me tell you my first impression of Matsuo Noda's scenario. It was legal, it was legit, and it was — as Joanna's teenage niece used to describe notable phenomena — totally fucking awesome.

What's more, he wanted me to stay on as tail-gunner. The truth? I felt the disorientation of a kid who'd been fooling around in the Soap Box Derby suddenly being handed a slot in the Indianapolis 500.

The most astonishing part of all was, I had the feeling he just might pull it off.

You're right. I should have said no, not on your life, this is *way* out of my league, never in a million years . . .

Instead I said I'd think about it.

Good, he said. Why didn't I stick around till Monday and get a feeling for the operation?

I didn't shake his hand. I just walked out and poured myself a cup of green tea from the huge urn there in the middle of the floor. Walton, you idiot, how did you get yourself into this?

Which is when I spotted a sporty-looking lady way across on the other side of the floor, over by the climate-controlled NEC mainframe. Something about her seemed vaguely familiar. Definitely not DNI staff. Wearing jeans, dark hair in a nice designer cut, handled herself like a mover. Not to mention a world-class bottom inside those tight shapely Calvins. From all appearances she actually seemed to be second-in-command. She was reading the riot act to Tanaka about something to do with the computer, had the self-important little fucker bobbing and weaving. Who was that? Hadn't seen her around here before.

Well, now, no time like the present to head on over and check into this. A fellow *gaijin*. Could be she'll explain what in hell's going on. Is Noda real?

Suddenly she turned around, saw me and stopped. I stopped. We both just stood there trying to remember. She hit pay dirt first, but I was only microseconds behind.

Want to know my first thought, my very first thought? Matsuo Noda, you son of a bitch, you're even smarter than I'd given you credit for. You've hired the best, the very best.

'Is this how you pick up your women these days, Matt? Given up on vegetable stands?' She was walking towards me wearing a smile. I tried to grin back. 'How are you, Matthew? Good to see you've still got your hair. Well, most of it.'

'Tam Richardson, I don't believe this. Now I know it all is a dream. Please tell me you were kidnapped. None of this is really happening, right? It's just a very big, very bad nightmare. We'll all wake up tomorrow and go to the beach.'

'Welcome aboard, partner.' She stuck out her hand. 'It's going to be a wild trip.'

'No kidding.' I looked her over as I took her hand. Nice and warm. Time had treated her well. Very well. 'How long have you known Noda?'

'Less than a month.' She was checking me over too. Wonder how I was doing. 'How long have *you* been helping him?'

It occurred to me that we both should have been using that classic hooker response where the guy asks his young companion how long she's been in her particular field of endeavour and she replies, 'long enough to know better'.

'Few months now. Noda is pretty impressive.' I tried to sound casual. 'Not to mention persuasive.'

'That he is.'

'Well, let's have a toast to winning this.' I turned to the urn. 'How about some tea, Professor?'

'Love it.'

'Tam, let's just hope these guys don't suddenly decide to eat us alive.' I passed it over. 'What do you think our chances of survival are?'

That one startled her. I got the impression she was half thinking the same thing. Then she managed a thin laugh.

'We'll eat them first if they try.'

'You still talk tough. I always told you you should have been a lawyer.'

But she was right. Once the cards are dealt, you play to win.

Which is exactly what I planned to do. Since my own part was still down the road, that weekend I just sat in their offices watching spellbound as Noda and Dr Tamara Richardson reviewed the data and put together the financial details. Next, a lot of coded telexes were sent out to pile up somewhere in Tokyo with instructions for routeing of the funds.

After I'd digested his opening move, I did have occasion to ask the chief a few pointed questions. Such as, wasn't he at all nervous that Wall Street might rebound before he could get rolling? He replied, correctly as usual, that the total collapse in the financial markets would last for a while. Even though the dollar was still down for the count (over forty per cent), he figured only the most intrepid foreign speculators would go plunging into the American stock market looking for bargains. As for American investors, most of them, including the institutions, were still in shock. He rightly forecast that the herd mentality of the Street hadn't been repealed. War stories of '87 were going around and nobody wanted to make the textbooks as a fool. Better a little profit forgone than more money lost. The mutual fund managers, most of whom had been caught with their pants at half-mast, were devoting their energies that weekend to composing creative explanations.

Events Monday proved him to be essentially on target. There was an eerie quiet over the financial landscape. Everybody was waiting for somebody else to try breathing life back into the corpse.

Then a few analysts noticed something peculiar. Anonymous buy orders were coming in, more and more, for stocks in the sector hardest hit, high tech. Maybe it was bargain hunters, but the buyers weren't any of the 'growth' mutual funds that might have been expected to lead the action. In fact, many of those hotshot managers were relieved to part with some of the dogs they'd ridden down that long lonesome decline of the week before.

Gradually the prices of certain securities began to edge up in this early thin trading, enticing more and more holders to 'sell on strength'. What issues? First off, anything to do with computers. Of course there weren't all that many hardware manufacturers left around by then, after the shakeout and mergers of the early eighties, but somebody was buying heavily into the few that remained. They were also actively purchasing little software outfits. Those stocks had taken a heavy beating over the past week, so prices were at an all-time low for most.

Other industries they started to nibble at were telecommunications, aerospace, biotechnology. They seemed to be looking for outfits with substantial R & D operations: the focus was on creativity, growth sectors, the sunrise industries.

Of course, what this mysterious new buyer was really doing

was snapping up outfits loaded with labs and PhDs. Dr Richardson and my new client Matsuo Noda had DNI acquiring companies short on competent management and market share but long on research, innovation — the one thing we were still best at. Looked at differently, what Dai Nippon was really buying was underused brainpower, the American smarts currently going to waste thanks to inept corporate management.

Explanations began to sprout all over the place — from the 'Heard on the Street' column in the *Journal* to Dan Dorfman, a guy with a bloodhound's nose for Wall Street shenanigans. But the hard truth was nobody could put it together. Who could have? The play was too ambitious even to imagine.

You guessed it. With the trillions and trillions now at its disposal, Japan was about to take charge of America's future.

FOURTEEN

The task ahead can actually be described very succinctly. I was going to help Dai Nippon acquire controlling stock positions in a bevy of ineptly managed American high-tech companies and she was going to be in charge of turning them around. I was DNI's takeover artist; Tam was the fix-it expert. That probably sounds a bit ambitious on everybody's part, but after watching the Dai Nippon assault forces for a couple of days I knew one thing for sure: we'd have plenty of heavy backup.

Why did I agree to ride shotgun for Matsuo Noda's 'Save America' project? Because, if he meant what he said, such a programme was long overdue. American industry was in trouble and it was hurting a lot of good hardworking people who didn't deserve to be hurt. Worse still, this wasn't some random act of God. It was largely the result of self-serving corporate management. Most occupiers of the executive suites these days were too busy merging and acquiring and leveraging to do what stockholders thought they were paying them for: building industry and creating American jobs. (Well, maybe that's an overstatement; they *had* kept Drexel Burnham's junk-bond cowboys working overtime.) In the mid-eighties, American corporations were spending two and three times more on mergers and acquisitions than on research and development. Uncaring industrialists here no longer bothered to try making anything as old-fashioned as competitive products; they preferred to make deals and sell imports. The net result was that America, the world's major economic locomotive, was veering off the track and seriously in danger of taking everybody else in the world along with it.

That's where Matsuo Noda came in. Part of the arrangement he'd made with the Japanese institutions putting up the funds was that he would be given proxy to exercise all voting rights. Face it, he had a pretty impressive performance record overseeing the long-range planning and investment of well-run corporations. So after I'd helped Dai Nippon acquire control of a long list of poorly managed companies, he and Tam Richardson were planning to move in, clear out the deadwood, and lay down priorities for restructuring. She was Dai Nippon's Technical Director for all US operations, which meant she was going to head up the team on the newly evacuated floor just above the financial section – Noda's management *samurai*.

Enough theory. Here's how it actually went. On Friday the story was finally broken by the *Wall Street Journal*, a little squib in 'What's News', with a short two-column analysis on page three. The piece revealed that all the heavy new activity building in the high-tech sector of the market represented buys being coordinated by a new Japanese investment concern.

This sudden, unexpected programme of foreign investment was heralded at first as a salubrious omen, refuting those doomsayers who were claiming the world had lost confidence in the US. In fact, if anything it was proof that overseas enthusiasm was actually increasing. Japan's previous practice of focusing on debt instruments was at best passive investment. But buying heavily into a sector of the economy that appeared weak was something else entirely. It was a rousing endorsment of America's prospects.

To be fair, there was still a modest case to be made in that direction. Our high-tech sector wasn't all struggling high fliers operating out of some one-storey cinder block on Route 128 or the Washington Beltway. America had plenty of solid industry in high tech – computers, aerospace, office machinery – and American laboratories and universities were the envy of the world. The problem lay with the downside. We'd lost our lead in electronics, drugs, scientific instruments, plastics, communications equipment . . . it's a long list. In fact, America's overall trade balance in high-tech products had actually gone negative, shrunk from a twenty-five-billion-dollar surplus as recently as 1980. The ignored question, therefore: Given the direction things were headed, why were the Japanese suddenly supposed to be so impressed?

The market's initial euphoria didn't last long, however. By the end of the second week the SEC was sniffing the air and the lunch talk downtown, from the AMEX traders at Harry's to the expense-account crowd at historic Fraunces Tavern, was focused on what appeared to be a major shift in Japan's investment strategy. Now that the stock market was in a shambles, they weren't just dabbling any more; they were cashing on the fire sale hand over fist.

Thus the Street's early cheering melted into apprehension. Japan had already taken apart our debt and currency markets, turned them upside down, and scored a bundle. Now Noda had Wall Street looking over its shoulder and reminiscing about the good old days when all it had to worry about was rich, crazy Arabs. When it became clear that Dai Nippon was assaulting the US securities markets with high-speed computers and a cheque-book that just kept coming, there weren't all that many wisecracks about camels and tents.

Wall Street, however, merely counts; it doesn't think. The real disquiet was reserved for the corporate boardrooms. Take it as a given that when the Securities and Exchange Commission reports some ten, twenty, or thirty per cent of your company's stock has just been swallowed by a cash-rich Japanese raider, your attention can focus most exquisitely. In a word, Matsuo Noda was the talk of industrial America. More to the point, and exactly what he had expected, the boards and CEOs of the companies being bought were beginning to be scared shitless. A major player with seemingly bottomless pockets was gobbling up heavy blocks of their publicly traded shares. Worse still, nobody had the slightest inkling why.

What all those entrenched CEOs didn't realise, in their wildest paranoia, was that seven-figure salaries and cushy executive perks were about to go the way of Cadillac tail fins. World competition, not executive compensation, would be the new game. Playtime was over; America was about to get serious again.

My early suspicions concerning my role in Noda's design had

been precisely on the mark. I was indeed the freelance gunslinger he wanted by his side when the companies he was aiming at started to shoot back, which they surely would. Needless to say, if his plan was ever allowed to reach the courts, it would create a virtual living trust for half the corporate lawyers in the land. He'd be in litigation through the twenty-first century as managements fought to the last stockholder's dollar to keep their jobs.

Enter Matt Walton. Time for some *samurai*-style legal swordsmanship.

The rules: If you're CEO of a company and somebody starts buying up a major chunk of your stock with the intent of taking you over, you've got roughly four basic ways to stop him. The first is to try to bribe that buyer to go away, paying him a ransom — politely called greenmail — to sell his holdings and disappear. (More than one corporate raider you've read about in the papers has made millions in a couple of weeks using that very play.) The drawbacks of trying to buy off a potential acquirer are, (1) it's expensive and (2) maybe he really *does* plan to eat you, in which case it won't work anyway. Matsuo Noda was in that category.

A second popular means to thwart a hostile takeover is to go out and find somebody else to buy you first, the proverbial 'white knight'. Ideally this friendly buyer should be, (1) too big to be taken over himself, and (2) willing to let you keep your playpen.

A third technique to stop somebody from acquiring a controlling chunk of your stock is to jack up the price, usually by offering to buy it yourself. Float some junk bonds, sell off a few divisions, do anything that will raise cash and then offer the shareholders more than the raider is willing to bid. This can be very expensive, but if you're a CEO with millions in compensation every year, why should you care if your stockholders' company is leveraged to the brink of ruin? You've still got *your* job and *your* goodies. It's used a lot.

The fourth and most fashionable way these days to stop hostile mergers is to try to make yourself unmergeable. To do that, you get your board of directors to vote a poison pill. What this does is make sure that any company that swallows you is going to be ingesting a piranha that will eat said company's own guts instead. The newest twist on this is to use phony bonds with a so-called flip-over provision, a killer pill invented by a clever New York law operation I won't name but whose initials might be WLR & K. The game is as follows. In order to protect yourself you invent some convertible bonds and stash them away somewhere, ready. Then, should a raiding company start acquiring your stock or make an unauthorised tender offer to your shareholders, you hand out these little bombs to everybody who owns your shares. If this unfriendly company is then unlucky enough to actually acquire you, those convertibles 'flip over' into the stock of that buyer. Your stockholders suddenly have the right to exchange their funny paper for huge, discounted chunks of real stock in the acquiring company – which would, naturally, be ruined should that happen. And usually, just for good measure, you also vote through a few golden parachutes for you and all your cronies, giving everybody in the executive suite severance pay in the tens of millions.

Those were the stakes. Now a lot of outfits suddenly found themselves being bought by a mysterious Japanese entity named Dai Nippon, International. What were they going to do? At first of course everybody just assumed DNI was merely angling for a little greenmail. No such luck. After a couple of days went by and we hadn't returned anybody's phone call, they knew that wasn't it. Next, a few went looking for a white knight with more money than DNI (a tough assignment). Not surprisingly, however, most corporate managers very quickly decided to call a board meeting and ram through a poison pill.

I got more than a few phone calls at my downtown office from CEOs wanting to know if I could pitch in and help them stave off what looked like an unfriendly Japanese buy-up. I had to say, sorry fellows, I'm unavailable. But why not give it your best shot and try the old 'pill'?

Most of them did. They had no option really.

Which suited me fine.

The time was late Friday – the afternoon was gorgeous, sunny and crisp – and the place was Noda's office. Naturally he understood all about poison pills, so he knew the problem. What he wanted to hear was our solution.

'I'd like to try something that's never been done before. A different battle plan.' I glanced out at the blue sky and wished I was already in St Croix, on holiday with Amy. 'However, I think it's possibly just unconventional enough to fly.'

'It has to be legal, Mr Walton.' Noda leaned back in his chair, waiting.

'It is. But in order to lay the groundwork, we'll first need to set up a string of dummy corporations.'

'Any particular state?' He was listening closely now, his mind clicking away. I was never sure what the man was thinking, but I figured he'd probably seen it all before.

'That old standby Delaware should do fine, though you might want to consider going for some offshore tax-haven places, if only because the paperwork is minimal. In the Caribbean I'd recommend the Turks and Caicos Islands, maybe the Cayman Islands. Then there's Bermuda or the Bahamas or the Channel Islands. If you really want to get esoteric, why not Vanuatu, used to be the New Hebrides, in the South Pacific.'

'I'm familiar with world geography, Mr Walton.' He was deadpan. A joke?

'Fair enough. These dummy corporations of course will have no assets.'

'I understand.' He smiled and ran his fingers through his silver hair, doubtless already miles ahead of me. 'Absolutely no problem. Please proceed.'

'While those corporations are being set up, you continue buying stock in whatever companies you need to control, making sure in all cases that you acquire just enough to deliberately trigger their poison-pill mechanism. We force them to issue their flip-over bonds. They can't stop the process since it's always set up to be automatic after a certain percentage of stock has been acquired. Not even the boards of directors can revoke it.'

'Yes, Mr Walton. I'm aware of that.' He seemed not the slightest bit ruffled by such an unorthodox opening move.

'Well, let me elaborate. The reason we want to trigger their poison pill first is so that nobody can later come in as a white knight and save them. They're totally isolated. They'll have made themselves into sitting ducks.'

'Very good.' He leaned back. Was he really that far ahead of me?

'While that's happening, you "sell" the stock acquired thus far to one of the dummy outfits we've set up, in return for debt paper. Which puts DNI at arm's length and untouchable. After that, you lend that dummy corporation the rest of the millions or billions necessary to acquire a controlling interest in the company, taking back as collateral more junk bonds at absurdly usurious rates. That makes it a financial leper, but you don't care: you're merely lending yourself the money. This paper corporation is all that can be touched when the acquired company's poison bonds flip over. So instead of being convertible into the stock of some cash-rich corporation, the way they were intended, those flip-bonds are going to give their holders a piece of some offshore phone booth with zero assets and enough debt to choke a horse. They're worthless paper. And you're in the clear.'

He smiled. 'Which means our programme can proceed on schedule?'

'Dai Nippon will be totally insulated from their poison pills. Like the guy who sells his house and boat to his company and then lets *it* file Chapter 11 bankruptcy in order to protect his personal assets from creditors. Nobody can lay a glove on you.'

'Mr Walton' – he leaned back, a twinkle in his dark eyes – 'that's exactly why I knew you were right for us. You have an intuitive grasp of tactics.'

'If you do this, there're going to be a lot of unhappy unemployed lawyers in this town.'

'Most regrettable. Some of them might even have to go out and find productive work.' He rose and shook my hand. 'You've destroyed the prospect of years of legal roadblocks in a single stroke. It's elegant.'

It was. Sun Tzu and Miyamoto Musashi would definitely have approved. But there still had to be more. An unexpected opening is not enough in itself; it needs an equally deft follow-up. *Bushidō*, the Way of the Sword, teaches that you should first surprise your antagonist, and then you must confound him. Both the initial attack and the carry-through are crucial to success. Among other things, that meant Noda's mechanism for calling a board meeting of the companies he'd be acquiring had to be instantaneous, without the usual niceties.

'This set-up should do the job, but only if it's used with finesse. Otherwise the whole system gets buried in paperwork.'

'What do you mean?'

'You have to be fast and flexible. Once you've taken ownership of a company, you've got to gain immediate control over its board of directors, in order to block any and all countermoves.'

'I understand.'

'Do you? I'm talking about the ability to call an executive session out of the blue. The *kesa* stroke of the sword. The power to cut a CEO in half before he can blink. No time for consensus and the usual Japanese niceties.'

He stood quietly, thinking. At last he spoke.

'In other words, I must be able to convene the board at a moment's notice. Is that the essence of what you are saying?'

'Nothing else is going to work.'

'Very well. After we have a commanding stock position, we can institute the necessary changes.'

'Good. Remember though, that's still merely half the battle. Besides being able to call board meetings, you need full authority to institute a shareholders' vote, which in this case will consist of nothing more than you signing your name.'

'Perfectly reasonable.'

'It is. But it also means you've got to be available to me at all times. Can I rely on that?'

He turned and strolled to the window, pensively. 'That may not always be possible.'

'Then you've got a potential problem.'

He revolved back and studied me a second, finally taking the bait. 'There is, of course, one very simple solution. I can merely assign you power of attorney, allowing you to act in my name if I cannot be reached.'

'That would do it. But you'd be handing over a lot of authority.'

'I envision no difficulty.' He looked me over with the self-assurance of a tiger contemplating a haunch of beef. 'I have every reason to believe you would always act in DNI's best interest, Mr Walton.'

It was possible he knew a few things I didn't. On the other hand, maybe Matsuo Noda had just overreached, taken too much for granted. Whichever it was, the manoeuvring just completed had been one small step for Tam and Matthew Walton. Should we ever need them, I'd just conned Matsuo Noda into giving me duplicates of the keys to his kingdom. It was our protection and, in a way, my secret price for putting our heads into Dai Nippon's noose.

'Then it looks like we have everything we need to move forward.'

'Excellent.'

Upon which I absented his office, safety net in place. The play was on.

Which brings us to Tam Richardson. If my approach to this new job was a little unconventional, what about the college prof who showed up in jeans as she readied to renovate corporate America? One thing, we suited each other. It was a tag team made in heaven. After I'd pried open the door to the companies DNI was buying, she was going to roll in, guns blazing, and shove everybody against the wall.

Let me add one important distinction, however. Whereas I may have been wary, even slightly sceptical, Tam was definitely the idealist. She was, by God, going to get this country moving again. America was once more going to lead, she declared, not follow. No defensive Fortress America claptrap. Hers would be nothing less than a full-scale assault, intended to win back and keep a solid manufacturing base here, toe-to-toe with the world.

Since no overall American programme existed to rescue industries now being killed by foreign competition, she was going to do it herself, create a coordinated battle plan for our strategic sectors. Backed by Noda's Japanese billions, she was about to try to redeem this country's future, leading us back to number one. She also was quick to add she had no intention of merely copying Japan's famous management techniques. Japanese industry, she insisted, hadn't invented long-term planning, sound capital investment, dedication. What they did over there these days was what the US used to do. The American work ethic was alive and well; it was just temporarily on the wrong side of the globe. She was about to bring it home again.

Maybe she could. One major impediment at least would be out of the way. Since the companies Dai Nippon was taking over would no longer have to answer to a lot of fickle fund managers every three months, they could start investing for the longer term. Also a lot of unnecessary fat was going to be sliced out of upper management. If things went as planned, Dr Tamara Richardson and Dai Nippon were about to become the ruthless architects of a new corporate America.

Unless . . . well, there seemed no reason not to take things at face value, at least for now. DNI's new Industrial Management Section on the twelfth floor had already begun filling up with young Tokyo University graduates, guys who embodied the work ethic in human guise. They meant business. Nobody was sipping coffee and critiquing last night's rerun of _Dynasty_. I got the definite impression that one of the unsmiling whiz kids in Noda's handpicked cadre could chew up about five American MBAs for breakfast. Tam currently had them working overtime putting together a reorganisation plan for an outfit in Boston, one of their new acquisitions, which I guess I'd better call XYZ. The previous week Dai Nippon had purchased some twenty-four per cent of its stock, presently at a historic low, and she was planning to make the company her showcase turnaround.

Stock in hand, she'd buckled down with her new staff and using DNI's analytical machinery confirmed some alarming suspicions. It turned out XYZ was practically a terminal case, living at the moment off its real estate assets, which were being systematically dribbled away to mask heavy losses. Layoffs would be next.

By Thursday of the second week, however, she'd put together a restructuring, including some painful austerity, that might just salvage the company and its American jobs. She went home that night feeling quite proud of herself, and Friday she flew up to Boston for her first official conference with XYZ's chief executive officer.

Since a quarter of a company's shares gives the holder reasonably high recognition, the CEO was understandably nervous about who exactly had acquired a fourth of his company inside a week and a half. He appeared at Logan with his Rolls limo to receive Dr Richardson personally.

She explained right off that she was there merely to pass along a few of DNI's recommendations. She took one look at the Rolls and added that, for example, one of the first was going to be to divest all limos forthwith, along with the new fifteen-million-dollar Gulfstream IV he'd bought for weekend fishing trips down in the Keys, and direct the proceeds towards capital investment.

From there on things progressed pretty much as might be expected. By the time they reached his panelled office she had been obliged to explain that his options were either (1) to get in line or (2) to watch DNI pick up another thirty per cent of his company's OTC shares, then march him and his golden parachute past a stockholders' vote they would call to review his career options. After that she had claim to his unalloyed attention.

It was a tough Friday. After she flew back late, she dropped by the office to pick up a few things and fill me in on how it went.

'Good. You're still here.' She popped her head around my office door.

'Who won? The Christians or the lions?'

'Want to hear about it?' She came on in and dropped her briefcase on the desk.

'Wouldn't miss it for the world.'

'Matt, you should have seen the look on that man's face.' She clicked open the case and pulled out the action plan she'd developed for XYZ. She was exhausted but still wired. 'These CEOs forget it's shareholders who own the companies and pay their salaries. They start thinking they're little Caesars.'

'Hey, those are the kinds of operators who used to be my clients. Believe me, I know the type.'

She then proceeded to give me the rundown. Outfit XYZ specialised in high-tech widgets it sold in the US, Latin America and Europe. Problem: their widgets cost too much, broke down more than they should, and consequently folks didn't tend to buy them the way they once did. As a result XYZ had dropped about five million last quarter and (unbeknownst to its workers) was currently on the verge of closing two of its three US plants and exporting the assembly operation someplace where it could exploit two-dollar labour, a move that would tank just over a thousand American jobs. Management says, gee, that's tragic and awards itself another year-end financial tribute.

Dr Richardson had just dropped a bomb in the playpen. First off, she told them, XYZ's damned widgets cost too much not because American workers are overpaid, but because its assembly plants were a candidate for the Smithsonian. Therefore, starting immediately, short-term profits as well as dividends and all management compensation would be slashed and the resulting capital, together with a new offering of long-term corporate equities, would be invested in automating its facilities and retraining workers. There would, in fact, only be workers in future, since all freeloading middle managers, attorneys and drones with titles like 'administrative assistant' were to be terminated. She gave them a list.

Henceforth, she went on, management would begin planning ten years ahead, not three months. XYZ would concern itself with world competition then, not now, and it would develop a substantially more diversified product line to cushion slumps. As part of that shift, it would double the budget for R & D immediately and expand the lab. Innovation would once again be brought to the product stage fast and adapted quickly to world markets. XYZ's new focus would be on making its market share grow in the decade ahead, which also meant cracking down on quality and halving the current customer-be-damned response time on deliveries and service. Concerning those last items, product managers would now be required to address customers' complaints personally. She figured that in itself would turn around XYZ's substantial quality-control debacle overnight.

Finally, there would be an immediate crash programme to rectify XYZ's costly illusion that English was the worldwide language of business. These days, she explained, the language of business is the one your customer speaks. Accordingly all XYZ's overseas operatives would be required to enrol in intensive language training, including formal study of the history and social customs of their territory.

'Sounds like you let him have it with both barrels. Keep on like this and the US of A may never be the same.'

'That's the idea. One company down and about three thousand to go.'

What's that saying about a journey of miles and miles starting with the first step? Well, she'd taken the step. The future lay ahead.

'Hey, can I buy you a drink?' I was winding up the day, the week. 'You've earned it.'

'Like nothing better.' She was repacking her briefcase. 'Matt, I'm having the time of my life. All the things I've always wanted to do. This is like a fantasy come true. We're going to pull this off, wait and see.'

'Could be.' I was switching off the lights in my office. 'Tell you something though, Doctor. I keep wondering what will happen when Noda gets through with us.'

'Thoughts?' She glanced back.

'Well, after Japan takes over half the companies in this country and starts running them right, then what?' We were headed for the security doors. 'But maybe we ought to talk about that some other time. And place.'

'I'll think about it tomorrow. Just now I'm bushed.'

'Tomorrow, in case you've lost count, is Saturday. Don't know about you, but I'm taking the day off. The hell with Japanese business hours. My daughter comes this weekend.' We were saluted by the heavies in the security airlock, then the doors opened. 'Matter of fact, we're going to eat somewhere down in Soho tonight. Care to join us? Be warned it'll be mostly soy by-products and brown rice.'

'I'd love to meet her.' She looked at me. 'Matthew Walton with a daughter. My God.' She laughed. 'Sorry, Matt, but you really don't seem the father type.'

'Amy's mother said approximately the same thing as she was packing her bags. But I'm now undergoing intensive on-the-job father training. Fact is, I'd planned to knock off around Christmas and take her down to our place in the islands, though now I'm not sure there'll be time.'

'Sounds very fatherly. You should go.'

'I'm still hoping to.' I looked her over again. 'Well, the hell with it, why mince words? Tell me, Tam, how's your love life these days?'

She burst out laughing again. 'You haven't changed a bit. Not at all.'

'Spare the commentary, OK? Just stick to the question.'

'Excuse me, counsellor. The honest answer is it's non-existent, which you surely must know, since I'm here every night till midnight just as you are.' She examined me pointedly. 'Matthew, could this conceivably be construed as a proposition? To a horny bone-tired woman in her moment of mental fatigue?'

'It might be a tentative gesture in that direction. I'm a slow mover.'

'You always were.' She finished buttoning her coat. 'What time's dinner?'

'I'll pick up Amy and buzz you. Give us an hour.'

'Think she'll like me? Some stranger competing for Dad's atten-tion.'

'If she does, it'll be a first.' I pushed the button on the ele-vator.

Guess what. Matthew Walton barely got a word in edgewise

the entire night. Then around eleven, in the cab headed home, Amy whispered to me she thought Dr Richardson was 'kinda neat'. Was she gonna be my new girlfriend?

Tell you, it's not always simple, learning to be a father.

FIFTEEN

Over the next couple of weeks I began to wonder if the scenario wasn't going a little too smoothly. Everything about Noda's set-up seemed surprisingly pat. The answers came too easily. Was it all really what it seemed?

I should also add that in the fortnight since Tam's first contact with America's shell-shocked industrialists, the situation had not gone unnoticed in Washington. Tuesday of the second week Jack O'Donnell called and left a message downtown with Emma, asking if I could arrange a meeting for him with the elusive Matsuo Noda. Although I'd tried to keep Jack informed as to developments, he still wanted to confront America's New Age maker face-to-face.

'Walton,' he said when I got back to him, 'I just heard your guy's too "busy" to meet the press, but maybe he'd chat with a close, longtime friend of his American attorney. That's me, in case you didn't recognise the description. Why not try and get me in to see him?'

'You're dreaming, Jack.' I told him that a US senator was about the last person Matsua Noda would be interested in meeting just now. 'Don't hold your breath, but I'll bring it up and see what he says.'

And what do you know! Noda declared that nothing would please him more. Naturally there had to be a few ground rules about confidentiality – this was after all a delicate corporate situation – but otherwise he'd be delighted to chat. You could have knocked me over with a feather.

Thus around 2.00 p.m. Thursday, Jack O'Donnell arrived at the new twelfth-floor operation, ready to get the truth or by God know the reason why. After he made his way past our Uzi-outfitted reception, I brought him on through the floor and

208

introduced him to Dr Richardson. Jack knew of her writings and hit the ground running, asking who, why, when, where, etc., but before he could get any real answers, Noda appeared and took over.

O'Donnell confided later that his first impression of Matsuo Noda matched perfectly my description of the man – every bit central casting's image of the in-charge Japanese honcho. After the usual routine pleasantries, Jack said he'd like to record their talk. Noda politely demurred, saying recording instruments stifled his spontaneity, then proceeded to laud Jack's own articles and speeches urging American industry to get its house in order. Senator Jack O'Donnell, he declared, was a visionary American statesman.

Jack accepted this praise warily, then asked if he could maybe have a peek at the computer operation on the floor below, the analytical armoury I'd told him about. Again Noda begged off, claiming he'd be honoured to guide the esteemed senator's tour personally, but surely they'd both prefer to postpone that until such time as they had the leisure to review the operation in detail.

Jack sensed, and I did too, that he was getting a polite runaround, so he decided to get down to business. He clicked open his briefcase and took out a notebook.

'Mr Noda,' he began, 'there's been considerable speculation in Washington this past couple of weeks regarding the specific intent of Japan's sudden heavy involvement in America's high-tech sector. My subcommittee has monitored foreign investment here for a number of years and frankly I've never seen anything remotely like what's now underway. I'd appreciate an informal briefing, unless you wish to open the regrettable possibility of a formal subpoena to appear before our subcommittee.'

Whereupon Jack received the first whoosh of what soon blossomed into a roomful of aerosol bullshit. Noda started with some malarkey about the great tradition of economic cooperation between our peoples, advanced to balderdash about Japan's desire to share her resources with the world's less fortunate, then outdid himself with triple-distilled crapola about the timeless trust and regard his country's ordinary citizens cherished in their hearts for our Christian nation (which had merely torch-bombed and nuked them a few decades past). Worst of all, Jack had to sit there and listen. I've never seen the guy so uncomfortable.

Clearly Noda intended to give him pure *tatemae*, soothing generalities that added up to zilch. The man was, by God, going to do exactly what he wanted, all of which was perfectly legal, so he didn't really see any point in drawing a picture for the US Senate.

Finally Jack just closed his notebook. 'Let me put this differently. I understand that your objectives are not merely acquisition, but also an attempt to rejuvenate US business. Beginning, I take it, with the lacklustre segments of our high-tech sector?'

'We hope to offer suggestions from time to time that may prove helpful.' Noda just sat there like a sphinx. 'Perhaps I can offer an example. As you doubtless know, Senator, Japanese firms build plants overseas these days primarily to be more competitive in those foreign markets. You Americans, however, are moving your manufacturing abroad now mainly to compete with foreign goods here at home in your own market. You appear to think it as comparable, but of course it is not. What you are doing is exporting your own jobs. Your strategy is defensive, ours is offensive.'

Jack looked him squarely in the eye. 'Quite frankly I must tell you that not everyone in Washington these days trusts Japan's "offensive" in international trade. I for one would be very interested in knowing exactly why Japan has chosen to invest billions of dollars in keeping America's manufacturing alive. Particularly when so much of it is competitive with your own.'

'Yes, Senator, I realise you Americans prize frankness.' He wasn't giving an inch. 'Very well. Quite honestly, no one in Japan believes it is in the interest of the Free World to allow your industrial base to continue its current decline. Our economic condition is linked to yours, like the vital organs of Siamese twins. We cannot afford to let you atrophy. For one thing, you are our only defence shield since we have none of our own. I might also add, though it is a comparatively lesser concern, you are Japan's primary customer.'

'So what you're proposing – if you'll permit me to paraphrase – is to take certain of our strategic industries, the ones in trouble, by the neck and institute the management, investment and research necessary to keep them competitive.'

Noda just smiled. 'Dai Nippon expects to offer occasional advice in the spirit of friendly cooperation. Which is why,' he went on, 'I am so happy to have this opportunity to review our programme with someone such as yourself. Your understanding of America's industrial malaise has not gone unnoticed by those Japanese who take the longer view, who worry about world economic stability.'

Jack tugged at his silk tie and nodded his thanks. Then Noda continued.

'You will be pleased to know I have been in contact with the Japanese trade organisations that have political action committees, or PACs as you call them, in Washington. Last year we distributed over fifty million dollars . . . at least if you believe the Senate Foreign Relations Committee's staffers . . . in an effort to clarify misunderstandings about Japan's trade and investment position here.' He smiled. 'That averages out to about a million dollars per state, to take a somewhat clinical view. Of course I will try to use my influence to see what our PACs can do to help you next fall.'

'Mr Noda, your expression of support is, naturally, appreciated.' Jack was turning politician again. 'However, you should be aware of Section 441(e) of the Federal Election Campaign Act, which states that "no foreign national shall make a contribution, or impliedly promise to make a contribution, in connection with any federal public office." I don't think this discussion is proper.'

'That law says nothing about PACs of duly incorporated American subsidiaries of foreign-owned organisations, Senator. For example, Sony of America and a coalition of Japanese investors recently contributed hundreds of thousands to legislators of Florida and California to encourage the defeat of those states' unfair unitary taxes on foreign-owned companies. Sometimes it's necessary to remind your federal and state governments that Japanese investment can be very problematical in an uncongenial environment.' He smiled. 'Americans investing overseas have a long history of making their interests known to those governments; why should Japanese businessmen be expected to do otherwise?' All of a sudden Noda glanced at his watch, rose abruptly, and bowed. 'Well, the afternoon seems to have slipped away from us. I wish you to know I am extremely honoured you've taken time from your undoubtedly busy schedule to visit with us, Senator. It has been most pleasant.'

He shook hands with Jack as he continued. 'Of course I have not yet had the opportunity to review the thinking of the man expected to oppose you in next fall's Senate contest. I believe he is Representative Mark Reynolds, is he not?'

Jack's polite smile sort of froze on his face.

'But I'm sure I will,' Noda proceeded blandly. 'Again let me stress that voices such as yours are important. There are so few opinion-makers in America, individuals such as Dr Richardson and yourself, who have the receptivity to appreciate the importance of Dai Nippon's programme and its objectives.'

I quickly offered to show the distinguished Senator to the door, hoping I wouldn't need that Christmas-gift dog muzzle. He was still closing his briefcase as we passed the guards, a couple of guys who looked like the heavies in an old Bruce Lee karate epic. Click, we were in the elevator, click, we were headed down.

'Good Christ!' He exploded. Before he could say anything else, I waved for silence. Around here the walls probably had ears. (Shortly thereafter I discovered I'd underestimated even that.)

In minutes we were on Third Avenue, autumn wind in our hair, with O'Donnell positively awestruck by Matsuo Noda's balls.

'Matt, did I hear what I thought I did?' His eyes were grim.

'That he's got X million bucks that say you get retired if you fuck with him?'

'My reading was, I play ball with him and his crowd and he'll write a blank cheque for my campaign next year. I cross him and

I'll be watching the Mark Reynolds show every night on prime time right through election day.' He was livid. 'Matt, take my advice and get out of this thing. That bastard thinks this country's for sale. If he expects me to run interference for him on the Hill while he gears up for World War III, he's making a big mistake.'

'Jack, I can't quit now. Who else is going to keep an eye on this guy? Besides, he'd never let me. I know too much.'

'So what? He's got to be stopped.'

'Look, if you're so worried, then deliver a major speech on the Senate floor. About all these Japanese billions rolling in, absorbing companies, with a lot of *samurai* fanning out to take names and kick ass across the boardrooms of America. It ought to get picked up by the *Nightly News*. Then we'll see what the country wants to do about it.'

The problem, obviously, was what *could* the country do about it? And more than that, where would it eventually lead? Did anybody — Tam Richardson included — seriously believe this was merely a temporary helping hand? History had a practice of going in one direction, forward. So after Noda had acquired a lot of our high-tech outfits, maybe even kept them from going the way of Mostek and others, what next? More and more I was beginning to wonder if this was really preferable to our blundering along as best we could on our own.

After gazing at the sky a minute, he declared he was going to do exactly what I'd said. Blow the whistle. He was about to write a speech that would be read the length of America, maybe even in the White House — unless, as Henderson claimed, nobody there these days read anything but Teleprompters. Nobody was going to buy off Jack O'Donnell.

I watched as he bulldozed a matron and her fur-collared pooch out of the way to grab the next cab for his midtown office. On the way back through the lobby I stopped off and grabbed a copy of *Time*. Had we made the weeklies yet?

Yep. Lead article, all about how the Japanese loved investing here. Going up in the elevator, though, I happened to flip past a profile of some recently disappeared luminary in the academic world, the guy who was supposed to have been the father of artificial intelligence. It occurred to me the piece might be of interest to Tam. She'd been so busy she was probably out of touch.

When I got back up to twelve, Noda was gone. Vanished almost as though he hadn't been there. I wanted to huddle with Tam about his evasive new song and dance, but since I was holding the magazine, I showed her the item. The rest of what happened you can probably guess. She *had* been out of touch.

'Oh, my God, Allan!'

'Friend of yours? I'm sorry.'

'Nobody told me.' She grabbed it and quickly skimmed the article. Finally she headed for her office. 'I've got to call Sarah.'

'Tam.' I caught her arm. I'd finally made the connection. 'I think I already know the story.' Then I recounted Henderson's bizarre tale.

That was the first time though not the last that I saw Tam Richardson look scared. She obviously knew something I didn't.

'Matthew, something is very, very wrong.'

'Just repeating what I heard.' I looked at her, now twisting the magazine in her hands, and decided to press. 'Is there more to this than you're telling me?'

'I don't know.' She glanced around. 'I really don't want to talk about it here.'

'Whatever you say.' I paused. 'How well did you know him?'

'He had dinner at my apartment not more than a couple of months ago.' She tossed down the magazine. 'And he asked me to do something for him.'

'Did you?' Don't know why I asked. It just seemed relevant.

'No. I guess you could say I did just the opposite. Now it all makes me wonder if . . . if maybe it has some connection with . . .' Her voice trailed off.

'What? What connection?'

'Nothing.' She was starting to clam up.

She didn't say anything more. And, so far as I know, that phone call never got made.

Besides, something else occurred that night to occupy her mind. When she got home, she picked up her mail and decided to crash. She'd been so busy she still hadn't finished with all the odds and ends that had stacked up during the Tokyo trip, but she was too knocked-out to bother. She poured herself a glass of white wine, quickly checked the mail and was getting ready for bed when she first noticed the light flashing on her answering machine. For a minute she considered just letting it wait. There was nobody she wanted to talk with who wouldn't still be there in the morning. But finally curiosity got the upper hand, and she pushed 'Play'.

There was only one message. In Japanese.

Ms Akira Mori wanted to see her Friday morning, at the DNI offices. It wasn't a request; it was a summons.

Wait one minute! Mori? When did *she* get into town? And more to the point, where did Mori-san come off summoning Tam Richardson for a command appearance? She had another glass of wine and finally went to bed wondering who exactly was now running the show at DNI.

Friday late she awoke still thinking about Allan. What was going on? She was beginning to get worried and maybe a little frightened. Finally, just before lunchtime, she got her briefcase and hailed a cab for uptown.

After she cleared the checkpoint at the twelfth-floor elevators, she spotted Mori-san, right there in the midst of the action. This woman wastes no time, she told herself. Mori, an incongruous peacock of designer elegance in the midst of the bustling short-haired staff, was poring over a stack of printouts assembled on a desk in the centre of the floor. Meanwhile, the office was going full tilt: the green print of CRT screens glowed; printers hummed all around; data bleeped between terminals; and staffers were hurrying over selected documents for Mori to review. Also, since heavy buys were underway, the latest SEC filings (required when one entity acquires more than five per cent of the stock of a given company) were being readied.

As it happens, I was already on hand too, over in Noda's office where we were going over some paperwork. The day's news as far as I was concerned also was Mori-san. She'd appeared bright and early, held a closed-door confab with Noda, proceeded to do some photocopying (herself), then commandeered an office.

By purest coincidence I was doing some copying of my own round about then and ended up on the copy line right behind her, inhaling her perfume. Next an odd thing happened. As we all sometimes do when rushed, she'd snatched up her copies while the last original was still on the machine. Then she asked me if I wanted regular size or legal. Legal, I said, and she reached to flip the switch. As she did, though, she accidentally clicked the 'print' button with those long fingernails, whereupon she stalked off, rummaging through her copies and forgetting the original.

Not for long. Two seconds later she was back to claim it, but by that time an unauthorised copy was lying in the output bin. I didn't even see it. However, when I scooped up my own pages a minute later, mixed in with them was a sheet listing some names and numbers with REVISIONS lettered across the top. I started to toss it, then paused to glance over the names for a moment.

Hang on, everybody, this is very out of line. That's when I decided to slip it into my briefcase.

When Mori saw Tam come in, she quickly stacked the printouts she was reviewing into a neat pile, then beckoned her towards the far corner of the floor. Tam noticed that Mori's new office was at the opposite end of the building from Noda's.

'I understand Noda-san has appointed you director of this division.' Mori was ushering Tam into the office, all the while running her fingers nervously through her sculptured black hair. 'Congratulations.'

Not exactly a great opener. It sounded even harsher in Japanese, since it was so at odds with the usual polite greetings.

'I've been hired to do a job, Mori-san, and I intend to do it.'

'Sō desu ne,' Mori concurred in Japanese, her voice a trifle strained. Tam thought she looked a bit bleary-eyed after her flight in from Tokyo, but there were no half measures about the woman. She was all business in a prim silk suit shading to grey with a bright blue scarf tied at the neck. She wore high heels, but they didn't slow her brisk stride as she paced around her desk. 'I am sure you will do it well. I would like you to know I am prepared to assist you at every step.'

Well, Tam had a pretty clear idea of how she intended to proceed, which didn't really include a lot of assistance from Akira Mori. What exactly had Noda been telling this woman? Maybe, she mused, Mori-san just hadn't been fully brought up to speed.

'I noticed that you're reviewing our analytical sheets,' Tam continued. 'Those are the firms we're going to begin restructuring first.'

'And if you do not receive the desired cooperation? What will you do then?' Mori asked evenly, as though she didn't already know the answer.

'We'll just keep up stock acquisition till we have whatever's needed. Also, I intend to appoint a representative to sit on the board of directors, to monitor performance and make sure our programme is implemented.'

'That is my understanding as well.' Mori went on, 'And concerning the matter of who will be assigned—'

'I've just finished putting together a list of management experts. They're dedicated people. Most of them will probably help us for a small honorarium instead of their usual consulting fees.'

'These personnel are an area I wish to discuss with you,' Mori pushed ahead, almost as though not listening. That was when Tam realised she was finally getting around to the real agenda of the meeting. 'It is our opinion that, at this stage, the heavy involvement of Americans in that capacity would be counter-productive.'

'"Our opinion"?' Tam didn't like the sound of this. 'Who exactly is "our"?'

'I have reviewed Dai Nippon's programme in some detail with . . . the interested parties in Tokyo.' Mori appeared to be making an announcement. 'They have concurred that at this stage it would be more efficient if we assigned our own specialists to assist in the management of these companies.'

'Your own specialists?' Now Tam was starting to bristle. 'Just whom do you have in mind?'

'Industrial experts such as Kenji Asano, for example, may be involved.' She continued, 'We have a great reservoir of talent to choose from, particularly within the Ministry of International Trade and Industry.'

'MITI?' Tam stared at her, dumbfounded. She couldn't believe her own ears. That was like calling in a fox to fortify your henhouse. 'You've got to be joking.'

'The decision was made last week.' Mori fixed her coldly. 'Noda-san has been informed and he finds the suggestion . . . acceptable.'

'Well, I don't,' Tam flared. 'It's outrageous.'

'There is something you must understand, Dr Richardson,' Mori continued in Japanese. 'The management of a company should represent its ownership. Since Dai Nippon will be holding what amounts to a controlling interest in these firms, we are obliged to assist them using whatever international specialists we feel are most qualified to contribute. For now we believe that the expertise in our Ministry of International Trade and Industry is most appropriate since it has guided corporate growth in Japan for many years with undeniable success.'

'That's irrelevant.' Tam steamed. 'First, most MITI executives don't necessarily understand American business. And second, MITI has no right involving itself in the operation of our industry. It's a flagrant conflict of interest.'

'There I must disagree with you. On your first point, many Japanese firms have begun manufacturing here and have an excellent record of labour relations and management success. As to your second point, using specialists trained by MITI is simply the most efficient way to transfer Japanese expertise.'

'It won't be allowed.'

'Why shouldn't it be? Any people we bring here will be on leave of absence. Hence they will no longer have any official ties to the Japanese government. No law prevents us from appointing whoever we wish.'

Ouch, Tam thought. She's right. Nothing could stop Dai

Nippon from restructuring the boards of directors of the companies in which it held a voting majority of shares. In fact, several Japanese firms had already taken over and reopened the manufacturing facilities of some of the very companies MITI's 'targeting' had decked only a few years before, bringing in Japanese board members as part of the deal. What's more, Americans loved it. Governors were falling over themselves to lure more Japanese plants and joint ventures to their states.

'Does Noda-San understand the significance of bringing in MITI personnel?'

'There are many interests to be addressed . . .'

At this point I wandered in, together with Noda, to talk about setting up a meeting that afternoon. We'd been reviewing DNI's plans for a new programme of real estate investment and construction, part of expanding the research or manufacturing facilities of the firms it was now in the process of absorbing.

I passed a pleasantry with Tam, then studied her, puzzled. 'You look a little distressed this morning.'

'I'm receiving an update on a change in our programme.' Tam glared back at Mori, then turned to Noda. 'What's this about bringing in people from MITI?'

Noda smiled, but he looked a trifle uncomfortable. 'Think of it as a temporary measure.' He nodded towards Mori, then looked back at Tam. 'We always like to operate by consensus. And that consensus among the fund managers who have joined us appears to be that our investments should initially be monitored by our own people.'

'I thought *this* office was going to be in charge of determining who our people would be, not somebody in MITI.' Tam fixed him coldly, then turned on me. 'Did you know anything about this?'

'Bringing in honchos from MITI? News to me.' I examined Noda. 'I understood the management end of this was going to be directed by Dr Richardson.'

He was smiling again. 'But it will be. She will continue to meet with the CEOs of the firms we intend to assist to provide our preliminary analysis of their operations and she will be with us every step we take.'

'It hardly sounds that way.' Tam was boiling. 'The way it looks now, I set up a reorganisation plan, then MITI's people come in and take over.'

'Merely for consultation, Dr Richardson. I assure you.' He glanced uncomfortably at Mori-san. Both Tam and I had the same hunch at that point: Noda's backers had started to get a little edgy about his investments, so they'd decided to send in some brass from the Delta Force to keep an eye on things. But you'd never have suspected that as he continued, 'Dr Richardson, surely you must be aware that MITI personnel are not in the habit of, as you phrase it, "taking over". At most MITI merely recommends policies to enhance competitiveness. Furthermore, the individuals we will engage will no longer be associated with MITI. They will merely be specialists in our hire. Their participation will be extremely beneficial, please believe me.'

'If making decisions like this is your idea of consensus, then I don't think much of it.' Tam was getting increasingly wound up. 'And I'll tell you something else. I intend to review the government connections of anyone you bring in. I'm going to have final say.'

'We all want to work together,' Noda continued smoothly. 'Our plans are continuing to evolve. Of course I will insist on full American-Japanese coordination and cooperation at every stage.' He looked squarely at Tam. 'You have my word.'

She glanced over at me, trying her best to keep cool. I was toying with my papers, still posing as a neutral observer, but I was equally puzzled. Why would Japan's Ministry of International Trade and Industry let its people be used to assist American companies? OK, MITI's élite technocrats were probably the cream of Japan's management talent, but they already had their hands full.

More to the point, given MITI's sorry history of rule bending and economic guerrilla warfare, why would it now cooperate in Dai Nippon's plan to restructure the high-tech segment of US manufacturing? I asked Noda point-blank.

'Mr Walton, if you choose to see Japan and the US as competitors, then I suppose you could regard this as our ancient tradition of "giving salt to the enemy".' He smiled awkwardly.

Bullshit. That's what I thought, not what I said, which was nothing.

Tam in the meantime had her own question to chew on. Mori had mentioned Ken Asano. Was he involved too? Since Mori had specifically named him as being on the MITI team that she or somebody now planned to enlist, was this a tip-off that Ken was in with them up to his neck? Was this the 'trust' he'd talked about?

Since Tam looked as if she was getting ready to resign on the spot, I figured a little cooling-off time for everybody might be in order.

'Dr Richardson, if we're about through here, could you help me a minute?' I thumbed towards the open door. 'Tanaka wants you to approve the final set-up for the partitions.'

I quickly discovered I was wrong about the idea she would quit. As we worked our way past the computer terminals and stacks of printouts, retreating towards the centre of the floor, she declared war. 'MITI or Mori or whoever's behind this is going to have a fight on their hands. We don't need them involved.'

'Hate to be the bearer of bad news, but I think we're being kept in the dark about a lot of what's cooking.' I kept my voice low, scarcely above a whisper, as the Japanese staff milled in and out. 'There's a sheet of paper in my briefcase that I'd like to go over with you. Yet another example of the curious new developments around this place.'

She poured herself a cup of green tea from the large urn stationed in the middle of the floor. 'What do you mean?'

'We'll talk about it later.' I poured some tea for myself. 'I think something's gone haywire.'

That startled her, and she began to tune in. 'Things are pretty haywire now.'

'This may be even worse. I came across something a while ago that doesn't add up.' I looked at her. 'I think we ought to talk about it.'

'Now?'

'Not here. How about tonight?'

'Can't. There's a damned faculty dinner I have to attend.'

'Then tomorrow night?'

'Where?'

'What would you say to my place downtown? I think you live right around the corner from me.'

'This has to be strictly business, Matt.'

'Guaranteed.' I raised my palm.

'Well, I've got a lot of work—'

'Shall we make it for seven?' I was handing her my card, address and number thereon. 'The cocktail hour?'

She was still glaring at Mori's office as she absently took it. 'Well . . . all right.' She glanced back. 'Seven.'

'See you there.'

Jack O'Donnell's speech, to be delivered to the Senate that Tuesday, sort of slipped to the back of my mind. Maybe it shouldn't have. After getting back to his office that afternoon he dictated about three versions before he had it the way he wanted it. Friday morning he messengered a copy down to my office, and I can tell you it was a beauty. He'd got it all and he'd got it right.

Later Friday, however, he received a phone call from Matsuo Noda. After the usual preliminaries, saying how much he'd enjoyed their meeting, Mr Noda confided he was calling as a personal favour to the Senator, since they'd hit it off so well the previous day. Turns out he'd just been talking to the CEOs of various Japanese outfits scheduled to set up manufacturing operations in some of the rust-belt mill towns in upstate New York. Here was the distressing development: seems they were all of a sudden taking another look at sunny Tennessee. The problem was, they were upset by the anti-Japanese tone a lot of New York publications were taking these days – Japan-bashing in the *Times* editorial pages, things like that. Noda, however, felt all this was very short-sighted of those Japanese investors; and he wondered if Senator O'Donnell would like him to put in a word for the Empire State. Pause. He hated to mention this, but people were even talking of closing certain Japanese-operated factories already in place, such as that big one in Elmira, Jack's hometown, and moving them south. But he thought threats such as that were very impolite and he was hoping he could find time to straighten the whole thing out.

Like I said, it would have been a hell of a speech.

SIXTEEN

That Saturday turned out to be the day when winter descended abruptly and with rare vengeance. Remember we're only talking mid-December, still a dozen full shopping days till you know what, but it could have been the depths of January. After things kicked off with what seemed a foot of snow around three, the elements really started to unload. Everything from sleet in historic proportions to a wind-chill that would have frosted the horns off a Bexar County billy goat.

While I waited for Tam, I battened down the garden, covered the outdoor furniture, and prudently provisioned the larder with a flagon of Remy antifreeze. Ben in the meantime was lumbering around downstairs, eyeing the snow-covered garden with an air of disgruntlement. The universe had turned unacceptable, something he never greeted with equanimity. I decided to try to divert his misery by hauling him up on the long Country French dining table and combing some of the knots out of his shag. When that merely reinforced his overall gloom, however, I called it quits, located a consoling rawhide stick for him to gnaw and poured a brandy. It was along about then, shortly after nightfall, that Tam finally appeared.

A cab with snow chains dropped her off (she'd come directly from the office, which Noda had just shut down for the weekend) and I helped her navigate the sleet-covered steps. I got the immediate sense that her first impression of my living quarters was unchanged from the old days. In spite of all the art, armour and antiques, the place had a poignant rootlessness about it. Boys like toys; they just get more expensive as the bank account grows. Also, since she'd been in the man game long enough to spot a divorce-rebound case a mile off, she probably had me figured from the start: part of that army of emotional paraplegics in our feckless day and age.

After the MITI twist, however, I suppose she was ready to consult with somebody concerning the direction things were headed. I warmly invited her downstairs to the sisal-carpeted den just off the garden and dumped some logs in the fireplace. Next I pulled out a few discs – Mendelssohn seemed about right for some reason – and offered to whip up a batch of margaritas. 'Twould be, I dared to hope, a long winter's eve. Alas, she said no thanks, a club soda and lime would do fine. Looked as though I would be working barehanded, without aid of that universal socialiser, distilled spirit, so I rustled up a Perrier then poured another snifter of brandy for myself.

Since she appeared exhausted, my first suggestion was she kick off her shoes and get comfortable. No argument.

After settling in, shoes off and feet to the fire, she announced she was ready to hear what I'd come up with.

Before an awkward silence could grow, I snapped open my briefcase.

'Dr Richardson, in keeping with the ground rule that this is a formal business meeting, let me introduce my first agenda item.' I flashed her my best smile, then pulled out the purloined page. 'This is part of the paperwork Mori seems to have brought with her. I don't understand too well what it's all about, but my first impression is that somebody has decided to do some major tinkering with your programme. Take a look at this and give me an opinion.' I passed it over.

She glanced down, then back at me. 'Are you supposed to be bringing DNI documents home?'

That was her first reaction, swear to God.

'Look, this just accidentally got in with some of my photo-copies. All it is is a list of companies. And I didn't want to talk about it there in the office.' I reached over and ran my finger down the string of firms, then to several columns of numbers off to the right. 'The question is, what are *these* outfits suddenly doing on DNI's buy list?'

She studied it a second, looked around the room and said exactly nothing.

'Doesn't that seem at all strange to you?' I finally spoke up.

'As I understand the plan, you want to shift more corporate funding into research in the companies you're buying into? I do have it right, don't I?'

She nodded.

'OK, then you're with me so far. But take a look at this.' I indicated the column of numbers. 'That's the current research budget for these firms – it says so right up there on the top. Presumably these figures came out of the analytical set-up down on eleven. Does anything about those figures seem out of line?'

She looked at it, her eyes widening then narrowing.

'Well, I don't know what this sheet is all about.' She glanced up. 'These companies aren't part of our buys.'

'Got news for you. I think they just made the team.' I pointed to the heading. 'See that – "ACQUISITION SCHEDULE: RE-VISIONS".'

When she said nothing, *nada*, I continued, 'But you're right; they weren't on the *original* list. The reason being, I would surmise, that they didn't need any of this so-called management R_x you guys are supposed to be cooking up. Look at that one, and that one. Even I know enough to realise those outfits are operating with a real cash surplus right now, have plenty of R & D funding already and hence are doing just fine, thank you. The figures, in fact, are right over there in that column on the right.'

'Matt, we don't know what this is for.'

'True, true. So let's just play pretend. And to make it fun, let me show you something else.' I rummaged through my briefcase some more, finally extracting another paper. 'I copied a corresponding page from the file on current buys.'

I laid it alongside the first.

She picked up the second sheet, checked it over. 'I helped compile this list.'

'Then maybe you'll see what I'm saying? Format's the same. The only difference is, some of the dogs have been dropped and replaced by some very well-run corporations.'

'You're right about that. All high-tech, heavy research investment.'

Progress? The first scale to fall from her eyes?

'Then let's play another round of this "pretend" game. As I understand it, you and yours put together this original list of companies for one main reason: lousy management. But all of a sudden the outfits in the worst shape on list number one have disappeared on list number two. Meaning, I would assume, that they're no longer part of the programme, at least as it's laid out on this revised version Mori must have brought in from Tokyo.'

'What are you trying to say?'

For chrissake, what did she think I was trying to say?

'Oh, nothing much, I suppose. Except that it looks to me like somebody's just knifed your programme in the back. All of a sudden DNI's going to start buying outfits that already *have* good management, not to mention heavy research commitments. So what exactly is anybody supposed to be doing to help them along?' I paused. 'Maybe a better question is, who removed those others, the ones now winging it on a hope and a prayer?'

She laid down the two pages side by side and began to compare them in more detail, a finger here, a finger there. But strictly no comment.

Along about then Ben got up and checked out the sleet-covered garden, then lumbered back and plopped down beside us, clearly expecting a pat for diligence in the line of duty. She remarked that English sheepdogs always reminded her of a big flotaki rug. After that put-down she returned to the lists. I hoped the poor guy's sensitive ego wasn't mortally fractured.

Well, she announced finally, my so-called discovery didn't add up to much.

'Matt, I officially have no opinion about this. It could mean anything.' She shrugged. 'Maybe the new twist is to start with the companies that can benefit the most from coordination. Take on the easy job first where the payoff will be greatest. Save the tough ones for later.'

'Oh, sure. Who knows? It could all be very innocent, right? I mean, for all we can tell the moon might really be green cheese.' I wondered what had gotten into her all of a sudden. It was plain as day what was happening. But instead of congratulating me on my sleuthing, she was turning obtuse.

'Tell me exactly how you got this sheet.'

'Like I said, more or less by accident.' I told her the story again. 'I was about to chuck it, then I took a second to mull it over. That's when I got to wondering why the numbers seemed so inconsistent. Next thing I noticed was the new list of players. All of a sudden the heavens opened. A vision.' I got up to freshen my brandy, then came back. She was still sitting there, maybe too exhausted to think straight. 'But I take it you don't believe my little epiphany means anything?'

'Since I don't know *what* it means, I'm not going to engage in a lot of uninformed speculation.'

Good Christ, I thought, what's happened to all her reputed brilliance?

'You know,' she went on, 'I don't think you should be taking any more documents out of the office. There's a reason for all the security.'

'Hey, back off. I just have boundless curiosity.' I still couldn't fathom her lack of interest ... no, make that hostility. 'Look, I don't claim to understand how birds fly, how fish swim or how this whole damned picture fits together. However, my new, albeit uninformed observation is that Noda and Company are not exactly giving us the fine print on their scenario. Exhibit A: this strange new list.'

'I think some fresh air would be nice.' She rose to her feet, located her shoes, and strolled over to look out at the garden. The sleet and snow was about a foot and a half deep. 'Why don't we go into the back?'

'What?' I stumbled to my feet. 'Do you have any idea ...'

She looked at me a bit funny, then made some hand signals. Huh?

Finally I realised she was telling me she didn't want to say anything more inside the house.

Talk about paranoid! Suddenly the reason for all her hemming and hawing over my little theft came clear. She actually thought we might be bugged! Get serious, lady.

Anyway, she gave me the cool-it sign, then calmly started putting on her coat. Astounded by the possible dimensions of human mistrust, I dug out a sweater from behind the couch and opened the door. She was still nursing that damned designer water.

Ben snapped to alertness and galloped to the door, whereupon he confronted the weather. His strategic decision, executed with lightning speed, was to switch into his patented 'zone defence' surveillance mode against backyard trespassers, which called for staying inside where it was warm. I gave him a pat, freshened his water bowl and followed her out into the snow.

There was a brief lull in the weather. The sky glowed red from all the streetlights, at least what you could see of it through the surrounding brownstones and the leafless ailanthus tree at the back. I looked around as Ben gave the fence one last survey, then plopped down and settled his chin on to his paws with a grunt.

Tam, I suppose, had finally concluded I wasn't pulling some kind of loyalty check for Noda, so that was when she opened the real can of worms.

'How long was she making copies? I mean, you were standing right behind her.'

'Mori? I don't know. Less than a minute.' I examined her, a trifle puzzled. 'Why?'

'How many pages?'

'Probably half a dozen or so.'

She just stood there a moment, gazing up at the sky, then she went back inside, stepping around Ben, and returned with the sheet. 'Did you notice this?' She pointed to the upper right-hand corner.

I took it and strained in the faint light from the back windows. 'It says "129/147".' I looked up. 'You think that means . . .?'

'I think your episode suggests at least two things.' She took back the page. 'The first one is, this is part of a much larger document.'

'With you so far. A hundred and forty-seven pages. And the second?'

'You said she only made half a dozen copies, then overlooked this?' She paused. 'Don't you think Akira Mori can count?'

At that moment the snowy night grew silent as a tomb.

'What are you suggesting?' I finally blurted it out. 'That she left this *on purpose*?'

'Maybe. But I don't have the slightest idea why.'

'Christ, you have a very mistrusting mind.' I slogged on through the snow for a few steps, then turned back. 'I'm convinced it was accidental.'

'All right, let's just say that's a possibility for now. But what we do know for sure is we'd better get our hands on the rest of this.'

'Hey, don't look at me. I'm already in this scam deeper than I ever intended to be. I say we either play their way or cut and run. We start getting too nosy and we could end up on the wrong end of one of those Uzis.'

'Matt, there's something else I noticed about the list. It's ominous.'

'Care to elaborate?' I kicked at the snow.

'Well, not out here. I'm freezing.' She pulled her coat a bit tighter. 'Is there someplace inside where we can talk?'

'I've got an idea. But let's warm up first.' I led the way back in. The fire had died down a bit, so she settled on the floor next to the hearth, the smooth contours of her cheeks golden in the flickering light.

'Sure you won't have a brandy after all? To combat the chill?' The quartet Opus 44, No. 1, was enveloping us, both violins emerging out of the shadows.

She looked up and smiled. 'Maybe it would be nice.'

I fetched it, slid on to the floor next to her, and stretched to stir the coals. Ben sauntered over to keep me honest, plunked down and was immediately out like a light.

'How're we doing for warmth?' I propped the poker against the side of the mantel, then reached over and touched her tangled hair lightly with my fingertips. To my everlasting surprise, she leaned next to me.

'Much better.'

'Maybe we should both bail out right now. Tonight. Why not just go down to my place in the islands and monitor the apocalypse off the satellite dish? Watch MITI eat America.'

Was I joking? Only partially. Down home we have a saying about folks with a certain . . . *je ne sais quoi*. They'd do to ride the river with. In my book Tam was definitely one of the riders.

The fire snapped and startled Ben, who glanced up, checked out the sleet-covered garden, then grimly resumed his snooze. She reached over and gave him a pat. The first time. 'You know, I can't believe MITI is behind all this. I know at least one MITI person myself.'

'You know somebody in MITI?' I was a trifle taken aback. 'Who?'

She stared at the fire. 'His name is Kenji Asano. You wouldn't have heard of him.'

I lay there for a moment listening to the quartet, my memory registers running a quick sort. Then it came to me. Kenji Asano was the MITI guy Henderson said had masterminded Japan's rape of the US semiconductor industry.

'You actually know him?'

'Sure do.' She smiled. 'Very well.'

Shit. I didn't really need to hear this. 'That sounds like a little more than a professional acquaintance.' I looked at her for confirmation.

'A little.'

OK, I thought. Guess we're getting down to the straight story here. Press on. 'Well, I have some news you may not like. This Asano genius personally engineered the destruction of the US industry in RAM chips. Probably the most devastating sneak attack on America since Pearl Harbor.'

She stiffened. 'Who told you that?'

'Let's just say I heard it. So what's this guy doing all of a sudden saving US high-tech industry? He's already cost this country tens of thousands of jobs and literally billions of dollars.'

'I don't believe it. I know Ken. Sure, he works for MITI, but his job is overseeing Japan's own research in supercomputers. He's very proud of their progress.'

Oops. I swirled my snifter. 'Whatever you say. If that's really true, then excuse me. I take it all back.'

She looked up – probably not believing my diplomatic reversal –and watched as I casually slipped my arm around her waist. I couldn't tell if she wanted it to happen or not.

Thinking I might have some momentum going, I reached back and pulled a couple of wide cushions off the couch, stationed them by the fire, then eased us both against them. I tried to do it with naturalness, finesse.

It wasn't happening.

'Matthew, underneath all that unnecessary bluster, which is just as I remember, you're still a half-decent guy, which I also remember. But I don't really think this is a good idea.' She looked at me, her face highlighted in the orange glow of the embers.

'I hope it's not because you have other commitments.' I heard my voice harden. 'Like maybe in Japan.'

'I'm just a little distracted tonight, that's all.' She watched as I trailed a finger around the hard tip of a nipple beneath her shirt. Gently she moved my hand away. 'Don't start.'

'Maybe I can at least get a rain check.' I was retiring from the field, gracelessly.

'It's possible.' She smiled, then gave me a telling glance. 'A while ago you said something about another place.'

My soundproof chamber?

'Right.' I rose. 'We're always open around here for travellers on a frosty night.' I helped her up. 'And for this evening's special introductory offer, there's a hot tub down the hall. Why don't you let me fill it and you can unwind those muscles for a while, Japanese-style or California-style or whatever? Do you good.'

She looked me over a second, then smiled. 'Lots of nice, loud running water?'

'Exactly.'

Off we went to the Italian marble bathroom there off the downstairs bedroom. I'd installed that little indulgence for Joanna back during happier times; these days I used it as the world's largest laundry hamper – ripping it out would have cost a fortune. Jo's revenge, I called the thing.

She marched in, took a look about the room, which had one of those big tubs trimmed in redwood, and said it reminded her of a place near Ise. She did at least have the discretion to omit the circumstances of that occasion.

What happened next sort of shook my cool, my being a good Texas lapsed-Baptist. You see, I'd never bought into the nudity-is-wholesome ethic of the Age of Aquarius. Passed me right by. I mean, where's the fun in life without a little forbidden fruit? But Tam just began chucking her clothes. Everything. Kept going till she'd even doffed her little beige knickers, piling everything one piece at a time in a neat heap on the counter. Just like that. While bold corporate raider Matt Walton stood there in terminal astonishment, grasping the edge of the sink as if it were a life preserver. My nonchalance was an Oscar-winning performance.

Now in the attire God gave her, she calmly inquired if I had any bubble bath.

'Well, ah, sure, I mean, I suppose so, probably somewhere around here. If not, there's probably a box of Tide in the basement.' I groped blindly in the cabinet and my hand fell upon a pink bottle whose label read 'Mr Bubble'. What's this? Then I realised it must have been some suds stashed there by Amy. Bet she saw somebody soaking on TV and concluded that's the way grown-up women behaved. My God, it's in their genes.

Then I turned around.

Tell you one thing, Dr Tamara Richardson was still in great shape. All of her. Was she pulling a tease number on me, or just doing what comes naturally? Sad to say, I fear it was the latter. I guess she'd somehow internalised this Japanese idea that nudity is no big deal.

'Tam' — I finally found my voice — 'you're something else. I know you're smart, and I'm beginning to remember you never were all that retiring. How about refreshing me on a few of the other things I seem to have forgot?'

'I think I wanted to be a boy.' She laughed as she sampled the water with her toe. 'I thought they had all the fun.' Now she was pouring in a test portion of Amy's Mr Bubble. 'Then I found out girls could do anything boys could, but usually better. So I stopped worrying about it.' She stepped in.

'Easy. You're talking to an unreconstructed male chauvinist.'

'What else is new? You all are at heart. At least you have the decency to admit it.' She dumped in the remainder of the pink gunk. Will somebody please tell me why women, all women, go for that stuff? An exaggeration, you say? Ever see one turn it down?

'Hey, I'm trying to deprogram myself, but it's uphill work.' I watched as a perfectly formed breast disappeared beneath the foam. 'I tend to be old-fashioned.'

'I recall all too well.'

'Well, give me a chance.' I leaned back against the sink. 'You know, this striptease isn't helping repress my primal male instincts a whole heck of a lot.'

'Matt, for somebody who's supposed to be an expert on Japan, you've understood very little about us.'

'Us?'

'You know. I'm half and half.' She flashed me a Mona Lisa smile as she was wrapping her hair in a towel. I found myself thinking that at least she shaves her underarms, a minor concession to conventional propriety.

'Well, so what. I'm an equal-opportunity seductionist. That is, when I *get* the opportunity.'

'Not making much headway tonight, I fear.' Another tricky smile. She was starting to drive me distracted.

'Thought you'd never notice.'

'Look, you're an emotional basket case. I've seen plenty.' She looked me over sympathetically. 'Sorry, but I've got enough problems of my very own. You'll have to manage your own salvation.'

'Could be you're just deceived by my sensitive nature.' I leaned against the counter, playing peekaboo with a tan nipple now half-concealed in the bubbles. 'Mistaking it for brain damage.'

'Uh, uh.' She shook her head in the negative. 'I read your gender pretty well.'

I was beginning to get a little annoyed. Who needed this?

'Tell you what, Dr Richardson, for all my putative failings, I do happen to possess a modest allotment of native wit. And my male intuition tells me your dance card is full right now. That same right-brain perception also suggests it has something to do with this MITI honcho Asano.'

'So?'

'So that upsets me for a couple of reasons, only one of which will probably be of any interest to you. I don't think you have an entirely open mind on the possibility MITI or somebody may be about to try and nail this country to the wall. Because if you admitted that, you would also have to admit something you apparently find distasteful to concede about your Prince Charming.' I watched her eyes grow sad. 'Stop me if I cross the line from preaching to meddling – to use a little expression from my youth.'

'Matthew, you've just ceased being nice.' She looked down. 'What do you do if you think you trust somebody and then you find out maybe that trust is . . . misplaced?'

'Old Ecclesiastes, back in Bible times, told us, "In the time of adversity, consider." As advice goes, that's still probably sound value for the dollar. Like for example, you might want to back off and do a little thinking on whether Noda and his crowd have been using you, and me for that matter, like a couple of patsies.'

When she said nothing, I pressed on. 'I walk into the office yesterday, the first thing I hear about is some MITI connection, then tonight I hear about your MITI connection, and it's starting to sound like the same tune. Like maybe these guys have been playing you like a violin.'

'But why me?'

'Credibility. And low profile for MITI's grab. By sending you out to meet the victims, they've thrown the hounds off the scent. Dr Save-American-Industry has come to help. You're so goddamn clean, Tam. Impeccable credentials. You're gold to those guys.' I was set to give her a blast, but I decided to try keeping the lid on for once. 'Maybe a better question than why they chose you is why you went for it. How did they brainwash you?'

235

'Nobody brainwashed me. I still think Noda's being straight. He can think in global terms. That's a rarity.'

'And how about this Asano character? You sure gave me the message to back off when I questioned *his* intentions.'

'Maybe I've been thinking with something besides my head.' She sighed and leaned back. 'But then, maybe not. I have no reason to believe he'd mislead me.'

'Look, I don't know anything about the situation. But I respectfully suggest you ought to reflect on that possibility.' I looked at her. 'By the way, I seem to remember you said there was something else about the list that struck you as odd.'

'It has to do with the *kind* of research being done by those new firms on the list. A pattern.' She paused.

'What pattern?'

'I'd rather not say just yet. Until I'm sure. It's probably just my imagination.'

Something snapped inside me about then. Anger. Tam Richardson, I was rapidly concluding, was being used by those bastards. And as best I could tell, this idealistic woman couldn't let herself believe it. The situation royally pissed me off. Even more when I also suspected this Asano operator had somehow been playing fast and loose with her heartstrings. I decided then and there I wasn't going to let them get away with it.

A strange psychology takes hold of you when you sense you've been temporarily outflanked; I think it's that primal human response somebody once dubbed flight or fight. You realise you've got two choices: you can either stand your ground, or you can make a run for the sidelines. So what to do about Dai Nippon and Noda and Mori and Asano? Right then and there I made a tactical decision. I decided that – like the caveman facing the sabre-toothed tiger – the best defence would be to try to make the beast back off.

More to the point, it wasn't merely Tam that was imperilled. Maybe Henderson's suspicions were right; maybe this was the handshake that turned into a karate flip, the beginning of World War II, Part B. So I figured I owed it to myself and everybody else to at least uncover the truth.

No entity, I've always believed, is unstoppable, no matter how massive. There's always a soft underbelly somewhere. After a while any big organisation gets cocky and makes a blunder. Sometimes, in fact, you can lure them into it. I concluded there was only one way to go head-to-head with Dai Nippon. You want peaches, you shake the tree.

'OK, you've got your theories, I've got mine. But for both our sakes, I think it's time we moved on them.'

'What do you mean?' She looked up.

'I suggest we start with a little information-gathering.' I turned on the hot water again, nice and noisy, then continued. 'What do you say we go up and take a private look around the offices?'

'Tonight?'

'What better time? Weather alert, right? Nobody's there. Should be perfect. We can fast-talk the security, get in and check the place over.'

'And where, exactly, do you propose we look?' She examined me sceptically. 'I'm there every day.'

'How about that new office Mori commandeered for herself? I think we ought to poke around and see what she's got. Maybe try and locate the rest of that document, if nothing else.'

'I'm not sure we ought to be doing anything quite that drastic, at least not just yet.'

'I didn't claim it was approved by Amy Vanderbilt. I just say we ought to give it a shot. If we don't look into this, who will? Maybe we'll find something to explain the so-called pattern you think you see.'

'Matt, for all I know, that may be nothing more than a coincidence. If Noda found out we'd done something like this, the whole ball game would be over.'

'That's the chance we take. Let's just see what we can come up with, OK? Personally, I'm beginning to think Noda and your pal Asano are both world-class con artists.' I poured a little more cognac for us both. 'But whoever's right, we should at least try to find out. Who knows? What if it's becoming a MITI show now, for some purpose neither of us can imagine?'

'All right.' She looked apprehensive for a second, only a

second, and then her eyes hardened. 'You know, Noda and Mori claim I'm Fujiwara ... on my mother's side naturally.' She laughed. 'And you know something else? I feel in my bones that it's true. I believe it. I'm Japanese, Matthew, and I'm proud of that.'

I glanced over at a set of *samurai* armour stationed just outside the bathroom door, glistening enamelled steel. 'Tell you the truth, I'm second to nobody when it comes to admiring Japan's ethic and their guts. But I tend to draw the line at "master race" talk. As a matter of fact, I wouldn't object too strenuously if they did manage to beat us in a fair contest. Hell, we won round one and they were remarkably sporting about it. But what I want is to make sure round two is fought on level ground. No inventing new rules, no rabbit punches or below-the-belt stuff. That's all I ask.'

'How about showing me some of those swords you claim you collect?' She came out with it, just like that.

'My pleasure. Like nothing better.'

Besides, it seemed a good time for a change of pace. I straightened up and headed for the back parlour upstairs, then around the corner to the sword room, its door now fully repaired from the strange break-in. I fished out the key and snapped open the lock.

Funny thing, but walking around fully dressed *I* had started feeling out of place. Maybe it is merely a state of mind.

All right now, where to start? This was a crucial moment. My first impulse was to go all the way to gold, that marvellous *katana* dating from the early Kamakura, or even before, said to have come from the forge of the Shogun Yoritomo Minamoto's personal swordsmith. But wait a minute. After that, what? Maybe the absolute tops should be saved for a more auspicious moment. That sword was, to my mind, an almost sacred work. Maybe instead we ought to start with something a little offbeat, then gradually work up to the best and sharpest.

The obvious choice, in fact, was a piece I considered a real curiosity, racked there on the left, top slot. As I lifted it off and slipped it out of its scabbard, the metal glistened like a mirror, reminding me how long it'd been since I'd oiled and pampered my playthings.

'I'm afraid nothing here was handed down by the Sun Goddess.' I was coming back down the stairs a little unsteadily, like a half-drunk *samurai*. 'But this one's kind of like the old style, at least the metallurgy is. Unusual. Heavy on copper and tin. In a way almost closer to bronze than steel.'

Then I proceeded to point out a few interesting features – the nice curve of the face line, the burl grain, the Shinto deities on the elliptical *tsuba* hand guard, that kind of thing – taking care to keep it out of the damned bubbles. I was starting to get wound up, as all enthusiasts do with a captive audience, when she tactfully cut me off.

'How's the handle attached, or the grip, or whatever it's called?'

'That's the hilt, the *tsuka*. Held on with a little wooden peg stuck through a hole in the metal. Here, let me show you.' I had a small brass punch on my key ring that was specially designed to push it out. 'Under the grip there's a wrapping of silk braid and then a layer of the belly skin of a stingray, to protect the steel. But you just remove this peg and the whole ensemble slides right off.' I removed the handle and laid it on the sink. 'Now you can see the untempered end of the sword, the tang or *nakagō* as it's called.' I passed the weapon to her, blunt end first. 'That's where a swordsmith engraved his signature, his title, the place it was forged. So you always should check. On a really important piece, there may be cutting tests noted there. Like maybe they tried out the blade on a criminal or two just to see if it worked. Quality control.'

'God.' She shuddered. 'Really?'

'Licensed testers did it and certified it in gold engraving on the *nakagō*. Some of the ones upstairs have it. But this one's an *ubu*, virgin.' I watched her turn it in the dim light. 'Careful now. That edge is *very* sharp.'

'How can you tell if it's really old?'

'Lots of ways. The grain, the signature, and then too a good one should have some rust there on the *nakagō*, black not red.'

She held it up a second and examined it.

'Virgin, huh? No signature?' She had a funny, almost embarrassed, expression on her face.

'Correct. But like I said, this one's not—'

'Then who was "*Nihon Steelworks: Nagoya*"? Somebody you bought it from?'

'Anybody ever tell you you've got a crummy sense of humour.' I wasn't smiling as I reached to take it back. Her crack annoyed me and I'm afraid I showed it. Some things you don't kid around about. 'That's a modern foundry that turns out crappy—'

'Don't get testy. I'm only reading. Right there.' She pointed to some very faint English engraved into the metal.

'Christ!'

I grabbed it back and held it under the light to look. No mistaking. There it was, plain as could be.

That's when I finally realised the thing was a copy. A goddamn *replica* of the original. OK, a remarkably good one, but a fake nonetheless.

How did *this* get in my closet?

Could somebody have broken in and . . .?

Suddenly it hit me. The robbery. Whoever had lifted my records must have also pulled a switcheroo on this *katana*, leaving this piece of Nagoya junk and disguising the deed by replacing the original grip and *tsuba* hand guard. I'd been too loaded to notice.

I wanted to crack the goddamn fraud over my knee like in the movies, but you don't do that with a *samurai* sword, even a phony modern one. So instead I flung it down on Jo's Italian-marble floor and headed back upstairs to check the others. What in hell had happened? Had they cleaned me out after all? My God, thousands . . .

I began yanking down swords, starting with the aforementioned centrepiece of the collection, scrutinising them in the light. But after about half a dozen proved to be all right, I started calming down. Nothing else seemed to have been touched. Well, what the heck, I thought. It wasn't exactly a crippling loss.

Finally I grew a little ashamed of myself and sheepishly wandered back down, collecting the ringer off the floor.

'Tam, I'm sorry. Somebody broke in a while back and they must have stuck this fraud in my collection. It's not the one I thought it was.'

'Sure.' She just looked at me, with some sympathy. 'Matthew, it's all right. Really. Lots of people own replicas of art. I have a few prints myself. It's not a crime.' She touched my hand. 'Don't worry. It doesn't matter—'

'*You*—' I bit my tongue to squelch the unpleasant word forming on my lips, stomped back upstairs and returned with a real sword. Then I gave my lecture all over again, dwelling on every insignificant detail. I was going to bore the woman till she cried uncle. Finally I succeeded.

'OK, you win. I apologise.' She leaned back in the bubbles. 'You really love this hardware, don't you?'

'Tam, I love the *samurai* ideals. I admire craftsmanship. I revere courage. The guys who made and used these blades had it all. If I'm going to collect art, why not something that inspires me?'

She just looked at me and nodded. I think she really understood.

'Then let's make a pact, Matt, you and me,' she finally spoke up. 'We'll face Dai Nippon or MITI or whoever honourably. And we'll keep them honest.'

'*Samurai*.' I smiled. 'Lineage to lineage. And may the best . . . person win.'

I returned the sword and locked up, then lounged in the bedroom and chatted through the open door while she finished her soak. It didn't seem proper to lug a chair into the bath and there was something too undignified about perching atop the loo. Why, I kept wondering, had somebody taken such elaborate pains to lift a single antique and plant a fake? So I wouldn't miss it? But why bother?

Finally she got into a robe and came out, whereupon we went downstairs and proceeded to put away more brandy, sleet slamming against the windows. That was when she refreshed my recollections of her early life, the peripatetic half-breed army brat. I think, truth be told, she was currently about as adrift as I was. She was too wary to admit it; I was too incapable of touching my own fractured emotions. So we talked around things, saying everything except that maybe we needed somebody. All the while, the storm outside continued to rage. But once again I was feeling those stirrings I'd kept on ice for way too long.

Alas, though, it had to end. About 1 a.m. we geared up. She retrieved her coat; I banked the fire; and we straggled out into the sleet. After finally managing a cab, we headed uptown. We'd agreed on the rules; now we were off to face the beast.

SEVENTEEN

As we rode, I tried to get into mental fighting trim. It wasn't easy. Walton, I kept telling myself, you're too old for this kind of intrigue. And why drag this innocent woman in? You're not shuffling paper and cutting deals and then going out for a drink with the other side's counsel after you've both finished impressing your clients by shoving each other against the wall. You're about to start fooling around with guys who carry submachine guns. When you wouldn't know what to do with an Uzi if somebody handed you one. If these boys start shooting, there won't be a lot of polite inquiries concerning due process.

Tam was leaning against my shoulder, still perfumed from the bubble bath, and totally relaxed. She seemed to know what she was doing. Or maybe she didn't want to think about the risk we were taking. As for me, this Sam Spade number was definitely not part of my legal arsenal.

My thoughts, however, kept coming back to her. Tam Richardson was the first woman I'd felt this comfortable with for a long, long time. She was a mixture of tough and soft, and she was smart. What I'd always been looking for. Exit Donna, enter Tam. Maybe life was going to give me another inning.

If we both lived that long.

We'd headed uptown on Sixth Avenue, rutted with slush; at Fourteenth Street we hung a right, east towards Third. The snowploughs were out, together with the salt machines, while abandoned cars were lodged in furrows of ice all along the kerb. This was definitely shaping up as the storm of the year. Since most of Tanaka's staff lived in the Japanese 'ghetto' up in Hartsdale and Eastchester (where there's even a Japanese PTA these days), they surely must have caught the Orient Express out of Grand Central before the trains got stopped dead by the weather. Certainly tonight of all nights the DNI offices would be empty. This had to be our shot. So shape up Walton and go for it.

While we listened to the sleet bounce off the back window, our Jamaican driver proceeded to compare New York City un-favourably with every armpit he'd ever known, as well as a few arctic locales he doubtless was acquainted with only by reputation. I finally tuned him out and began asking myself one question over and over. What exactly are we going to *do* if we figure out there's some kind of skulduggery afoot? Is there any way to stop them, even if we wanted to?

Probably nothing short of Congress's cracking down could keep Noda's money out of the country, and who's going to support that kind of legislation? Most solons, in fact, were hailing DNI and its Japanese billions as the salvation of America. No lawmaker was staring at the cameras and 'viewing with concern' this new godsend of cash. Ditto the stock exchange. They were nervous downtown, sure, but given the avowed purpose of Wall Street – attracting money – there wasn't exactly a groundswell of sentiment against Dai Nippon's massive investments. Noda had come into the market at its darkest moment and begun shovelling in capital. How could this be anything but positive? So every time another Japanese billion rolled in and prices ticked up some more, everybody merely leapt for joy. The Japanese were coming to rejuvenate our land, cheered the *Journal*. Billions from the cash-rich Japanese capital markets were voting with their feet to be part of America's resurgence.

Maybe they're right, I told myself. About the only discordant voices in this chorus of hesitant hallelujahs belonged to a few op-ed sour-grape academics. I recalled one piece in particular from late last week. Who was it: Robert Reich, Lester Thurow, 'Adam Smith'?

This must be how it felt all those years in Europe as they helplessly watched the invasion of American money. Has the US now joined the Third World, capitalised by rich 'Yankees' from the East? Now at last we realise that setting up plants here for 'co-production' was merely the foot in the door. Does it matter if US industry is owned by American pension funds or Japanese insurance companies? Guess not, unless you happen to care whether we still control our own destiny. America, soon to be the wholly owned subsidiary . . .

The writer was just blowing smoke and knew it. These days a harangue in the *Times* and a token will get you on the subway. Even Henderson was taking a new look at Noda – astounded by his market savvy. The Georgia po' boy who once summarised his own trading style as the four Fs ('find 'em, fleece 'em, fuck 'em and forget 'em') had met his match. What a play Noda had made! To Bill, my new client had acquired the aura of some omnipotent invader from the depths of space – The Creature That Ate Wall Street. His eyes glazed over whenever he reflected on Noda's masterful one-two punch. Billions skimmed inside a week.

'Tam, take a good, long look.' I was pointing up into the night as we emerged on to the slippery sidewalk. 'The house that Noda built. Did all of this happen since only late September?'

'Time flies when you're having fun.' She slammed the door and headed for the lobby, calm as could be. OK, Walton, you'd better toughen up too.

I rewarded our grumbling cabbie with a vulgar tip and watched the vehicle slowly roll off into the sleet, tyres crunching, to end another of those passing New York intimacies so vivid yet so forgettable.

As it turned out, lobby security was a breeze, since yours truly had approved the application of the night guard personally right after DNI took over. Eddie Mazzola, blue uniform and grasping a styrofoam cup of coffee, glanced up from the Sunday *Daily News*, his face generic Staten Island.

'What brings *you* out on a night like this, Mr Walton? Nothing wrong, I hope?'

'Do me a favour, Eddie. Burn this place down. We'll split the insurance and both retire to Miami Beach. Who needs New York?'

He concurred the idea had merit. I then went on to mention that we'd just come from uptown; Dr Richardson here had forgotten some kind of gobbledygook up on twelve and we wouldn't be a minute.

'Tell you the truth, Eddie, my fingers are too damned numb to bother signing the visitor's book.'

He saluted and returned his concentration to the Knicks' perennial slump.

We took the night elevator up, and somewhere around the time we passed the ninth floor, we managed to settle on a story. Noda, we would say, had called Tam and asked her to hurry up a special report on one of the firms for Monday. We'd just left a dinner party on the East Side, thought we'd drop by and pick up some printouts since she wanted to work at home tomorrow. Shouldn't be more than a minute.

As the number above the door hit twelve, I tried to remember how to pray.

In the hallway we waved at the TV eye and the steel door opened. Standing there was Shiro Yamada: cropped hair, trifle burly, grey uniform. One of the regulars. He shifted his Uzi as we came through. Then he recognised Tam and bowed low.

By the wildest of good fortune Yamada only spoke Japanese, a linguistic limitation that turned out to be crucial. Tam began by observing the niceties: she commiserated with him about the weather, the late hour, would the next shift be able to get through and relieve him? He was all bows and deference and 'hai, hai'.

Finally she worked around to why we were there, almost as though that were a nuisance and the real reason had been to drop by for a chat. By the way, she added, there were a couple of things she needed from her office. She gave him the story.

Yamada listened, bowing, hai, hai, then sucked in his breath to demonstrate we'd presented him with a serious conflict of obligations — which for a Japanese can be the most distressing prospect imaginable. This situation entails great difficulty, he said, drawing in more air through his front teeth. Hontō ni muzukashii desu.

Muzukashii deshoo ka? inquired Tam. Difficulty?

Hai, sō desu. Yes, and he was deeply apologetic. Lots of *sumimasen*, very sorry.

At first I thought he just hadn't bought the story. But then it turned out that there were these rules, you see. No one was allowed on the floor at weekends without a pass signed personally by Tanaka-san. He glanced at his watch. It was nearly 2 a.m. More heavy intakes of air and *muzukashii*'s. Of course the honourable Dr Richardson-san, being an honourable director herself, should be able to come and go as she pleased, but the rules . . .

He seemed to be pleading with Tam to help him find a resolution for this towering dilemma.

'What's the problem, Tam?' I inquired, *sotto voce*.

'No fucking pass.'

After an extremely awkward pause a light bulb clicked on in my simple mind. With great theatrics I suddenly slapped my own forehead, gave Tam a tip-off in English, and began rummaging my pockets. When we left the house I'd grabbed an old topcoat, not worn since that rainy night I met Noda, and in it somewhere was . . .

She started explaining that Walton-san may have brought the pass with him and had merely let that fact slip his mind.

Then I felt what I was looking for, in the bottom of the inside pocket. Noda's *meishi*, his business card, complete with the English note scribbled across the back.

'How stupid of me,' I apologised. 'Had it all along. Noda-san's "top priority" pass. He gave it to me only yesterday.'

Yamada took the business card and studied it with a puzzled look. What did this have to do with anything?

That's when I impatiently turned it over and pointed to the English scribbling on the back. Noda's initials, I groused, right there at the bottom.

'*Hai, wakarimasu.*' He understood that Noda-sama surely had written this, but so what? It wasn't the official form that the rules specified. More *muzukashii*.

Noda-san was in a rush, I apologised again. Didn't have time to locate the regular form. Tam passed that along in better Japanese.

'*Soo desu . . .*' Yamada thoughtfully agreed that such oversights sometimes happened. Everybody knew the big *daimyō* had a tendency to override official channels. He shifted his Uzi uncertainly.

'Noda-sama insisted I finish this report by Monday,' Tam stressed. 'We should only be a minute.'

Yamada scrutinised the back of the card a moment longer, holding it up to the light. What was he going to do?

Finally he handed it back, bowed reluctantly and looked the other way. It was a go.

'God, that was close.' Tam closed the door behind us and clicked on the lights. 'You don't know how lucky we were. If Morikawa had been on duty tonight, forget it. He'd never have bought that cock-and-bull routine.'

About a dozen computer workstations had been installed on twelve to link up with the mainframe and data centre on eleven. As we moved quickly past the sleeping screens, blind eyes staring vacantly into space, there was an eerie, ghostlike abandonment to the place, all the more so because of its hectic motion during regular hours. The phantoms of regimented analysts seemed to haunt the rows of empty desks. Tam remarked she'd never seen it like this: the nerve centre off duty. Only the storm of the decade, together with 2 a.m. Sunday morning, could create such solitude. It took God to shut down Dai Nippon.

'OK, time to move fast. Let's hit Mori's lair.' I was whispering as we neared the corner office. Ahead was the closed door, solid oak. I took a deep breath and reached for the knob.

It was locked.

'No dice.' I looked around at Tam, who was still wearing her lamb coat, grey against her dark hair, sleet melting on the shoulders.

'Let me try.' She gave it a twist. Nothing. 'I don't suppose we'd be very smart just to kick it in. Though that's what I feel like right now, after all our trouble.' She turned to me. 'Maybe there's a key somewhere in Noda's office? Think there's a chance?'

'Could be.' I was rummaging my pockets. 'First, though, let me check something.'

I pulled out a ring and began to flip through it. 'I ended up with a master, courtesy of the RM & S floor manager the day they turned in their keys. Now, if this internal door lock hasn't been changed yet, maybe . . .' I selected one and kissed it for luck. 'Here goes.'

The key, a large silver model, was resistant, the way masters always are. Undeterred, I wiggled it forcefully and slowly it slipped into the knob. A couple of jiggles more and the thing began to revolve under my hand.

We emitted matching sighs of relief as Tam shoved the door wide and reached for the light switch. 'Now I've got to regress into the past. A lot of their reports are in Japanese.' She went on to explain that although she could read the *kana* syllabaries easily enough, she'd forgotten a lot of the *kanji* ideograms. She could piece together enough to work through a simple newspaper story, but heavy technical prose was always tough.

She quickly sorted through the papers piled in neat stacks atop Mori's desk, but who knew what most of them said? Nothing looked like my stolen list. Next she checked the drawers of the desk. One contained a heavily marked printout; the others, nothing.

Time was ticking. If Yamada decided to make the rounds, no quantity of creative fiction would save us.

She quickly grabbed the printout. At least we had one item that might give us something. What, though, we still weren't sure. Nothing resembled the page I'd lifted, but locating that document now appeared increasingly like a long shot anyhow. Guess everything seems easy till you actually try doing it.

Where else to look?

I glanced around the room, wondering about the file cabinet. Probably locked, and besides . . .

That's when I saw it. On a side table next to some technical books was an item we'd both failed entirely to notice. A large leather attaché case.

'Tam, I think we've hit pay dirt. Check that out. Do you suppose she could have forgotten it last night when they shut the place down?'

'Maybe she didn't need it. Anything's possible. I remember seeing her carrying it around yesterday afternoon.'

'Well, could be this is our find.' I lifted it . . . and realised it was empty.

'Shit.' I slammed it down and just then detected a faint rattle inside. Hold on a minute.

I carefully shook it again and listened. 'Tam, there's something in here.'

'I vote we take a peek.'

Which is what we did. No harm, right? I mean, the darned thing was just lying there. No 'break and entry'.

Guess what was inside. Not paper. Not a MITI report. Not lunch. Nothing in fact except for a shiny little compact disc, a CD.

'What the hell is this doing in here? Did she bring along some Beach Boys?'

'Matt, that's an optical disc, a CD-ROM.' She suddenly seemed very pleased.

'Huh?'

'Compact disc, read-only memory. Except this one looks to be erasable and writable. This is the latest thing in computer storage technology.' She held it up to the light, which reflected a rainbow of colours off its iridescent surface. 'Maybe we've found what we came for. Let's take it and go.'

'Is this like the CDs in record stores? The ones you play back using some kind of laser gizmo?'

'Same technology, only this is for text and data, not music. These can hold 500 megabytes, about 150,000 pages.'

'Then I have some disquieting information to impart. I saw somebody come in here one day after shopping at Tower Records and a CD he'd bought tripped the metal detector out there in Yamada's anteroom like he was wearing sleigh bells. Down inside this shiny plastic must be aluminium or something. We can't take it out.' I turned it in my hand. 'And besides, what would we do with it anyway? Stick it in a Walkman and listen to all the little digits spin by? In hi-fi?'

'I've got a reader at home . . . but wait, there's a better way.' She lifted it from my grasp and headed out on to the floor. 'Ever hear of computer crime?'

'In passing.'

'Good. Then what you're about to witness won't shock you.'

I watched as she kicked on one of the NEC desk stations and loaded in a program. Next she walked over, flipped a switch on a little box and a drawer glided out. In went Mori's shiny disc. Another button was pushed, the drawer receded and the disc was spinning silently.

Well, I thought. You want peaches, you shake the tree, right? Maybe she's about to kick hell out of the orchard.

'I'm going to dump this into the memory of the mother ship downstairs.' She did some fiddling, then typed in her password to sign on the mainframe on eleven. 'Beam us down, Scottie.' In moments she and all those silicon cells below us were beeping away at each other. She didn't look up, just kept typing away, the hollow click-clack that's become the signature sound of our computer age. Finally she leaned back and breathed. 'OK, it's reading the disc. After it's in memory down there, we can pull up the contents here on the screen and see what we've got.'

I don't know how long it took to read the thing. Probably no more than a minute or so, though it seemed forever. Finally something flashed on the screen and told us the disc had been dumped. Tam took it out of its little player and passed it to me.

'Here, put this back in her case. While I start pulling up the file.'

I'd just finished snapping it shut when I heard an expletive from out on the floor that would not be judged suitable for family audiences.

'Watch your language.'

She was sitting there staring at the screen. Finally she turned and looked at me. 'So close, yet so far. It's *encrypted*.'

'It's what?'

'Come and look.'

I did. On the screen was a mass of numeric garbage. What was this all about?

'Matt, when this disc was written, whatever went on it was scrambled using some key, probably the DES system, the "data-encryption standard". It keeps unauthorised intruders like us from snooping.'

'How does anybody read it?'

'A decrypting key must be in the hardware down on eleven. But we can't get through to that level of the machine without an "access code". Which we don't have.'

'Very smart. The electronic keys to the kingdom.' I watched, wondering all the while what Yamada was doing out there. Should I blunder out and chat him up with my Berlitz Japanese, just to keep him occupied? The clock above the door was ticking away.

'Tam, why not just try activating the key using your own password as the access code? Maybe it'll get you into that level on the mainframe.'

She gave it a go, without much enthusiasm. Predictably the message came back, 'ACCESS CODE NOT RECOGNISED'.

'Well, try some others.' I was grasping. 'Hit it with "NODA" or "MORI".'

She did, but after both were rejected the workstation suddenly signed off. Click, out of the system.

'What's happened now?'

'More bad news. I forgot the mainframe is programmed so that you get three tries at a protected code and then it breaks the connection. That's to keep crackers like us from sitting here all day and running passwords at random. Another security precaution.'

'Three chances to guess the secret word and then you're out. Sounds like a game show.' I just stood there and scratched my head. Seemed we were, to be blunt, shit out of luck. 'What now, Professor? I assume there are about a hundred million alpha-numeric combinations they could use.'

'Close.' She was clicking away at the keyboard. 'So let's think a minute.' She glanced back at me. 'Why don't we assume for a minute that this is a MITI disc.'

'Safe bet.'

'So the decryptor key in the machine here would be from MITI, right, since Mori obviously brought the disc to be read?'

'Sounds good.'

'You know, I was in Ken's office once, and I recall watching some of his staff playing around with the information on one of these discs. Don't know why I still remember this, but the password they used was . . . I think MX something, three letters, followed by six digits. The digits were always changing, but the prefix was the same.'

'So if your wild guess about this being a MITI disc is right, and the first two letters of the three-letter alpha part are still MX, that means there are exactly, what — twenty-six letters in the alphabet times a million numbers — twenty-six million combinations. We're looking for one number in twenty-six million? So if it takes, say, five seconds to type one in and try it, we're talking roughly a hundred and thirty million seconds to go the course.' I glanced again at the door. 'Besides which, we get kicked off after every third try. Working around the clock, we ought to have it sometime about, what, 2001?'

She glanced back at the screen, then suddenly whirled around, a funny look on her face. 'What do you have in your office?'

'What do you mean?'

'Don't you have a PC downtown?'

'Just a little IBM AT, 512K. And also a Mac, a toy I use to draw cutsey-poo pictures now and then and do covers for reports.'

'How about a telephone modem?'

'Built in. How else could I handle all that trading?'

'And it's up?'

'The IBM? Never turn it off. Little twitch left over from playing the Hong Kong exchanges. Habits die hard.'

'OK, I'm going to try and use it to crack the code in DNI's mainframe.'

Honestly, for a second there I thought my hearing had gone. 'My little IBM against that monster? How, for chrissake? There're twenty-six million—'

'We'll have to do something not very nice. Since the Japanese aren't used to hackers, those bearded malcontents in firms who screw up business computers for spite, these workstations aren't buffered off sensitive parts of the system. We are now going to exploit that trust in Japanese culture. We're going to organise these terminals, hook them to your computer, and then direct that network against the mainframe downstairs. Something no Japanese would ever dream of doing.' She got up and went down the row clicking on machines. 'There's a list of names in my office, there by the phone. Can you bring it?'

'Coming up.' I fetched it. It was a temporary 'phone book' of the staff on the floor. She took the list and went back down the line of stations, typing something on each keyboard.

'What are you doing, Tam? This is crazy.'

'It'll just take a second. Everybody here has a password to sign on to the mainframe, but it's just the name of the person.' She came back to the first workstation. 'Now the mainframe thinks ten people just signed on to the system. We'll use these terminals to try access codes on the main computer. Your PC will control them so that each terminal hits it with two codes and then the next one goes on line. That way we'll never get kicked off. It should get around the "three times and you're out" filter downstairs.' She began frantically typing again.

'What are you doing now?'

'We could try alphanumerics sequentially or randomly. I think randomly is probably better. It'll be faster. So I'm writing a little program for the mainframe, a random-number generator. It'll start making up random access codes of mx followed by a letter and six digits and sending them to your PC downtown, which will immediately feed them back in pairs to these terminals. Out one door, in another. Maybe that will fool it.'

'Christ, woman, you've got a criminal mind. Is this the kind of stuff you teach at NYU?'

'What's your number downtown?' She was typing away again.

I wrote it down and handed it to her. 'I don't have the foggiest idea how you're going to be able to swing this.'

'That's all right. I do. Just let me get your IBM networked into these terminals here. Fortunately it's compatible, and all it's going to be doing for now is bouncing back numbers generated by the mainframe.' She slipped some switches, then typed my number on to the screen. I momentarily wondered if the sleet had knocked out the phone system. It hadn't.

Again the seconds crawled by, but as soon as she'd finished her chat with my IBM downtown, the row of terminals suddenly started beeping away. Two shots, beep, the next one came alive; two shots, beep, right down the row.

'OK, your computer is running the show now. Sooner or later maybe something will click.' She punched a couple more keys then got up.

'It's done?'

'Ready to rock and roll.' She was putting on her coat. 'We'll be running millions of numbers.'

'Isn't anybody going to know you've pulled this?' I was, I confess, totally dumbfounded.

'Not unless they discover my little program in the mainframe downstairs. But it's just a random-number generator, something any sophomore could write. The trick is, we're hitting it with so many terminals it won't be programmed to keep track of all these little elves trying to sneak in. And when we're through we'll turn them all off using your modem downtown.'

'Good God, whatever happened to pen and pencil?' I was still dazed. She'd done it all so fast. 'If you can find the decryptor key and get into the files, then what? You going to dump all the info on Mori's sexy little CD down at my place?'

'I hope you've got lots of paper. Who knows what's on it?' She was shutting off the lights. 'Come on, let's get out of here.'

'Aye, aye, Professor.' I walked back, clicked off the light in Mori's office, then paused to double-check the lock.

'We came for printouts, remember. We only have Mori's.' I was joining her. She glanced at the stack on her desk, then grabbed a pile and handed them to me.

'You'd better carry these. And don't be put off by my "ugly American" routine at the door. It'll be for a purpose.'

After she'd doused the rest of the overheads, we passed through the first security door and greeted Yamada. While I fiddled with Tam's printouts, she proceeded to give him a very Japanese-style dressing down, disguised as a series of pale compliments. She reviewed all her work for Dai Nippon, just happening to mention Noda-sama this and Noda-sama that every other breath. The hapless guy sucked in his breath and bowed a lot and *hai*, *sō*-ed about once a second and then *sumimasen*-ed some more. By the time the elevator appeared, she'd destroyed him. He'd lost so much face he'd never dare mention our visit to Noda or anybody.

About two minutes later we were out on the sleet-covered sidewalk, looking for a cab. It was a heroic effort, but eventually we were headed back downtown. Secure and holding.

Although my upstairs office was freezing, I was mesmerised watching the flashing green numbers spin on my little IBM screen. It was like playing one of those 'fruit machines' at the local bars, except we were sitting there witnessing a gigantic intelligence turned against itself, searching for the crack in its own armour. There was something ironic about the fact that the Japanese were such a homogeneous, disciplined people they didn't need vast arrays of American-style safeguards to keep crazies off their computers. Unfortunately for them, they weren't expecting a couple of American criminals with no such scruples.

By 4 a.m. we had watched three million random numbers tried; by first light we were up to six.

'Tam, I'm beginning to get this sinking feeling MITI must have changed the prefix.' I was bringing a new pot of coffee, half staggering up the carpeted stairs. 'Or maybe we should have done it sequentially.'

'Maybe, but that would mean wasting a lot of time on numbers that are improbable. This is our best chance.' She poured another cup of java while I just stretched on the floor. 'Damn. I wish I could remember what the other alpha was. MX what? That could save us days.'

'We don't have days.' I closed my eyes. 'Try hypnosis.'

She sat staring at the screen for a few moments, then slowly wheeled around. 'I know why I couldn't remember it. It was a repeat. Matt, it was X.'

'Go with it.'

'Hang on.' She did some quick typing and hit the play button. Her face was showing the strain, but I loved her looks. What a champ. We were together; us against the beast. Unfortunately, though, the beast was still ahead.

At 7.30 a.m. Ben roused himself and lumbered expectantly up the stairs. With a silent curse I put on my boots and took him out for a stroll on the ice. He hated it. When we came back, I decided to give up and crash. Come on, this was insane, a billion-to-one shot and we didn't even know what the prize was at the bottom of the box. We were getting nowhere. MITI had changed the code and screwed us. Fortunately, however, I heroically vowed to try to stay awake till 8 a.m. That was it. The end.

At exactly 7.49 the numbers abruptly stopped. 'ACCESS CODE MXX909090 CONFIRMED – DECRYPTOR KEY ACTIVATED.' Confidential MITI memos started scrolling in orderly green clumps up the screen.

'My God, Matt, turn on your printer.'

EIGHTEEN

'Jack, doing anything today?'

'Walton, what in hell . . .?'

Jack O'Donnell and Joyce Hanson had been working through the ten-pound Christmas catalogue known as the *Sunday Times* — she was up to Arts and Leisure and he'd advanced as far as Business — when my call interrupted their mutually agreed-upon vow of silence. Now that her apartment in the West Seventies had become Jack's weekend hideaway, his escape from phones and conferences, the number was as carefully guarded as a Minuteman launch code.

The time was shortly after noon. He'd just braved a foot of snow and sleet to retrieve the paper and a couple of fresh croissants, while Joyce was still recovering from a 2 a.m. session editing a speech one of his staffers had drafted for some ILGWU holiday blowout the following week. Since he was still chewing over Noda's ominous phone call, wondering what to do, the last person on earth he wanted to hear from right now was Dai Nippon's lawyer, even if it was me.

'Feel like coming down for a Bloody Mary? An academic lady we both know is here and we've happened across something you might find interesting. Very interesting.'

'Care to elaborate?'

'It's a little complicated, Jack. How about coming down?'

He glanced out the frosted kitchen windows, puzzling what in blazes was up, then finally agreed.

'Keep the coffee hot.'

'You've got it.'

Joyce claimed to be unamused, though in truth maybe she wasn't all that heartbroken to have the place to herself for the afternoon. He grabbed his coat and said don't throw out The Week in Review.

The streets were now at a standstill, so the prospect of finding, let alone travelling in, a taxi was implausible in the extreme. As a result Senator Jack O'Donnell shared the Broadway local with several hundred of his lesser-heeled constituents and finally managed to get down to Sheridan Square, from which it was only a few mushy blocks over to my place.

Ben greeted him at the door with me not far behind, doubtless looking as if I'd just stumbled in from a three-day forced march. Without a word he passed over his coat, then followed me downstairs where Tam was still going through the line of print-outs spread across the dining-room table, translating on to one of my yellow legal pads.

I pointed him in the direction of the coffee urn stationed in the kitchen. He poured a cup, then came around and plopped down on the couch.

'Walton' – he sampled his brew, then set it down – 'you're not going to believe what your goddamn client did Friday. Swear to God, your man actually threatened me, the bastard, a not-too-subtle warning to back off.'

'Jack, that's small potatoes.' I straddled one of the dining-room chairs. 'What would you say to a possible play by our friend Matsuo Noda that makes Pearl Harbor look like a gesture of Japanese–American solidarity?'

'Two days ago I might have thought you'd been smoking a controlled substance. Now, I'm not so sure.'

'Well, we're still piecing it together. I don't think anybody could even imagine what's really afoot. One thing's for sure, though – this is big.' I paused. 'It might even be that Noda is somehow fronting for MITI, though I'm still not totally convinced.'

I'd been turning that possibility over, but I somehow couldn't buy it all the way. Wasn't Matsuo Noda's style. He was a loner.

'MITI?' He looked at me. 'That's government, right? The Ministry of . . .'

'International Trade and Industry. Japan's "War Department" for trade.'

'Yeah? Go on.'

'Listen. All Noda's talk about helping American industry? Of course it's bullshit. But I think it's just half the bullshit. What we suspect is, he's buying a little of everything so nobody will figure out their real agenda.'

'You'd better back up and take this from the beginning.'

'Wait a minute.' Tam got up and started the turntable. Mendelssohn was still on the platter. Maybe we were taking too many precautions, but she still nursed the idea we might be bugged.

With the music cranked up to '8', we proceeded to give Jack a quick summary of how the stack of memos on the table had come into our hands. In a way, though, they raised as many questions as they answered.

'Jack, nothing here is spelled out in detail. We have to take everything and sort of rotate it by ninety degrees to see how Noda fits in.' I walked over to the table. 'Tam, where's your translation of that one by what's-his-name ... Ikeda?'

'Right here.' She handed it to me.

'Here, Jack, start with this. Just to get up to speed on the background.'

He fumbled in his pocket, retrieved his bifocals, and began to read the yellow sheet.

OPERATION MARKETSHARE—90
Internal Memo No 22
From: Hiromu Ikeda, Deputy Minister of Industrial Technology
Sector Ministry of International Trade and Industry (MITI)
Subject: SUPERCHIPS

World dominance in semiconductors will provide the basis for Japan's control of the global information industry by the turn of the century, which will be the key to our economic leadership and military strength. The critical path to achieving this lies with the coming generations of semiconductor technology – the submicron, giga-scale *superchip*. Accordingly, the objectives of Operation Marketshare—90 in the semiconductor sector should receive

the highest possible priority. Areas of research should include semiconductor grade polysilicon, silicon wafer
production, ceramic packaging, quartz photomasks, X-ray
lithography, supercooled Josephson junction circuits, and
optoelectronic chips for optical switching. R & D should
also be focused on digital signal processing, application-
specific integrated circuits (ASICs), specialised dynamic
random-access memories (DRAMs), very large-scale
integrations (VLSIs) for supercomputers . . .

'Walton, I can't make heads or tails of this gobbledygook.' He
tossed down the sheet. 'What's this all about?'

'What it means,' Tam spoke up, 'is that Ikeda has targeted
every emerging area of semiconductor research. Everything. A
clean sweep. If he succeeds, sooner or later nobody else will even
be able to make the really advanced chips. A few more years and
America joins the Third World.'

Jack looked a little sceptical. Truthfully I found her extrapolation somewhat fanciful myself. But then, who knew?

'Tam, how about showing Jack that other memo? You know
the one.'

She didn't say anything, just turned back and sorted through
the stack of yellow pages till she had it. Out came Jack's glasses
again.

OPERATION MARKETSHARE—90
Internal Memo No 37

From: Kenji Asano, Deputy Minister for Research and
Planning
Ministry of International Trade and Industry (MITI)
Subject: CURRENT STATUS OF R & D

This office has now completed its review of the recent
survey of research and development (R & D) by Japanese
firms compiled by the Science and Technology Agency,
the results of which are the subject of this memorandum.
Of the companies surveyed, 70 per cent maintain that their
research is equal or superior to leading firms in the US and
Europe, although only 18.2 per cent consider themselves
in unchallenged top position. Furthermore, the remaining
30 per cent believe their research is inferior or lagging

behind the West (ref. to Table 1). Of those who reported inadequate R & D in high technology areas, the following reasons were given . . .

'Whoever wrote this is just poor-mouthing.' He flipped on through the sheets, then looked up. 'Saying he needs more money for basic research. I hear this kind of stuff all the time. Hell, Japan already spends nearly twice what we do per capita on non-military R & D. What does he want?'

'Keep reading, Jack, and you'll see that the main R & D he's pushing is in computers and semiconductors. It ties in exactly with Ikeda's targets. This is backup consensus for the big drive.'

'You still haven't told me anything I didn't already suspect.' He tossed the pages on to a side table. 'So how about answering a few less obvious questions?'

'Shoot.'

'First off, what's this Operation Marketshare—90 all about?' He took off his glasses and pocketed them.

'Jack, remember the famous Hitachi directive that got loose a while back, the one on how to market their 256K memory chips, ordering their salesmen just to keep underpricing American manufacturers till they had the sale, loss no object. According to Henderson, by the time the International Trade Commission got around to convicting them of dumping, they'd demolished America's domestic industry and nailed down ninety per cent of the market.'

'Ninety, you say. Well, that's getting to be a familiar number.' He slumped back against the sofa. 'Out of curiosity, what's included in this MITI Marketshare—90 operation?'

'Computers, of course. But also pretty much everything in high tech where the US still has a leading position — from biotech to aerospace. These guys don't think small.'

I gave Ben a pat, then pulled Mori's printout around, going on to explain that we'd come across it in the drawer of her desk. It was, I added, obviously some kind of special computer sorting of the firms DNI was targeting. The categories in the sort were a breakdown of high-tech areas, with individual firms listed underneath, together with a summary of their research expenditures.

'Take a look. First, notice that this printout has been sorted and converted into this list here.' I placed it alongside the page I'd found in the Xerox machine. '*Voilà*, they're identical.'

'So?'

'OK, now compare that list with the R & D areas targeted in Ikeda's memo.' I laid Tam's translation down next to Mori's pages. 'See? Everything on Ikeda's MITI wish list for research in semiconductors is now being done by the American outfits named here in Mori's sorting, which is the latest revision in DNI's acquisition programme.'

'What are you getting at?' He looked it over.

'It's a pattern,' Tam spoke up. 'These new buy-ups cover Japan's last remaining shortfalls in R & D. I spotted it right away. But what I didn't realise till we got these memos was that the areas covered by Mori's companies exactly dovetail with MITI's goals. I probably wouldn't have noticed it without her sorting. Mixed in with all the other companies Noda's buying, he's targeted those that fill the gaps in MITI's semiconductor push.'

Jack looked at us quizzically. 'Are you telling me MITI's behind Noda's programme?'

That's where Tam and I parted company. She argued it was obviously a MITI play: why start from scratch when you can just buy what you need? Sound business investment. For some reason, though, I wasn't so sure. Somehow that explanation seemed too simplistic. Unfortunately, however, there's a law in science or somewhere that says you should always pick the least complicated theory that fits all your data. Hers appeared on the face of it to address the facts perfectly. Except for one unknown: if Mori did "accidentally" feed me the sorting that blew the whistle on Noda's design, why?

'I think this has to be what the buying program on this list is all about,' Tam answered. 'He's taking over firms whose R & D coincides with MITI's targets. Matsuo Noda has been put to work simply acquiring what they need, but to make sure nobody suspects the real agenda, he's worked up this elaborate "management assistance" story, buying all kinds of companies.' Her voice was bitter. 'The next step will be to set up joint ventures between these firms he's bought and their counterparts in Japan. Then all American R & D would be shared.'

'Which means' — Jack's face began to redden — 'that since we always seem to lose out when it comes to commercialising what we invent, the US ends up becoming one big think tank for Japan in the twenty-first century. We do the research, and they manufacture and market. They pick our brains and then cash in on it.' He turned back to Tam. 'Do you really think it was Noda who planned all this?'

'I wish I knew what to think.' Her voice grew hesitant as she continued to stare down at the memo. 'It's hard to believe Ken would do something so unethical — especially a grab like this — when I'm sure he's convinced Japan ought to be advancing its own R & D.'

'Ken? Who's—'

'Did you see who authored that second memo?' She pointed to the name.

'Kenji Asano is apparently a close friend of Dr Richardson's,' I broke in, my tone unnecessarily sharp. 'Unfortunately, he seems to be an even closer friend of his cronies at MITI.'

Tam didn't respond, just sat there looking betrayed.

'Matt, let's be constructive here.' Jack walked over and shook the coffee pot, then sloshed the last dregs into his cup. 'We damn well ought to take some kind of action.'

'That's why we wanted to talk to you.' Tam came back to life. 'Do you think you could leak something about this? Maybe to the *Times*?'

'And say what?' He laughed, a little sadly. 'That I've happened across a set of secret MITI memos that bear a coincidental similarity to some stolen DNI printout? Don't think that's exactly "Fit to Print".' He frowned. 'But I'm glad our Mr Noda has finally let slip his true intentions. I never believed all that pious malarkey about propping up American industry.' He snorted. 'The man gets a few suckers like you to help him destabilise our bond markets, in the process of which he turns the high-tech sector of American industry into a bargain basement for MITI.'

Tam sipped at her coffee, maybe trying to act as if Jack's comment hadn't stung her the way I suspected it did. I decided to try to handle her defence.

'Jack, hold on a second. You've got to admit that a lot of these outfits Dai Nippon is buying are currently on pretty thin ice. If somebody doesn't come in here and help run them right, they're probably headed offshore anyway.'

'We're not talking about first aid now, Walton. We're talking about Matsuo Noda taking over the most strategic segment of our economy after pulling the biggest scam in the history of world finance.'

'That looks to be the story.' I watched his cheeks redden with frustration. 'So what do you propose we do? There's no law against foreign investment. Securities exist to be bought.'

'Well, dammit, Matt, we've both seen enough by now to realise this Noda genius is up to no good. We've got to stop him.'

'Couldn't agree more. So why don't you just arrange to have the SEC shut down trading in every stock DNI has in its gun-sights?'

'You know that's out of the question.'

'Exactly. So what legal remedies are there? How do you squelch a takeover programme that's not even against the law?'

'That's *your* speciality, counsellor, or so I hear.'

'Jack, be realistic. We can expose this thing, maybe even try and lean on Tokyo to back off, but aside from shutting down trading there's no legal way to actually stop Matsuo Noda from buying whatever he likes. You can't shut Japanese investors out of Wall Street. There'd be a riot downtown. We're talking about the open market here, not some inside deal.'

'Forget legalities.' He scowled. 'Tell me how your damned corporate raiders go about shenanigans that don't quite match the letter of the law.'

'Jack, I've officially quit the business. Retired. Guess you hadn't heard.'

'That's what you think. You just got unretired. As of this moment. Now give me one of those high-priced consultations you're so famous for.'

'For you, Jack.' I looked him over. 'One last play. Trouble is, there's not much that's do-able, at least on short notice.'

'You say "not much". Which means there's something.'

'Well, one possibility might be to try and slow him down some, make him think twice, say by punching up the prices of the stocks he's aiming at. Make them less of a bargain.'

'That's a start.'

'Not much of one.'

'Well, how could it be done?'

'Since you're such a Boy Scout, Jack, you probably won't like what I have in mind. This one's not exactly in the rule book.'

'Try me.'

'OK, it's a long shot, and we'll definitely need some help. If we're going to tinker with the market, then we have to have somebody Wall Street trusts. And also somebody who's got a lot of money to play with, short term.'

'Sounds like our mutual friend from Georgia.'

'Well, Henderson can play the Street like a symphony. What I'm thinking of involves tricking the smartest guys around, the "risk arbs". We'd need to suck them in. If anybody can do it, he's the man.'

'Then I say let's give him a buzz.'

'Fine. Why don't I get him on the squawk box so we can all listen in?' There beside the couch was an old conference phone some client once gave me as a Hanukkah gift. At long last it might be good for something.

The risk arbs, by the way, are the risk arbitrageurs, those speculators who live with one ear to the ground. The minute they hear word, inside or otherwise, that a company is 'in play', meaning it's a candidate for a possible takeover or merger, they immediately grab up and stockpile huge blocks of its publicly traded shares. Then they sit back and pray for a bidding war. Since company A has offered so much a share for company Z, maybe company B will step in and offer more. Or maybe company Z itself will outbid them both and offer even more in a stock buyback. They're the hyenas of the hunt, getting plenty of leftovers no matter who ends up buying Z. Besides, they don't really care anyway. They're not investing in American industry, they're laying side bets.

Tam and Jack settled back while I punched in Bill's number.

The doctor was in, and after a few profane formalities — tempered when we informed him of a female presence — he listened with uncharacteristic attentiveness. I gave him an update, concluding with the view that we ought to try heading off MITI's presumed play.

Henderson, despite his admiration for Noda's style, didn't take kindly to the possible buy-up of America's remaining R & D in semiconductors, a spectre that coincided all too closely with his own fable about how MITI had already eaten one segment, memory chips. I decided to start by seeing if he and I were on the same wavelength concerning countermeasures. Without tipping him to my own idea, I asked what he thought could be done.

'Tell you, it won't be easy. One thing, though, we could maybe try and scare 'em off with a little brushfire.'

'Try that in English, Bill,' Jack interrupted.

'Don't know, maybe a few hot rumours could hit the Street . . . mergers, takeovers, your usual quick-buck action. Say a few of the CEOs of these outfits on Noda's Christmas list had a little pow-wow, a "secret" meeting everybody manages to hear about, and supposedly talked about gettin' themselves bought out. Naturally they'd deny everything on the *Evening News*, which in itself will tell the Street we're talkin' wedding bells.'

'Is that really going to do us any good?' Tam was talking to the box.

'Afternoon, ma'am. Liked that last book of yours a whole lot. Hope you're keeping them boys sober.' I could almost see Henderson turn up the charm, sculpting a voluptuous, horny divorcée in his ardent imagination. Tam, to my surprise, was not totally immune to his Georgia sweet talk. She sort of smiled to herself as he continued, 'But to answer your question, a takeover rumour can do marvels for your stock price. What happens is the "arbs" come in, snapping up blocks of stock and holding them, just in case. It can take a lot of securities out of circulation, at least short term. So if we could get the arbs to chasing those companies on Noda's list, they'd give the Japs a little competition. At the very least it'd kite the market, hurt their pocketbook.'

'Bill, that's why we wanted to call you. How about putting your finances where your flag-waving is? Be an arb yourself for a few weeks. Lead the herd. Start picking up some blocks of stock and shooting off your mouth a lot about your "inside" information. I'll even kick in my modest retirement fund to help the action.'

'What if somebody pulls the rug out from under us? Shoots the whole thing down? We'd be left holding all that stock we'd bid up. We could lose our shirt.'

'Then protect the downside by buying puts. I have full faith you'll think of something. Come on, Henderson, be a market maker. You've got the credibility. All you have to do is set a spark to this, then we'll quietly head for the sidelines to make way for all those investment-house yuppies who love to shoot craps with their clients' money.'

'Have to be a quick in and out for damned sure. This hot-air balloon won't stay up for long.' He paused, clearly not wild about the idea. 'Tell you what, though, maybe if we had a real good story.'

'Ideas?'

'Well, how about this? Maybe we've just heard on the grapevine that those outfits on Noda's play list have started a little "white knight" talking. And since this is just speculation, we might as well think big. Know who I mean?'

'The pride of Armonk.'

'Give that man a gold star. We both know IBM headquarters ain't talked to nobody but God since Watson outgrew his short pants, so it'd be weeks before they'd stomp on some horse-pucky rumour about how they were looking into saving whatever's left of the chip business here. Just covering their ass, we'll say. Friendly mergers. No poison-pill stuff.'

'That's exactly the kind of specious "supporting detail" that always triggers the Street's greed,' I concurred. 'Offhand I'd say that sounds just about perfect for tomorrow's hot tip on the Exchange floor.'

In truth it did seem like a workable first draft of an idea. No law against deep background sources that turn out to be 24-carat bullshit down the road. The antitrust implications would be front page for a couple of days, but since the Administration adhered to the 'see no evil' school of regulation, that angle wouldn't impress the smart money. America starts thinking big, chucks the myth of garage entrepreneurs, and staves off Japan using a dose of MITI's own medicine. IBM rides in to rescue what's left of Silicon Valley. It might just make Matsuo Noda back away. He'd learn America could play hardball too.

We told Bill to take the rest of the day off. Jack was, I can report, noticeably encouraged. Tam also. For my own part I just crashed, with a few wistful reflections on my rocky nonseduction. But if we pulled off our little scam, she might be more inclined to take me seriously.

As Shakespeare said, Lord, what fools these mortals be. I realised the true extent of Matsuo Noda's reach on Monday, just after noon. I was still home when Tam called from the office uptown to inform me of the latest developments. I was so busy on the phone just then, planting merger rumours with a few friendly columnists, that I was almost annoyed to take time out for her call. However, she quickly captured my attention.

First, the revisions on DNI's acquisition programme were in full swing. Noda had started purchasing those healthy semiconductor outfits on the new list.

Then she went on to say that an additional set of buy orders had just gone out over the wire. Noda had been on his satellite hook-up to Tokyo all morning and he'd now finalised official authorisation for a minor expansion, so to speak, in DNI's programme. Apparently Tokyo had agreed with him that his portfolio should include a certain high-grade issue to achieve better overall 'balance'.

She didn't say much more, for obvious reasons, but we both had a strong hunch what must have happened. If anything was bugged, for chrissake, it wasn't my apartment. That's B-movie stuff. It had to be my phone.

Matsuo Noda had just kicked off a new buy programme to the tune of three and a half billion. For what? More high-tech stragglers? Not precisely. One company, and in an amount intended to stay safely just below the Securities and Exchange Commission's Form 13-D mandatory reporting. Twenty-five million shares of IBM, roughly a full four per cent of Big Blue.

It was a massive variation of the 'Pac-Man' takeover defence: you eat anybody you think wants to eat you. Noda's message to us was loud and clear: he could buy the USA any time he wanted. Dai Nippon was unstoppable.

NINETEEN

I hung up the phone very slowly.

'We've "moved the shadow".' I spoke the words to myself hesitantly, maybe even a little apprehensively. That was the name for a famous strategy of the seventeenth-century swordsman Miyamoto Musashi, using a feint to lure your opponent into prematurely disclosing his battle plan.

The way I saw it, Matsuo Noda now stood revealed. It had all been a set-up. The financial scam, the 'help-American-industry' cover, the MITI 'guidance'. This was a takeover, all the way. A global takeover. What else could it be?

And the only people on this side of the Pacific who knew were Matt Walton and Tam Richardson.

For some reason that thought brought to mind the professor at Stanford, the AI guy who'd disappeared. What was it Tam had said? He'd had dinner at her apartment? Asked her to do something for him in Japan? And her MITI friend, whose name was all over that stack of memos on the table downstairs? Asano. Where did he fit in?

One thing, he'd helped Noda recruit her. They'd worked together and their play had been flawless.

But now our friend Matsuo Noda had a small headache. Tam Richardson and Matt Walton had exposed the underside of his game. The shadow had moved. Which meant it would only be a matter of time before he struck.

Where was our weakness, hers and mine? What would cause us to lose our rhythm, to blunder? He'd already outmanoeuvred Jack O'Donnell with ease. He had a master swordsman's unerring instinct for his opponent's weakness. So where was mine? I had to know it before he found it.

He'd realised Jack could be blackmailed, if the stakes were his constituents' jobs and lives. But I didn't need a job. And the only life . . .

Of course! It was obvious. Amy.

Could it be I was dealing with a madman who made people disappear?

If I was about to take on a pro like Noda, I had to cover every possibility. Which meant I had to get her out, away, beyond his reach. Today.

Still, though, there were so many questions. Who was really behind all the moves, the master puppeteer? Was it only Matsuo Noda, or was this possibly, just possibly, something that wound its way even higher. If so, who was the point man on that? Akira Mori?

The only rational countermove now was to back off and 'survey prevailing conditions'. Miyamoto Musashi's *keiki o shiru to iu koto*. But to do that we had to remove ourselves beyond the reach of Dai Nippon's sword. How long did we have?

I glanced at the clock on my desk, the little Sony digital. The number 12.18 stared back, the two dots in the middle flashing once every second. Amy was still at school, and for the moment I couldn't think of a safer place. They wouldn't even let *me* in without a pass. She didn't get out till 4 p.m.

So now what?

Simple. In swordsmanship, vigilance is everything. And there are two things you always have to keep in view. The first is called *ken*, the surface actions, the moves your opponent wants you to see. The second, and more important, is *kan*, the essence of things, the real truth. *Ken* covers the superficial moves; *kan* gives you the big picture.

Instinctively I still believed we had only been witness to *ken*, the distractions, the insignificant feints of our opponent. The deeper wisdom of *kan* still lay beyond us. Time to probe.

We had three and a half hours.

I got up and headed downstairs to retrieve a couple of very important memos. If we needed them, we'd have them. The rest of the pile I brought back upstairs and locked in the sword room (the closest thing I had to a safe). Finally, I reflected a second and paused to scribble Emma a note, asking her to feed and walk Ben in case I wasn't around for a while. That taken care of, I retrieved my heavy topcoat from the front closet, walked out into the street, and grabbed a cab for the offices of Dai Nippon, International.

Maybe our opening move should be *uromekasu to iu koto*, to feint a thrust that would induce a state of confusion in Noda's mind. Then we could stage a tactical retreat to plan the final, all-out attack.

Retreat to where? Well, that part at least was easy: the obvious hideaway was my place down in the islands. The thing to do was to quietly catch American 291 and head for the Caribbean. If Noda did manage to track us down, he'd be in for a surprise. Let me explain.

Back when the world was young and Amy was still a gleam in our eye, Joanna and I acquired a rambling white fortress, complete with pool, that was being offered to the first tourist appearing on St Croix that day with ready cash. Seemed its Cosa Nostra owner back in Sicily (so the story went) suddenly needed a transfusion of a hundred grand in bail money. Fortunately I'd had a good year and happened to have the necessary liquidity. It was luxurious beyond vulgarity. Hardwood parquet floors, heavy tile roof (to withstand an Interpol bombing run? Who knows?), manicured grounds, satellite dish, a bar worthy of Caesar's Palace, three bedrooms and music in every room. It was oversize and garish and pretentious and . . . who cares, I loved the place. Sort of a Roman villa in the middle of paradise. However, because of the peculiar requirements of its former tenant, it also had a security set-up to shame Fort Knox, including a six-foot fence, two-inch-thick doors, and TV monitors all over the grounds.

If we could locate a little hardware to match Noda's Uzis, he'd be in for a surprise should he try to send down a Dai Nippon hit squad for an unscheduled visit.

But first things first. Right now we needed somehow to lure Matsuo Noda into revealing more of his overall strategy.

After the cab dropped me off, I rode the elevator up to twelve and passed through security. The complement of guards, I noticed in passing, had just been expanded. Instead of two, now there were four. And when I walked out on to the floor, nobody said anything, but there was an almost palpable air of tension. Stony silence, analysts nervous. Bad vibes, very bad vibes.

I just ignored the stares and headed straight for Tam's office. She was waiting, and she had an identical reading of the situation. The minute I walked in, she got up and shut the door. Her first words . . .

'He just brought in more security. That, and the IBM thing. Matt, he's getting worried.'

'Bet your ass he is. We're moving in too close. But I think Noda figures he's just toying with us now. Having some fun before he cuts us in half.'

'I'm not afraid of him. No matter what he tries.' She glanced at the door. 'Did you bring the memos?'

'Here in my briefcase. But I think it's too soon to show him everything we have. Right now he doesn't know *what* we've got. That's better.'

'Well, I've just begun to fight. I'm going to Tokyo to get the truth out of Ken.' She paused, and her voice trembled slightly with anger. 'He's got some heavy explaining to do.'

'You're incredible.' I just looked at her. 'I almost believe you still can't accept that your friend Asano is in on Noda's play. Since he's such a terrific guy.'

'Matt, I don't believe it. He wouldn't be part of this. You don't know him.'

'That I don't.'

'All I'm saying is, this doesn't feel right. He wouldn't involve MITI in whatever Noda's planning.' She sat down, running her hands through her tousled dark hair. 'You know, the fact is we still don't know for sure who's really behind what.'

'Exactly. How does everybody fit in, including us? We've got pieces of a puzzle lying around – a section here, a section there – but something fundamental is missing.'

'So what do we do next?'

'How about a little joust with our friend downstairs? Try and feel him out. Maybe we can lure him into making another move, something that'll give away more of his game.'

'You don't think he's actually going to talk.'

'Not really. He'll feint, parry. But if we watch carefully, maybe we'll glimpse more of the outline of his strategy. Then we'll know what our counter scenario has to be.' I decided to hold off on telling her the getaway plan. Assuming the walls had ears, we'd already said too much. 'Look, make you a deal. First let's see what happens with Noda, then we decide what to do about your friend Asano.'

'All right. But let's stay cool.' She was locking her desk.

'You read my mind.'

With that settled, we strolled out, past the doubled security, and headed down to eleven. The way people looked at us, I felt as naked as Tam had been in the bath Saturday night. How much did they know?

Matsuo Noda was in his office. His secretary buzzed us right through, almost as though he'd been waiting for our appearance.

'Dr Richardson. Mr Walton.' He rose to greet us. 'How timely. There is an urgent matter we have to discuss.'

'We want to talk about MITI.' I decided to try and break his rhythm as quickly as possible. Take the action *to* him.

'Then this *is* a coincidence.' An easy smile as he resumed his seat. 'That happens to be the very matter I wanted to explore—'

'What we want to know,' Tam interrupted, 'here and now, is whether our programme is being run by the Ministry.'

'Dr Richardson, you . . . and Mr Walton, are in the employ of Dai Nippon, International, not MITI.' He leaned back in his chair. 'Though of course nothing in this world is entirely simple. Certain . . . interests of the Ministry are germane to our programmes here.'

'Then we'd like to hear about it.' She glanced at the leather chairs but decided to remain on her feet. I did the same.

His face was like granite. 'Well, you are aware we've occasionally received input from MITI's Industrial Technology arm.'

'How about Research and Planning, Ken's section?'

'Only a few informal—'

'Nothing to do with Marketshare—90?'

He betrayed a hint of confusion, quickly masked. 'Dr Richardson, with all due respect, I fear you may not be entirely aware of the various forces at play here.' He leaned back. 'This programme of ours must succeed. There are many avenues of responsibility, but all difficulties will be overcome.'

'What do you mean?'

'All in time, please believe me.' He smiled once more. 'I'll readily grant you our acquisition programme may have evolved slightly as of late in the direction of more solid securities, but you can be assured that is merely a response to the concerns of certain conservative institutional investors in Tokyo.' He continued, a silver tongue to match his silver hair, 'Risk is involved. Not to mention an enormous quantity of funds. There is pressure on us just now to try and maintain a prudent balance in our portfolio.' He glanced at his watch impatiently. As if he was anxious to move ahead. 'Which brings us to the matter we have to address.'

'Just to set the record straight' — I decided to do a little parrying of my own — 'you have nothing to say about any kind of MITI involvement? Including Marketshare—90?'

'Well, this Marketshare—90 proposition you refer to probably should be thought of as merely one of the Ministry's more ambitious trial balloons, nothing more. It has the quality of — how do you say it? — woolgathering. Whatever its purpose, it should in no way be confused with Dai Nippon's objectives.' Such was Noda's reply. Then in a remarkably convincing tone he added, 'How could the Ministry's planning possibly have anything to do with our programme here?'

Tam wasn't buying. 'Looks to me like it has a lot to do with it.'

'Dr Richardson, since I am no longer directly affiliated with MITI, I am not in a position to speak for every proposition arising there. However, we both know that the Ministry's responsibility is to provide long-range industrial planning. They often circulate scenarios for comment. It's part of their job.'

We were rapidly losing our footing. Noda was a top-ranked swordsman. He'd kept his discipline and revealed nothing. He was telling us we hadn't found an opening. He was right. It was a classic standoff.

Or it should have been. Strategically, we should have taken that moment to back away and analyse Noda's style, searching for his weakness. But instead Tam made what turned out to be a fatal move. She struck, exposing herself.

'Since according to you MITI is not involved in this programme, there should be no problem if I contacted them directly and talked this over. In Japan.'

I wanted to yell *no*, don't tell him anything.

But it was too late.

'An excellent idea.' He nodded gravely, then turned to me. 'Do you intend to be part of this expedition as well, Mr Walton?'

What to do? The only moves left now were defensive. No way was I going to let Tam face the beast alone. Also, if Noda had me, he wouldn't need Amy.

'I assume you can spare me here for a few days.'

'But we will all be in Japan together.' He removed his thin, wireless spectacles. 'That is in fact the very matter I needed to discuss with you. It is time you both were brought more closely into the matters at hand. Beginning today. I've already made reservations on New York Helicopter, departing for Kennedy in two hours. From the East 34th Street heliport.'

He had us. He'd seized the initiative, feinted us off balance and defined the terms.

She tried to recover. 'When and where we go is something *we* intend to . . .'

'Ah, Dr Richardson, one must seize the moment. It is past time you and Mr Walton understood more fully the many levels of concern involved here. There are a number of things you need to see.' He smiled as he replaced his glasses. 'Because of the expected frequency of my travels in the coming months, I have just leased a Concorde. We refuel in Bahrain. I've been looking forward to having you both as my guests.'

'The answer is no.'

'Mr Walton, I urge you not to forgo this opportunity too rashly.' He looked me over. 'In fact, since you are known to be an authority on Japanese arms, I could even arrange for you to have a first-hand look at the Imperial Sword.'

'Forget it.'

'But the timing couldn't be more ideal. At the moment the sword has just been transferred to one of the metallurgy labs at Tsukuba Science City for minor repair work. Since Tsukuba is to be our destination as well, I can just telex the Imperial Household and instruct them to arrange a viewing date.' He smiled again. 'For a connoisseur such as yourself, nothing would please me more.'

There was something about the way he said it. I don't know. Maybe a strange glimmer flashed through his eyes. Looking back, I think that was the moment I first should have realised Matsuo Noda had decided he was God.

'You didn't hear me. We're not leaving now. At least not on your terms.'

'Mr Walton, I really must insist.' He glanced over at Tam. 'What I intend to show you should be of extreme interest to you both.'

'I'll go when *I'm* ready.' She turned and headed for the door.

'Dr Richardson, I'm afraid we all have no alternative.' He spoke quietly, his tone masking the harshness as he continued. 'These offices have been sealed. As a temporary security measure. There appears to have been an unauthorised access to the NEC mainframe here. However, I've decided to postpone criminal charges for the moment.' He smiled again. 'Besides, the time has come for you both to know everything.'

We were on our way. I looked out of the window on my side, down through the haze covering New York's East River just below us, and took Tam's hand. The NY chopper was a Sikorski S58T, twin engine, two pilots. Events were moving so fast it was hard even to think. No doubt about one thing, though: we'd been outmanoeuvred, outplanned, outfought. The only good part was, he had me as hostage, not Amy. In a final face-off with Noda, whatever he had in mind, I still figured I could take care of myself, MITI and all. The battle had just begun.

When we walked out of Noda's office, there was no longer any mistaking the new security arrangements. Dai Nippon was on red alert.

'Well, Matthew, looks like we're about to get the big picture, like it or not.'

'On Noda's terms. Which wasn't the way it was supposed to happen.'

'I just need to confront Ken.'

For whatever good it may do, I found myself thinking. We were knee-deep in confrontations and we still didn't know a damned thing. What did Noda have planned for us? Whatever it was, I had a strong feeling I didn't want it.

Back in my own office at Dai Nippon, there was only time for one phone call. The first name that came to mind was Joanna. I wanted to say, Look, if I don't make it through this, you and Amy are well provided for. She's got a trust fund that's now seven figures, and you can have the house, the bank account, the whole damn works. Just don't ever let a man named Matsuo Noda anywhere near you or her.

But I couldn't force myself to dial the number. It wasn't Joanna who was in over her head now; it was me. The subtle or not-so-subtle difference was enough to stop me cold. I'd vowed to manage life on my own and this was no moment to waffle.

So, instead I did the next best thing and called the West Side Free School — which, I might add, may have been free in its disdain of classical curriculum, but it had very non-free tuition practices. I identified myself, announced an emergency, and asked to speak to Ms Amy Walton. In about a minute she was there.

'Dad, we're in the middle of our Monday Geo-Two exam.' She lowered her voice. 'What's the capital of Somalia?'

'Honey, haven't a clue. Just try and do the best you can. Employ that exceptional brain of yours.'

'Thanks.'

'Adults don't have to know the capitals of Third World countries. That's a small perk we get for putting up with old age.' I paused. 'Amy, about this weekend.'

'Uh oh.' She sighed. 'Betcha I know what's next.'

'Well, a problem's come up. I've got to take care of a few things.'

'Dad, the snow leopards. This weekend is when they're supposed to—'

'Honey, we'll hit the Bronx Zoo the minute I get back. I absolutely promise.'

'You going off somewhere?'

'Just a quick trip.'

'Where?' She perked up.

'We'll talk about it when I get back.' I wanted to say 'if I get back'.

'Big secret, huh?'

'Amy, I just wanted to ... darling, be careful.'

'What's the matter? Dad, are you in some kind of trouble?'

How could I answer? Damned right I was, but that wasn't the point of the call.

'Sweetie, just ... just be especially careful. That's all. I'll try my best to make it up to you at Christmas. Maybe we can still get down to the islands somehow. And Amy ...'

'Yeah.'

'I love you, honey.'

'Love you too, Dad. Look, I gotta get back.'

'I'm sure Ms Winters will give you some extra time.'

'Don't bet on it. She's an old grouch. She's twenty-eight and an old maid.'

Twenty-eight. Old? Good God. I keep forgetting what it's like to be thirteen and think of the future as the next three weeks, followed by a gaping void.

'Sweetheart, that's not exactly ancient. Believe me. She's probably still got half a dozen good years left.'

'Tell *her*. Look, I've gotta run.'

'All right. Just advise your mother something unexpected came up. Maybe you and I can make it next weekend. We'll do the snow leopards, that's an absolute guarantee.'

'Great. So long, Dad. Have fun.'

I almost said 'goodbye'. Bad luck, I thought. So instead I said, 'take care'.

Shortly thereafter Matsuo Noda, Tam Richardson and yours truly were headed over to New York Helicopter's midtown pad, Noda's bodyguards in the limo with us. The battle was drawn.

Now as I looked down at the boroughs of New York gliding below, all those little strings of metallic beads lined up on the ribbons of asphalt, the backyards of New York's solid middle class glimmering with remnants of snow, I found myself wondering what Noda had planned for *them*.

Another imponderable still nagged at me as well: what about Akira Mori? Tam reported that by the time she'd arrived at the DNI offices that morning our friend had vanished. Ditto her information-packed attaché case. As quickly as the lady had come, she'd disappeared back to Tokyo. But not with Noda. She'd gone on her own terms. Was he now using his new Concorde to try to head her off? What had she been doing here? Just hand-delivering MITI's latest 'guidance'?

Maybe we were finally about to uncover everybody's real agenda.

Again my mind went back to *ken* and *kan*, Miyamoto Musashi's famous discourse on mental attitude in *The Way of the Warrior*, which he called *heihō kokoro mochi no koto*. What was merely appearances, *ken*, and what was *kan*, the global picture, the essence?

Noda had temporarily gained the upper hand, but now I realised that was almost to be expected. After all, he was a swordsman with decades of experience. So much for *ken*, my superficial observation. The real truth, *kan*, lay much deeper. And like all such truths it had to be elementary, elegantly simple.

Which left only two possibilities. Either Matsuo Noda was merely an insane genius about to show us the inner workings of the massive organisation he now controlled, or he planned to kill us.

Or both.

TWENTY

Dr Kenji Asano gazed out of the window of his office at the Institute, the last shafts of sun casting long shadows in the canyons below. It was late Tuesday afternoon and gales of December wind tunnelled around the skyscrapers of Tokyo, chilling the grey steel and glass. The blank computer screens reflected back his smooth, trim face, his glum eyes. Technology. It was divorcing man from all sensibility. What Kenji Asano found himself wanting at that moment was not high-tech but high-touch, to be seated on the *tatami* of his Tokyo teahouse, smelling the fresh straw, gazing out over the manicured evergreen shrubs of his garden, the clumps of leafless black bamboo. He recalled again the tea ceremony in Kyoto and the sight of Tamara approaching down the stepping stones of the 'dewy path'. She was a rare American, one who understood the essence of *cha-no-yu* — inner power shows itself in outer restraint.

As he lit a Peace cigarette with a wooden match and continued to examine the cheerless skyline of Tokyo, a thought flickered past — Bodhidharma, the first Zen master, who had plucked away his eyelids to prevent sleep as he meditated. That reflection led naturally to ruminations on the master's disciple, Hui-ko, who sat *zazen* for days in the snows outside Shao-lin monastery, then finally severed his own arm and offered it to the master as testament of his devotion.

Bushidō, the code of the *samurai*. Who today would cut off an arm to prove determination? Or be Benkei at the Bridge, the servant who breaks the rules of society and cudgels his own master to protect their disguise and deceive their foes. That famous episode, he told himself, would be his model. Sometimes *bushidō* required you to circumvent tradition and honour for the greater good.

What was happening in Japan? These days many thoughtful Japanese were expressing open concern, even fear, over their country's rising nationalism. Although high officials still couched their flag-waving in coded language intended to elude foreign notice, many prominent voices were now suggesting 'it's wrong to think prewar Japan was all bad'. The latest school textbooks spoke glowingly of the country's Imperial traditions. Encouraged by this jingoism, in truth veiled racism, many superpatriots were beginning to emerge from obscurity. Now, with the Imperial Sword as symbol, the Japanese Right was openly on the march. Surely Noda had known it would happen, had counted on it.

He recalled the line by Yeats, 'And what rough beast, its hour come round at last . . .'

The 'beast', Kenji Asano feared, had arisen in Japan. And its monstrous head was none other than Matsuo Noda. Who could have suspected the dark side of Noda's grand design or the extent of his determination? Violence, money in the billions and accomplices where they were least suspected. Perhaps even inside MITI.

This last disturbing prospect had convinced Kenji Asano that the time for operating within the rules was past. He had already taken a first step, aided unwittingly by a bureaucrat of immense ambition within the Ministry. His first counterploy against Noda had bought time – how much he didn't know – but the next move must be decisive.

He glanced around his office, then at the MITI reports stacked high on his desk. Benkei at the Bridge. For Kenji Asano only one course was left. He would now have to use his own master, MITI, to destroy Matsuo Noda.

His mind went back to the meeting at his MITI office Monday of the previous week. Although he was on temporary assignment at the Institute, he still checked in daily at the Ministry. Filing into his office at nine-thirty sharp had been the three men whose 'consensus' was crucial. The difficulty was, they must never know what he planned.

Michio Watanabe, International Trade Policy Bureau, Trade

Research Section: heavyset, early fifties, a professional bureaucrat with powerful eyes and a permanent expression of scepticism. He had been a close colleague of Noda's for decades.

Tanzan Kitano, Industrial Policy Bureau, International Enterprises Section: grey hair tinged with silver, immaculate dresser, spoke five languages. He had been in MITI over twenty years and had maintained the same mistress for fifteen: a man respected for his long-range thinking.

Hiromu Ikeda, Industrial Technology Agency: late thirties, thrived on expediency, doing the job no matter the consequences. Part of a hard new breed, he was Japan's future. And MITI was *his* future.

While the men moved towards the wide couch across from his desk, Kenji Asano opened with offhand pleasantries, directed mainly towards Watanabe, partly because he was eldest and partly to sound out his mind-state. Next he welcomed Kitano with a few inquiries concerning his wife and son, a transparent formality since he was known far and wide to despise them both. Finally he greeted Ikeda and indicated that the meeting would be short, knowing the younger man liked to move directly to matters at hand and regarded the usual preliminaries as an old-fashioned waste of time.

Agenda: the American companies Matsuo Noda was acquiring. A proposition had 'surfaced' (in Japanese bureaucracies, all ideas are anonymous and thus devoid of repercussions) that certain MITI personnel be put on leave of absence to serve on the boards of those US concerns. Given the heavy participation of Japanese monies in Noda's American programme, perhaps a more formal monitoring mechanism would be helpful to head off potential anxiety in Tokyo's financial community.

The idea, of course, was Kenji Asano's. He had first laid the groundwork with a few oblique hints to several of Dai Nippon's major institutional backers, particularly the Dai-Ichi Credit Corporation, Ltd. That move had borne fruit. Within days they had begun wondering aloud whether the Ministry might wish to consider helping oversee Noda's American investments. So far, so good. Now MITI itself had to be convinced. This meeting would undoubtedly be the first of many, resulting eventually in a 'consensus'. Would the Ministry go along?

Having set forth the topic, Kenji Asano surrendered the floor to Watanabe, the senior man present – and therefore the one whose views, in keeping with convention, would be listened to and applauded by everyone else in the room whether they agreed or not.

'In my judgment, the original objectives of Matsuo Noda and Dai Nippon are the most desirable means of maintaining the long-term security of Japan,' Watanabe declared. 'It is in our strategic interest that he be allowed to succeed. Which is why MITI should stay hands-off, should limit its participation to an advisory capacity, nothing more. Anything further could well prove extremely counterproductive in our relations with the United States. We do not need more friction.'

'*Sō deshoo*, Watanabe-san.' Kitano, the man second in seniority, nodded after a moment's pause. 'I totally concur with the basic aspects of the viewpoint you have expressed.' He was telling everybody he hadn't made up his mind.

'I also support fully Watanabe-san's insightful summary of the relevant issues,' Ikeda spoke up, his honorifics far more polite than necessary, a signal. '*Keredomo* (however) . . . it might possibly be prudent to examine briefly the considerations advanced by those who differ with this wise assessment in order that we may counter their concerns more thoughtfully.'

That was it. Kenji Asano had a head count. Watanabe was against sending MITI personnel. Kitano was waffling. Hiromu Ikeda was foursquare and hell-bent in favour of the idea. He had just announced it to the room.

Was Watanabe in league with Noda, willing to give him free rein? Was he one of Noda's operatives inside the Ministry? Or was he merely advancing his own ideas, genuinely fearful an influx of MITI personnel into the US could precipitate a severe diplomatic flap?

On the other hand, why was Ikeda so in favour of having MITI move in on Noda? The answer to that was hardly a puzzle. MITI's young prince of ambition, Hiromu Ikeda, scented the possibility of grabbing a part of Matsuo Noda's new American empire for his own. Handled skilfully, it might well catapult him directly to vice-minister inside a decade.

'Perhaps it would be useful to review once more the main elements of the situation.' Kitano knew he had the middle ground and thus was offering to arbitrate. 'The condition of America now is very troubling. The question is, how can we best aid it and ourselves? We in Japan realise that a nation's true strength is ultimately not in armaments but in the health of its economy, its industry. Yet the Americans, by making themselves a military state, have paradoxically imperilled their real security. How long can we continue to rely on an ally so blind to the main threat to its own strategic well-being? Matsuo Noda is correct. Our very safety may soon be imperilled. Something must be done. The only question is how best to proceed.'

'Sō desu ne.' Watanabe pressed, realising he would have to force his point. 'The Pentagon is, ironically, America's most insidious enemy. Japan's greatest benefit from America's defence umbrella has not been the billions we've saved on sterile arms; it has been the technical manpower we have free to support competitive industries. But the price has been the industrial decline of our foremost ally. This cannot, must not, be permitted to continue.' He paused. 'Matsuo Noda, a man I've known and respected for years, who guided this Ministry to greatness, should be allowed to assist the Americans in rebuilding their civilian sector unhindered by us. If MITI involves itself at this time, the American government may well grow alarmed and step in to stop him. Then their industrial stagnation will merely accelerate.'

'Sō deshoo.' Ikeda finally spoke. 'I agree. Unfortunately, however, there are some who believe the task Noda-sama has undertaken cannot succeed without direct MITI assistance. Again it is a matter of our own security. The question has arisen concerning whether we should continue to rely on the Americans to rescue their industrial base unassisted by any formal direction. Of course I disagree with such pessimistic views, but some would say we ourselves must now step forward and assume global leadership in technology to prevent a vacuum from developing in the Free World. By taking charge of America's floundering high-tech sector, we could rescue it from continued mismanagement, while – incidentally – satisfying our own R & D needs in a way that is extremely cost-effective. However, this can only be achieved if we are in a position to provide hands-on guidance. Which means direct MITI involvement.' He paused. 'These opinions of course are not my own, merely ones I have heard voiced. I am told, though it is difficult to comprehend, that this viewpoint has been entertained by Nakayama-sama of the Secretariat, and even discussed in his weekly conference with the Parliamentary Vice-Minister.'

The hand of fate! Asano exulted. Hiromu Ikeda has already done my work *for* me. He's gone over everybody's head. He swallowed the idea like a carp snapping a hovering dragonfly, then went off and peddled it to the Vice-Minister as though it were his own.

A man to watch out for in the future, he thought. But a perfect ally at the moment.

Watanabe said nothing. His ancient face was in shock. Everybody realised the meeting was over. It was clear Ikeda had trampled on consensus and seniority in order to further his own fortunes.

'Watanabe-san, I think we all agree your understanding of the situation is entirely proper,' Kenji Asano said soothingly. 'But solely in the interest of continued theoretical discussion at some later time, it might be prudent if all Sections prepared a contingency list of staff, fluent in English, who would be suitable for reassignment to an American sector.'

'It is always wise to cover contingencies, Asano-san,' Watanabe said drily.

None of them realised it, of course, but Hiromu Ikeda's ambition could well turn out to be the salvation of MITI itself. But for now, Asano mused, that was something none of them needed to know.

Looking out of the window at the freezing streets below, glimmering from headlights and neon, Kenji Asano told himself that a dangerous game lay ahead. Noda's first gambit had been countered, but there would be more. What he needed was a preemptive strike.

He had made the plans for that strike, a play of pure, absolute genius. The catch was, Tamara would have to cooperate.

With that thought he reached down and unlocked the top right-hand drawer of his metal desk, then drew out a large red and blue envelope. It was air express from a university address in California. As he fingered the stripes along its side, he recalled how it had arrived here at his office at the Institute for New Generation Computer Technology while he'd been in Kyoto with Tamara.

Finally he opened it again and slipped out the contents. Inside was a confidential memo on the old Nippon, Inc. letterhead, unsigned but obviously authored by Matsuo Noda, a top-security document that had been clocked in at a document station at Tsukuba Science City. How had Allan Stern stumbled on to this? Had he stolen it? Picked it up by accident? It was in Japanese, so how could he have sensed its real import?

American ingenuity, he told himself, defied all understanding. The memo, which outlined the timetable for a massive scenario, had been the first step on a long path of discovery leading Kenji Asano to indisputable proof of Matsuo Noda's real objective. Allan Stern must have had this translated or somehow intuitively guessed Noda's plan. And then ... Allan Stern had tried to warn MITI. Why? Out of past regard for Dr Yoshida, former head of the Institute and a close friend?

Stern reportedly had vanished the same day this envelope was postmarked. Noda had acted, but not swiftly enough.

Who at MITI had been the original recipient of this memo? Maybe, he thought, it no longer mattered. There was only one real way to stop Dai Nippon ...

At that moment his phone buzzed. As he punched the button, his flustered secretary announced that an in-flight call was waiting, channelled through MITI's satellite security link. It was the president of Dai Nippon, International.

TWENTY-ONE

Tsukuba Science City can be awe-inspiring or a spectre, depending on how you choose to look at it. The time was Wednesday morning, and Tam and I were viewing the place through the tinted windows of Matsuo Noda's personal DNI limo, the black Nissan she knew so well. From the vantage of an elevated freeway packed with rows of sleek Hondas and Toyotas sparkling in the cold December sunshine, we could see the silhouettes of cluster after cluster of modernistic concrete towers, an urban complex of 150,000 souls rising above what was, only a few short years ago, mostly farms. Be that as it may, take my word for it that nobody's growing radishes there today. Science City, nestled in the foothills of Mt Tsukuba some fifty kilometres north-east of downtown Tokyo, represents a government investment, including the industrial park once the site of Expo '85, of over thirty billion dollars.

Tsukuba is holy ground, the place of heroes, where kamikazes once trained for their suicide missions against the American fleet. Now it is one of the largest research centres in the world, with almost ten thousand scientists and fifty separate laboratories and scientific institutes. As we neared the first complex, I tried to make sense of all the Dáli-esque curved buildings that housed Japan's new brain trust. From the outside you can tell something is going on, but it seems secretive and proprietary. It is. The thing I had to keep reminding myself, though, was that none of this was for military boondoggles. It was aimed dead-on at industrial technology. For example, there's research here on high-energy lasers all right, but they're not intended for zapping some hypothetical Soviet satellite; they're part of the world's largest laser-radar telescope, which can project beams out more than thirty miles to analyse air quality. In short, the work here was applications-oriented, practical, and – get a firm grip on your wallet – commercial.

Together with Noda and his bodyguard/chauffeur we were headed for the Electrotechnical Institute, where he was about to give us our first glimpse of Japan's new high-tech empire. That lab just so happened to be the place where heavy work was underway on applications of the artificial-intelligence effort of Kenji Asano's Fifth Generation shop. It was merely the first stop, however, in an odyssey Noda claimed would take us through the hidden heart of Japan's industrial future.

Noda reported that he had spoken with Kenji Asano, who was unfortunately tied up in meetings and couldn't join us until tomorrow. Thus Tam had not yet had her chance to hear his account of MITI's sudden new interest in Dai Nippon's programme. All the same, Noda claimed to welcome Ken's arrival.

'Whatever concerns you may have, I'm sure he will be more than happy to address them,' declared the president of Dai Nippon.

Tam had tried on her own to reach Ken at his office, without success. Maybe, I thought to myself, he just didn't want to talk. In any case that quandary remained unresolved.

The way I saw the situation, though, we had enough to deal with merely getting through today. Noda's game was no longer a game. He was going to take us to the top of the mountain, show us the other side and then . . . what? Whatever it was, that part would have to be handled in due time. For now his intentions seemed to be to drive home a singular point: if you think Dai Nippon has been playing hardball with money, wait till you see Japan's real action. He was going to lay bare the empire, the awesome machine he now had at his command. The payoff of Tsukuba, he explained, was intended to be nothing less than total technological supremacy.

The limo was slowing to a stop in front of an oddly shaped concrete building, brand-new, that covered several acres with cones and hexagons and various geometries. We'd arrived.

'This is the Electrotechnical Institute, research centre for Japan's Advanced Robot Technology Project.' He pointed. The laboratory appeared to be somebody's idea of what architecture would be in the twenty-first century, a sort of Japanese spaceship splattered across a vast acreage. 'The work underway here and over at the Mechanical Engineering Lab is intended to coordinate all government and private research on industrial robots.'

He stepped out and motioned for us to join him. Our top-secret tour had begun. As we walked towards the main entryway, he delivered an opening summary.

'Here we have allocated twenty billion yen, about a hundred and fifty million dollars, for an eight-year research programme to perfect a range of industrial robots.' He continued while we walked past the small grey metallic sign, in both Japanese and English, that identified the Institute. 'It is being closely coordinated with the spin-offs of the Fifth Generation AI work.'

I noticed that no guards were posted, though the metal doors were tightly sealed. Noda didn't bother to take out a key as he proceeded. 'The Advanced Robot Technology Project coordinates the research of over twenty corporations as well as R & D at various universities, and this lab is where we integrate all the results of that work.'

'You mean different parts or robots are being created at separate research operations, then brought together here?' I probably shouldn't have been surprised by the tight, nationwide coordination. Typical Japan.

'Precisely. Robots have a multiplicity of elements. There are manipulators, the mechanical versions of our hands; then there are the senses of vision and touch; and finally there is movement, locomotion. Each of these is being developed individually, then combined here. For example, if a robot is to understand voice commands — in effect make its operator a programmer — then it must incorporate the speech-recognition work of the Fifth Generation Project, which will supply the eyes, the ears, the brain.'

Maybe that's where Asano comes in, I thought. Could it be he's the point man here for artificial intelligence, on board to oversee creating the computerised brains for all these babies?

Was he yet another DNI operative, witting or unwitting, just as Tam and I had been?

Noda's lecture was still underway. 'The first generation of robots does things by rote, the same motion repeated dumbly over and over again. What we call the second generation are those with crude sensing abilities, perhaps touch pads or video, though they are still stationary.' He placed his hand over a small screen by the door. A light flashed under his palm – presumably allowing a computer somewhere to analyse his handprint – and a second later the door slid open. Then he continued, 'The goal of the work here is a third-generation robot. You might almost call it a functional "android", since it will be able to move, see and think much as we do. Whether it will actually look like a human is another matter, but that's not necessarily even a useful objective.'

Intelligent monsters in silicon and steel, I found myself thinking. All our fantasies, or nightmares, come to life.

I didn't have to look far to see that they were already in the womb. We were entering the main laboratory floor now, surrounded by what seemed a Martian landscape of mechanical creatures. The place was bustling, yet spotless as a hospital ward. Noda acknowledged the deep bows of several of the shirtsleeved staff, then continued.

'Although visitors are not normally permitted in the sensitive areas here, I have arranged total-access priority for you both. I consider you among the few Americans today who can understand the strategic significance of this programme.'

If Matsuo Noda was really saying that he intended to give us a sobering dose of Japan's impending high-tech clout, he was off to a bang-up start.

Then he turned and greeted a short white-uniformed man. 'Allow me to introduce Dr Noboru Matsugami, who is Senior Staff Specialist for the programme here. Dr Matsugami will be your guide today.'

Matsugami was close to fifty and balding, with short-cropped hair that seemed to stand out on the sides of his head like the bristles of a metal brush. He was bowing to Noda every other second, as though he'd just been summoned by God. He attempted a smile, then greeted us in Japanese, followed by accented English.

I surveyed the floor — steel and aluminium and computers — feeling as if I could have been on another planet. Tam, strangely, had said scarcely a word the whole time. She probably knew about a lot of this, but surely not the proprietary advanced devices.

Noda's glimpse of Japan's industrial 'Manhattan Project' was one of the most memorable experiences of my life. Although I suspect the devices he let Matsugami show us were just the toys, they still were enough to leave no doubt where things were headed.

Without going into the classified details, let me attempt to describe a few of the items I still remember. I was particularly impressed by the Waseda University/Hitachi walking robot WHL-II, which uses advanced machine technology and computer control to move just as a human does, two-legged style. Its hydraulic steel joints and carbon-fibre muscles, together with its computerised foot sensors, give it walking skills better than most young humans. Its brain of course is a microprocessor, programmed to let it walk in different styles, just as we do. Other mobile robots had four legs, even six — such as the Titan III, which we saw climb up a set of stairs like a metallic sci-fi spider.

As for robot hands, the most advanced also were from Hitachi's mechanical engineering research lab. Unlike most robot grippers, little more than glorified vices, this one had three fingers (which Matsugami claimed were more agile than a version at MIT) whose 'muscles' were a heat-sensitive metal (invented in the US) that would contract when an electric current passed through.

Vision research was also well advanced. A Matsushita robot equipped with a computerised 'eye' was able to analyse the lines and shadows on a human face and then draw a black-and-white sketch like a sidewalk artist. Even more amazing, a robot with a TV-camera eye — developed jointly by Waseda University and Sumitomo Electric — could read sheet music and play it on a keyboard using mechanical fingers. This android pianist employed recent advances in artificial intelligence to determine the best fingering for each phrase and even took requests for tunes in spoken Japanese. Play it again, HAL. Other robots with 'voice-recognition' capability allowed a human operator simply to sit in one spot and command the mobile machine where to go and what to do.

At one point Tam asked Matsugami for a candid opinion on how far along he thought the Advanced Robot Technology Programme had progressed. Well, he replied, sucking in his breath pensively, the manual-dexterity problem was about licked: the robot arms now being perfected could pick up anything and move it anywhere. Vision and programmable intelligence were harder, but he felt their research was getting close. Already he had robots that could analyse and interpret 3-D objects and scenes, enabling them to manoeuvre around a factory floor and make decisions of almost human complexity. The ultimate objective was factory-wide systems for Computer Integrated Manufacturing (CIM) that would allow every operation of a company, from design to engineering to manufacturing, to be controlled by computer via a single data base. It was cheap, and it elevated quality control to a hundred per cent. No doubt about it, he said, as Japan moved to automate manufacturing and get on with an information-industry future, these smart robots would be their secret weapon.

The Institute's mechanical menagerie, I realised, was what the next century was going to look like. Except it was here now. As Matsugami took us through lab after lab, it became clear that the Japanese 'third-generation' functionoid robot was all but a reality.

Noda's message was clear. Already Japan was spending twice as much on new manufacturing technology as America was. They led the world in robotics and that lead was growing. With the coming of that third generation – robots that could see, move and think – world industrial leadership would be up for grabs. These were the stakes Japan was betting on the twenty-first century. Anybody who planned to play against them better have something on the table too.

At the end of the tour as dusk was beginning to settle in Noda reappeared and escorted us back to the limo. And that's when he laid it out.

'Dr Richardson, what you and Mr Walton have just seen is merely a glimpse of the real peril to America's future.' He was closing the door of the car. 'There is much, much more ... projects such as the rapid commercialisation of superconductivity. America's world supremacy is at a crossroads.'

'Why are you showing us this?' Tam was still troubled by the same question that was eating at me.

'Very simple, really. Thus far we have, together, attempted to address some of the more egregious ineptitudes in America's corporate management. Our success in that, if I may say, has already been substantial. However, even the best-managed organisation cannot flourish without the tools required to take it the next step. That translates as technology.' He paused, then looked at us both. 'Do you understand what I'm saying?'

'Japan now has the technology, just as it has the money,' Tam answered.

'You are correct. Thus far Dai Nippon has merely provided a conduit to infuse capital into the American industrial scene. That was the easy part. The task remaining will be much more difficult.' He looked at us. 'Difficult because, for this, America must share in return.'

'You want to make a deal, I take it.' I finally spoke. Funny, but I thought I sounded a little like Faust beginning negotiations with the devil.

He smiled. 'That is a blunt way of describing what I am about to suggest, Mr Walton, but it does capture the spirit of my proposal. America excels in basic research, Japan in applied research, in engineering. The time has come to join forces.'

'How?'

'As you have seen, the monetary resources at Dai Nippon's disposal make it possible for us to wield significant influence.' He smiled. 'Japanese capital has been brought to America; Japanese technology can be brought as well.'

'At a price.'

'At a price, yes. But a modest one really.' He smiled again, then buzzed for his driver to start the car. 'Let me put it like this. If you choose to proceed with me in the next step of Dai Nippon's programme, I will arrange for everything you have seen today to be my gift to America. All I ask from you both is complete cooperation in the days ahead. Together we can forge an informal alliance between Japan and America that could alter the course of world history. But it must be done in an atmosphere of complete trust.'

Tam was astonished. 'You'd make this manufacturing technology available to American industry? Why?'

'As part of a *quid pro quo*, Dr Richardson. It's quite simple. In return I would expect complete access to the R & D in the firms Dai Nippon has acquired.' He stared back through his rimless glasses. 'Which, I gather, is a notion you find a trifle unsettling.'

You bastard, I thought. You did have my phone tapped. How else could you have known what she was thinking.

She shot me a telling glance. 'How does all this fit in with the new MITI "guidance" we're suddenly getting?'

'That is a separate matter, Dr Richardson, which we will address in due course. What I am concerned with now is something else entirely – the final step in restoring America to economic health. The first requirement was long-term capital and better management, which Dai Nippon has now begun to provide. The next is technology, a small foretaste of which I have shown you today.'

Was this, I wondered, the big picture, the *kan* we'd been trying to get a handle on?

'What I'm proposing,' Noda continued, 'is that together we become partners in the creation of a massive Japanese–American consortium. Perhaps we could call it NIPPONICA.'

'NIPPONICA?' She kept her tone even.

'The name has an interesting ring to it, does it not? As I envision the organisation, you would be its American CEO.' He paused. 'I would chair the board.' Then he turned to me. 'And you, Mr Walton, could be invaluable as chief corporate counsel.'

The man had gone totally mad. Or had he?

'I still don't understand how this venture could be brought together. You'd be dealing with hundreds of companies, a worldwide management headache.'

'Mr Walton, what other choice do we have? Given the precipitous decline of America's global leadership, together with Japan's economic and technological rise, there can be only two possible outcomes of the inevitable direction affairs are headed: bankruptcy for us both, or war. The time has come for risk-taking, for a belief in the human spirit. We each need the other more than our political leaders can allow themselves to admit, and thus steps must be taken outside normal diplomatic channels to bring us closer together.' He continued, in perfect form, 'Both America and Japan would benefit from a comingling of our industry and research. We would learn from each other, find strength in unity, realise a common perspective on global concerns. Our economies would be joined, our peoples united. Instead of friction and the sabre-rattling of trade disputes, we would have the harmony of a single enterprise.'

'Who exactly is going to finance and operate this undertaking?' I was listening to him describe his planned-for utopia with increasing scepticism. But he had already rocked America, and Japan, to the core. Not a man to underestimate.

'As you might suppose, Dai Nippon would, by virtue of its present situation, be ideally suited to lay the groundwork.' He glanced out the tinted windows. 'Afterwards the political processes of both countries would naturally have no choice but to follow our lead, ratifying – as they always do – conditions that have already become a *fait accompli*.'

It had all the easy resonance of a grand historical undertaking, except ... except what if this was still *ken*, superficialities, not *kan*, the real truth?

'Before we go any further, I think Dr Richardson and I should talk this over.' I looked up to see the Tsukuba Hotel, where we were scheduled to stay overnight. Noda had made other accommodations for himself, saying he also needed to drop by the Metallurgy Lab and check to see how work was going on the sword. My scheduled viewing was to be tomorrow.

'I agree.' Tam looked at me sharply. 'We can discuss this more in the morning.'

'As you wish.' The limo was pulling to a stop. 'Tomorrow should be an interesting day for you both. We will pursue our discussions then.' He smiled. 'However, be aware that time is of the essence.'

With that parting shot, the long black Nissan sped away.

'Tam, let's see if this place has a bar. I need a drink.'

'Double.' She was carrying the small overnight bag Noda's New York staff had handed her as we left. I had one too, just a shirt and essentials.

The hotel saloon was modernistic, vinyl, and leaned heavily towards Japanese beer and Suntory whisky. By now some middle-level executives were getting off work at the labs and dropping in to start their usual evening round of drinking, but at this early hour it was still sparsely occupied.

We headed for a corner table and ordered a couple of draught Kirin. After the beers arrived, we got down to brass tacks.

What the hell was Noda's real agenda?

Two heads, so the saying goes, are better than one. I don't know, could be they're worse. Because as Tam and I sat there, Noda's offer to head up some kind of new world consortium dangling before us, what our two heads came up with was the scariest thing that'd ever crossed my path.

Maybe it was the thought of America's working stiffs, whose jobs Noda supposedly was so determined to save. Trouble was, I didn't buy that in the slightest any more. So what made any sense?

Simple. Why not the most obvious answer of all? Noda wasn't doing this for them. Or for Japan. That wasn't his game. Noda was planning this grandiose design for Noda.

'Tam.' I sipped at my beer. 'Did you believe a word of what he said?'

'Of course not. At least not the United Nations speech. It's pure hogwash.'

'Totally agree. But he's about to do something big, I'm convinced.'

'Got any ideas?'

Luckily the place was getting noisier now, so nobody could have been listening even if they'd tried. Which was the very reason I wanted to talk in the bar and not in either of our rooms. Who knew the reach of Noda's electronic ears?

'Not really. But what if we stepped back a second and tried looking at this latest move from a longer view? Maybe we've been tangled up in the trees, missing the forest.'

'We've seen plenty of forest lately.'

'But what if it's the wrong one? Let's try the *teki ni naru to iu koto* strategy, become the enemy. Pretend for a minute we're Noda, a guy who's got it all – money, clout, everything. So why does he all of a sudden want to come across the Pacific and buy himself a load of industrial headaches, then hand them Japan's technology?'

'It's MITI somehow. I'm convinced that's the key. Which is why I'm going to nail Ken.'

'Well, let's not jump to conclusions. I'm wondering. What if Dai Nippon is taking over American industry not because it's strategic to MITI, as those memos we found would lead us to think? What if the reason is because it's strategic to Noda?'

'But why?'

'What if his relationship to that Ministry is something totally different from what it seems?'

'Well, if MITI's not behind the buy-ups, then who're they for?'

I sat a minute, again trying to think like Noda. 'What if this scenario is actually aimed at . . . what if it's a global power play?'

She looked at me sceptically. 'I don't get it.'

'OK, granted it sounds crazy, but let's chase that for a minute. I think we agree this whole scenario is not what he wants it to seem. So what are some of the other things in all this that aren't what they appear to be? Does anything dovetail?' I sat musing a second, searching for an opening. 'What are some of the twists about Japan that're obviously misleading?'

'Well, acceptance of *gaijin*, for one. It goes only so far, then stops like a brick wall.' She was obviously speaking from personal experience.

'Maybe that's because they've always been isolated. Some things never change,' I pondered aloud. 'Which is probably the secret of their success. Take the ruling clique. Sure, Japan is a democracy, but is it really? Not the way we understand the word. What they actually have, after you get past all the slogans, is just a retread of the old system. The truth is it's still run as it was a thousand years ago. By the old families, the old money. Elections never decide issues. They're handled by the power structure. Half the seats in the Diet are practically hereditary, going back generations in the same family. There's only one real political party. The ministries are fiefdoms. I mean, the goddamn country is still feudal. They don't even have a word for democracy. They had to borrow it. *Demokurasu.*'

'Well, Japan's a pragmatic place. The old ways work. Remember the *zaibatsu*, those industrial conglomerates that ran the war machine? MacArthur dismantled them, but they reappeared almost as soon as he left.'

'Right, the power structure restored those right away. The *zaibatsu* are back and chewing up world commerce. But the *demokurasu* eyewash is still around. The job's not finished.'

She stared around the room. 'Matt, I don't like where I think you're headed.'

'I agree it's sick, but let's push it a little more. What is it about Japan that's made it such a dynamo the last couple of decades?'

'Hard work, organisation, drive.'

'Exactly. But where did that come from?'

'They had to have it. Over the centuries most Japanese were dirt poor. They had to hustle just to survive. Matthew, Japan is a collectivist society driven by capitalism, an idea so alien to the West nobody can even *see* it.'

'Perfect description. Only problem is, all this *demokurasu* is sooner or later going to start cutting away the very thing that's made Japan so successful – a country powered by obedient, collective action and glued together by hierarchy and tradition.'

'You're saying Noda wants to turn back the clock?'

'Don't know. But what if these industrialists, these *zaibatsu* honchos, are fed up with having to deal with all the cumbersome *demokurasu* machinery? And they're especially fed up with a certain ministry making them jump through the hoop? Tam, what if Noda's real agenda is to go to America and buy himself a gun to hold to MITI's head?'

'You don't think he's buying America's companies to help MITI?' She looked unconvinced.

'If I had money to bet, I'd almost be willing to put it on the possibility he's buying leverage to use *against* MITI, and through them the whole inefficient government set-up. How come MITI's suddenly sending staff over to look in on Noda's play? Could it be somebody there's figured out what he's up to and they want to head him off? They realise Matsuo Noda is the only man on the planet who could conceivably beat MITI at its own game? Bring it to its knees? First he acquired control of half the capital in Japan, then he came to the US and started grabbing up all the R & D that'll be competing with MITI through the end of the century. When he's got it, he'll have a power base to match theirs. He's set to call the new tune.'

'Which is?'

'Who knows? But try this for an agenda: time to cut the crap, Noda's thinking, get rid of all the clumsy Western-style *demokurasu* charade, tighten up, lean and mean. Go back to the only system that's ever really clicked for Japan. Imperial rule. Make the "Land of the Gods" sacred and invincible.'

'This is getting wild.' She lowered her voice. 'But maybe . . . maybe you could be right. He just happens to locate the Imperial Sword, and suddenly the Emperor is resurrected from a discredited figurehead back to a symbol of Japan's greatness.'

'Here comes that old-time religion. Everybody goes traditional, right on cue, and the nutty Japan Firsters are thriving again, just like the thirties.'

'Good Lord.'

'Doesn't it all fit somehow? Matsuo Noda started off by creating this shadow outfit, Dai Nippon, in order to get his hands on all his countrymen's money. Now the next step will be to start phasing out the *demokurasu* frills and the powerless Prime

Minister and the MITI bureaucrats and turning the place into a kick-ass machine again. Look out, world.'

'One small problem. The Emperor can't rule Japan. Not really. He's a living god. Which means . . .'

'See? That difficulty's nothing new. For a thousand years the Emperor's had no real clout anyway. The nitty-gritty of running Japan was always the job of his stand-in.'

There was a long pause. We both avoided speaking the word, but there it was. Finally she leaned back and closed her eyes, her voice barely audible above the din of the bar.

'Shogun.'

TWENTY-TWO

'*Komban wa*, Tamara.' The voice emerged from the dark as her key turned in the door of room 328. 'How are you?'

'Ken!'

'Good to see you again.'

'How did you . . .?'

He chuckled as he switched on the light by the chair. 'Rank in MITI has its moments.'

'I thought you were coming tomorrow.'

'I am, officially.' He rose and moved towards her. 'But tonight I'd hoped we could be together.' He smiled. 'Alone.'

She stood in the open doorway, unmoving.

'Ken, we have a lot to talk about, all right?' She closed the door. 'And I don't mean in bed.'

Truthfully, she wasn't even sure she wanted to see him at all. The Dai Nippon scenario was getting too complicated, too insidious. Noda's play was turning into something with worldwide implications.

'Tamara, I came because we need to talk. I think you're in danger. Maybe we both are.'

'From Noda? Just because he's a megalomaniac—'

'You think it's that simple?' he interrupted. 'Don't be so sure. For now let's just say he's very, very clever and very powerful.' He reached out to welcome her. 'But whatever he is, the time has come to stop him.'

'I think Matt and I just figured out why. He's a threat to MITI, isn't he, Ken? A peril to your power base.'

'He's a threat to everybody. But yes, MITI is definitely in his way at this point. Or at least I'm in his way. Somebody has to be.'

'So what do you expect me to do about it? As a matter of fact, what has MITI done for me lately except try and move in on my work?'

'Tam, you can't stand up to Noda alone. But maybe together we can, at least for a while.'

'What makes you think . . .?'

'I have a weapon at my disposal. A powerful weapon. The Ministry. If we can use it to focus attention on what he's—'

'How?'

'I want to speed up the Ministry's involvement. Bring in lots more people. We do that and we'll—'

'I see.' She slipped past him and headed for the second chair. 'That's a terrific idea. Give it all to MITI.' For a moment there she'd almost been ready to start trusting him again.

'Tam, we only have to make it *seem* that's what is happening.' He turned to face her. 'It'll be like waving a red flag under the nose of your Congress. Surely that'll wake everybody up to what he's doing. They'd move in and stop him cold. Guaranteed.'

'Ken, Matsuo Noda made me a very intriguing proposition today. Matter of fact, it sounds better than yours.' She got up and walked over to the small refrigerator fitted under the sink. 'Want a beer? I'm going to have one.'

'All right.' He looked at her. 'What were you saying just now? About a proposition?'

'Noda asked me to head up a Japanese–American consortium run as a single industry. It's almost as if he wants to put together an American version of MITI, an organisation that can oversee and coordinate American R & D nationwide.'

'Do you believe he means what he says?'

She turned and stared at him for a moment. 'I guess the honest answer is no. I think it's just a smokescreen to get his hands on everything he wants in the US, disguised under the rubric of assistance.' She retrieved two cans of cold Asahi and popped the tops. 'On the other hand, you're suggesting we have to give America's industry to MITI in order to save it from Matsuo Noda.' She extended a can of beer and a glass. 'Right now, I don't trust MITI any more than I trust him.'

'Tamara, this is a high-stakes game. Against a man with more money and power than the world has ever seen in one place. It's not going to be easy to stop him. It's also going to be risky. For us both.'

'And you think a MITI takeover is the answer?'

'It's the only thing that's left.' He sobered. 'Unfortunately it'll also damage MITI's political credibility badly worldwide. But that's the price I'm willing to pay to stop Noda. What other choice is there?'

'Hurt MITI? I'm not so sure. Taking over all of DNI's American research labs should give quite a boost to your Marketshare–90 programme, shouldn't it? You'd be acquiring America's high-tech sector for Japan all nicely wrapped up in a bundle.' She poured from her can. 'Ought to trim years off your timetable.'

'I don't know where you heard about that, Tam.' Vague surprise in his voice. 'But that's not a real programme. Marketshare–90 is just a planning exercise over in the General Affairs Section. Part of some training for their new people.'

'When we asked Noda about it, he seemed to think it was real enough.'

'Then he was just bluffing. He had to be.'

'Ken, what do you take me for . . .?' She wasn't sure how much more double-talk she could stand.

He waved his hand to stop her. 'Please. Just trust me for this once. That's all I ask.'

'You're sure as hell not making it easy. I think it's time you told me what's *really* going on.'

'All right. I'll show you the bottom line. Maybe then you'll accept the truth.' He got up and went over to his briefcase. 'I have something in here you ought to see.'

'What?'

'It's an advance text of the speech His Majesty delivers on 2 January.'

'That's his annual New Year's appearance at the Imperial Palace, right? When he bestows his blessing on everybody.'

'Exactly.' He pulled out the sheet. 'I think this sheds light on a lot of things. Here. I made a rough English translation, just to hear how it sounds.'

She took the paper, torn from a yellow legal pad, and began to read.

The speech began with a long-winded celebration of the famous Yasukuni Shrine, home of the spirits of all Japanese warriors. That shrine, His Majesty then went on to declare, was increasingly misconstrued by the world as a symbol of Japanese militarism, a misapprehension both unfortunate and untrue, since Japan had indeed renounced martial force forever. However, to reinforce that commitment in the eyes of a nervous world, he was now announcing the dedication of a new national shrine to Japan's spirit, one that would have no such misleading overtones. This new shrine, at Tsukuba Science City, would be a memorial to the peaceful use of technology, to man's mastery of the physical world sanctified so long ago by the Shinto gods.

She looked up. 'A new national shrine? Nice political move.'

'Better read the rest before you jump to conclusions.'

She glanced down and continued.

It had further been decided, the Emperor would say, that the newly recovered Imperial Sword would not be housed at Ise after all. It would instead be the centrepiece of this new memorial to Japanese technology.

Well, she thought, it still sounds OK. Theme shrines are perfectly within tradition. After all, the Meiji Shrine in Tokyo commemorates the nineteenth-century Emperor who began Japan's modernisation. However, the thing to remember was that new shrines can have a philosophical subtext. The Meiji told the Japanese that their country had accepted Westernisation. So, given that the creation of a new shrine can embody a message to everybody, she found herself wondering what word was being sent out this time.

The Emperor would go on to spell this out, lest any of his subjects were too dense to get the picture. Unlike the Yasakuni Shrine, he would say, this new memorial at Tsukuba would not commemorate Japan's warrior past; rather it would celebrate a modern Japan whose world eminence would be fashioned not with arms but through economic struggle. In so doing, it would symbolise the regeneration of Japan's ancient spirit, *Yamato damashi*, of which the *bushidō* of the *samurai* was merely one manifestation, only a stage. Grander things were on the way. Japan's rightful place in the new world order was only now coming into its own. The new *Tsukuba damashi* would harness modern technology to Japan's ancient traditions, would put the new at the service of the old.

What he was really telling his people, she realised, in oblique language only they would comprehend, was that Japan was now prepared to wage open confrontation through commerce — their trading state pitted against the world's military states, whose economic base and martial ascendancy they would now proceed to challenge through technological superiority and cut-throat trade.

'Ken, does this mean what I think it means?' She passed back the yellow page.

'If you think it means Noda's got him now, then the answer is yes. He's co-opted the Imperial house.' He took the sheet and returned it to his briefcase. 'I'd bet you anything Noda himself wrote that speech. He's begun, Tamara. His total takeover, of America *and* Japan.'

She sat a moment in silence, a strange sensation in her stomach. Did she believe it? She wasn't sure.

'Ken, there's something you should know. A colleague came with me this trip. An American lawyer. Knowing him, he's probably still down in the bar. I'd like him to read this. Why don't we go down and I'll introduce you?'

'Who is he? Can he be trusted?'

'As a matter of fact, he's an old friend. From a long time past. But we've been through a lot together lately.'

He leaned back and sipped his beer. 'Am I to assume this travelling companion is more than a casual friend?'

'That's not exactly your worry, is it? I don't pry into your life when I'm away.' She got up to retrieve another can of beer.

'You can't blame me for being curious, Tam. It's a simple, reasonable question.'

Nothing Kenji Asano does is ever simple, she told herself. There's always a subtext.

'Don't try to change the subject. One thing at a time.' She sipped from her glass. 'And regarding your plan, as far as I'm concerned, there's been too much MITI dabbling already. Frankly it pisses me off.'

'I'm sorry if you choose to feel that way.' His eyes darkened. 'Please believe me when I assure you we're on the same side. I've told you what I propose doing about Noda. But I haven't heard any of your ideas.'

She sighed and sipped her beer. 'I don't have any. Yet.'

'Then why not trust me?'

Trust. There was that word again. Trouble was, she wasn't sure she trusted anybody any more. She rose, strolled to the window, and reached for the curtain. Should she let him stay the night? Maybe that was just asking for more heartaches. Letting Japan screw America two ways. With that dismal thought she pulled open the curtains.

It had begun to snow, a swirl of drifting white.

'Ken, come and take a look.' She beckoned him. 'I think I'd like to go outside for a while. I'm weary to death of arguing.'

He rose and came over to the window, standing next to her. 'It's just started.' He glanced around the room. 'Did you bring any boots?'

'No, and I don't care. I just want some fresh air to help clear my head.'

'All right, but we'll have to use the service elevator. I can't be seen walking through the lobby, not till tomorrow.'

'We can take the stairs. Come on.'

By the time they emerged on to the driveway leading out towards the road, traffic had slowed to a crawl and the futuristic shapes of Tsukuba's labs seemed like a fairyland. She noticed that the hotel had its own helicopter pad, undoubtedly to accommodate MITI officials who needed to pop up for a quick consultation. The place was high-tech, powerful, frightening.

Just like Kenji Asano.

'You know, I'm afraid maybe we've lost it, you and me.'

309

'Lost what?'

'Whatever we had there in Kyoto.' She sighed.

'Maybe you've lost it, Tamara.' They were striding through the first thin film of white that now blanketed the sidewalk paralleling the road, leaving a trail of flattened footprints. 'Nothing has changed for me. You're welcome to come back and be part of my life any time you choose.'

'Well, right now I just want to walk in the snow.' She glanced at him, wondering if she still felt anything at all. 'You know, it's a funny thing, but this snow tonight reminds me of a trip I once took, years ago, up north to Hokkaido. The innocence, the simplicity, it was all captured in that pure, endless white.' She looked around them. 'How could Tsukuba Science City even be part of the same country?'

He smiled. 'As the tour books always say, "Japan: land of contrasts". Well, the old ways are going fast, Tam, except in our hearts. Some things will always be the same.'

'Tell you the truth, that's what scares me the most. Things like the sword, which can cause this whole country to go crazy overnight.'

'Ah yes, the sword. Matsuo Noda's magic talisman. You know that's the real reason he'll be so hard to stop. What a genius. He delivers it to the Emperor, almost the same way the Sun Goddess supposedly once did, and in the process makes himself a living god.'

'Speaking of the sword, by the way, Matt is going over to the Metallurgy Lab tomorrow to see it. Live and prime time.'

'Matt?'

'The lawyer I told you about.'

'So his name is Matt?'

'Short for Matthew. Walton.'

'But why . . .'

'Well, besides being a corporate attorney, he's supposed to be an amateur expert on swords. Hobby of his.'

'And Noda is actually letting him see it?' There was a faint note of surprise in his voice. 'Very unusual. That sword has been kept very tightly under wraps, or so I've heard.'

'Believe it. Tomorrow Matt Walton gets a command presentation. Courtesy of Noda. He's arranged everything with the Imperial Household.' She gazed up at the sky, now a white mantle reflecting back the lights from the traffic.

'Tam, I'd like very much to see it too. Think you could arrange something with Noda-san?'

'I can try.'

'You know, not many people outside the Imperial Household have actually viewed it really up close. I hear it's almost perfectly preserved.'

'Then this could be your chance.' She reached and took his hand. After all, the weather was cold. 'I'll ring Noda in the morning.'

'Thanks. But no matter what happens, with that or anything else, just seeing you again will make this trip worthwhile.' He gave her hand a squeeze.

'All right, Ken, dammit, you win.' She turned and slipped her arms around his neck, then drew his lips down to hers. The snow drifted on to her eyelids. 'You're right. I don't have any answers, to anything.'

Again she felt almost as though time was running in reverse. The smoothness of his skin, the ease of his touch, the firm muscles.

'It'll be over soon, Tam. It has to be. And then we'll all look back on this like a bad dream.' He held her in his arms. 'We'll even go off to Hokkaido if you like it so much there. Together. Just you and me.'

'Why is it all the men I know keep offering me trips?' She laughed and brushed the snow out of his hair. 'Matt keeps trying to get me to go down to the Caribbean. Now you want to take me to Hokkaido. I sound like everybody's getaway girl.'

'Nobody's called you a girl. You're a woman. You decide what you want.'

'Well, at the moment I just want to go to bed with you.' She pulled his lips down again. 'After that I'll worry about the next move.'

311

'We just have to trust each other. That's all that matters.'

Well, she thought, how could she not trust this man?

At least for tonight. Tomorrow she would think about tomorrow.

TWENTY-THREE

Kenji Asano was a very complex human being – Western on the surface, but with his own personality always glimmering through at the unexpected moment. He seemed to capture the best of both worlds: the forthrightness of an American and the intuitive self-confidence I've come to think of as a hallmark of the East.

The Japanese are a subtle people, in the finest sense of the word, and I normally feel slightly oafish in their land. I always know I'm missing about three levels of the nuance in whatever's going on. By the same token, a Japanese venturing into the West frequently seems to be moving as though he were following the numbers on one of those old Arthur Murray dance diagrams. The steps are precise and correct, but there's no glide to it, no natural rhythm. Ken, I must say, had long since gotten past that kind of awkwardness. His motions were fluid, his reactions quick and natural. Also, he managed to achieve this while retaining qualities that always reminded you he came from a culture that was writing Kyoto romances and wearing perfumed silk when London and Paris still had pigs in their garbage-strewn streets.

'Ken, you're a phenomenon.' We were climbing into his blue Toyota sports car, which he'd driven up from Tokyo. Low profile – the car and the trip. 'This play could blow up in your face.'

Over our leisurely three-way breakfast in the hotel bar, he had given me a reasonably detailed sketch of the situation, after which Tam headed off in the DNI limo for her second day of appointments in the robot labs. My honest reaction, despite the prickle of jealousy, was instant liking for Asano. Furthermore, in the absence of anything better, his scheme seemed worth a shot.

Now came the sword. A phone call established that Noda had no objection to Ken's seeing it too, so we were set to head over to the Metallurgy Lab together. Not a bad time for straight talk.

'I know it's a gamble, Matthew, but I'd like to think of it as repaying my debt to America.' He inserted his key in the ignition and started the engine. 'In a way I feel some personal responsibility for the current condition of your technology.'

Was he about to come clean on the subject of MITI's semiconductor blitz?

'You know, I once heard you were the brains behind Japan's memory-chip takeover.'

'Our strategy seemed prudent at the time.' He sighed, then turned around to begin backing out of the hotel parking lot. 'If you're planning for the long term, the sectors you focus on are obvious.' He paused to light a Peace, then crumpled the wooden match in his hand and exhaled as he shifted into drive.

'And you play hardball?'

'Otherwise why bother? I guess we had no idea the US could be so inept. We assumed your semiconductor people, like your baseball teams, were major league.'

He was right about that part. America fumbled away its lead chasing quick profits. While MITI was playing the only way it knew how. Long term.

'I can't tell you how much I regret what's happened since,' he continued, glancing occasionally at the rows of research labs gliding by on both sides of the roadway. 'I now realise that a more cooperative approach would have worked to everyone's benefit. In the long run we each need the other. Now, it's going to take plenty of cooperation to prevent the US from becoming a back office for Matsuo Noda.'

'You really think a big MITI move will blow the whistle?'

'Matthew, the Ministry is the closest thing Japan has to a strategic deterrent. By exploiting it, I will become the Japanese Rosenberg in the eyes of many, but if I can cause a worldwide scandal, perhaps everyone here and in the US will start thinking about the implications of Noda's takeover.'

'Friend, you're throwing your career in front of a train.' I said it with respect. 'Matsuo Noda could eat us both for *hors d'oeuvres*.'

'Us, maybe. But not MITI. At least not yet.' He smiled. 'You know, we Japanese have a tradition of committing ritual suicide, *seppuku*, to emphasise a principle. You might say I'm doing that, but it's only professional *seppuku*. No unseemly knives or blood on the *tatami*.'

'I understand now why Tam feels about you the way she does.'

'Matthew,' he spoke quietly, 'I am here, you are there. I think she needs someone she trusts, and you seem to be that person just now. Stay by her.'

'I'd like nothing better.' And with that we lapsed into pensive silence.

It took only about ten minutes for the drive over to the laboratory, another structure that could have been a hangar for flying saucers. Somehow the idea of viewing a sacred relic of Japan's imperial past in this sci-fi setting was incongruous in the extreme, pure George Lucas.

We alighted in the executive parking lot and headed up the sidewalk together. At the sealed entrance Ken showed his palm to the computer's eye, a synthetic voice cleared us and in we went. Waiting on the other side was a senior staff man who greeted us at the first security check, bowed, and motioned us to follow.

One area of the lab had been cordoned off, top security, with gun-carrying guards posted about every ten feet. There were also about two dozen plainclothes types wearing a white arm band emblazoned with the Imperial insignia. Seemed that nobody, but nobody, got close to the Sun Goddess's sidearm without clearance from the top.

The staff man said Noda was currently tied up in a meeting with the Director, so we should wait. No need, I replied, flashing my DNI *meishi*. He bowed and we were waved past the guards, then ushered directly into the top-security workroom – where the team of white-frocked technicians was said to be cleaning and retouching the gilding on the sword's *tsuba* hand guard, the decorative little disc that separates the hilt from the blade.

Since the *tsuba* on swords are interchangeable, not necessarily connected in any particular way to a given piece, they're actually a separate art form, interesting but not overly serious items. Fact is, the Imperial Household could just as well have sent this one up here for work and kept the sword in Tokyo.

Such, however, was not the case. The main attraction itself was undoubtedly over there on the back workbench, in a big stainless-steel box half the size of a coffin, an armed guard stationed next to it.

Noda must have told everybody we were coming in today because the technicians parted like the Red Sea at our approach. Although the president of Dai Nippon was still nowhere to be seen, the *tsuba* was there all right, lying exposed on a worktable right next to a pile of cleaning pads and the gilding apparatus.

And it was a stunner, take my word. One of the most tasteful I've ever had the pleasure to view. Iron, of course, and about ten centimetres across, circular. Actually it was shaped like a chrysanthemum, with the raised image of a mirror on one side and a beaded necklace on the other. The exquisite metalwork was enhanced by the fresh gilding, which made the embossing even more striking. My unprofessional opinion? Very, very ancient. Older than twelfth century? Entirely possible. I really couldn't say. But a wild guess would be early Heian, certainly no later than Kamakura. Fact is, back in those days metalwork didn't change all that much for long periods of time, so there's no real way to date with precision.

'Hijō-ni omoshiroi desu' – very interesting – I said after a respectful interval, hoping to get into the spirit of the occasion and impress everybody with my Berlitz Japanese. 'And now, would it be possible to see the actual sword?' I pointed towards the stainless-steel coffin. 'Sealed in there, I presume.'

The head technician bowed and suddenly looked very troubled. Then he mumbled something in rapid Japanese to Asano. He didn't budge.

'Problem?' I turned to Ken.

'He says Matsuo Noda has given strict orders that the sword is never to be viewed by the public when disassembled.' He shrugged. 'Noda-sama, he says, has declared it to be sacred and therefore it must be displayed with the proper ceremonial reverence always. Of course we'll still be able to see it, but only after the *tsuba* is replaced. Perhaps later on this afternoon.'

We'd come all this way, and now we were going to be stymied by some middle-management lab technician?

'Of course' – I bowed back, hoping to bluff – 'weren't you informed why we are here? I have the honour to be Matsuo Noda's senior American corporate counsel. Noda-sama has ordered me to check and make certain the hilt remains in place while the *tsuba* is undergoing repair. So if you'll kindly open the case, I'll verify that and the matter will be ended.' I bowed again.

'*Sō desu.*' He turned pale. Obviously the grip had been removed. Whoops. I'd just bungled, creating a problem worse than the one I wanted to circumvent.

'On the other hand,' I continued quickly, trying to recoup, 'as long as it's locked in the case, I'm sure there'll be no problem.'

Again he bowed, looking relieved. Noda had these guys scared.

'However, it will be necessary to actually see the sword, so I can report to Noda-sama that I have carried out his instructions. Otherwise Noda-sama may be upset and I will be deeply dishonoured.'

Couching the ploy in personal terms seemed to tip the scale. He bowed again, hesitantly, then led us over to the box. Throughout my little white lie, Ken hadn't said one word. Guess he was as curious as I was to take a look.

'Do you realise what you are about to witness?' The senior staff man stood before us, his dark eyes haughty and grave. Time to put the barbarian *gaijin* in his place. 'Physical proof of the divinity of His Imperial Highness, the Emperor of Japan. This sword is the most sacred object in the world.'

I nodded reverently and moved to the side to let the head technician begin. He slipped a magnetic card into the handle of the steel case, punched in some electronic numbers on the pad next to the latch, and slowly raised the lid.

Since photographs of the sword had been officially forbidden by the Imperial Household, neither Ken nor I had seen even so much as a snapshot. We were literally holding our breath.

317

The interior of the coffin had been partitioned into a front and rear section, both draped with satin. First he lifted away the back shroud – to reveal a long gold box. That, I figured, must be the watertight case Noda's scientists had originally detected. Ken emitted a low hum as we looked at it. Gleaming, the purest of the pure, it had to be 24-carat, like something you'd find in the tomb of a pharaoh. Along the sides were some elegant, playful Heian-style reliefs. Birds, musical instruments, Shinto goddesses. Breathtaking, that's the only word I can find.

'It's beautiful.' I was staring, dazzled. 'And the sword?'

The technician hesitated. Guess he was still worried.

'I'm sure Noda-sama will be pleased to know of your cooperation,' I said soothingly. 'There should be no difficulty.'

He got the message. We weren't going to rock the boat. *Wa*. Harmony.

He nodded again, reassured, then reached down and lifted away the satin cloth covering the front section. Underneath was a bolster of deep purple velvet, and nestled in the middle was . . . the Imperial Sword.

Ken emitted a quiet, reverent exclamation, the hissed Japanese 'Saaaa' that denotes pensive regard, and for a second we both just stood there. Dr Kenji Asano was clearly awestruck. I was too.

As well we should have been. For one thing, it was a superbly well-preserved piece. The blade was delicately curved and its edge could probably still do damage. A few flecks of rust were visible here and there, but overall it was in mint condition, just as Noda had claimed.

Even more interesting was that, sure enough, the grip had been removed while they worked on the *tsuba*. So we were being treated to a glimpse of the Sacred Sword the way Noda had specified it should never be viewed – except by a few crew-cut technicians there in the lab – with the *nakagō*, the steel beneath the grip, exposed. We were seeing it all.

It's gratifying to report that his publicity people had told the truth: there was indeed no signature on the *nakagō*. (I guess if you're swordsmith for God, you just naturally go easy on the ego.) That omission notwithstanding, it was definitely a first-class *katana*. Looked to be some kind of off-alloy, heavy on copper. If you had to guess what the early swords were like, say at a time in between the late-bronze and early-iron ages, this would be a knowledgeable estimate for appearance. The alloy was plausible; it was clearly very old; and with an antique hilt such as the one lying there, the overall look was very reasonable. I was impressed. Put the handle back on the way you normally see a sword and everything about it clicked.

Sorry, but out of habit I have to do something now. What follows is a technical description of the Imperial Sword, including the part usually hidden by the grip — which nobody else has been able to supply because nobody else had seen it disassembled as it was there in the lab. There may be some collectors who'd feel cheated by anything less. This was, as the senior staff man had sternly brought to our attention, a once-in-a-lifetime moment.

'Early Shinto *katana*. Very long and active *sunagashi* and *utsuri* extending into a *kaen boshi*. Slender *nakagō* with one *mekugi-ana*. Shallow *koshi-zori* with *chu-kissaki* and *bo-hi* along either *shinogi* extending into the *nakagō* . . .'

Enough. Actually, that last part made me a little sad. Truthfully, I think Noda was absolutely right. Nobody should sully the divinity of this piece by exhibiting it disassembled, with the grip removed. The problem is that anybody with the slightest experience might possibly have his Faith shaken a trifle, since it's common knowledge that a tapered *nakagō*, the sloping edge there extending back into the section normally hidden by the hilt, didn't come into its own till around the mid fif—

'Mr Walton, I hadn't expected you until later. You should have contacted me.'

It was the voice of Matsuo Noda, directly behind me. I looked up to notice that the faces of all the technicians around the room now matched their bleached lab coats.

'Sorry. Guess we needed to coordinate better.' I turned around and smiled.

Walton, I lectured myself, don't be a smartass, just this once.

Be reverent. Who the hell knows how the Sun Goddess liked her *nakagō*'s tapered?

Besides, the simple truth was the Imperial Sword of Emperor Antoku really knocked me over. Superb workmanship, excellent balance, elegant shape. And overall, surprisingly good condition . . . well, except for one thing.

'It's almost flawless.' I revolved back to examine it again. 'Except for that little scratch on the *nakagō*. Too bad.'

'What scratch, Mr Walton?' He stared down.

'It's actually on the other side, as best I recall.'

There followed a long pause as Noda's eyes gradually narrowed to slits. Finally he said, 'I wasn't aware you were so conversant with press descriptions of the sword, Mr Walton.'

We both knew the scratch on the *nakagō*, on the side not showing, had never once been mentioned in the papers.

Which was as it should be. A minor blemish really. All the same I now felt very guilty about it. I do hope it was an unavoidable accident, like the metallurgy guys at the Princeton lab claimed in the apology that accompanied their bill after I shipped it down last summer for tests.

This was turning out to be quite a day. Seems New York's crime statistics were looking up; a theft had actually been solved. The son of a bitch was MINE.

'Ah, well, Mr Walton, I trust you are suitably impressed all the same.'

'Only you could appreciate how much.' My head was swimming. Judging from the surrounding technicians' reverent gaze, I got the definite impression they had totally missed the significance of our exchange. Kenji Asano was now wearing a pure poker face. What was *he* thinking?

My own concentration, however, was elsewhere at that particular instant. The new realization: *Matthew Walton is a dead man.* As of this moment. Noda would never let me live to tell what I knew.

Just then an official wearing some sort of formal-looking black kimono emblazoned with the *kiku* crest of the Imperial Household Agency came walking briskly out of the office behind us. He was carrying a silver case, about cigar-box size, something etched across its filigreed lid. He walked over to Noda, bowed deferentially and settled it on the workbench next to Kenji Asano's briefcase.

Nobody paid him much notice, however, since we were all still admiring the Sacred Sword. Finally my brain started to function. Dates? Right . . . the night I met Noda . . . which got me out of the house . . . his hirelings cleaned out my office . . . that was about, what, two weeks before the sword was 'discovered'. Perfect. Just enough time to salt the thing in the Inland Sea, let his high-tech research team fish it up . . .

The technician bowed to us once more, then started spreading the satin cloths back over the two compartments. Down came the stainless-steel lid. Click. History time was over.

That was when, finally, Ken looked over and noticed the silver case. He stared at it, puzzled, then glanced at Noda, for whom it obviously was intended, and inquired politely concerning what it might be.

Noda cleared his throat, mumbled something about official DNI business, and started thanking the Household rep who'd brought out the case.

However, the Household man showed his breeding. He picked up Ken's question, smiled and bowed, then proceeded to explain that it contained the only copies of DNI's original technical analyses of the sword — X-ray crystallography scans, non-destructive radiation tests, various scientific data he didn't actually understand but which had been used by Dai Nippon to establish the sword's alloy composition and therefore its sacred authenticity. These data had been forwarded to the Imperial Household with instructions they be kept under lock and key. He'd understood all along that they had merely been on temporary loan to the Emperor, and thus he had no objection now that the honourable Noda-sama had requested their return for additional study by DNI scientists. All Japan was in the debt of the esteemed Matsuo . . .

Kenji Asano turned to stare at me, his eyes gradually filling with an enormous realisation.

You know, I used to have a hobby of reading biographies of the geniuses who'd come up with the truly original insights of modern times. How, I puzzled, did they manage it? I mean, did Newton really watch an apple fall and intuitively sense it was responding to some invisible force? Maybe. Or how about Einstein's insight that matter and energy are really the same thing? Or that space can be curved? Whatever happened, they made a connection that nobody else in history had ever come up with.

Who can explain how these breakthroughs happen? They're always the result of standing off and viewing reality in a wholly new perspective.

With apologies, I've invoked some heavy names. But the point is, there are transcendental moments when a given set of circumstances is suddenly seen to fit more than one paradigm of how the universe functions.

Standing there looking at the silver case, Kenji Asano saw the apple fall from the tree. And I was only seconds behind him.

New insight number one: Something very fishy was going on with the Imperial Sword, something which would not necessarily stand the light of day. (On *that* one I was actually several seconds ahead.)

Number two: If the truth came out, Japan would be a laughingstock worldwide. Worse, His Imperial Majesty would have egg all over his Imperial face. As would Matsuo Noda. Hence the box, having served its PR purpose, had to go.

Number three: The first two insights pointed to the very real possibility that Matsuo Noda had long since passed around the bend, sanity-wise. But whether he had or not, one thing was clear — that silver case contained everything we needed to nail Dai Nippon.

Who knew for sure what was in it? But Ken and I both realised at that instant the contents had to be pure dynamite.

What happened next I probably wouldn't have believed if I hadn't been standing there to witness it with my very own eyes. Kenji Asano was calmly extracting a Peace cigarette from the packet in his left breast pocket and inserting it in his mouth.

Then his right hand came up and out of his thumbnail flared one of those wooden matches he liked so much.

'Asano-san, *sumimasen*.' The senior staff man stepped forward and blurted out, 'No smoking, please.'

'Sorry,' replied Asano, and flicked the still burning match towards the waste bin there at the end of the table – which just happened to be piled high with the solvent pads they'd been using to scour the *tsuba*. A lab can be a dangerous place and this one was no exception. A microsecond thereafter the floor was carpeted in flame.

Later I theorised what must have occurred, remembering a long-ago personal disaster that almost got me kicked out of college. The heavy aromatic solvent they were using, probably a benzene compound, had vaporised off the cleaning pads, drifted down over the sides of the container, and was hovering as an invisible heavier-than-air cloud just above the floor at knee level. The exact same thing happened to me once in a Chem 201 lab – during an after-hours endeavour wherein I was steaming out a twenty-gallon benzene container preparatory to an experiment on the propensity of brewers yeast to convert grape sugar into potable ethanol. The sink happened to be situated next to a gas-fired hot-water heater – which suddenly kicked on. Next thing I knew, the heavy fumes around my ankles detonated. Along with the lab fire alarm.

That explosion, as this one, was actually minor, mostly noise, though it sounded like a bomb. The fumes flashed and it was over, leaving no damage other than to the nervous system of any bystanders. This time, however, there was an added ingredient. The waste container. It had become an instant inferno, billowing dark toxic smoke into the room.

As yelling lab technicians began rushing in with fire extinguishers, everybody else was bolting for the exits, including the security people. All in all, it seemed a reasonably propitious moment to make our own departure as well, since we'd been the cause of the ruckus. Ken fumbled around in the smoke now obscuring the workbench till he recovered his briefcase, and then we headed out.

At the door I caught sight of the Household official and bowed my thanks.

'*Domo arigatō gozaimashita*. We were deeply honoured by this opportunity to view the Imperial Sword of Emperor Antoku.' I bowed again. He nodded back and glared at Asano.

I'd planned to thank Noda too, but he was still in there with the confusion, undoubtedly standing personal guard over his Sacred Sword. Let him stay. There was no real danger. The fire should be out in no time. It was mainly smoke anyway.

Ken was also bowing his farewells to one and all. Then, as though on cue, we both started edging towards the main hallway. By now security people were running down the corridors and the place was in pandemonium.

When we reached the lobby, I almost wanted to bolt for the outer door, but we managed to keep our exit dignified, business-like. Finally as we cleared the last security checkpoint, I turned to him.

'You really should be more careful with your smokes, Ken.' I lowered my voice. 'Manage to grab it?'

'In my briefcase.'

'Then let's get the hell out of here. Noda's going to figure out what happened any second now and go totally bananas.'

'I doubt he will be pleased.'

'Tell you one thing, that silver case has got to disappear, fast. Or we're likely to vanish ourselves. We may anyway.' I quickened my pace towards the parking lot. 'You know, I've got a wild hunch what's in that box. But whatever it is, I *do* know for sure we'd better get the thing somewhere for safekeeping. Quick.'

'Should we tell Tamara?' He glanced down at the smoke-smeared briefcase in his hands, as though holding a cobra.

'She's got to know everything. For her own safety.'

'Matthew,' he said, looking at me. 'You're supposed to be an authority. So tell me the truth. You were behaving strangely in there. It *is* a fake, isn't it, just like I'd always feared?'

'Ken, during the Middle Ages about fifty different monasteries in Europe possessed the authentic, consecrated relic of Christ's circumcision. Who's to say? Remember Francis Bacon's "What is truth?" Japan's Emperor is now and forever. That's the only "truth" that matters.'

'What are you saying?'

'That sword belongs to the people of Japan. Ask them if it's real.'

'Well, you've learned enough about this country to be able to get your message across without actually spelling it out. Very Japanese.' He stared at me. 'You'll have to concede one thing, though. Matsuo Noda is an absolute genius. Think about it. He claimed to have analysed the sword, then loaned the data to the Imperial Household – knowing there would be only one place on earth where it could be right out in public and yet never actually examined. In a fancy silver case kept by a bunch of Household bureaucrats, not one of whom would have the presumption to open it. Or be able to understand anything if he did.'

My own nagging thoughts at that moment were on a different track. *Why* had Noda offered to let me see my own piece? To flaunt the dimensions of his balls? Or was he starting to believe his own trumped-up fantasy? Had Matsuo Noda convinced himself he was God? That he could turn water into wine? Or a fifteenth-century metallurgical screw-up into ... The more I thought about it, the scarier it got. Or maybe, just maybe, he thought I wouldn't recognise it with a different hilt. Could be he was right. But Ken and I had accidentally viewed it disassembled. That wasn't part of his little inside joke. For once Matsuo Noda had gone too far.

'Ken, everything I've learned about Noda so far tells me he's going to do something totally unexpected the minute he realises we took that.'

'Let him. I want to know what's in it.'

'Do the world a favour. No. Never, never open it.'

He paused a second and looked down at his briefcase.

'Maybe you're right. It's better for everybody if it just disappears.'

By then we'd fully cleared the outer doors. The day was turning gorgeous, sunny and brisk, while the thin film of last night's snow was beginning to soften.

Abruptly he stopped. 'Wait, Matthew. Think a minute. We have to at least make a copy of the contents. And that copy needs to be out of Japan.'

'To protect ourselves?'

'Precisely.'

'OK, I'll buy that. Got any ideas?'

'Well, first let's go pick up Tam. Then I'd like to transmit digital facsimiles of whatever's in here to New York. She can set up a file in DNI's big NEC mainframe, and only the three of us will know the file name. It'll be your, and her, insurance policy.'

'Can we do that from here?'

'In fifteen minutes. There's the Teleconferencing Centre over next to Electrotechnical. They've got everything we'll need.'

'Then let's collect her and get it done fast.'

He opened the door of the Toyota, then turned to me. 'You know, Matthew, I think you and Tam ought to be gone from here, too, as soon as possible. There's a copter pad by the hotel. I'm going to phone for a MITI chopper to pick you up and take you straight to Narita.' He patted his briefcase. 'After we've transmitted the contents of this, I want you back in New York. I'll call my secretary and have her book the next flight out; we'll just have somebody bumped if it's full.'

'Why don't you come with us? No need for you to face Noda alone.'

'Not yet.' He hit the ignition. 'But I'll be there in spirit.'

How prophetic.

TWENTY-FOUR

Our major concern at that point was time. We had a lot to do, and we weren't sure how long we had to do it. Furthermore, it would be foolhardy to assume everything was going to proceed smoothly. That apprehension was, in fact, soon to be thoroughly vindicated.

First, it wasn't all that simple to track down Tam. We finally discovered she'd already left the Robotics Lab and was back at the Tsukuba Hotel lunching with Matsugami and some of his senior staff. Returning there, however, did provide a perfect opportunity to grab our bags. Ken dragged her from the lunch with a phony excuse, and minutes later we were checked out, solving at least one logistics problem. Unfortunately, it also tipped off Matsugami and anybody else who might be interested that we were departing.

Next were the details of arranging for the chopper. While we were driving around trying to locate Tamara, Ken had been on his car phone pulling strings to commandeer one of the two MITI helicopters. After three calls he managed to locate one at their auxiliary pad, currently being refuelled and serviced. I listened as he leaned on the service people, doing his diplomatic but firm Deputy Minister routine. End of long story: it would be on its way shortly, arriving in about an hour and a half.

Good, we thought. Plenty of time to handle the transmission of the still unseen documents in Noda's silver case. In the car we brought Tam fully up to date on the extraordinary circumstances by which it had fallen into our possession, including its potential for use as leverage against Noda. Then we headed for the Teleconferencing Centre, where we planned to open the thing, scan the contents with a reader and bounce the pages to New York via satellite. Ken revealed that the Ministry had a high-security channel it used to communicate with the New York offices of JETRO, the Japan External Trade Organisation over on Sixth Avenue, MITI's public-relations arm. He declared we would just link up with that office and have them patch us through to the DNI computer. Nothing to it.

Which was correct, theoretically. When we marched in, Ken again flaunting his Deputy Minister walk-on priority, the white-shirted staff bowed to the floor, led us to the hard-copy scanner, turned it on and diplomatically excused themselves, closing the security door. The place was ours.

Don't know why, but until that moment none of us had really wanted to know what was in Noda's case. Maybe a part of me still didn't, even then. Whatever the reason, however, we hadn't bothered to take it out of Ken's briefcase for examination. Turned out that was a mistake.

He settled his satchel on to the desk, clicked it open, and out came the box for our first real look. As he wiped off the smoke, my initial reaction was to be dazzled. It was magnificent, a silversmith's masterpiece, engraved with all manner of myth-ological beast and fowl. A work of art in every sense. Never seen anything remotely like it.

The problem was, it wasn't merely locked. It was soldered shut. The silver lid had literally been welded on, leaving it essentially a solid piece. Noda, it turned out, left nothing to chance. Only a silversmith could crack the seal and divulge the contents. So we still had no idea what was inside, and worse, we'd managed to fritter away a valuable half hour coming to that fruitless discovery. Now what?

'Shit,' said Tam. 'When will we ever get a break?'

'Looks like we've got two choices,' Ken announced ruefully, gazing down at the intractable chunk of metal in his hands. 'We can do what we probably should have done in the first place: simply stash this for the moment and let Noda think we know what's in it. Or we can drive into Tokyo and locate somebody there who can open it, then transmit from MITI headquarters downtown.'

Neither of these plans seemed particularly inspired. The first gave us nothing but presumptions for leverage, and the second could take hours. Noda, we all realised, was not a man who dallied.

'Actually,' Tam spoke up, 'there's a third option. Surely Noda's going to find out sooner or later we came here to the Centre. Believe me, he always learns everything eventually. So why not transmit something else now, anything, and then after you get the case open you can send the real data?'

'You mean, give him circumstantial cause to assume we've got the goods on him?' Sounded good to me. 'Buying ourselves more time?'

'Right. It'll take him a while to find out exactly what was transmitted. All he'll know for certain is that we sent something. In the meantime Ken can go on to Tokyo and proceed with plan B: open the case there and transmit the real contents.'

He looked sceptical. 'That might deceive everybody for a while, but not for long. There're too many links in the chain between here and DNI's New York office.'

'But sending something now will gain time. It has to. Then you can go on to Tokyo and do what you need to from there. Tomorrow.'

'Maybe.' He still wasn't totally convinced. 'But all right — rather than waste time arguing, let's just go ahead and do it. No harm in any instance.'

She peeked into his briefcase, a jumble of documents. 'What have you got in here that we could send?'

'Today's *Asahi Shimbun* . . .' He laughed.

'Ken.'

'OK, OK.' He laid the newspaper aside and was riffling through his paperwork. 'How about a few MITI memos?'

'Nothing to do with Marketshare—90 I hope,' said Tam.

'Promise.'

The apparatus was already humming, so he put through the connection to JETRO's New York office, whereupon Tam took over and gave them instructions for the phone link over to the DNI mainframe. It probably required all of a couple of minutes. Welcome to the Brave New World of global information transfer.

Since we were just shooting in the dark, they transmitted some twenty or twenty-five pages. Actually it would have been almost better to send too few rather than too many. At four pages a minute, though, we were finished in no time. As something of a joke, Tam suggested using the file name NIPPONICA, homage to Noda's takeover pipe dream. Somehow it seemed poetic justice.

Whether the transparency of our ruse would be immediately evident to Matsuo Noda remained a big unknown. But . . . maybe Noda would have no real way of discovering we'd sent garbage, at least not for a while. The transmission done, we signed off, zipped up Ken's briefcase and marched out as if we knew what we were doing. Still, it was only a bluff, and a shaky one at that. Which set me to thinking.

'Ken, it seems to me you're the critical path in this scenario now.' We were walking back to the executive parking lot, where we'd left his car. 'It's more important to have a real copy of the data stashed somewhere than it is for us to blow the country in the next two hours. Which means maybe you ought to take the chopper back yourself, find a way to send the stuff today and let us just drive down to Narita in your car?'

'I agree.' Tam nodded concurrence. 'We can leave it there and you could have somebody pick it up tomorrow.'

'That's dangerous, for both of you.'

'Maybe so,' she said, 'but he's going to come after this case, guns blazing, as his first priority. Ken, you're the one who's going to have to stay out of his way now, not us. The quicker you move, the better.'

'You've got a point. All right, if you want me to, then I could take the copter back to Tokyo myself and you can use the Toyota.' He was fishing for his keys. 'In fact, maybe you should just leave now.'

'Let me check the schedule.' I'd asked his secretary for a listing of the afternoon and evening flights in case we got delayed. It was now one-thirty. The next flight that looked like a sure thing was a United at 7.42 p.m., or maybe the JAL at 9.00 p.m. Then there was a North-west at 10.15 p.m. Loads of time.

'Look, we can wait for the chopper and at least see you off. Why don't we head back over to the hotel and have a drink? Solemnise the occasion – the final screwing of Matsuo Noda.'

'Fine.' He started the car. 'But both of you get only one, at least whoever's driving does. I want you back in one piece.'

The hotel bar was beginning to feel like a second home, though now it was deserted, the lunch trade long departed. Our ceremonial libation also provided my first real opportunity to study Ken Asano at leisure. I sat sipping my Suntory while he repeated once again the details of his upcoming political move at MITI. Given any kind of luck, the flap would render Noda's takeover a worldwide scandal.

Great. Tam and I had been Noda's point men, had done everything we knew to assist him, and now it was clear he'd been using us all along for his own ends. He was bent on bringing American industry back to life for the sole purpose of skimming the cream.

What other reason could there be? Noda's noble intention supposedly was to help rejuvenate American corporations doing basic research – but the price was then to let Japan lift that R & D and translate it into consumer technology, thereby keeping for his team all the elements of real economic value in the chain from laboratory to cash register. They would be the ones refining their strategic capacity to transform new ideas into world-class products and economic leadership. Japan would retain the advanced engineering segment of product development, while tossing a few low-skill assembly plants to the US to make us think we were still part of the action. It would, of course, be a fatal delusion. The high-tech hardware of tomorrow's world increasingly would be Japanese, while America became an economy of paper-shuffling MBAs and low-paid grease monkeys assembling products we no longer were able to design or engineer.

That depressing conclusion required the space of one Scotch. By then I was ready to order a second, hoping it would bring forth a solution to the problem the first had evoked with such alarming clarity.

But there wasn't time. At that moment we heard the MITI copter settling on to the pad next to the hotel parking lot.

'Ken, here's to success.' I saluted him with the last melting ice cubes.

He toasted back, then signalled for the bill. Time to get moving.

The chopper was a new Aerospatiale AS 365N Twin Dauphin, big and white, a VIP four-seater. Single pilot, capable of 180. (The Japanese love those high-rotor French copters.) Guess Ken had called in a lot of chips to arrange this customised three-wheeler for a couple of *gaijin*. The seat-mile costs alone must have been staggering. But there it was, fully serviced and set to go.

He walked over, ducking the rotor, and advised the pilot that there had been a slight change of plans. They'd be returning directly back to Tokyo. The man, wearing a blue uniform, bowed and gave him a little salute. They seemed to be old friends. Well, I thought, if Deputy Ministers don't use this gold-plated extravagance, then who's it for?

Then he returned to pick up his briefcase (Noda's silver box safely therein), have a brief farewell and give us his keys.

'Tamara, telex me the minute you get back. We'll proceed immediately. Full speed.'

'Let's go for it.' She smiled and drew his face down for a long languorous kiss. I then shook his hand and we headed for the car. Since our bags were just little carry-ons, we looked solid to catch the United flight with a couple of hours to spare, assuming traffic cooperated.

'Tam, how about taking the wheel? This left-hand side of the road driving takes practice. I almost hit somebody once in England.'

'Sure.' She reached for the keys, then turned back to wave to Ken. But he was already climbing aboard and didn't notice.

'Isn't it odd?' I mused, 'we still haven't heard zip out of Noda. He must have realised by now we have his silver case. What's he planning to do? Where'll he try to head us off?'

'Good question.' She turned the key in the ignition. 'I'm not going to feel safe till we've got the actual goods on his phony sword. Not just some dummy data.'

'My guess is he'll try and nail us at the airport. It'd be his best shot.'

'At least Ken was smart enough to make the reservations under fake names, so he won't know which flight to watch.'

'There're not that many. He could be covering them all. On the other hand, he'll assume we're arriving via the MITI chopper, so maybe we can dodge his hit squad.'

'I feel like I've been run through a wringer.' She was pulling out of the slot, backing around to begin making her way through the rows of staff vehicles, all with special Tsukuba parking stickers.

'You can say that again. Who could have guessed all the—'

I'd reached around to check the back window, hoping to get the heat going, when my field of vision turned an incandescent orange, bright and glaring, as though the sun had just come in for a close encounter. Before I could turn to see what . . . the dashboard rose up and slugged me in the teeth, as a shock wave flung us both against the seat belts.

We're dead, I thought. We've been bombed. Noda's just dropped . . .

Then I looked up.

The MITI Aerospatiale, about two hundred feet off the ground, had become a blazing sphere, a grotesque nova. Now its rotor blades were clawing the air, askew, while it circled downwards like a wounded bird. An instant later it nosed into the parking lot behind us, hurtling fragments of tail assembly through several empty staff cars.

I sat mesmerised as a second ball of fire erupted where it had crashed. One of the fuel tanks had ignited, just like in the movies. . .

'Ken!' Tam let out a choked cry after the first few seconds of disbelief. Then she slammed the transmission into 'Park' and began ripping off her seat belt.

Where's she going? Doesn't she realise—

Her door was open and she was stumbling out. That's when I

finally came to my senses, which included the sobering thought that there might be more fuel tanks, such as the auxiliary, that hadn't yet blown.

'Wait!' I'd ripped off my own seat harness by that time and had rolled out to begin running after her as she stumbled across the snowy stretch of asphalt separating us from the flames.

She was moving like a gazelle, but I managed to catch up about thirty yards from the wreckage. Using a modified shoulder lock, I pulled her around and tried to get a grip.

'Tam, nobody could survive that. We've got to stay back . . .'

At which point we both slipped and collapsed in a patch of snow . . . just as the last fuel tank detonated with the impact of a sonic boom. Memory can be a little unreliable under such circumstances, but I still remember more wreckage sailing past us, including a strut off the landing gear that gouged a furrow in the asphalt no more than ten feet from our heads.

'Tam, he never knew what hit him. It had to be instantaneous.' I was trying to brush the wet snow off her face as I slipped my arm around her shoulders. She was still holding back the tears, but only just.

'We didn't even have a real goodbye.' Her words were jagged. 'There were so many things . . . I was hoping we . . .'

Her voice trailed off into tears.

'Look, I only knew him for a day, but that was enough to learn some things. Kenji Asano was a wise and noble soul. Everything about him was good.'

She took my hand and held it against her cheek. 'Matt, he was so kind. That was what . . . He was . . . all that I . . .' Her eyes were reflecting back the flames, now billowing into the pale afternoon sky. Around us the labs were emptying as technicians raced towards the lot, white coats fluttering.

'You know, he said something to me today. About you . . .'

'What?' She glanced up, her face streaked. 'What did he say?'

'He must have known there was danger. He sort of asked me to look out for you.'

'Danger?' She looked back at the wreckage, and a new tear

trailed down her left cheek. 'I guess we don't really know for sure, do we? Maybe it was just a fuel-tank rupture, or . . .'

'You don't believe that.'

'No.' The tears, abruptly, were gone. 'Matsuo Noda just took away the one . . . Matt, I'm going to kill him.'

It was a sentiment I shared in buckets. The question was merely how. Medieval torture seemed too kind. I started to say something inane and then, finally, the shocking truth landed with the force of that last explosion.

'Tam, that was supposed to be *us*.' I was gazing at the flames, watching talons of metal contort in the heat. 'Noda thought *we* were going to be on that copter.'

'My God, of course.'

'We've got to get out of here. Now. There's nothing anybody can do for Ken.'

'I'm not leaving till I've settled the score.'

'Be reasonable. There's no way we can do it here. This is Noda's turf.' I was urging her to her feet. 'We'll find a way. All I ask is that he *know* we were the ones who did him in.'

'But how can we just leave?'

'What else are we supposed to do? There's nothing left.' I tried to take her hand. 'Come on.'

She finally relented and, with one last tearful stare, turned to follow me back to the car. By then a crowd of technicians was surging in around us.

Ken's blue Toyota was still running. Without a word she buckled in, shoved the stick into gear and turned for the exit, whereupon she barely avoided colliding with the first racing fire engine.

'Look, are you OK? I can drive if you . . .'

'Matt, don't say anything more, please.' The tears had vanished. 'Can I just think for a while? Just give me some quiet to think.' She was gripping the wheel with raw anger. 'Please.'

By the time we reached the highway, she was driving mechanically but with absolute precision, almost as though tragedy had somehow sharpened her reflexes, her logical processes.

It's a curious thing, but different people respond differently to

335

disaster, and Tam was one of those rare few who become harder, not softer. I could see it in her eyes. As the minutes ticked by, and we reached the packed thoroughfare that would take us south, it even got to be a little unsettling. What in hell was going through her head?

Finally, after about an hour of bumper-to-bumper freeways, I couldn't take the silence any more. Without asking anybody's permission, I reached over and clicked on the radio. It was set for a classical station, the music Chopin. Was this Ken's regular fare? I wondered. Was he a romantic at heart or a classicist? Guess I'd never know . . . that, or much of anything else about him. Which thought brought with it a renewed sadness. Kenji Asano was a man of the East who was as much of the West as anybody I'd ever met in Japan. I'd wanted him for a friend.

When you get to be my age, you don't make too many new friends, not real ones. After forty, it's acquaintances. The roots of true friendship extend so deep that there's never really time to plant them if you start too late. Maybe it's because there's always a part missing, that shared experience of being young and crazy and broke. Those times back when you both still believed anything was possible. New friends can't begin sentences with 'Remember that weekend before you were married when we got drunk and . . .' Getting old is tough, and that's one of the toughest parts. But somehow I felt, with Ken, that I'd known him forever. Could be that's absurd, but I really did. So quite apart from the tragedy of his death, I felt cruelly robbed. It sounds selfish, maybe, but it's the truth. A sad but true truth.

I was still thinking those thoughts when the four-o'clock newscast came on. For a moment neither of us noticed, but then Tam snapped alert and turned up the volume. The report was opening with a live remote from Tsukuba Science City. I couldn't really follow very well, but she realised that and began to translate as it went along.

'. . . *was the first tragedy of its kind for the Ministry, and there are widespread calls for an official inquiry. Dr Kenji Asano, nationally known director of the Institute for New Generation Computer Technology, died today here at Tsukuba Science City when a MITI heli-*

336

copter, an Aerospatiale Twin Dauphin, crashed due to a malfunction. No cause has yet been ascertained for the accident, which also took the life of the pilot, Yuri Hachiro, a MITI veteran with fifteen years of service. The condition of the wreckage has made it impossible to determine how many other passengers may have been on board, although MITI sources report that two visiting American scientists are also thought to have been travelling with Dr Asano. Their names are being withheld by the Ministry at this time, pending the completion of a full investigation . . .'

Next came an interview with a MITI official, after which the reporter offered a wrap-up.

'. . . believe Dr Asano's death represents a significant blow to several vital sectors of MITI's computer race with America. However, the Vice-Minister has assured NHK that MITI's research effort will redouble its commitment to . . .'

Tam clicked it off. 'Two birds with one stone.'

'What?'

'Matt, by bringing down the copter with all three of us in it, he was planning to stop MITI and us both. Now he may think he did.'

'You're right.' I looked at her, and finally understood the real import of the crash. 'Which means we're now officially dead. If nobody else knows we weren't on that chopper, why would Noda?'

She didn't answer for a long moment. Finally she said, 'Maybe that gives us the time we'll need.'

'Time to nail him.'

'Right. I've been thinking. About what it all means.'

'Noda's play?'

'Not just that. I'm talking about Japan. Everything. You know, this country could lead the world some day, maybe even now, if it wanted. It has the finest schools, the most disciplined people; it's not hung up on a lot of "superpower" male-macho bullshit. It could be a beacon in the dark, a force for good. But what has Noda done? He's turned it all upside down. He's exploited the noble things about Japan for his own selfish ends. Greed and power.'

'Lucifer, the fallen angel? Who walked out on the Kingdom?'

'I guess so. But I'm also thinking about what he did to me. He exploited the fact I was part Japanese, that I understand the potential this country has. He made me think that's what I would be helping him realise. But all along he intended to pervert it. He's perverted us, Matthew. Both of us. Perverted us and used us. And now that we're no longer needed, he's tried to kill us.'

'High time we evened things out.'

'Damned right. I learned a lot when I lived here. About the Japanese mind. And you understand legal tactics. Swordsmanship. I think we're ready.'

'Ready?'

'To turn our knowledge against him.'

'Start probing for the niche in his armour?'

'No. There's no time for that.' She was silent for a moment, as though preparing her words. 'We've got to just sink him. Obliterate Dai Nippon totally. And with it Matsuo Noda.'

'You mean . . . go public about the sword? The problem with that is . . .'

'Exactly. Everything's destroyed. So why not forget about the sword for a while? Whatever you know about it, at this point that's just your word against his. I mean we have to bring the whole thing down.'

'Tam, we're talking billions of dollars. This could take a while. That number is a little hard to argue with.'

'But what if that's both his strength *and* his weakness.' She glanced over at me. 'Look, I've been thinking about what we might try. Maybe there is a way.'

'To assault him on the money front?'

'Right, but we'll need your friend Bill Henderson. Think he'd help?'

I nodded. 'If you want him, I'll see that he pitches in.'

'Good.' She turned her eyes back to the road. 'Matt, I'm Fujiwara. Did I ever tell you that? And a Fujiwara's duty is to protect the Emperor of Japan. For a thousand years it's been their job.'

She'd cracked. Begun talking gibberish. 'What's that got to do with—'

'Noda thinks he's going to exploit the Emperor. Well, he's got a big surprise in store. I am now going to use Dai Nippon to destroy him and then drive a stake into DNI's heart. Matthew, I'm going to make Matsuo Noda's billions just disappear.'

'That's impossible.'

'Watch me.'

TWENTY-FIVE

Guess Tam's Shinto *kami* were on our side, since we made it through Narita Airport with no hassles; or maybe being dead keeps you off anybody's hit list. Now that MITI was determined not to release our names until they located our remains, we looked to be in limbo as far as Matsuo Noda and Dai Nippon were concerned. Given the fact that the chopper had been demolished and then burned down to metal, nobody knew anything. Yet.

The scenario Tam laid out on the 747 flying back, while we drank a lot of airline cognac in the upstairs lounge, was destined to be yet another first in the annals of American finance, one way or the other. If we bungled it – and lived to face the consequences – would we end up like those grim-faced executives you see being hustled into the federal courthouse downtown, flanked by G-men in cheap trench coats? Later, eyeing the network cameras, we'd have to smile bravely and declare that American justice, in which we had full confidence, would surely vindicate us after all the facts, etc.

To go with her play meant we were headed either for the history books or jail, or both. But we would definitely need Henderson and his 'Georgia Mafia'. The questions were actually pretty simple: (1) Could it be done, and if so, (2) how and how fast?

We got back Monday, the day before New Year, and the first person I called after Amy was Henderson, casually mentioning that something potentially very disrupting to the Street was in the works.

'Bill, fasten your seat belt. Bumpy weather ahead.'

That captured his attention in a flash. What in hell, he inquired, was I talking about?

'We need to get together, tonight,' I continued.

'Where?'

'How about your place? Matter of fact, there's a real question just now, at least in Japan, concerning whether Tam and I are actually alive.'

'Walton, what in God's name is going on?'

'In the fulness of time, friend, all things will be known. Now we see as through a glass darkly ... well, actually we're seeing through the smudgy windows of the Plaza, Suite 325, where we're presently holed up. But we've got to stay low profile for a few more days.'

'Whatever you say,' he replied, still puzzled. 'Then how about dropping by here tonight for a quick one, and then afterwards we can all mosey over to Mortimer's on Lex for a quick bite?'

'OK. As long as we go late. I want to miss the happy-hour crowd.'

This did not please him, but he agreed. My suspicions were that he wanted to use the occasion to reconnoitre the glittery jet-set ladies at the bar. Henderson, whose style and drawl undoubtedly distinguished him from the B-school competition there like a white-maned palomino in a herd of draught horses (investment drones who wore a beeper on their belt and used 'bottom-line' as a verb), surely found the place a fertile hunting ground. Mortimer's was custom-made for his idiosyncratic style.

About nine that evening Tam and I slipped out of the Plaza's 59th Street entrance and headed up Fifth Avenue towards Bill's. He was headquartered in one of those solid granite-faced buildings near the Metropolitan that are constructed like small fortresses – presumably so New York's upper one tenth of one per cent can repel the long-feared assault of the homeless hordes at their feet. In the lobby, Henderson vouched for us over the TV intercom, after which we were given a visual search by the doorman, his uniform a hybrid of Gilbert and Sullivan and crypto-Nazi, and shown the elevator.

A quick doorbell punch and the man from Georgia greeted us, Scotch in hand. His little pied-à-terre was about three thousand square feet of knee-deep carpets, Old Masters (I loved the

Cézanne and the Braque) and masculine leather furniture. A padded wet bar, complete with mirror and a bank of computer monitors — for convenient stock action — stretched across one side of the living room, while the sliding glass doors opposite faced on to a balcony that seemed suspended in mid-air over Central Park. While Tam, with her designer's eye, was complimenting him politely on the understated elegance of his Italian wallpaper, French art and English furniture, I tried not to remember all those early years back in New Haven when his idea of decor was a feed-store calendar featuring a bluetick hound.

Although the balcony doors were open, the living room still had the acrid ambience of a three-day-old ashtray. He poured us a drink from a half-gallon of Glenfiddich on the bar, gestured us towards the couch and offered Havana cigars from a humidifier. I took him up on it, out of olfactory self-defence.

'So tell me, ladies and gents, what's the latest?' He settled himself in a leather armchair and plopped his boots on to an antique ottoman. 'How're the Jap assault forces doing these days? They gonna take over the Pentagon next?'

'Not that we've heard.' I was twisting my Havana against the match. 'Though it might lower procurement costs on toilet seats and ashtrays if they did.'

Henderson sipped at his drink, then his tone heavied up. 'Who are we kidding, friends? My considered reading of the situation is your boys on Third Avenue are unstoppable. They can do whatever they damn well please from here on out.'

'That's not necessarily in everybody's best interest, Bill.' I strolled over to look down at the park. 'Got any new thoughts?'

'Can't say as I do. Our IBM play didn't get to first base; Noda saw us coming a mile away. Thank God I didn't get in deep enough to get hurt.' He leaned back. 'What makes it so damned frustrating is the market's tickled as a pig in shit. Ain't nobody too interested in dissuading your friends from buying up everything in sight. Street's never seen anything like this kind of bucks before. It's a whole new ball game downtown.'

'That's right, Bill,' I mused aloud. 'The question is, whose ball game is it?' Tam still hadn't said anything.

'Damned good question. What happens when foreigners start owning your tangible assets? The answer, friend, is they end up owning *you*.'

'Henderson, all that could be about to change.'

'Says who?' He leaned back. 'Looks to me like Noda's going all the way.'

'Bill, let's talk one of those hypothetical scenarios you like so much. What if Dai Nippon suddenly had a change of plans? Switched totally? And instead of buying, they started selling?'

That pulled him up short. He even set down his glass. 'Come again.'

'Call it a hypothetical proposition. I'm asking what would happen on the Street if Dai Nippon decided, unannounced, to make a significant alteration in its portfolio? All of a sudden started divesting? Massively.'

'When'd this happen!' He squinted. 'How much action we looking at?'

I didn't want to say it for fear he might need CPR for his heart. Finally Tam set down her drink and answered him. 'All of it.'

'Christ.' He went pale. 'What's that add up to, total?'

'We figure it'd run to several hundred billion,' I answered.

He sat there in confusion. 'Over what kind of time period?'

'That's part of the reason we wanted to see you. If, strictly as a hypothesis, they were to do something like that, as fast as possible, how long would it take? Just throw your hat at the number, wild guess.'

'Time, you mean?'

'Exactly.'

'Well, let's look at it a second here. I'd guesstimate that all the exchanges together – Big Board, American, Merc, CBOT, NASDAQ, Pacific, and the rest – probably have a dollar volume upwards of . . . how many billions a day? Say twenty billion, easy, maybe more, the way volume's climbing. But that figure's purely hypothetical. If Dai Nippon dumped all those securities on the table at once, the value of their portfolio would go to hell.'

I glanced at Tam.

'That's how we see it too,' she said. And nothing more.

'What are you two suggesting?' He was visibly rattled. 'Noda'd never pull anything that crazy.'

'Bill, with all due respect, let's proceed one step at a time here with this hypothesis,' I went on. 'Assuming, just for purposes of discussion, he did decide to do something like that, unload everything, what's the fastest way?'

'Hell, I'd have to think.'

'Come on, man. Financial derring-do is your special trade.' I pressed him. 'What if DNI's mainframe was used to set up a global trading network? Began dumping worldwide?'

'Well, that'd probably be the quickest approach.' He was slowly coming awake. 'Jesus Christ! It's not Noda we're talking about.' He looked at me, then at Tam. 'It's *you*. You're going to try and . . .'

'Possibly.'

'Then we sure as hell *are* talking theory, 'cause you'd never be able to do anything like that without Noda gettin' wind of it.'

'Henderson, as usual you're not listening. Plausibility is not the topic under discussion. Right now we're looking at the impact.'

'Well, you'd damned well better start with some plausibility.' He settled back. 'Say you could get around Noda. The next problem is, the minute word hits the Street DNI's dumping, all hell's liable to break loose. It'd be front page. And first thing you know, the market's going to be headed the wrong way. If you've got a heavy block of shares you want to divest, you damn well do it on the QT, 'cause the price can start to nosedive. Folks tend to figure you know something they don't. The Street's about ninety per cent psychology and ten per cent reality . . . if that much.'

'Just concentrate on the technical part, Henderson.'

'Well, friends, any way you cut it, we're talking what I'd call a very dubious proposition. Those Jap institutions would lose their shirt if DNI dumped all at once.' He exhaled quietly. 'You start rolling billions and billions in Japanese money, how you plan on keeping the thing from blowing sky-high? You'd have Nips climbing all over your ass in ten minutes flat, if you tried something like that.'

'Henderson, relax. What if we did it anonymously? Like I said. Used the DNI mainframe, funnelled orders through accounts everywhere, dummy accounts in banks all over the place? Wouldn't that give us some elbow room?'

'Maybe, maybe. If you played it right. I'd guess a few wiseguy analysts would probably sniff something in the wind, but nobody'd have a handle on the real action, at least not for a while. Things might stay cool temporarily.'

'Are you saying that, in theory, the market side is do-able, at least initially?' Tam pressed him.

'I'm just guessing it's vaguely conceivable.' He got up to freshen his drink. 'Be that as it may, though, the real problem is the Japanese end. I'd guess the shit's going to be all over the fan in Tokyo the minute you start selling. Those pension funds are not going to roll over and let you wreck their portfolio.'

'Bill,' I spoke up, 'they're not going to be able to stop us. Count on it. DNI holds the stock as trustee. Noda's rules. Ironclad power of attorney.'

'So?'

'So,' I said very carefully, 'we are going to *take over* Dai Nippon.'

'What the hell are you talking about?'

We told him. The Rambo part.

'Jeezus!' He stared at the two of us. 'What you're proposing is a major felony. I could get accessory and five years for just listening to this.'

'Who's going to file charges?'

'How about Mr Matsuo Noda for starters?'

'Bill, we just happen to have a little leverage with Mr Noda-san at the moment. The minute he finds out we're still alive—'

'You'd damned well better, or you could be looking at a long interlude of pastoral delights up at the Danbury country club.' He was still dumbstruck. Finally he grinned. 'After parole, though, you could probably sell your memoirs to *Newsweek* for a couple of million and land a guest slot on Carson.'

There was a long pause as silence filled the room, broken only by the distant sound of a siren from the street below. For a minute I had the paranoid fantasy it was the first wave of the police SWAT team heading downtown to shoot it out with us.

Finally Bill turned back and fixed me with a questioning look. 'Are you really serious about this asshole idea?'

'It's not without appeal.'

'Walton, you dumb fuck, do this and you'll never work in this town again.'

'I'm well aware of that.'

'Nobody'd hire you to fight a dog summons, let alone a takeover.' Bill turned to Tam. 'Talk sense to this man.'

'It was my idea.'

'You're both crazy.' He walked over to the bar and poured some more Scotch into his glass. 'But what the hell. I've seen enough to know we'd damned sure better start taking this country back into our own hands one way or other.'

'So you'll help?' She was watching him like a hawk.

'Well now, what's life for, gentle lady' — he grinned — 'except to kick ass now and again? Somebody's got to throw a monkey wrench into Noda's operation. If you think you can do it, then count me in. If nothing else, maybe we can cause a few waves down on the Potomac.'

What am I hearing? I found myself wondering. Dr Willliam J. Henderson, capitalism's pillar of sober reappraisal, entertaining a scenario straight from a CIA handbook?

Of course, Bill still hadn't heard the second half of the play.

'Fine, we could use your help on the set-up.' I glanced at the row of CRT screens behind the bar. 'First there's the matter of getting control of DNI's supercomputer and then we'll need somebody with trading experience. Is there any chance you could bring in one of your boys to oversee that end?'

'How do you figure on running it?'

'I'd guess our best shot is to stay off-exchange as much as possible. Use Jefferies, third-market outfits like that. And also keep the money offshore, international, with a lot of separate bank connections to handle the transfers. Maybe also float some of the interim liquidity in overnight paper to cover our tracks, just so we can generally keep the lid on everything as long as we can.'

'Then it so happens one of my boys might just fill our bill. That's his thing. He operates freelance now, but he's good. Damned good. Trouble is, he knows it and he don't come cheap any more.'

'I think we can cover a few consulting fees. Can he keep his mouth shut?'

'If he couldn't, we'd both probably be in jail by now.' He drained his glass. 'Though remember, you'll be moving a lot of bucks and there *are* folks who keep track of such things. But I know a few smokescreens that'll hold the SEC and that crowd at arm's length for a little.' He looked at me for a second, his face turning quizzical. 'What was that you said just now? About parking the money overnight? What are you going to do with it after that?'

'You're getting ahead of things,' Tam replied calmly.

'Bill, why don't we head on over to Mortimer's?' I looked out at the park one last time. 'You may need a stiff drink for the rest of this.'

'Jesus, I'm dealing with maniacs.' He got up and headed for his coat. 'Let's move it.'

TWENTY-SIX

Bushidō. Take it apart, *bu-shi-dō*, and you have 'military-knight-ways', the rules of chivalry that governed every moment of a *samurai*'s existence. This code of honour of the warrior class, this *noblesse oblige*, was also known as 'the way of the sword'. For a *samurai*, the sword was a sacred icon, an emblem of strength and inner resolve. Casual handling was unheard of. You never stepped over a sword, you never treated it with insouciance or irreverence. It was an extension of your character. A *samurai* regarded his *katana* as the symbol of his caste: a weapon, yes, but also a constant reminder of who he was, his obligations as well as his rights.

Which was why I needed the prize of my collection in hand when we entered our final battle with Dai Nippon. I wanted to face Matsuo Noda with classic dignity, with the Japanese honour he had scorned, to let him know he had a worthy opponent, one who understood the meaning of *bushidō*. I also wanted in that process to stick those DNI guards' Uzis up their ass. I'd be needing a *katana*.

Our meeting with Henderson was Monday night. Tuesday morning we all buckled down and began working around the clock, each of us handling a separate area. Tam called in some favours with the head of the NYU computer centre and adapted an off-the-shelf program for stock transactions to suit our unique requirements. Then she booked time and scheduled a few debugging runs. In the meantime Henderson was taking care of our banking preparations, opening a string of accounts, mostly offshore where we could move with comparative anonymity. Also, we all got together at his place a couple of times and blocked out exactly what we wanted to unload first, names and dates.

While Tam and Henderson were setting up the financial end,

the electronics were my responsibility. I was on the phone all day Tuesday knocking heads with Artie Wilson, an old friend who operated a maritime radio business down on the island of St Thomas. Together we assembled a piece of gear needed to address one of the essential telemetry elements, and Wednesday night he took his boat over to St Croix to install it.

I think I've already mentioned the marvellous Caribbean beach house that had practically fallen into my and Joanna's hands a few years back. It also sported, as do a lot of island places, a TV satellite dish, and it so happens that this one was massive, a twenty-footer. Now, what is not commonly appreciated is that those concave parabolas can be used to broadcast as well as receive.

Artie and a couple of his cronies worked all Wednesday night and got it rigged the way I wanted it, including a deadeye bead on the commercial satellite currently being used by DNI for proprietary communications with Noda's Kyoto office. I figured it like this: if 'Captain Midnight' could override Home Box Office's satellite network using a receiving station in Florida and broadcast a Bronx cheer to Time-Life, we could by God knock out DNI's high-security channel for an hour or so. Artie would be on standby Friday, ready to flip the switch.

Noda was apparently still in Japan, presumably busy throwing obstacles in MITI's path, or maybe searching for the remains of his silver case. Let him. We were about to start handling his communications with the DNI office for him, via a set-up of our own devising.

One nice thing about global electronics is that if you get a network far-flung enough, nobody can trace anything — which was what we were counting on. After we'd killed Noda's primary communications system, we intended to substitute some Japanese hardware we'd had installed at Henderson's — together with a little help from a mutual friend in Shearson Lehman's Tokyo office. The arrangement was complicated, but it looked workable on paper. Thing was, though, we'd have to get it right the first time. No dry runs.

All of which tended to make me uneasy. You don't leave

anything to chance when you're playing our kind of game; you need to have a backup. This feeling brought to mind an admonition in an old sixteenth-century text on swordsmanship, the *Heihō Kaden Sho*, something to the effect that 'you should surprise your opponent once, and then surprise him again.' So, strictly on my own, I went about a bit of *bushidō* lawyering, using that power of attorney Noda gave me back when we started out to set up a fallback position in case Tam's scheme somehow failed. This twist, however, I decided to keep under wraps. Nobody needed to be diverted just then worrying about worst-case scenarios. That's what corporate counsels are for.

It was the most hectic week of our lives, but by 3 p.m. Friday we were ready, assembled at Henderson's place and poised for battle. Using his new hardware, we got on line to Shearson's Tokyo office, Bill cashing in a decade of stock tips with a longtime acquaintance there. We then fed in the MITI ID codes we'd picked up from Ken during that ill-fated episode at the Tsukuba Teleconferencing Centre and he used these to patch back through to their New York JETRO offices. Finally we got St Croix on the phone, holding.

'Time to synchronise everybody's watches.' Tam was wearing her usual designer jeans, a blue silk shirt, and had her DNI flight bag freshly packed for the long days ahead.

'That thing says 3.28.37.' Henderson was watching one of his monitors behind the bar, now blinking off the seconds.

'Then let's all get ready to set at 3.29,' said Tam.

Which we did.

'OK, time to roll.' I punched the speakerphone. The line to St Croix was still open.

'Ready, Artie?'

'Say the word, my man,' the voice from the box came back. 'We got the watts.'

'You on frequency?'

'Loud and clear. Sound like they runnin' some kind of coded transmission. Don't read.'

'Double-check, Artie. We can't mess up. You're on 26RF-37558JX-10, right?'

'Yo, my man. Who doin' this?' He bristled. 'Think I can't hit nothing 'less it got hair round it?'

'Just nervous up here, OK? Settle down. At 3.30, exactly 27 seconds from now, go to transmit.'

'No problem.'

'Stay on channel, Artie. Don't wipe out *The Old Time Gospel Hour* or something. We're about to be in enough trouble as it is.'

'*You* the one 'bout to be up to yo' ass in bad news, frien'. Me, I just some oyster-shuckin' jive nigger don't know shit.'

... Except, I found myself thinking, how to make a monkey out of the US Coast Guard and DEA and God knows who else for ten years. Artie was the best.

Disconcertingly, I might also add, Artie Wilson had demanded cash in advance for our job, which didn't exactly reflect a high degree of confidence in the endeavour. However, there was no way we could test what we planned to do. This was it.

'You've got fifteen seconds.'

'One hand on the switch, boss, the other on my—'

'Artie, stay focused—'

'Thing is, jus' hope I remember which one to yank.'

'The big one.'

'That's what you think, white boy ... zero. Blast off ... yooeee, they gone.' Pause, then. 'Yep, we pumpin'.'

'Got it?'

'Just hit that little birdy with enough RF to light up San Juan. They eatin' garbage. Decoder up in Apple Town's gotta be goin' apeshit. Can't be readin' no telex, no nothing.'

'OK, keep it cranking.' I turned to Tam. 'You're on.'

'We're already patched through, on hold.'

'All the way through Tokyo and back?' It was still a bit dazzling.

'We're going to look just like an auxiliary MITI transmission. All I have to do is put in the DNI code, then request the connection over to Third Avenue.'

She tapped away on Henderson's keyboard, sending the ID through Shearson's communications centre in Tokyo, then back through JETRO on Sixth Avenue, from whence it was routed into the communications room at DNI's Third Avenue offices. Since she was using the standard DNI transmission format, we would look authentic. Right now, with their primary satellite channel gone, the JETRO link should be DNI's only high-security connection to the outside world. She began the transmission, in Japanese *kana*:

'Attention: Eyes only; J. N. Tanaka. Special instructions regarding operations. Please confirm routine satellite communications channel currently inoperative.'

Moments later the message came back: *'Confirm communications malfunction.'*

Then Tam: *'Due to technical difficulties with transmitter, weekend operations terminated. Staff advise alert number, message J9.'*

That last was DNI's special set-up that caused the computer to automatically dial the home number for all members of the staff, giving special instructions. Message J9 told everybody not to come in until further communication. God, was DNI efficient! The mainframe just kept dialling each number till somebody picked up. It even talked to answering machines. We figured that would head off most of the next crew. All we needed was a window of a few minutes between the goings and comings.

Then a message came back. As Tam began translating for us, though, a strange look was spreading across her face.

'Operations already suspended as of 2.57 NY time per security-link instructions. Staff leave of absence. Is this confirmation? Repeat. Is this confirmation?'

'What in hell?' Henderson stared at Tam, then me. 'Whose damned instructions?'

'Matt, what do you think's going on?' Tam's fingers were still poised above the keyboard. 'Why on earth would DNI Kyoto order a shutdown here?'

'That's a big question.' One that had no answer. 'Better just fake it, and fast.'

'What else can we do?' She revolved back around to the keyboard and began to type.

'Confirmation. What personnel remain?'

Back came Tanaka's reply: *'As instructed, security personnel only.'*

'Tam, get off the line. This feels wrong.'

She wheeled back again: *'Transmission concluded. Stand by for further instructions.'*

Tanaka's reply was brief and to the point. A man of few words: *'Confirmed.'*

'Whatever's going on, we've got to get over there.' I hit the speakerphone line again. 'Artie, keep them jammed till 5.05. That should do it. If we're not in by then, we're dead.'

'You got it, boss,' came back the voice. 'Any longer, some gov'ment honkie's gonna put on a trace. Be our ass. Correction, yo' ass.'

'Just pack up your gear and haul out of there. The FCC's the least of our problems at the moment.'

'You the man. Down again soon?'

'Can't rule it out. Take care.' I punched off the phone.

Tam was already headed for the door. Downstairs waited the car and driver we'd hired. No point trying to hail a cab in rush hour, particularly with so much depending on the next thirty minutes.

'OK, Bill, keep that Shearson link up. Maybe it'll block anybody else from reaching DNI's message centre.' I was putting on my coat. 'Where's that package?'

'Right here.' He reached behind the bar and retrieved the one item I wanted with me when we confronted security. It was nicely wrapped in brown paper. 'Look out for yourself, Walton. I got a few good drinkin' years left. Be a shame to have to do it all by myself.'

'Your guy ready?'

'Says he's on his way. Due here inside fifteen minutes.'

Without further farewells we headed for the elevator.

The trip over brought forth various thoughts on what lay immediately ahead. For some reason I found myself remembering Yukio Mishima, who once voiced a very perceptive observation on the nature of swordsmanship. He claimed that the perfect stroke must be guided towards a void in space, which, at that instant, your opponent's body will enter. In other words your enemy takes on the shape of that hollow space you have envisioned, assuming a form precisely identical with it.

How does this happen? It occurs only when both the timing and placement of a stroke are exactly perfect, when your choice of moment and the fluidity of your movement catch your opponent unawares. Which means you must have an *intuitive* sense of his impending action a fraction of a second before it becomes known to your, and his, rational mind. The ability to strike intuitively *before* your logical processes tell you your opponent's vulnerable moment has arrived requires a mystical knowledge unavailable to the left side of the brain, because by the time that perfect instant becomes known to your conscious mind, it has already passed.

The point is, if you allow yourself to think before you strike, you blow it. Which is why one of the primary precepts of *bushidō* is 'To strike when it is right to strike'. Not before, not after, not when you rationally decide the moment has come, but when it is *right*. That moment, however, is impossible to anticipate logically. It can only be sensed intuitively.

My intuition, as we rode the elevator up towards Dai Nippon's centre of operations, was troubled. The offices had been cleared in advance of our arrival by somebody from DNI's Kyoto operation. We had struck at the proper void in space, all right, but our opponent had deliberately created that opening. Things weren't supposed to happen that way.

Then the elevator light showed eleven and the door glided open. We were there. Before us lay the steel doors of the Empire. While Tam gave the computer a voice ID, I stood to the side readying the surprise I planned for Noda's security twosome. Off came the brown paper, then the scabbard, and in my hand gleamed a twelfth-century *katana* from the swordsmith who once served the Shogun Yoritomo Minamoto. The prize of my collection. It was, arguably, the most beautiful, sharpest, hardest piece of steel I had ever seen. With the spirit of the Shoguns.

'Ready?' Tam glanced over as the doors slid open.

'Now.'

Awaiting us just inside the first doors were the X-ray and metal detector, the latter a walk-through arch like you see in airports. Then past that were the second doors, beyond which were stationed the two Uzi-packing guards. The detector was set to automatically lock the second doors if metal was detected on the persons of those passing through and the wires leading out of it were encased in an aluminium tube, attached there on the left. This would have to be fast.

The sword was already up, poised, and as we entered, it flashed. Out went the electronic box with one clean stroke, the encased wires severed at the exact point where they exited from the grey metal. There was no alarm, not a sound. We'd iced it.

Beautiful.

I figured there would be time for exactly two more strokes, but they had to be right, intuitively perfect. So at that moment I shut down my rational mind, took a deep breath and gave my life to Zen. Mental autopilot.

The connecting doors slid open and there stood the guards. We'd caught them both flat-footed. So far, so good. Now the sword . . .

Yukio Mishima, whom I mentioned earlier, once asserted that opposites brought to their logical extremes eventually come to resemble one another, that life is in fact a great circle. Therefore, whenever things appear to diverge, they are actually on a path that brings them back together — an idea of unity captured visually in the image of the snake swallowing its own tail. According to him there is a realm wherein the spirit and the flesh, the sensual and the rational, the yin and yang, all join. But to achieve this ultimate convergence you must probe the edge, take your body and mind to the farthest limits.

I'd been reflecting considerably on what this meant to us. Noda's two heavies personified brute physicality, the body triumphant; Tam and I were meeting them with the power of the mind and, I hoped, finely honed intuition. Whereas these may seem the farthest of opposites, as with the symbol of the snake, they merged at their extremities. They became one. I knew it and the two startled guards now staring at us understood it as well. Mind and body were about to intersect. The circle had joined.

Their Uzis — about two feet long, black, heavy clip, metal

stock – were hanging loosely from shoulder straps several inches away from their hands. I saw them both reach for the grip, but that sight didn't really register. My cognitive receptors were totally shut down.

While the first man's left-hemisphere neurons were telling his right hand to reach downwards, the sword was already moving, milliseconds ahead. It caught the gun's heavy leather strap, parting it like paper, and the Uzi dropped, just eluding his fingers. He stood naked.

That was all for him and he immediately knew it. If you're looking at a razor-sharp *katana*, you don't get a fallback try. However, the second guard, dark eyebrows and bald head, now had time on his side. Up came the automatic, one-handed.

Right here let me say you've got to admire his pluck. If I'd been staring at a four-foot *katana* that could have bisected me like a noodle, I might have elected to pass. But he'd weighed the odds and concluded he had a chance. Again, though, his rationality bought us time. The neurons firing in his brain were setting in motion a sequence of logic. He was thinking.

The sword wasn't. My blank mind was centred on the void, the place where the Uzi would be when it was levelled at my chest. The overhead stroke caught it just where intuition said it would be, point-blank, his finger a millimetre from the trigger.

Cheap Israeli steel. The eight-hundred-year-old *katana* of Yoritomo Minamoto's swordsmith parted the Uzi's perforated black barrel like Hotel Bar butter, bifurcated it into two identical slices. Guard number two just grunted as it clattered to the floor.

By my reckoning we'd been in the inner chamber for about three quarters of a second, but Noda's two human mountains were now standing there holding nothing but time in their hands. Nobody had to draw them a picture. The game was over. *Bushidō.*

I motioned Tam towards the first guard's weapon.

'Matthew . . .' She hesitated a moment, then snapped into action. 'You weren't kidding about that sword. I never realised—'

'Let's go.'

'Right.' She now had the one remaining automatic. The other was no longer usable. Didn't matter. One was all we needed.

We now had to kill the automatic ID on the outer door and put it on manual. Otherwise the two guards upstairs might come calling. While Tam stood there with the Uzi, I went back out and yanked the wires that hooked the voice reader to the computer. There was probably a scientific way to turn it off, but who had time for science? Besides, just then my veins were still pumping pure adrenalin. Facing the business end of an Uzi, even for a fleeting instant, is no way to begin an evening.

Tam ordered the guards to open the last door and in we marched. Tanaka was standing outside his office, his dark eyes glazed, his bristle-covered skull rosy with shock. He turned even redder when he saw the *katana*. Nobody had to tell him what it could do.

'Mr Walton, why are you here?'

'We're about to undertake some corporate restructuring.'

Tam proceeded to herd Tanaka and the guards into his office, pausing just long enough to kill the phone wires. As he began to recover, he commenced sputtering about legal action and jail and general hellfire. Who cared? As of this moment, the offices and computer of Dai Nippon, International belonged to us.

Henderson was informed of our progress when his phone rang at exactly 4.48 p.m. He arrived, along with his Georgia Mafia computer expert, at 5.17, and Tam met them at the security doors.

I wasn't actually there to welcome them aboard, since I was guarding Tanaka just then and engaged in a small one-on-one with the man, explaining to him that Matsuo Noda's ass was ours. The president of Dai Nippon, I advised, was a few short days away from becoming everybody's lead story, featured as the Japanese executive who'd (apparently) rebelled against his homeland. Noda was no stranger to headlines, of course, but he preferred to engineer them himself, so this definitely wasn't going to be his style. Matsuo Noda was, albeit unwillingly, about to make history. As I broke this news to Dai Nippon's chief of New York operations, I sensed he was definitely less than enthusiastic about the prospect. Well, he'd have a few days to get used to the idea, since nobody was going to enter or leave the eleventh floor for a while.

It was still a bit difficult to believe what had happened. Or even more, what was next. But sometimes reality can have a way of outstripping your wildest powers of imagination – a Space Shuttle explodes, a nuclear meltdown in the Ukraine, ten-dollar oil, all of it too farfetched to make credible fiction. It could only exist in the realm of the real.

We were about to start moving billions and billions of dollars, fast. And since we didn't know how long we could continue before Matsuo Noda figured out a way to stop us, we were going to adhere to a schedule that covered the most vital sectors first – those outfits whose R & D Tam considered strategic to America's future technological leadership. Our goal for the first day was five billion, worldwide.

Thus the countdown began. Henderson's financial artist loaded Tam's new program tape on to DNI's big NEC supercomputer and cranked up. We had roughly sixty hours till the opening bell on Monday.

TWENTY-SEVEN

'It's the worst of times, buddy, and the best of times. Whatever dude once said that didn't know the half of it. He oughta be around now to check out the Street.'

That was Henderson's Georgia Mafia co-conspirator, an irritatingly smug young man with red hair and acne who dressed entirely in white, right down to his skinny Italian tie. We were told he went by the handle of Jim Bob. As he meditated upon Wall Street's macroeconomic incongruities, he punched a Willie Nelson tape into his boom box and popped a Coors, pregame warm-up for programming a full-scale assault on the US securities markets.

Jim Bob allowed as how he'd arrived in the Big Apple four years earlier with a cardboard suitcase, a finance degree from Georgia Tech and a larger than regulation endowment of natural cunning. After a couple of years' toil in Henderson's quasi-legal vineyards, he'd gone out on his own, whereupon he'd parlayed his winnings with Bill and the remnants of a baseball scholarship into what was now a high six-figure 'haircut', the name options players use for their grubstake. The way he figured it, he was just hitting his stride.

How, I inquired at one point during that long weekend, had he managed it?

'Chum, it's idiot simple. You buy into fear, sell into greed, and fuck fundamentals. Main thing is, if something makes sense, don't do it. It's like everybody's bidding up standing room on the *Titanic*. But who cares? You play options like I do and all you have to worry about is not getting stupider than the herd. Which ain't necessarily much of a trick.'

Stock options, he went on to assert, were like having a credit card in a whorehouse – a ton of action for what amounted to tip money up front. No wonder Las Vegas was in trouble, when Wall Street was beckoning our high rollers to take odds on the direction of the market. Only widows and orphans, he observed, bought actual securities any more. That action was reserved for the halt and lame.

While country singers twanged beer-hall soliloquies on the general increase in faithless women, Jim Bob coded in the brokerage houses and offshore banks we'd be using, the catalogue of stocks in the DNI portfolio, and our sequence of transactions.

As noted earlier, the financial set-up had been handled by Henderson and friends. Using his connections, he'd opened accounts for hundreds of dummy corporations in about two dozen offshore banks. He stuck to the usual no-questions-asked operations like Banca della Svizzera Italiana and Bank Leu in the Bahamas – the latter a Swiss-owned Nassau laundry that had, in years past, reportedly destroyed records and lied to the Securities and Exchange Commission as a favour to certain of America's more inventive inside traders.

Since the volume of money to be moved was staggering, it would all be handled by sophisticated telecommunications networks. We would pass it through the anonymous accounts we'd established, accessed both ways by computer, and it would never be touched by human hands. DNI's cash would flash in and out with total cover. Added to that, anybody who tried to trace us would first have to break through a traditional Swiss stone wall.

To dump the stock we were planning to exploit fully the new 'globalisation' of the financial scene. Now that the National Association of Securities Dealers had struck a deal with the London and Tokyo stock exchanges to swap price quotes, worldwide market makers were buying and selling American securities around the clock. Plenty of active market-making was happening off the exchange floors as well, at places like Jefferies out on the coast, which had recently handled a massive Canadian takeover of an American company *overnight*, entirely off-exchange. With all the avenues available it was almost impossible to track the movement in a given issue. DNI's computers would be routeing sell orders to brokerage firms around the globe, a block here, a block there, none of them in quantities that would raise eyebrows.

Maybe I also should add that none of the 'corporations' Henderson had set up would be allowed to show a profit, which would simplify Treasury Department reporting requirements. As a matter of fact, before we were through, DNI was going to *lose* billions. But it would all be done legally, in accordance with SEC regs. It would also lead to a world financial flap of notable proportions. Nobody would ever take Noda's money for granted again.

While Tam went over her new program with Jim Bob, pointing out her special features, Henderson and I found ourselves at reasonably loose ends. We sat around drinking green tea (God, how I came to hate that stuff) and puzzling how we'd all managed to get into such a mess. The major plus, however, was that we finally had Matsuo Noda by the short and curlies.

Or so we hoped. The problem was, he'd been a player longer than any of us, and he'd already demonstrated plenty of stamina. How would he counterattack? The question wasn't if, it was when. For the moment, though, we seemed to be on our way with clear sailing; in fact, the communications link with Kyoto was entirely empty. Tanaka also had clammed up, refusing to talk – beyond a rather firm prediction that our wholesale divestiture of DNI's assets was an insane act doomed to failure. I might also add he didn't appear nearly as concerned as the circumstances would seem to merit. In fact, he was so complacent I started getting a little uneasy. Finally Bill and I ran his prediction past young Jim Bob. Could somebody get through to Tam's program and devise a way to shut us down?

Henderson's increasingly glassy-eyed protégé took out enough time from popping 'uppers' and swilling Coors to assure us to the contrary.

'Hell, no way you could stop what we're settin' up here. We got ourselves what you call a closed system. Everything's going to be handled by that green-eyed monster over there in the corner. We got these numbered brokerage accounts all over the place. Zip, in go the sell orders; zap, out go confirmations. And since none of the cash sits around, our bank accounts are all just gonna churn. We'll have billions of buckaroos rollin' at the speed of light. Ain't *nobody* gonna be able to get a bead on the action, take my word for it.'

Our computer-generated buying and selling, he went on to declare, was conveniently similar in appearance to the 'program' trading of the big institutional investors, the arbitrage players who routinely sold millions of dollars of securities in minutes using computers. Thanks to them, the market these days had been conditioned to accept huge, unaccountable trades as part of the territory. If somebody dumped massive blocks of stock un-expectedly, it could mean anything – such as, the spread between those stocks' prices and some 'index future' had gotten moment-arily out of sync. Shuffling securities like poker chips was the name of the game on the Street these days, so nobody would really notice or care. The turnover we'd be generating would merely suggest to the market that various investment-house arbitrage desks were unwinding positions.

What the heck, I said to Tam, maybe we *could* unload the better part of DNI's holdings before Noda struck back. The real key to our attack on Dai Nippon, however, depended on what happened to that cash after we turned it around. When I men-tioned that, she just crossed her fingers.

By late Sunday night the DNI offices were a clutter of empty Chinese take-out containers, Kentucky Fried boxes, and computer printouts. However, Jim Bob claimed the system looked like a go. He'd completed a long sequence of test runs, and he was predicting he could probably swing at least four billion the first day, something in the nature of a warm-up for grander things to come.

Jim Bob, I should say, was fully as efficient as advertised by Henderson. Even if he was now flying higher than a moon shot, thanks to all the pills. He worked methodically, carefully an-alysing the program at every step, double-checking the codes, poring over his verification printouts for obscure glitches. Mainly, though, he kept one unfocused eye on the clock, saying he always delivered on time. Point of honour.

Thus it was that, when Monday morning rolled around, we were primed to move on Wall Street. Tam's program was poised inside the mainframe like some lurking id, ready to be unleashed. We decided to start modestly, sticking to the exchanges in New York, and only later in the day expanding outwards as we gained firmer footing.

At the stroke of 9.30 a.m., Jim Bob inaugurated our maiden run with yet another beer. Henderson and I poured ourselves a bourbon. Tam even joined us, accepting a respectable shot.

'Fasten your seat belt, boys and girls.' Jim Bob shakily peeled back the tab on his Coors. The screen in front of him focused our attention down to one small flashing green dot.

'Ignition.'

He hit a key on the terminal, and Merrill Lynch got a computerised 'sell' order for ten thousand shares of Texas Instruments. The time was exactly 9.31.

It was a textbook lift-off. Rows of green numbers began to scroll up the screen, only to blink and disappear. By God, the thing seemed to be working. We had just pulled the plug on DNI. All that was left now was to sit back and watch it sink.

As the morning wore on, Tam fielded phone calls from staffers, always claiming that Tanaka was not available just then. Of course, we weren't sure how long we could get away with that excuse, but for now none of us wanted to set the man free to start jabbering in Japanese on the phone. On the other hand, we were loosening up a bit on security. Partly, I guess, because we were all increasingly wrecked, but also because it seemed to fit the situation. By Monday, Tanaka and his two retired sumo bone-crushers appeared to have grown resigned, one might even say philosophical, and I don't mind admitting it bothered me a lot. Tanaka was watching us destroy Noda's grand design right before his very eyes, yet he just sat there as though none of it mattered. How could this be? All he did was busy around brewing tea for everybody (except, of course, for Jim Bob, who stuck to Coors). However, I was too tired by then to think much about it.

Around 2.30 p.m. Henderson began complaining of a splitting headache and declared he had to go home and get some rest. I started to protest, but the man looked half dead. Tam and I weren't much better off, so we flipped a coin to see who would take the first watch. She won, which was great by me, since the long hours without sleep were really starting to unravel my concentration.

To understand what happened next, you have to try to en-vision the scene. It was 3.00 p.m. and things were going letter perfectly. The dollars were sailing through the accounts we'd set up and along about noon we'd even kicked in our buy program.

Yes, *buy*. That's not a typo. You see, we had to lose billions, not necessarily a trivial task. Think about it. If you merely want to drop a few million, all you have to do is just invest in some high-flying start-up and then sit there till the venture craters. But billions?

That's the part where Tam really showed her mettle (no pun intended). Look, she said, the Brothers Hunt managed to blow millions by trying to corner silver, bidding up the price and then seeing it collapse. But we've got to get rid of some *serious* money, so why don't we do the same thing, only with a com-modity worth something?

Platinum.

All life's great ideas have an inevitable simplicity. That's right, we were programmed to sell DNI's stock and buy platinum. From anybody, anywhere, at any price. We were planning to just swallow the worldwide commodity markets in the stuff, starting at the NY Merc and ending at Cape Town. Of course, what we were also doing was boosting its price into the stratosphere – we were even bidding against ourselves through different brokerage houses. Anything to drive it up. I mean we had a lot of money to get rid of. We figured that by the time we were finished, DNI would be the proud owner of a couple of hundred billion in platinum metal, platinum futures, platinum mining stocks, pla-tinum storage companies, platinum dealerships, platinum reserves, platinum investment coins. All of it at a price as high as we could push. I was betting on two thousand dollars an ounce by Friday.

The nice part was, what central bank was going to step in? Platinum was strategic, sure, but it wasn't a monetary metal. And if we had to bid against governments, so much the better. We were playing a drunken speculator's dream, going all out for the most volatile of all the world's commodities. After we'd squeezed that scam for every ounce it was worth, we would deliberately puncture the bubble and let the price nosedive. We were going to destroy the cancer of Dai Nippon by gorging Noda's takeover machine with financial poison. The eventual collapse should wipe out Matsuo Noda totally.

Platinum. I asked Jim Bob to check the waning moments of Monday's spot market, the latest prices down at the NY Merc, and he reported it had scooted up about twenty dollars an ounce. A little slow maybe, but then we were just starting out. I figured it would probably double in a couple of days.

Such was my fond hope as I drifted off for a nap on my desk. Tam was in Tanaka's office, half-nodding in her chair, while Jim Bob was sitting before his monitor, still nourishing himself with beer and coloured pills. I gave him the Uzi and told him to help Tam out by keeping an eye on Tanaka and the two guards, all now sleeping like a baby. My last vision was of Jim Bob sitting there, the Uzi draped over his wrinkled white lap, clicking away at the keyboard.

I slept right through Emma's four-o'clock phone call from my office downtown. When I awoke around 9 p.m., Jim Bob mentioned she'd rung. No message, he said. Then don't worry about it, I mumbled to myself; get back to her in the morning.

Tam didn't seem to remember the call, which momentarily troubled me. Had we both been dozing at the helm? Well, who could blame her? In spite of my own nap I still felt like hell, so I dragged myself up, stretched, wandered around the office, drank some more green tea, and inquired of Jim Bob how things seemed to be proceeding.

'Looking good,' he grinned. He was now working Hong Kong

and the Asian exchanges, limbering up the satellites as he flashed our (DNI's) money around the globe. Anybody heard from Henderson? I asked. Not a word, he said in a tone that seemed disconcertingly pat.

I briefly toyed with heading down to the street and trying to locate an early, 'bulldog' *Times* to see what kind of a splash we were making in the press, but since Tam was now sound asleep, I figured I'd better stick to duty.

I vaguely recall stumbling into my office to rummage for an old box of NoDoz stashed somewhere there in the desk, and thinking how nice it would be just to lean back in the chair . . .

A phone was jangling in my ear. As I pulled erect, the clock on my desk was reading ten-thirty – My God, a.m.! – and I felt like I'd been run over by an eighteen-wheeler. What the hell was in that green tea Tanaka had been brewing?

Inside the receiver at my ear was Emma, and what she had to say brought me awake like an ice-cold shower. In a voice brimming with triumph, she announced she'd just resigned and I could consider this official notice thereof. In fact, she was price-shopping Florida condos this very minute – what did I think of Coral Gables? – and I was lucky she'd bothered to take out time to inform me of her intended plans. By Wednesday she expected to be able to loan money to the Rockefellers, in case they should need a little liquidity on short notice.

How'd you come by this sudden fortune? I asked.

Where, she snapped back, have you been? The Dow Jones Average was about to double, if it hadn't already. Funny, but the rest of the market was going nowhere. Oddest thing she'd ever seen. However, it only went to show what she'd always told me, and if I'd listened to her instead of those smarty-pants uptown brokers, I'd be rich now too. Stick with the blue chips. IBM was up thirty per cent since yesterday, AT & T was flying, GM was selling for a price that would make you think they were back in the car business.

What the hell was she talking about!

That's when I noticed a copy of Tuesday's *New York Times* lying there on my desk, right next to the phone. Only at first it didn't seem like the *Times*. Or maybe Punch Sulzberger had just been swallowed whole by Rupert Murdoch, because I hadn't seen a headline that arresting since the *Post*'s immortal 'Coed Jogger Slain in Bed'. It was banner, right across the top; the *Times*' headline writer was practically orgasmic. But whereas the *Post* gets off on mere sex, the good grey *Times* reserves its libidinous juices for that ageless aphrodisiac, money.

NEW YORK STOCK EXCHANGE PRICES EXPLODE

NEW YORK — Volume skyrocketed on the floor of the New York Stock Exchange yesterday, as buyers for Big Board issues responded worldwide to a renewed confidence in American industry. Analysts are calling this the first leg of the Great Bull Market of the 1990s, saying this surge has been overdue for a decade. Leading the phenomenal rally were a number of America's foremost corporations . . .

I came off my chair like a shot and headed for Tam's office. 'Is anybody following what's going on outside?'

Her face was down on the desk, dark hair tousled across her cheeks. She looked up and rubbed her eyes, obviously knocked out too. Strange.

'What . . .?' Her voice was slurred.

'Something's gone crazy,' I yelled. 'Where's Henderson?'

Then I remembered he wasn't there. However, I did locate Jim Bob easily enough. He was in Noda's corner office, wide-awake and still carrying our Uzi. Only now there were two of those long black automatics present, the other lying atop the wide teakwood desk.

One more thing. Seated behind that desk, his silver hair framed by the sunlight streaming through the wide back windows, was . . . Matsuo Noda.

The Shogun had arrived.

And with him came the dawn of a new, powerful reality. My drugged mind was flooded with the ramifications. Matsuo Noda, I now realised, had been on to us from the start. Once again he had used us. *He* had been the one who had emptied the office, the better to lure us in.

But the guards ...

Noda-san, I bow to a true *samurai*. A swordsman's swordsman. Of course, it was as simple as it was elegant. You were testing us, allowing us a plausible opening, just difficult enough to force us to reveal our true strategy. The dictum of the masters: 'If you want to strike your enemy, let him try to strike you first. The moment he strikes at you, you have already succeeded in striking him.' Pure *bushidō*.

Everything up till now had only been feints. What I'd assumed was the battle turned out to have merely been staking out terrain, jockeying for position. At last, though, we were ready for the real engagement. Trouble was, Matsuo Noda had just secured the high ground.

'Come on in and have a seat, Walton.' Jim Bob beckoned towards the vacant chair as he sipped from a glass of California champagne, its plastic-looking bottle stationed on the floor beside him. Coors time was over.

'Jim Bob, what's happening with the market?' I was ignoring Noda for the moment, trying to get a firmer grasp on the new 'prevailing conditions'.

''Bout what we figured,' he replied, his white suit now greasy and wrinkled. 'Yep, looks like we're roughly on schedule.'

'It's a relief to know there's a timetable.' I finally turned to Noda. 'Wouldn't want this takeover to be half-cocked.'

'Mr Walton, if you would be so kind.' He smiled and indicated the chair. 'It would be well for you to join us.'

Jim Bob waved me over with his Uzi. 'Fact is, we're all about due for a little show and tell.' He glanced up as Tam entered the doorway. 'Be a good idea if you got up to speed on what we're doing here, too.'

'I just scrolled some prices,' she said, glaring groggily at Noda, the morbid realisation descending rapidly now. 'You don't have to tell me anything. I know exactly what you're doing.'

'What we're doing is, we're pulling this country out of the shit. That's what we're doing. We're saving this country's ass. Which is more than anybody else here's doing,' Jim Bob continued, satisfaction in his voice. 'How in hell did you ever think you could pull something like you were trying? Mr Noda here could squash you all just like a June bug any time he gets a mind, take my word for it.'

Noda still hadn't amplified the new Dai Nippon scenario, but he didn't really need to bother.

'Jim Bob, don't spoil the fun and tell me. Let me try to guess.' I glanced over at Noda, then back at him. 'He suckered you in with his "Rescue America" spiel. World peace at a price.'

'Well, tell you the truth, the man did buy me lunch.'

'I'll bet that's not all he did, you opportunistic son of a bitch.'

I examined Noda. 'How does it feel to have Japan about to be sole owner of IBM and AT & T and GM and ... guess I could just check the supercomputer out there for the full list.'

'Certain strategic corporations.' Noda smiled benignly. 'It had become the only meaningful direction to proceed, Mr Walton. I'm afraid our other measures were clearly too little, too late.'

'Why bother with the small fish, right? If you're going to buy up American technology, do it right.'

'Mr Walton, we both know it is inevitable. Neither you nor I can alter the tides of history.' He sighed. 'Perhaps Japan *can* provide the management guidance required to save America's industrial base, but it cannot be achieved merely by dabbling. Stronger measures, much stronger, were required. I finally came to see that. The problem was how to do it without a major psychological disruption of the market and more Japan-bashing. Then by the greatest of good fortune, you solved my problem for me.' He nodded towards Tam. 'Your new trading program, Dr Richardson, which allowed us to operate anonymously, was ideal. Why not make use of it? Particularly since Mr Henderson had the personnel to render it operational.'

While digesting that, I returned my attention to Jim Bob. 'Let me guess some more. Ten to one you bought "call" options on the Big Board issues he was planning to take over.'

'Well, they were bound to go up.' He flashed a reptilian grin as he adjusted the Uzi, now a bolt of black against his rumpled white suit. 'If you're standing by the road and a gravy bus comes along, what are you going to do?'

'Terrific. Be a pity for this insider windfall to go to waste. Just wanted to make double sure you got a piece for yourself.'

'Does a bear crap in the woods?' he inquired rhetorically, then tipped back his head and drained the champagne glass.

'Right. So naturally you bought call options on the Blue Chips, locking in a cheap price just before Noda's money boosted them into the clouds.'

'Safe and simple. Of course, some traders go for index options, S & P 500's and indicators like that, but that's always been too airy-fairy for me. When the market's set to head up, I just buy calls. Heavy leverage. No risk.'

I concurred. 'Nothing too abstruse.'

'The thing of it is, I'm more comfortable dealing with reality,' he went on. 'I like to kick the tyres, check under the hood, so that index crap's not my style. Like I always say, if you've got hold of something you can't figure out how to drink, drive or screw, maybe you oughta ask yourself what you're doing with it.'

A pragmatic criterion, I agreed. 'Though it's rather a pity you didn't cut me in on the play. I could have used the money.'

'Walton,' he replied, 'it downright pains me to have to be the one breakin' the news to you, but you could have used the money more than you think. Whose bank balances do you figure I've been using to test out that platinum program?'

'In the spirit of intellectual curiosity, Jim Bob, does our new system for blowing capital show promise?'

'From the looks of my early churning, I'd say you got yourself a winner.'

The fucker. How in hell did he get access to my money? I decided to just ask, whereupon he obligingly explained.

'Well, we're hooked into every bank computer in town.' He was unblinking, a drugged-out zombie. 'Account numbers aren't exactly a state secret, given the right phone call. Same goes for trust funds.'

Trust funds?

'Let me be sure I've got this straight. You've also wiped out my daughter Amy's college money? She's now penniless too?'

'We're close, real close.' He reached down and retrieved the

370

bottle, then sloshed more of the cheap bubbly into his glass. 'I'm figuring I can have everything down to a goose egg by some time round about . . . lunch, probably.'

I decided then and there I was going to kill him, and Matsuo Noda, with my own bare hands. The only question was whether to do it at that moment or later.

'Jim Bob, for the record, you two've just fucked with the wrong guy. When somebody starts messing with Amy's future, I tend to lose my sense of proportion.'

'Nothing personal, Walton. You just had to be stopped, that's all.' He grinned. 'Figured it'd get your attention. Besides, way I see it, this man here's absolutely right. He's got the only answer that makes any sense.'

'As long as sellout artists like you get rich in the process.'

'It's in the grand American tradition, buddy. Enlightened self-interest, better known as looking out for number one. Everybody else here's hocking this country's assets to Japan and gettin' rich doing it. So why not? Besides, we've still got a ways to go. Time to give you all a piece of this thing too.'

'If we play ball?'

'Exactly.'

'You greedy prick.' I was considering just strangling him on the spot, nice and uncomplicated. 'Noda's not here for anybody but himself. He's—'

'That's not the way I see it.' He glanced over towards the Man, who was still silent as a sphinx.

'You wouldn't have the brains to understand even if we told you. But maybe there's something you *can* comprehend.' I glanced at the metal grip of the Uzi on Noda's desk. One lightning move and it was in my hand. 'I'm not going to let you do this.'

'It's already done, pal.' He lifted his own Uzi and levelled it at my forehead, grinning, his little idea of a joke. 'I've got the NEC mainframe out there programmed for weeks of trading. Billions . . . *Pow!*' he jerked the barrel upwards, then continued, 'Way I've got it rigged, ain't nobody can turn it off now. We'd just as well all go fishing.'

'Jim Bob, take care with that gun. Somebody might just decide to ram it down your scrawny throat.'

'Ain't gonna be you, buddy.' He reached for the champagne bottle again, no longer grinning.

'Mr Walton.' Finally Noda spoke again. 'I assure you this is for the best. What you two were planning was very ill-considered. Not to mention that, if I'd actually permitted you to sink Dai Nippon's capital into some volatile commodity and then manipulate the markets, you might have given our institutional investors an enormous loss of confidence in my programme. I have a responsibility to make sure that never happens.' He studied Tam. 'Dr Richardson, you especially disappointed me. You betrayed my trust, something I always find unforgivable.'

'You betrayed *my* trust.' She looked ready to explode. 'Lied to me, exploited me, used me. You perverted everything I had planned—'

'As I've explained, this had become necessary. There was no other way.'

'How about Ken, and probably Allan Stern?' she interrupted. 'Was taking their lives "necessary" too?'

'You have no proof of that,' he continued smoothly. 'I would further suggest that too much speculation is not a healthy pursuit, Dr Richardson. In the marketplace or in life.'

'I'm not speculating.'

'As you wish. In any case I think we both realise it is never prudent to meddle in matters beyond one's concern.'

'There's a small detail you may have overlooked, Noda-san,' I broke in. 'That bogus sword. What are you planning to do when we blow the whistle?'

'My timetable for NIPPONICA is now proceeding on schedule, Mr Walton.' He glanced at the Uzi on the desk, his voice ice. 'Consequently you are expendable as of this moment.'

TWENTY-EIGHT

> If the swordsman casts aside two thoughts,
> life and death, nothing can defeat his mind.

That was the credo of the formidable warrior-*samurai* Bokuden, who lived during the early seventeenth century. Focus on Noda, I told myself, not on staying alive. What we had to do was overcome him and the money of Japan by the power of mind. By beating him at his own game. That was the only way we could win.

As I saw it, we might actually have the advantage. We knew his strategy, so all we had to do now was move inside his defence perimeter. In a way we were even closer than he realised. Noda was obsessed with NIPPONICA, and a *samurai* concentrating on his sword is not able to attack. The thing to remember was rhythm, the beat. We had to get out of sync with him, disrupt his pacing.

When Tam and I retreated to my office, I noticed that my *katana* was missing. No surprise, but it didn't really matter. We would be using the 'no sword' technique anyway, moving under his hilt, then going in for the kill. Jim Bob would be our new weapon.

At the moment Noda's new hatchet man was strolling around the floor in his dingy white suit, toting his Uzi and monitoring us with an occasional vacant stare as he watched the terminals flash. His bumpkin façade, incidentally, had to be the best acting job I'd seen since the Royal Shakespeare. He may have been a spaced-out options hustler at heart, but he could coach Machiavelli on duplicity. A worthy opponent.

'Just hit nine per cent of IBM.' He glanced at a CRT screen as he ambled down the row next to my office, swinging the automatic. 'Telephone looks good for twelve per cent by opening bell tomorrow. Good thing we've got a computer and these fake accounts. Otherwise we might have to cut the SEC in on the news a little too early.'

Well, DNI was nothing if not organised; 'global trading' was on a roll. There would be no way to trace Noda – or to stop him. By the time anybody realised what was afoot, he'd be well on the way to having us literally bought out. God knows, Japan had the money.

'Jim Bob,' I yelled across. 'Mind telling me what the hell it is you really think you're up to?'

'I'm making history.' He grinned and waved his Uzi in the air. 'You're getting to watch the dawn of a new age.'

'For your wallet.' I beckoned him over. 'Tell me something. You didn't actually sell any of the high-tech stocks on Tam's list after all, did you?'

'Hell, no.' He was still grinning. 'All we did was play games a little. Whenever I sold anything, I just turned around and bought it back a few minutes later.'

'So where's all the money coming from for this big blue-chip takeover?'

'We got a whole new financial network in place. Mr Noda worked it out with the pension funds over there.'

'Well, it seems to me you ought to be doing this thing right. Why think small? Pick up some more shares of those high-tech issues in the old portfolio too.'

He stared at me with his bloodshot eyes. 'How come we'd want to bother with that?'

'Just thought maybe you'd like to make a score.'

'Huh?'

'Besides, down the line it'd probably impress hell out of Noda. The man admires initiative.'

'What was it you said about a score?' He was blinking in erratic bursts, still flying on uppers.

'Forget it. Just a crazy idea that crossed my mind.' I turned and walked back into the office . . . where Tam was waiting.

'What was *that* all about?'

'Tam, did you hear what those bastards did?' I was steaming. 'They blew my daughter's college money.'

'I heard.'

'Well, it pisses me off like I can't begin to describe.'

'I gathered that.' She looked at me strangely. 'He finally got to you, didn't he? Noda finally pulled your cork. No more Mr Cool.'

'You got it, lady.'

She continued to study me, and into her eyes crept a kind of affection I didn't even know they possessed. 'Guess that makes two of us, Matt. He found out how to get to me and now he's found out the one thing *you* care about.'

'Guess he did at that.'

'Well, now you know how I feel.'

'He broke the rules, Tam. That's not part of the game. But do you understand what this means? Now I'm free to do anything I want. Honour is out the window.'

'This isn't a game.'

'You're right. It's a battle. But even battles have rules.'

'My God, macho to the end.'

'Call it what you want. But I am now going to destroy them both, totally. Wipe them out. They've given me no choice.'

'How exactly do you propose doing that?'

'I made the opening move just now. Next I'm ... later.' I glanced up to see Jim Bob approaching. He was staring at me, glassy-eyed.

'What was that you were saying a while ago?'

'Don't remember, Jim Bob.'

'Something about a score.'

'Oh, that. Nothing really.'

'Don't start getting cute, Walton.' He sighted his Uzi around the office.

'Nobody screws with you, right?'

'Better believe it, sport.'

'Well, I was just wondering, since Noda's tied up at the moment, if you might want to go ahead and make a little money on the side.'

'I'm not doing so bad.'

'Fine. Since you're not interested anyway, we can just skip it. No big deal.'

'Hang on a second.' His eyes seemed to be trying to focus as he stared through his gunsights. 'What's the play?'

'Merely a wild idea, that's all. I was wondering what would happen if you bought a few call options on those stocks already in the portfolio, then boosted the prices on those too?'

'You mean on those high-tech outfits we were supposed to start selling?'

'Well, the set-up's just sitting out there. You've got all that Japanese pension money and Noda's computer. No reason not to kite those high-tech issues a little and pick up some pocket change. Fun and games to while away the time. But then maybe you've already made all you want to.'

'Hey, asshole, there's two things you can't ever get too much of, and one of them's money.' He was rocking mechanically. 'Matter of fact, this action we're generating is driving up the March calls for our new buys to the point where the price is gettin' way out of line.'

'Had to happen. Everybody else in town has figured out somebody's driving the market. They're getting on the options bandwagon too, bidding them up. So why not play a little market shell-game with those issues already in the portfolio, buy some calls and then kite the price on them as well? Show Noda a thing or two.'

'Kind of stick it to the boss man.' He paused.

'Think of it as insurance. Just to make sure you come out of this play whole. Tell you a secret about Noda. With that guy, you know you've got a deal when the cheque clears.'

'He's a crafty fucker, grant you.'

'You might want to give it some thought. But if you're going to make a move, it's probably now or never. Be the early bird or forget it.'

All this time Tam was looking at me as if I'd gone over the edge. I began to deeply regret not having filled her in on the fallback scenario.

The door to Noda's office was now closed, his two guards posted outside. Guess even a *samurai* needs some rest and tranquillity after flying halfway around the globe in a chartered Concorde.

'Well, gotta admit it's an idea.' Jim Bob continued to weave unsteadily. His motor mechanisms were now on automatic, along with his venal corn-pone brain.

'Matt, what in hell are you doing?' Tam was pulling me back into the office.

'Stay cool. Swordsmanship is like Zen. You can't ever let your mind get attached to anything. Do that and you're stuck; your mind stays with the past and makes you neglect what lies ahead. So I figure the best thing to do here is to adjust to the new "prevailing conditions".' I glanced out at Jim Bob, now just beyond the door and absently humming some Waylon Jennings tune as he swayed solo.

'Well, I want to know what you're up to.'

'OK, here's the play. While you were setting up your sell-off scheme, I did some fiddling on my own. Remember back when we started out, I fast-talked Noda into giving me power of attorney? Well, it finally paid off. Last week I convened an instant shareholders' meeting for every company where DNI owns a majority of the stock and personally voted through a new set of resolutions.'

'Mind filling me in on what they were?'

Before I could reply, Jim Bob came dancing in, licking his pale lips. 'Walton, tell you what. Think I'm gonna go for it.'

'What?' I looked up.

'That options play. Comes a time you gotta look out for yourself and fuck everybody.'

'That's the kind of thinking made this country what it is today, Jim Bob. Right on.'

'Fuckin' A, baby.' He did a quick dance step. 'Go for the gold.'

'You know, as long as we're at it, how about a little piece of the action for me too? Nothing big. Just a couple of bucks for old times' sake.'

'Why the hell not!' He let out a whoop as he turned and

headed for a terminal. 'Give you sloppy seconds on this one, ace. Just long as I get first pop.'

'Matt, I don't know what you're up to, but I'll kill you if you start helping him.' She looked like she would too.

'You know, you once said you wanted to drive a stake into DNI's heart.' I turned back. 'Well, this is your chance. But we've got to get moving and do it before Noda catches on.'

Whereupon we joined Jim Bob in front of his monitor. He was now busy pulling up quotes for March calls on the Chicago Board Options Exchange, the CBOE. He checked them over, then got on the phone directly to the market makers on the floor. When you're operating in hyperdrive, you don't dawdle around with brokers.

'Jim Bob, while you're doing that, I think I'll just start setting up the buy orders for the stock. If we want to move prices, we've got to have coordination.'

'Yahoo. Let's kick some ass.' He'd just entered a wholly new dimension of exuberance. 'Shit fire and save your matches; fuck a duck and see what hatches.'

My sentiments precisely. I started scrolling up DNI's portfolio of high-tech securities, looking for the biggies. If things went as planned, our screwing of Matsuo Noda was definitely going to be memorable.

Now Jim Bob was chortling quietly to himself as he punched up more numbers, moving on to bilk options traders on the AMEX.

'Matthew, you'd better finish explaining what you're up to.' Tam was standing behind me, her hand gripping my shoulder.

'Look, we have to do this fast. Switch a beat on Noda, break his rhythm. Just trust me.'

'My favourite word.' She didn't move.

'Now' — I pointed to a column of green numbers on the left-hand side of the screen — 'are those the percentage holdings DNI has?'

'Looks correct.'

They were about what I remembered. DNI's positions varied from around fifty per cent to the low sixties.

'OK.' I turned to face her. 'Which of these do you want to knock out first? There may not be time to torpedo them all.'

'What are you going to do?' She was frowning, but I could tell the idea had appeal.

'Set dynamite under them. Just blow them sky-high.'

'How?'

'Using an obscure corporate anti-takeover tactic not many people know about yet. Jim Bob's right. We're going to make history. Nobody's ever done this on the scale you're about to witness. Just pick the stocks you want detonated first, but please hurry.' I shoved a pen and paper at her, then turned to watch Jim Bob, now dancing around with a phone in his ear, still buying calls on the old DNI portfolio. 'How're we doing over there, chief ?'

'Don't want to push March too hard, tip off the market, so I'm picking up some Junes too.' He yelled my way, 'We're going *long*, baby.'

'Jim Bob, I was just wondering. Don't you think you ought to hedge a little, just in case? Maybe buy a few puts to cover the downside?'

'With the kind of volatility I'm about to goose into this market? You're starting to sound like some pussy, Walton. Get naked, go native. Only way to fly.' He did a twirl, then a kick. 'Just buckle in, dude, cause I'm gonna take that Jap money and pump my underlying stocks right into orbit. This play's a lock. Taking money from a baby.'

'Well, I wasn't blessed with your brand of raw courage, Jim Bob. So what do you say I do a little hedging for you? We'll be partners. I'll cover the downside with my own money, assuming I've got any left. I'll buy a few puts, and then if these stock prices just decide to go crazy and crash, we can still sell at the current quotes. Protect ourselves if things head south for some reason.'

'Suit yourself. But that's the best way I can think of to piss away what little "haircut" you've got left.' He was grinning again.

'Guess I'm a masochist. What can I tell you?'

While my new 'partner' was laying the groundwork for his

scam, loading up on options to buy stocks at today's prices just before he turned around and shoved enough Japanese money into the market to send them sky-high, I did the opposite. I got on the phone to various brokers, including a currently jubilant Sam Kline, and started buying 'at the money' puts in Amy's name.

Jim Bob was betting the market would head up, buying calls; I was betting it would go down, buying puts. I was laying a wager with anybody in America who would agree, for my front money, to buy a stock from me at today's quotes any time through mid-March, even if the real price had since dropped to zilch. Which I fully intended to make happen.

Insider trading? Well . . . yes. You see, I was literally the only man on earth who actually knew what the stock market was going to do next, after DNI started buying more of those stocks I'd planted with land mines. But I was a driven man just then. Maybe I'd go to jail eventually, but by God Amy would still make college.

Amy. What was she doing today? I wondered. This was, what? Tuesday? So she must be back at school, probably thinking about lunch. Strawberry yoghurt and a bar of Tiger's Milk 'health' candy. God, I loved that little dark-haired prize more than life itself.

Where were we headed, she and I? Was I going to learn to let go? Maybe that wasn't going to be the problem, I thought, at least for her. Face it, I was about to become a fixture, just a stuffy impediment to nature's raging hormones. She'd already started rehearsing feminine wiles on me, practising that coy, downcast glance that didn't quite break subliminal eye contact. *Where* did she learn stuff like that? And she almost had it down cold. Next it'll probably be eye shadow and coloured bras.

Damn. This Christmas was going to be my last real chance to get to know her, to bore her silly with all my eminently ignorable fatherly advice. And I blew it. That in itself was enough to make me want to deep-six Matsuo Noda forever, the bastard. The money I fully planned to recoup; her thirteenth Christmas was gone forever.

With which sombre thought, I returned to buying puts. By the time I'd finished, Tam had her 'death-wish' list ready. And Jim Bob was just wrapping up his new program of call-option acquisition. Now for phase two.

I strolled over to his monitor, carrying her paper.

'Jim Bob, these might be a good place to start.' I tossed the sheet down beside his keyboard. 'Why not just set up a lot of buy orders to hit the market tomorrow at the opening? Doing it all at once should drive the prices straight up.'

'Right.' He leaned back, twitching. 'Wonder how much buying it'll take?'

'Well, why not play it safe? Use the computer and just boost DNI's high-tech portfolio another . . . oh, five per cent, straight across the board. Every issue. Program it and let her rip. You've already got Tam's sell set-up. All you have to do is turn it around.'

'Sounds good to me.' Now he was swaying to and fro, humming tonelessly.

'Then let's get rolling. You hit AMEX and the Big Board; Tam and I'll see if we can't drop orders for a few blocks on Jefferies, the off-exchange network. We have to make waves at the opening bell tomorrow.'

'Hear you talkin'. These issues gotta look like major movers.' He was beaming from ear to ear as he revolved shakily back to his terminal. 'Damn if I don't jus' love screwing the market.'

We went to work, and for the next half hour we transmitted buy orders to the farthest reaches of the globe. Once they were posted, it didn't matter when they'd be executed. Even if Noda killed us, a hand from the grave would come back and destroy him. The time bomb I'd set would blow the minute the SEC tallied up DNI's new holdings. There were about to be a lot of rich, happy workers in this Land of the Free. But the one man certain not to be among their number was Matsuo Noda. Speaking of which . . .

'Mr Walton, would you kindly explain what you are doing?'

I froze, realising he was standing directly behind my chair. How long had he been there? I'd been too absorbed to pay attention. Stupid, Walton, extremely stupid.

'Tell you the truth, Noda-san,' — I wheeled around and looked him in the eye, shielding the screen — 'sometimes you have to make the best of things. Discretion's the better part of valour, so we're told.'

'I'm familiar with the expression.' He appeared less than convinced.

'Who knows? Maybe NIPPONICA is the way to go.' We needed time, just a little more time. 'In any case I'm a firm believer in riding the horse the direction it's going. So I persuaded Jim Bob to buy a few options for me. Trouble is, the guy's a little tentative on reality just now.'

'Decidedly.' He glanced over at our mutual friend, now typing away obliviously, then turned and moved on towards the water cooler next to my office. Did he believe me? Maybe he actually thought we would just roll over and give up.

Or possibly Noda was in that unconscious mind-state that goes along with real mastery in swordsmanship. When a Zen archer discharges an arrow, his concentration must never be on that shaft. It must be on nothing. And the same is true with swordsmanship. Your mind must be in its natural state, empty of distractions. So if Noda allowed himself to focus on the small stuff right now, he'd forfeit his 'no mind' edge.

Well, we were about through anyway. The only thing left was to keep him occupied just long enough for Jim Bob to finish sending out the last of our buys.

'The sword was a masterful idea, Noda-san.' I got up and walked over to join him. 'How'd you manage it?'

'Mr Walton, what exactly do you know about the Emperor Antoku's Imperial Sword?' He sipped from a plastic cup, eyes squinting behind his rimless specs.

'Probably more than I should.'

'Then you will understand its recovery is a turning point in the history of Japan.'

I looked at him and realised he believed it. Actually believed it. Matsuo Noda had become a legend in his own mind. Why tamper with perfection?

'Have to admit, too, the idea of using our international bank cover to gobble up America's blue chips incognito was a stroke of genius. Congratulations. You're about to scare MITI and the rest of Japan half to death. Not to mention the world. With DNI heading up the management, who knows what could happen? You can probably write your own ticket back home after this.'

'Your friend Dr Henderson's young colleague was invaluable.'

Was?

Alas, poor Jim Bob. Did that mean he wasn't going to live long enough to spend the new fortune he thought he was about to make? Maybe Noda was planning to do half of my work for me.

'I guess a few of those phone taps you like so much led you straight to him, right? You were probably at least a day ahead of everything we did.'

'Good intelligence is vital to any successful endeavour, Mr Walton. You should remember that from Sun Tzu's classic *Art of War*.'

The man was right on.

'All these dummy corporations.' I was still running the stall. 'A little stock bought by each one, the SEC will never suspect. You just roll trades worldwide, till . . .'

'As long as necessary.'

'Who knows you're doing this?' Was it possible some rogue financier such as Noda really could pull a fast one on the whole world, use Japanese institutional money for whatever he pleased? 'Have you cleared this with the fund managers . . .?'

'It was not necessary, Mr Walton. I have long since earned the trust of my colleagues.' Again he had a weird look in his eye. Matsuo Noda, I realised, was currently operating from a distant planet.

Needless to say, our dialogue hadn't done a lot to calm my nervous system. The obvious solution to Noda's secrecy requirements didn't include a lengthy life span for a lot of loud-mouthed *gaijin*. Time to wrap up the stock-market games and get back to swordsmanship.

'At this point there's only one problem left, but I suppose you've already thought of it too. If word of this anonymous takeover breaks too soon, the exchanges might just decide to shut down trading and stop you. Which means we're all a threat to you at this point.'

He stood unmoving. 'That matter will be addressed presently.'

How soon, I wondered, was 'presently'?

'But haven't you forgotten somebody? Bill Henderson. The man's no fool. The minute he figures out your play, which he surely will, he's going to start blowing word all over the newspapers. You'll never get away with this.'

Noda smiled lightly. 'It *would* be helpful if he were here now. Perhaps you could be good enough to arrange for it.'

So with Matsuo Noda standing over me, Uzi next to my head, I called Henderson on my speakerphone. He picked up after eight rings.

'Bill. Getting rich?'

'Walton, what time is it? Goddamn, you woke me up.' He yawned into the receiver. 'Jesus, I feel like hell. What's going on? Everything still looking OK?'

'Couldn't be better. Quite a party around here. Want to come back down and help us celebrate?'

'Well . . . what the . . .! It's after eleven already. Hey, let me check out the market first. Be down there in a little.'

I looked up as Noda fingered his Uzi. 'Just come on over now. Don't putz around with the market. We could use the company. And Bill . . .'

'Yeah.'

'This shindig's BYOB. So how about picking up a fifth of Scotch? That way we can all get into the spirit of things here on the eleventh floor.'

'Walton, that's a hell of a—'

'I know bringing your own booze is not your style. But why don't you check in with Eddie, the security chief downstairs? He always keeps me a bottle of Suntory there in the utility room. See him about it.'

'That Japanese crap. Matt, what are you talking about? You know I hate—'

'Just ask for Eddie, Bill' I cut him off. 'Tell him Matthew

Walton wants his *black* label Japanese juice sent up here immediately. Understand?'

I hung up before Henderson could say anything more. Such as tell me we both knew there was no such thing as 'black label' Suntory.

'Guess he'll be here shortly.' I turned back to Noda.

'He should be here in no time at all, Mr Walton. Two of my guards have been posted outside his building since he returned there yesterday. For his own safety. They will bring him.'

With that chilling bit of news Matsuo Noda proceeded to yank out the phone cord then head back to his office. *The Art of War.* You leave nothing to chance. In fact his two sumo heavies were now standing outside my office, keeping a close eye on us. Guess he no longer had full confidence in Jim Bob.

'Tam, did you catch what just happened?' I'd walked back over to the terminals.

'I did.' She was staring into space.

'Henderson was our best hope to get out of here alive. He has a suspicious mind the equal of Sherlock Holmes's. But now—'

'Matt, what's he going to do to us all?'

'Don't think it'll be pretty.'

'Then . . .' She'd turned and was staring at the security entrance, wearing a quizzical expression.

I wheeled around to look too, and at first I thought I might have been hallucinating. A female figure was emerging through the doors, wearing an outfit whose style I couldn't quite place. Maybe it was one of those bulky creations such as Yohji Yamamoto or some other avant-garde Japanese designer might dream up, but it didn't resemble anything I'd ever seen before. Silk like a kimono, yet with a flowing quality. Ancient almost.

Then I had a vision, just offbeat enough to fit. An ink illustration out of the *The Tale of Genji* flashed before my eyes, and I realised I was seeing a *hakama*, something that hadn't been around the streets of Japan for roughly eight hundred years.

The woman in it was wearing peculiar make-up, not punk, though it might have been. It was pale, like the delicate ink shadings on a Heian hand scroll. She looked for all the world like a court lady of ages past; she'd have fitted right in at some 1185 Heian linked-verse soirée. Old Kyoto come to life.

Is this the latest neo-New Wave? What in good Christ . . .

The only uncoordinated touch was the handbag, leather and starkly modern, with a lock attached.

Jim Bob gave her a glazed stare as she moved right past him, headed for us. The sumo pair were bowing to the floor.

Well, well, the Emperor's most devoted courtier had finally arrived. Into our presence on this day of days had returned none other than Ms Akira Mori. One look at her eyes told me she'd come to kill somebody.

TWENTY-NINE

'Mr Walton, where is the silver case?' She'd walked straight up to us and now was just standing there, awaiting an answer.

'Mori-san, that silver box is long gone, thanks to Noda.' I suddenly felt as if we'd just dropped out of the twentieth century and back into the twelfth. Time warp. 'Let me tell you something. It was like the apple in the Garden of Eden: bite into it and out would spew the knowledge of good and evil. Better to forget the whole thing.'

'You don't know anything.'

'Definite point. We've just discovered there was a heck of a lot we didn't know.' I thumbed towards Noda's office. 'Including the scope of Dai Nippon's impressive new investment programme.'

She ignored that response entirely as she whirled on Tam, her voice increasingly strident. 'Dr Richardson, you have betrayed His Majesty.'

'Mori-san, you and everybody who's helping Noda are the ones who've done the betraying.' Tam stared her in the eye, daggers.

'Even though you are Fujiwara, you still let him continue,' Mori pressed on, oblivious. 'His scheme to manipulate the Emperor, to undermine MITI—'

'That's got nothing to do with . . .'

'It is the duty of a Fujiwara to protect His Majesty.'

'Speaking of His Majesty,' I cut in, 'how much did you have to do with Noda's fake sword? Guess that "protected" the Emperor too. Nothing like being handed a new lease on divinity.'

'The sword was to be his gift to me.' She said it hesitantly. 'To restore—'

'Perhaps we can clarify what it's really intended to restore, Mori-san,' I interrupted again. 'The Shogunate, with Noda as—'

She turned on me. 'And you helped him too.'

'What?'

'You and Asano-san stole the only thing I could have used to stop him. The contents of that silver case. And then this operation. After I'd tried to warn you both.'

'Mori-san, could be we're all acting under certain misunderstandings here today. For starters, buying up every American blue-chip issue in sight was not exactly our idea.'

She stared at me for a second, disbelieving. 'But that is precisely what you are doing.'

'Think again.' I pointed towards Noda's office. 'That's *his* game. Helped along by that sharpshooter over at the console.' I waved to Jim Bob, who toasted us with his champagne glass, still too zonked on uppers to comprehend the revised ground rules. 'Maybe you'd like to run through it with them.'

She seemed to notice him for the first time. 'Who is that person?'

'Noda's new hired gun. We've been retired. Without even so much as a gold watch.'

'*He* is the one responsible?'

'He's good, tell you that. Fooled us all.' I settled on to the office couch. 'Noda's got him this supercomputer. Looks like goodbye America.'

Noda's office door, incidentally, was still firmly closed, so presumably he wasn't yet aware of Mori's arrival. Were we about to see history replayed before our very eyes, that fateful battle of Dan-no-ura staged all over again, eight hundred years later, as a loyal retainer of the Emperor fought to thwart the armed takeover of a would-be Shogun? Wonder who was going to win this time around.

'Mr Walton, this must be stopped.' She was turning the key on her new leather handbag, unlocking it. 'I also insist you return your copy of the contents of that case. Having that is the only way I can—'

'Mori-san, not so long ago the contents of that silver box were very dear to our hearts, which is one reason we took the precaution of storing a facsimile on the hard-disc memory of the mainframe here. Now, there are about ten zillion files in that computer, so all you have to do is figure out what file name we used and you can just run off all the copies you want.' I got up and faced her. 'At the moment, though, there're more pressing worries.'

'You are playing with fire, Mr Walton.' She glanced at the computer room down at the other end of the floor.

'No kidding. This is a tough game we've got going. Maybe you'd like to get an update from the other team too, Noda and his new crony.'

'Are you saying *he* is the one?' She was pointing towards Jim Bob, who was now winding up the last dispatch of our new buy orders. I noticed it was the third time she had inquired.

'Don't take our say-so for it. Go ask him.'

Without a word she spun around, leaving a cloud of exquisite floral perfume in her wake. Tell the truth, I rather liked the designer outfit, what you might call a real classic. What I didn't care for all that much were the vibes. Very, very ominous.

As she strode towards Jim Bob, he watched her with an unfocused gaze. He apparently assumed it was all some costume-party gag. Definitely a major mistake.

'I am Akira Mori.'

Probably by then he no longer knew *what* he was seeing. He revolved around, adjusted the Uzi leaning against the console, and extended his paw.

'Pleased to make your acquaintance. Jim Bob McClinton. You work for Mr Noda?'

'In a manner of speaking.' She ignored the proffered handshake. 'Is it true you are now in his employ?'

'I was. At the moment, though, I'm taking care of myself, American-style if you want to know.'

'Whatever you are doing, I hereby order you to terminate all activities in this office. Immediately.'

Jim Bob just stared at her, not quite sure his brain wasn't playing more tricks. 'Well, now, I'd normally like to oblige a pretty lady like yourself, but I'm afraid I just don't have any intention of doing that.' He grinned, eyes flashing.

'Are you telling me you refuse?'

'You hear real good.' He reached down for the Uzi and his bloodshot eyes began to blink. 'Far as that goes, where I come from we're not used to takin' orders from cute little twats. So the best thing for you to do would be to shake your ass on out of my way and mind your own business. Or maybe go talk things over with Noda.' He thumbed towards the office. 'In there.'

She was opening her handbag, reaching inside.

Jim Bob, I was wanting to yell, this woman is neither 'cute' nor 'little'. Above all, she is definitely not a 'twat'. You are now face-to-face with a world heavyweight ball-breaker. Who may be about to take that Uzi you're so proud of and tie it around your scrofulous neck. This game is way over your head. Can't you see where it's headed?

'Matt, what's she doing?' Tam bolted forward...

Sad to say, everybody was too late, including Henderson. By probably no more than a second or so. I watched Jim Bob swing around his automatic ... and then the lights went out. We heard the dull 'thunk' of a silencer, followed by another, and next the sound of a chair crashing backwards, an Uzi clattering across the floor. It was indeed Dan-no-ura all over again, only this time the Shogun's forces had just taken the first hit.

But at least Henderson must have eluded Noda's gorillas. How'd he do it?

Whatever had happened, he'd gotten the message. Suntory black. He'd had Eddie yank the master switch for the eleventh floor. He 'blacked out' Dai Nippon.

For what good it did. Not much, as things transpired. He'd only cut the overheads. The computer must have had its own backup power, some circuit that didn't run through the main utility room. The office was now eerily illuminated by CRT screens, still buying blue chips. As usual, Noda had prepared for all eventualities.

Gingerly we inched out on to the floor. Jim Bob was sprawled beside his console in a spreading pool of blood. Maybe he was still alive. Maybe not. Tam reached down to check the pulse at his neck.

'It's gone.' She looked up, stunned.

Who was next? More to the point, where the hell was Mori?

Then we saw her, moving like a ghostly figure in a Noh play, gliding through the bizarre lime-coloured light of the terminals. We watched as she disappeared into Noda's office, trailed by the two dumbstruck guards.

What a standoff, I reflected fleetingly. The would-be Shogun versus the Emperor's number-one fan. This time, though, the Imperial side is hopping mad and loaded for bear. Wonder who'll . . .?

There was, however, something more important to think about. The next few seconds could turn everything around. This was hardly the time for historical meditations. With deliberate haste we might even live long enough for some history of our own later.

In the dim glow of the screens Tam grabbed Jim Bob's Uzi and we both dived for Noda's office. The door, happily, had just slammed shut. Since it was the kind that opened out, all we had to do was shove a desk against it and they were contained.

Now, how much time did we have?

'The mainframe.' She was staring through the green shadows towards the glassed-in room that contained the massive NEC. 'Matthew, we've got to shut it down somehow. That's the only way left to stop him.'

'Is there an on-off switch?' Who knew how you went about disconnecting a twenty-million-dollar supercomputer?

'We're about to find out.' She led the way.

The entry door was glass, half-inch and locked. Beyond it stood the string of six-foot-high modules, off-white and octagonal, lined up like squat soldiers on flooring elevated about six inches above that outside. The nerve centre of Noda's empire rested there on its platform, silent and secure.

'Tam, pass me that thing.' I reached for the Uzi, turned it round, and rammed the steel butt against the glass. Then again. It just bounced off.

'Harder.'

'OK, but stand away.'

I hauled back and swung at it with all my might. With a sickening crunch the glass shattered inwards, spewing shards across the icy tiles inside. An alarm went off somewhere out on the floor, but we just ignored it. After I punched away the few hanging pieces, we stepped in and up.

I handed back the Uzi. Now what?

'It's freezing in here.' She shivered from the cold, then pointed down. 'You know, all the wiring must be underneath this raised floor. There's no way to even know where the power conduit is, let alone reach it.'

'OK, guess we'll just have to start ripping . . .'

My heart skipped a beat. As my eyes adjusted to the dim light, I finally noticed what I should have seen immediately. Lying atop the big computation module was a thin, four-foot-long bundle, swathed in silk.

So that's where he decided to put it – in the one room that would always be locked. Or maybe he thought it should be kept in the most powerful location on the premises.

I reached up and retrieved it, then pulled away the silk. The blade had just been freshly oiled, and it literally glistened in the dim light. It was every bit as razor-sharp as the day it had been consecrated eight hundred years ago, at the zenith of *samurai* metallurgy.

Guess Noda knew a prize when he saw it. And this *katana* was definitely a one-of-a-kind piece – an Old Sword, *kotō*, from the Sanjo branch of the Yamashiro school of swordsmiths, late Heian. Signed by Munechika, said to have fashioned *samurai* swords for the Shogun Minamoto Yoritomo himself, the man who destroyed the Imperial forces at Dan-no-ura. No wonder Noda had treated it with special reverence.

'Welcome.' I held it up.

'Why do you suppose he put it in here?' She was admiring it too.

'You know, I think I understand. But it's the kind of thing that can't be explained in words.'

'Well, at least you've got it back again. Samson's hair. Are you pleased?'

'Maybe Noda was trying to tell me something. Send a message. But now I'm going to send one back.'

'Do you really think . . .?' She was already ahead of me.

'Guess we're about to find out.' I bowed to the blade ritually, then to the NEC's head-high main processor. 'From the first Shogun to the last.'

This, I muttered silently, is for Amy. Her answer, Noda-san.

The great masters of swordsmanship all will tell you something very ironic. If you train for years and years, all your moves eventually become instinctive; you literally no longer 'know' what you are doing. You become oblivious of your mind, as unknowing, consciously, of technique as the day you started. Thus the greatest masters and the rankest beginners actually share something very similar. Both are totally unaware of technique.

Was I closer to the mindless beginner or the 'no-mind' master? Friends, that's one confession you'll need medieval torture to extract.

I will, however, admit to thinking about which stroke to use. There are several that might have done the job. Of them all, though, the *kesa* seemed best for some reason. It slices diagonally, from the left shoulder down and across to the right, and a swordsman pure in spirit can literally bisect a man, slice him right in half.

As the blade sang through the cold and struck with a ring true as a bell, I felt nothing, thought nothing.

The hexagonal computation unit standing in front of us wasn't halved, not even close, but it was severely disoriented. I felt a small tingle in my fingertips as the sword sailed through the outer steel casing and severed its first layer of silicon neurons, sending forth a shower of sparks.

It wasn't dead, but then the sword had some backup. There is a long tradition in Japanese culture of cooperation, support from others. For example, in *seppuku*, the ritual disembowelment sometimes called *hara kiri*, there is always a second participant who stands behind you and ceremonially lops off your head as your body topples forward. It is an honoured assignment.

My action may have been satisfying symbolically, but it wouldn't do the job alone. Fortunately it didn't have to. There was one simple way to disengage Noda's electronic brain, now and forever. Tam didn't even hesitate.

For a second there it could have been the Fourth of July. An Uzi blasting away in the dark is a marvel. I watched spellbound as she emptied about twenty rounds into the processor bank as well as into everything else in sight, continuing until smoke started to pour out of the flooring below, followed by the crackle of electrical shorting. Then several storage modules began to arc, their high voltage mating in mid-air. In moments Noda's NEC supercomputer was transformed into a shorting, sputtering junk heap.

After that, electrical fires erupted down below and the linoleum squares beneath our feet proceeded to heat and buckle. Next, something flashed somewhere in the dark, and a stack of computer printouts lying next to the door burst into flame.

Originally I'd planned to retrieve the blade, but then I reflected a second and decided just to leave it. The sword in the supercomputer. A six-figure gesture, maybe, but one worth every penny in satisfaction. Noda would definitely understand.

By the time we made our way back through the shattered glass doorway, picking a path among the splinters, the fire was already spreading to the main office.

'Let's get out of here.' Tam was still grasping the Uzi.

'Not so fast.' I reached for the grip. 'You don't get to have all the fun. How do you operate this thing?'

'Just pull there.' She pointed, then raised the muzzle. 'Careful. You might need that foot some day.'

I lifted it up and it coughed a burst of flame. The water cooler outside my office exploded.

'Uh, I think you have to be Chuck Norris to do it like that. On a scale of one to ten, that round scores down in the fractions. Better aim.'

'Spoilsport.' But I did. I took a critical bead on a leering green monitor, squeezed, and felt a light kick from the metal stock. Out blinked one of the dying monster's eyes. Then I methodically took out half a dozen more workstations, just for the hell of it. Automatic weapons fire can be great therapy. Not to mention fun.

'OK for a beginner . . . Matt!' She was pointing at the desk of Noda's secretary. A phone light had just flashed on. 'He's calling in reinforcements.'

'Time to make our not-so-graceful exit.'

'Bring the automatic.'

'You've got it . . . and, uh, I'm a little embarrassed to ask you for money, but would you mind grabbing your purse? We may need it.'

'You're now broke, right?' She dashed for her office.

'So we're told.' I was wrapping the Uzi in some computer printouts that hadn't yet caught fire. The place was really starting to blaze, thanks to all the paper. Smoke everywhere.

While she was coming back I decided to go over and kick the desk away from Noda's door. Sure it was a risk, but we couldn't let him burn to death. Or Mori. Besides, we were home free. With the NEC supercomputer blown to pieces, as well as Jim Bob, there was absolutely no way Noda could cancel that stack of buy orders we'd seeded all around the globe. Nothing could stop the bomb.

As we made our way through security, we saw Mori coming out of the office, choking through the smoke and looking crazed as ever. Apparently the battle of Dan-no-ura, twentieth-century style, was still raging. Then Noda appeared in the doorway behind her and just stood there surveying the blazing ruins of his empire. With his customary discipline, he appeared totally unperturbed by it all. Not her, though. She lunged for the remains of the computer room, now billowing smoke and tongues of fire. The last thing on her mind, apparently, was us.

Which was just as well, because the second we hit the hallway we heard the elevator chime. It had to be Noda's backup forces. Without a word we both ducked for the stairwell and, as the metal door slammed behind us, Tanaka and a host of armed DNI security guards poured off the elevator like gangbusters. Turns out there'd been a small army poised downstairs just in case.

They could have the place, what was left of it. My last memory of that office was a raging torrent of smoke and flame. Nothing remained. This had to be the grand finale for Dai Nippon and Matsuo Noda. The end. *Finis.*

Barring unforeseen developments.

THIRTY

When we emerged into the lobby, calmly as we could muster, fire engines were racing up outside, cops were crowded around the elevators and Eddie was so frantic yelling about the holocaust up on eleven he didn't even bother to say hello. We searched in vain for Henderson as we worked our way through the milling throng, headed for the pay phone in the corner. Bill had to be somewhere; nobody else would have blacked out the DNI offices.

My first thought, though, was that we needed to make tracks. The brouhaha to come would best be handled from the safety of a foreign shore. Fortunately in my pocket was just enough change for one call and, as luck would have it, our man was in.

'Sure, Matt, no problem. But this is damned sudden.'

'Right now, Patrick. And hurry. Could be the perfect moment for an extended vacation. How about just sending the car around? Over on Third, near—'

'That Japanese place you told me you work for?'

'Worked for, Patrick. No more. Just got laid off.'

'Hell, I know where they are. It's all over the tube. I'm sitting here right now watching Jack O'Donnell blow his stack at a press briefing down in DC. Wish you could see the guy. It's live on CNN. Is this thing for real? What was that Dai Nippon outfit trying to do? Buy up every—'

Incredible. Henderson had *really* come through.

'Patrick.'

'Yeah.'

'Fill you in on all the details over a drink some day. Right now, though, we could really use Charlie and the car ASAP. We'll be waiting outside.'

'We?'

I looked at the smoke-smeared woman standing beside me. 'Truthfully, I'm hoping for some company.'

Tam smiled, then reached out and took my hand. Not a word about 'strictly business'.

'OK, Matt, Charlie just walked in. I'll send him straight on over.'

'Thanks a million. Owe you a big one.'

As we moved on out through the revolving doors, we finally spotted Henderson, wearing his grey topcoat and mingling in among the crowd on the sidewalk. The lowest of low profiles. For a second I almost didn't recognise the man. He looked a wreck, standing there shading his eyes and squinting up. Then I followed his gaze and realised smoke was pouring out of the windows on eleven. Seems we'd demolished a little exterior plate glass, too, along with everything else.

'Bill.' I signalled. 'Over here.'

'Walton, thank God.' He waved and pushed our way. 'I was worried stiff you two might still be up there. What in hell happened? Did you just blow up—'

'Long story. There was a small war, a new one and an old one. But how'd you get here? Noda said he was having your place watched. A couple of . . .'

'Yeah, I saw those two apes. They were in my lobby in handcuffs, being grilled by New York's Finest when I came through. Our doorman figured they were casing us for a robbery and called the cops. What's Noda think — I live in a fucking tent? I *pay* for top security, friend. The best.'

'Anyway, nice work with the lights. Much appreciated. The bad news is, you might want to get out of town for a while. Maybe go skiing someplace. The whole thing fell apart. Noda just brought in a whole new load of funding.'

'Hell, I figured that out the minute I saw the *Times* lying there outside my door. Only one place the market could be getting this kind of dough. Tokyo pension funds. So I went back in and called Jack.'

'You made the right move, tipping him off.'

'Maybe he can get trading shut down. Stop it somehow.'

'We stopped it ourselves,' Tam interjected, then indicated the paper bundle in her hands, black metal stock protruding out of one corner.

'God Almighty.' He stared around at the policemen racing by, walkie-talkies chattering. 'Where's Jim Bob? I got a good mind to—'

'Your hotshot screwed us, Bill. Noda got to him and bought him off.'

'I figured that out too. Little fucker.' He grimaced. 'Guess I trained him too well.'

'He didn't deserve his payoff. Somebody'd better hustle a medic up there fast.'

'Let them take care of it.' He thumbed at the firemen piling off their trucks, then bent over and pecked Tam on the cheek. 'Well, Professor, it's been short and sweet. Keep 'em honest.' He reached for my hand. 'Walton, you know how I hate to travel on short notice, but considering the situation . . . St Moritz might be nice for a while.'

'Drink some Pear William for us.'

'Will do. Best of luck.'

'Same to you.' I watched him flip up the collar on his coat as he turned. 'Oh, by the way, Bill, one last thing.'

'Yeah?' He glanced back.

'Want a little insider information?'

'Wouldn't dream of listening.' He returned like a shot.

'Might not be a bad idea to short every high-tech stock DNI currently holds. There's a finite possibility all hell's going to break loose at the opening tomorrow.'

'What's the story?' He was all ears.

Tam turned to me. 'Are you finally going to explain what that scam with Jim Bob was all about?'

'Well, now there's some time. What I did was sucker him into posting buy orders for an additional five per cent of every company on your kill list.'

'I'm well aware of that.' She just continued to stare.

'Which means that when the SEC reports those holdings, it'll trigger the new provisions their majority stockholder — with whose power of attorney I acted with full legal authority — voted last week.'

'Which were?'

'It's a little like what's being called a "tin parachute" these days, the latest twist on the anti-takeover "poison pill".'

'Isn't that where managements have their boards vote that a hostile buyout will trigger big disbursements of a company's assets to the rank and file? What's that got to do with . . .?'

'That's the play. Great takeover defence, by the way.'

'But Noda had already taken those companies over.' She frowned, puzzling.

'Right. Obviously, nobody's supposed to institute one *after* a takeover, but that's what Dai Nippon voted to do last Wednesday and Thursday for every company it owns. The way it's set up now, if the majority stockholder in any of those companies, which just happens to be DNI, acquires another four per cent or more, all that shareholder's stock is automatically disbursed to the employees.'

'Just like that?'

'Fully legal. Like a "tin parachute".'

'But what will . . .?'

'Let me finish. In my version, there're some strings attached. The money can't be used to just go out and buy Toyotas. I arranged it so that all the stock will be held in escrow for ten years and used as collateral for loans specially earmarked to finance expansion and R & D. In other words the employees are about to become those companies' new bank partner.'

'What in holy hell are you talking about?' Henderson appeared to have just entered shock. His bloodshot eyes were like saucers. 'Noda's piece of those high-tech outfits is just going to be given to the troops, then locked up as security for new financing?'

'Bill, try and think of it as a different kind of "restructuring", that grand new corporate scam. But instead of the standard rip-off where managers entrench themselves by loading up a company with debt and bribing their shareholders with the money, I turned the whole thing upside down. Gave the control of those companies to their *workers*, who'll now have a stake in dividends and profits.'

'Walton, you idiot. Stock prices for those outfits are going to nosedive the second news of this hits the Street. It'll scare the institutions shitless. I've never heard anything so crazy.'

'Who knows what'll happen? Let the "supply-side" economists try and figure it out. My guess is we're about to find out if anybody here still believes in the working man. In any case it can't make things worse, and it should be great fun to watch. At least American industry is about to be owned by the people who punch the time clocks. Maybe working for ourselves instead of investment bankers will help things get rolling again.'

'I don't *believe* you did this.' Tam fell against me laughing. 'Do you realise what it really means? Noda's totally destroyed. He'll have to sell off that new portfolio of blue chips just to have enough profit to cover the claims of his original Eight-Hundred-Year-Fund investors. After this, no Japanese money manager is going to give him a yen. He's history.'

'*Bushidō*. When you break the rules, things like that can happen.'

'Jesus, I'm not going to screw around short selling. I'm just gonna load up on puts before the opening tomorrow. You oughta do the same, Walton. When the Street gets wind of this and all those stocks crater, you could clear millions.' Bill headed briskly up the avenue.

'Stay well.' We watched him disappear into the crowd, then started searching for Charlie Morgan and the car.

Incidentally, the recipient of that phone call wasn't really named Patrick. Since there are laws about smuggling firearms in and out of countries, and we damned well were going to take along the Uzi, it seems only right to give him a pseudonym. His charter outfit, which works out of that hangar off to the side of the majors at Kennedy, keeps a Lear that can make the Caribbean in one hop if it's not too full. He even picks you up in a limo, his come-on for the carriage trade.

About ten minutes later we saw Charlie working the Rolls around all the fire engines double-parked on Third and waving for us.

'Good to see you again, Matt.' He glanced back as we settled in. 'Christ, you two look terrible. Were you up there?'

'Just left.'

'Must have been a hell of a fire from the looks of it.' He hit the gas and made a right turn. 'Where to? Straight down Fifth to your place?'

'One quick stop first. Over on West Seventy-eighth.'

'The West Side? In *this* traffic? Come on, Matt. I still haven't had lunch.'

'Just cut through Central Park. Should be a snap.'

While he and Tam waited outside the West Side Free School, I went in to try to kidnap Amy. It wasn't easy. I finally explained to Ms Winters that my daughter's Christmas vacation had merely been delayed a little this year, but better late than never. After some haggling, we struck a deal on homework. Then, in a limo piled high with school books, class projects, lunch boxes and a black Israeli Uzi, we headed downtown.

'Dad, you've gone nuts.' My only offspring was in heaven.

'Honey, we're going to snorkel for two weeks solid. Think you can stand the old man for that long?'

'Can we have a Christmas tree? You promised.'

'I'll cut it myself.'

'And a Christmas party too?'

'Might have to call it something else, but I suppose we can give it a try. If you keep up on the homework.' I looked at her, failing as usual to understand the movements of her mind. 'Sweetie, why do you want to throw a party? This is supposed to be a vacation.'

'Dad, *really*. Don't you remember that *neat* boy from Sweden whose parents have that house across the bay? He was teaching me windsurfing last summer. He's in junior year now, but if he's there, we've *got* to have a party. Don't you understand?'

'Guess we'll have a party.'

What can you do? Nobody said you're supposed to win them all.

*

Bad news, or maybe it was good news, travels with amazing speed in this day and age. The late edition of the Tuesday *New York Post* found its way to the Caribbean on an evening flight, and since it took us a while to get out of town, it actually reached the Virgin Islands shortly before we did. However, since we flew directly into St Croix instead of the main island of St Thomas, we missed the delivery.

As it happened, though, an old acquaintance was passing the house that night on a personal mission and he was kind enough to drop off the *Post*.

The time was around 10 p.m. Amy was sound asleep, conked out from twilight windsurfing, and Tam and I were working on a pitcher of planter's punch by the pool when there came the sound of honking out front. I went in and unlocked the entry, then peeked out to see who it was. The red, white and blue jeep belonged to none other than Artie Wilson, dressed to the nines.

'Walton, my man, you done gone and got yourself famous.' He grinned with delight, then threw a rolled-up newspaper towards the door. 'Tole you it'd be yo' ass.'

'Artie, what in hell. Turn that thing off and come in for a drink. Somebody I want you to meet.'

'Hey, late for a reception at that new place down the beach. Think all them hot New York divorcées jus' come down here for nothing but sunshine an' Vitamin D? Gotta keep the tourists satisfied.' He revved his engine and began backing out of the drive. 'Tomorrow, maybe, Feds ain't nailed yo' honkie butt by then.'

With which enigmatic pronouncement he sped into the humid night.

I picked up the bundle, then snapped on the yard lights and strolled back out to where Tam was sitting, still wearing her pool robe. What was Artie talking about?

As I settled down beside her and unrolled the paper, staring back at us from the front page were two very familiar faces.

'Off one of my book jackets,' she said. 'I never much cared for it.'

'Mine's from their photo morgue, during some takeover circus.'

Guess we should have been keeping closer tabs on the news. Seems that Matsuo Noda, President of Dai Nippon, Int., had held a press conference mid-afternoon Tuesday to refute all the misinformation being spread by Senator Jack O'Donnell. As he claimed, it was actually two Americans, former employees of DNI, who had been responsible for Dai Nippon's secret hostile takeover of the US's largest corporations. He made this point to dispute Senator O'Donnell's assertion that they had been the ones who'd stopped it. (See photo, page 1.) He went on to apologise for what apparently had been a severe communications mix-up within DNI, which brought about this unauthorised action, and he was pleased to report he personally had taken steps to terminate the buy-up this very morning, as of 11.53 a.m.

Run that whopper by Jack's subcommittee, Noda-san.

There was more. Seems the body of an unidentified male — young, Caucasian, and badly burned — had been recovered by firemen on the eleventh floor of DNI's offices. Noda had no idea who this person was, perhaps an unfortunate prowler . . .

'Matt, look!' She was pointing at a paragraph on the lower half of the page.

There'd been a second casualty, although not as serious. The well-known Japanese financial commentator Akira Mori had been borne, unconscious, from the premises. Acute smoke inhalation. As of press time she was in intensive care at Mt Sinai Hospital.

'We saw her come out of the office. It was pretty smoky by then, but how could . . .?'

The answer followed. Firemen reportedly had discovered her in the computer room near the mainframe's burned-out storage banks. Speculation was she had been attempting to save the hard discs, the vital DNI files.

'Mori wasn't trying to *save* anything.' Tam tossed down the paper. 'She wanted to make sure all the discs were destroyed. To protect the Emperor from a scandal over Noda's sword hoax.'

'Another victim for the Imperial Sword.' I looked up at the starry sky, a mosaic of silver and black as the Milky Way floated above us. The night air was symphonic with the sound of crickets. 'How many more?'

Then she retrieved the *Post* and we finished the item. After Noda's prepared statement there'd been a Q & A – during which he reaffirmed his intention to use all available means to block Senator O'Donnell's subpoena of DNI's remaining records, an action he declared confiscatory and groundless. Privileged information, etc.

He did, however, manage to wrap things up on a forward-looking note. Today's unfortunate, indeed tragic, accidental fire should be understood as merely a momentary setback. Nothing that had happened would in any way diminish his programme of capital infusion and open-market acquisition in America's high-tech sector. Wall Street need not worry; Senator O'Donnell's 'harassment' notwithstanding, Dai Nippon's money was here to stay. We were now partners. His grand new alliance, NIPPONICA, would shape the world to come.

'That's what he thinks.' She laughed. 'Wait till he wakes up tomorrow and discovers he just donated all his high-tech acquisitions to their employees. Don't think that fits the big strategy. One thing, though, America's overpaid, golf-playing senior executives could have some wild and woolly board meetings ahead.'

'Life's full of surprises.' I pulled her over and slipped my arm around.

'And the biggest one for me, this week at least, has been you.' She turned and kissed me softly on the mouth, then again. My heart skipped.

Whereupon she abruptly rose and dived headfirst into the pool. Without her suit.

Looked to be a second chance coming up this year, for us all.

AFTERWORD

Contemporary tales of technology and economics engage a moving target, which means they must necessarily include an element of forecasting. Inventing the world to come is always more an art than a science, and the results can never be precise. Trends, however, do have a way of continuing. Sometimes, in fact, you look into the crystal ball and hope what you see never happens. This fable is offered in that spirit.

Those who have critiqued this manuscript all or in part include agent, editors and friends. Special thanks are due, in alphabetical order, to Virginia Barber, Susan and Norman Fainstein, Joanna Field, Linda Gray, Joyce Hawley, Fred Kline and, perhaps most importantly, Gary Prideaux, who introduced this writer to the magic of Japan two decades ago. Others who were kind enough to offer suggestions include N. R. Kleinfield, Pamela McCorduck, Ellen Solomon, Anna Stern, Karen Sunde, Christopher Martin, Eric Allison, Susan Stoller, Michael Cavallo, Makiko and Kazuyoshi Morikawa, Jim Piper, Tim Richards, Paul Bove, Eric Bove, Charles Gordon, Janet Miller, David Palmer, Arthur Blatt and Malcolm Bosse. If this story succeeds in any measure, it is because of them. Its faults are the author's alone.

RICHARD HUGO

FAREWELL TO ★ RUSSIA

Running desperately. Shouting breathlessly. His voice screaming itself
to soundlessness for want of air: 'Get away from here! Get away from
the water!'

The unthinkable has happened at the Soviet nuclear plant at Sokolskoye.
An accident of such catastrophic ecological and political consequence that a
curtain of silence is drawn ominously over the incident. Major Pyotr Kirov
of the KGB is appointed to extract the truth from the treacherous minefield
of misinformation and intrigue and to obtain from the West the technology
essential to prevent further damage. But the vital equipment is under strict
trade embargo . . .

And in London, George Twist, head of a company which manufactures the
technology, is on the verge of bankruptcy and desperate to win the illegal
contract. Can he deliver on time? Will he survive a frantic smuggling
operation across the frozen wastes of Finland? Can he wrongfoot the
authorities . . . and his own conscience?

'Immensely well-researched . . . growls with suspense . . . even without
the recent memories of Chernobyl the novel has an authentic ring'
Independent

'Diverse loyalties are suspensefully stretched and nerve ends twanged'
Guardian

0 7474 0061 X   THRILLER   £3.50

JUNIPER

James Murphy

'Knowing your enemy is not the primary consideration.
You have to know what you are defending first of all.
Then the enemy will show itself.'

Oliver Maitland joined MI5 to defend his country. To
defend freedom and democracy. He's served his time in
the hell of Northern Ireland, battling for a peaceful
solution. Now he's transferred to counter-subversion,
fighting, not the IRA but ordinary men and women.

Phone tapping, mail interception, burglary – it's a dirty
war. And when Maitland finds out the truth behind the
Mountbatten murder he begins to wonder who the
enemy really is.

Operation JUNIPER, brainchild of Maitland's sadistic
boss, 'The Butcher', is the deadliest campaign yet. It's
going to smash the peace movement and sabotage
disarmament talks. Maitland knows the butcher doesn't
care how many British agents have to die to fulfil his
plans. What he doesn't know is that he's top of the
hit-list . . .

Also by James Murphy in Sphere Books:

CEDAR

0 7474 0059 8   ADVENTURE THRILLER   £3.50

Deeds

JOSEPH AMIEL

The world of real estate has dominated the lives of the Behr family for three generations. And now the young, dynamic Ralph Behr intends to ensure the family's immortality in the shape of the Behr Centre – three 150 storey towers, to dominate the Manhattan skyline.

But overnight Ralph's elaborate plans and wild lifestyle are brought to an abrupt halt. The unwelcome arrival of a figure from the past throws Ralph into an intricate plot to save the family name – and into a bizarre marriage with Gail, a spirited, highly moral woman whose life has been a crusade against everything Ralph has ever stood for. His passion is to make money. Hers is to save the world. They met once in childhood. They will meet again at the altar . . .

Also by Joseph Amiel in Sphere Books:
BIRTHRIGHT

0 7474 0246 9   GENERAL FICTION   £3.99

A selection of bestsellers from SPHERE

FICTION

THE FIREBRAND	Marion Zimmer Bradley	£3.99 ☐
STARK	Ben Elton	£3.50 ☐
LORDS OF THE AIR	Graham Masterton	£3.99 ☐
THE PALACE	Paul Erdman	£3.50 ☐
KALEIDOSCOPE	Danielle Steel	£3.50 ☐

FILM AND TV TIE-IN

WILLOW	Wayland Drew	£2.99 ☐
BUSTER	Colin Shindler	£2.99 ☐
COMING TOGETHER	Alexandra Hine	£2.99 ☐
RUN FOR YOUR LIFE	Stuart Collins	£2.99 ☐
BLACK FOREST CLINIC	Peter Heim	£2.99 ☐

NON-FICTION

HOW TO GET A SAFE TAN	Dr Anthony Harris	£2.99 ☐
IN FOR A PENNY	Jonathan Mantle	£3.50 ☐
DETOUR	Cheryl Crane	£3.99 ☐
MARLON BRANDO	David Shipman	£3.50 ☐
MONTY: THE MAN BEHIND THE LEGEND	Nigel Hamilton	£3.99 ☐

All Sphere books are available at your local bookshop or newsagent, or can be ordered direct from the publisher. Just tick the titles you want and fill in the form below.

Name_____

Address_____

_____

Write to Sphere Books, Cash Sales Department, P.O. Box 11, Falmouth, Cornwall TR10 9EN

Please enclose a cheque or postal order to the value of the cover price plus:

UK: 60p for the first book, 25p for the second book and 15p for each additional book ordered to a maximum charge of £1.90.

OVERSEAS & EIRE: £1.25 for the first book, 75p for the second book and 28p for each subsequent title ordered.

BFPO: 60p for the first book, 25p for the second book plus 15p per copy for the next 7 books, thereafter 9p per book.

Sphere Books reserve the right to show new retail prices on covers which may differ from those previously advertised in the text elsewhere, and to increase postal rates in accordance with the P.O.